The Sarajevo Hypothesis

Altered State 3

The Sarajevo Hypothesis

J. G. Jenkinson

VULPINE
PRESS

Published by Vulpine Press in the United Kingdom in 2023

ISBN: 978-1-83919-519-8

Cover by Claire Wood

www.vulpine-press.com

This book is dedicated to everyone who persevered, whether it be with reading this series of books, a polar expedition or anything in between.

Prologue, 1952

This was the first time Henry had trusted him to take the roadster out without his supervision and he refused to allow Olga's obvious frustration at his lack of speed ruin it for him. Rudi Kessler had rebuilt the car for his guardian Henry Clive over the winter of 1951/52 and dragged the Jaguar XK120 into the modern age. Starting with the brakes, he began tearing out inferior parts like the Zenith carburettor, the ancient steering and, to Clive's great apprehension, the unsynchronized gearbox. The project had been both fascinating and rewarding in equal measure; a warm-up for his next great undertaking.

The cherry red machine roared through the Hampshire countryside at sixty miles per hour and Rudi allowed himself to become immersed completely in the experience, pushing thoughts of other twentieth birthdays from his mind. Though one in particular persisted, a depressing affair in a drab colourless apartment typical of the workers' paradise. His mother was doing her level best to inject some of the joy they had known before the war, some of the colour of the early days of the Third Reich, but despite this, the mood was muted and he remembered finding it hard to return her smile. His sister, Carla was unrecognisable from the woman he knew today, a sullen creature in practical brown clothing and painfully scraped-back hair, her features flitting from pinched disapproval to furtive, almost fearful glances at her husband Lothar.

Both were party functionaries and their presence brought the fear of accidental incrimination and with it a nocturnal visit from the Stasi, followed by a one-way trip to Normannenstrasse. Today

-- in this life -- she was a strong, successful academic with an infectious laugh and an ambition to save the world. This ambition was shared by Rudi and their adopted family: Together they planned to alter the key nation states of Europe enough to prevent the death and destruction brought by the twentieth century.

Both Clive and Olga agreed that the Jaguar handled like a completely different car since his modifications, and the hours spent tuning the triple Webbers on that huge straight six were well spent. Rudi watched the sky and trees reflected in the long bonnet for a moment before returning his attention to the winding lanes of the South Downs between Petersfield and Broadlands: The Clive family's Palladian mansion. Rudi had taken Olga to a lake he had found, hoping to recreate a cherished memory they shared of a day in 1961. It had worked, and the only difference had been the standard of food and drink.

"You know I love you Rudi Kessler, but you do drive like an old woman and I expect that she only drives that way because her eyesight is failing and she's not a sharp as she once was."

She was baiting him, a casual attempt at pushing him to push himself. She did it all the time, in the gym, in the workshop and even in bed. Olga knew that soon this charmed life they had led for the last seven years would be gone, not over, but gone, like it had never existed. She knew that she took it more seriously than the others, waking earlier, training harder and never taking her eyes from the goal. Carla and Rudi were serious and committed, there was no doubting it, but not on the same level as Olga. Clive, she knew, affected the disinterest of every Englishman of his class, but he spent long periods away from the house and when he was in residence, he was rarely out from behind his enormous mahogany desk.

She placed her hand on Rudi's as he shifted into top gear and he risked a look at her, they were both agonisingly beautiful to behold, but something else drew people to them. The bright sheen of youth combined with a wisdom emanating from the eyes and encompassing their whole beings. This was the wisdom of age, of lives spent pursuing a goal far greater than most could hope to understand, but this pseudo immortality came at a price.

Rudi tore his eyes from the most beautiful woman he had ever known to focus on the road and the tight bend approaching, he shook Olga's hand away shifting down to assist his braking and causing the engine to roar plaintively. He knew she would have taken the corner faster, but he also knew that she feared nothing and no one. Rudi feared both Henry and Sir Gerald Clive. These men, affable, polite and impeccably dressed, had another side to them. Deep down, in a part of himself that he refused to acknowledge, Rudi knew that the cold-hearted bastards who had fought tooth and nail for their country lurked beneath the surface, the idea that he should damage this car or upset these men in any other way did not bear thinking about.

Though a wonderful day out with the man she loved, the lake was a ruse and as Rudi crested the hill that gave out to the Test valley, the pieces fell into place. The dozen or so cars on the drive, the marquees, and the army of servants swarming like ants to ready Broadlands for a party the rival of any that the landed gentry of England cared to throw.

"Drive straight around to the barn," Olga said, when she caught the knowing glint in his eye, "I've had our evening dress laid out for us in that apartment, so we can really make an entrance."

She smiled wickedly at the implication that they should be alone and undressed once more before the festivities began.

"Olga, my darling, you must have gone to so much trouble," Rudi beamed, his German accent lost, echoing among the hallowed halls of Balliol College, where the memories of the upper class were long and without mercy. His momentary lapse caused Rudi to misjudge a corner and for a brief moment of screeching tires and thumping hearts he lost control of the back end of the Jaguar. Olga didn't flinch, cool radiated from her placid countenance as Rudi shot her a nervous glance.

"Eyes on the road champ," said sardonically, whilst giving his thigh an affectionate squeeze.

~

To the young lover's frustration, Olga's lady's maid was waiting in the apartment over the barn to fix her wild blonde locks into something that the Clive's friends would find acceptable. Olga hated Morris, not because she was a bad maid or even a bad person, but she reminded Olga of the life she had coveted back at Grunewald, the life Altstötter had promised her all those years ago. She dismissed the obsequious old woman after the briefest of cursory brushings, only to find that Henry had sent his valet down to see that Rudi looked presentable too.

"I think that Master Kessler is perfectly capable of dressing himself," she said with an edge to her voice that could have cut through steel.

"Very well, Ma'am, Sir Gerald said to remind you that the guests are meeting for drinks at six," the valet said, doing a commendable job of appearing unflappable, though she knew he'd seen what she could do when tested and how hard she trained – he was the poor bugger who added to the ever-growing pile of punchbags

4

and the splintered wreckage of a wing chun behind the barn. Rudi watched the man leave and pounced.

"We don't have time," Olga sighed, reluctantly pulling away from Rudi's embrace. "I gave Henry my word that we wouldn't be late."

"Since when do you care about punctuality?"

"He said that you would never be trusted with the roadster again if we were late and I do care about you," she admitted, straightening his bowtie, and planting a lingering kiss on his lips.

As they walked through the barn, Rudi felt drawn to the plans and parts scattered about his workshop, the beginnings of his first attempt at what he simply referred to as the gadget. The name was an homage to Oppenheimer and his team of wunderkind, they had been responsible for the Manhattan Project and in an attempt to lessen the horror of their work they had referred to the bomb they were developing as the gadget.

The buzz and mood of the party were palpable as they emerged from the rose garden, still a few hundred yards from the house. When the pair were in hailing distance, Clive and those he'd assembled for the soiree began to sing for he's a jolly good fellow, with a vigour quite unlike their usual reservation. As the final note died away, Olga and Rudi entered the marquee and champagne corks popped to cheers and a round of applause.

His sister Carla stepped forward and kissed him on the cheek before whispering, "alles Gute zum Geburtstag Bruder," producing a small wooden box from behind her back, she pressed it into his hand. "Open it later."

Confused, Rudi thanked her and passed the box to a servant.

"Happy birthday, dear boy," Sir Gerald called from his chair.

Rudi strode over to man he saw as a grandfather and took his trembling, liver spotted hand, "thank you. How are you feeling this evening?"

"Positively dreadful, but I mustn't whinge," he said with a conspiratorial wink. "Go, go and enjoy your party!"

"Rudi," Clive said, clapping him on the back and shaking his hand firmly, "happy birthday old man." Clive seemed to have reversed the aging of six years behind enemy lines and now looked about twenty-five. He'd put on a bit of the weight he'd lost and appeared to be sleeping better. Rudi was glad, he had grown fond of Henry over the last seven years and felt he owed him a great deal.

"Thanks, Henry, this is a jolly fine show you've put on for me here."

"Think nothing of it, we'll all be off on our adventures soon, and I thought we could use one last hurrah before the off."

"Mmm," Rudi said, through a mouthful of Vol-au-vent, "have you tried the salmon ones? They're smashing."

"Have as much as you like my boy," he beamed, helping himself to a pink-topped pastry, "come and find me later, I'll let you have your present then." Henry took a delicate bite and smiled warmly at his ward, before re-entering the throng of revellers.

"Rudi," Olga whispered as she wrapped her strong arms around him from behind.

"Yes, my love?"

"I've got your present for you indoors. You can have it whenever you'd like."

"Now?"

"If that's what you want? Maybe we should wait a short while though?"

"Fine, look, there's Bertie Hancock from college, we must say hello. It's a bloody long way from Lancaster."

"I'm never doing that again," Olga hissed and they hurried through the empty house towards the light and noise of the party.

"Don't say never," Rudi Pleaded. "That's a long time for the likes of us."

"Fine, but it'll be your birthday again before I even consider it!"

The band had retired and the dancing was over when the pair returned, but plenty of guests remained and the atmosphere was still one of merriment with laughter and singing from all corners of the lawn. Rudi looked back at the house to see Henry's silhouette in the high window of the study, watching as it twirled a brandy glass in one hand and held a cigar in the other. Reminded of his gift, Rudi made an excuse to Olga, now deep in conversation with a friend from Oxford and headed back inside.

The study sat at the end of a wide corridor with light pouring onto the carpet from a crack in the door. Rudi strolled up the passageway, a bounce in his step from the gentle buzz of just enough champagne, as he drew closer, he heard muffled voices from within.

"Just listen to me, I want everything he does catalogued, I want drawings and I want idiot proof instructions." The voice was Henry's and he was angrier than Rudi had ever known him to be.

"Certainly sir, but he is so much more intelli—"

"Is someone there?" Clive called. Moments later the door opened and his friend Bertie stood nervously behind a glowering Clive.

"Rudi?" he said, his whole face changing with recognition. "I suppose you've come looking for your gift?"

"Err… yes sir, hello Bertie?" Rudi stumbled, confused and a little unsure of what to do.

"Bertie here was just asking if I would loan him the money to stay on at Oxford. Now, now, my boy it's no secret that you father has made some poor financial decisions lately and it's understandable that he might not be able to pay your fees, but don't worry, I'll sort something out for you. Now off you go, enjoy the rest of the party."

Bertie hurried out, unable to look his friend in the eye as he passed.

"Best we say no more about that sordid business, his father has made rather a mess of things," Clive said, as he rummaged one-handed in a draw of his desk, holding both the brandy and cigar in the other. "Ah, he we are, happy birthday, Rudi."

"Thank you, Henry," he croaked, still a little put out by what had just transpired. Looking down, he found that he was holding an ancient looking six-shooter, the wooden grip curled around like the head of a walking stick and was heavy, heavier than any weapon he'd held before.

"That's a Reichsrevolver, the weapon you'll be carrying when you go back to 1904. You're to practice with it daily, learn everything about it until it becomes an extension of your own arm, understood?"

"Yes, sir."

"Very good, now hand it over and I'll meet you at the range tomorrow morning," Clive instructed, holding out a hand for the peculiar gun. "Oh, and it looks like Bertie will be joining us after

Trinity term, his father might have to go away for an extended period and close up their house, he can help you with your project. Don't worry, we can trust him to keep quiet."

Clive dismissed him with a conspiratorial wink.

Rudi did as he was told in both the pistol practice and by not embarrassing his friend over a half-remembered conversation from his birthday party. Bertie did move down to Broadlands in the summer and the pair worked hard together on the final stages of the gadget. Rudi was able to forge on while his new partner made all the notes, insisting that for him, that this was what science was all about.

By mid-August, the device was ready, a completely new machine, far simpler and far less constraining than previous iterations. With Henry, Sir Gerald, Carla, and Olga assembled in the barn, Rudi stepped forward and smiled at his family.

"Hello everyone, I'm very excited to show you all my new gadget and demonstrate to you how it works. Unlike the previous time machines, it works using—"

"A rudimentary tear in spacetime, caused by a phased singularity," Bertie interrupted, in his drawling public school accent. Olga hated him, a mealy mouthed, sycophant who took every opportunity to steal Rudi's thunder.

"Why don't we let Rudi explain it, it is his, gadget after all," she called over what she feared was fast becoming a monologue.

"Well, there isn't much more to say," Rudi added, "I'm not going to bore you with the quantum mechanics involved in generating the singularity. Let's move straight onto the demonstration. Bertie!"

His partner flipped a switch on the rudimentary console and the space behind Rudi began to wobble like heat haze on the desert.

"I've decided to keep it simple. I wanted to show you something iconic that was destroyed at some point in the war and the first thing I thought of was London, then I realised that Olga and Carla wouldn't have seen it before the Blitz. Then it hit me. Berlin. We've all seen Berlin before the bombs, so here it is."

Rudi stepped to the side to reveal a cityscape of Berlin circa 1925, it hung in the air like the opening of a tent and showed Unter den Linden, undamaged and teaming with people, cars and carts.

"I forgot how beautiful it was, before…" Carla cried, leaning into Olga's shoulder to hide her tears.

"Before the British, Americans and Russians destroyed it."

She was surprised by the strength of her bitterness, by the hatred she felt for the western Allies. Her hatred of Russians had been there since the day she had rescued Olga from the lock outside Brandenburg and it burned like a fire, it was the fuel that drove her and the light behind her eyes.

"Is it safe? For the likes of you and your sister I mean?" Clive asked, oblivious to Carla's gentle sobbing.

"Perfectly, we have tested it with animals and now—"

"Now, I will try," Bertie announced triumphantly, and without preamble, he changed the settings on the console and Berlin became a hazy version of the back of the barn, though the shadows were slightly off.

"Wish me luck!" he called, as he stepped casually through the tear.

"It works," came the same voice from behind them. "I am the first human being to travel through time!"

10

"Ha!" Olga barked, stifling the rest of her laughter with a balled-up fist.

"Right," Clive said, standing and addressing the family, "finish up your preparations and be ready for the first jump…oh, say the day after tomorrow?"

Afrika, 1904

Rudi Kessler awoke face down on an expansive beach. Coarse sand filled his mouth, nostrils, and eyes. The impossibly hot sun had dried his Feldrock uniform, leaving it stiff with salt and abrasive to the skin. He spat the sand and snorted in an attempt to expel the ground-up shell and ancient minerals, realising how desperately he needed water in the process. This was Africa's Skeleton Coast; hot, dry, and generally inhospitable. He knew he'd messed up and quite probably killed himself. He vomited more seawater and wept in despair.

Rudi had stepped through the tear from 1952 carrying a Reichsheer issue haversack containing a meticulously prepared inventory. All items were dated to prevent incrimination, sealed against water damage and selected for their singular significance to his mission. He had stepped as discussed through into 1904, but not as planned onto the solid earth of the highlands to the south of Windhoek. Instead, Rudi stepped with confidence into the boiling seas of the Southern Atlantic Ocean.

Weighed down by his pack and gasping for air, Rudi wrestled from his burden as he kicked and writhed, straining every muscle and sinew to push his head through the surface of the water. The cold, briny sea filled his lungs and caused him to draw in more of it. He finally broke free of the lifesaving haversack, managing to claw his way to the surface and inhale the sweet, salty air, the irony lost along with his consciousness.

Eventually washed up on the beach, Rudi forced himself onto all fours and brought up more seawater as he dug his fingers into the sand, retching his life away onto the beach. He staggered violently as he tried to stand and forced himself to focus, to think about what to do, because the next few hours would decide if he lived or died out here. Patting himself down, he found the papers identifying him as a subaltern of the Schutztruppe of German East Afrika. He found a pipe and tobacco pouch, one tin of petroleum jelly, one cigarette lighter, one hipflask filled with Schnaps, one silken map of German Southwest Afrika and a pocket watch that appeared to be contemporary. Hanging from his belt, he wore a water canteen, a bayonet, and his Reichsrevolver. Exercising the discipline of a much older man, the twenty-year-old sipped gently at his canteen. The liquid inside was an electrolyte solution designed to replace the minerals lost through sweat and in this case, vomit.

A relentless sun retreated from the zenith whilst beating mercilessly at the exposed skin of Rudi's face and hands. It shrank the rapidly drying leather of his Hessian boots and slowly turned the vice at his temples. He took out the watch, noted the lateness of the hour and the direction of north on the integrated compass. The watch was state of the art in 1952 and powered by the latest in battery technology, with an unbreakable glass face. The smaller mechanism allowed space for a roll of microfiche containing hundreds of pages of information. Also wedged in there was a telescopic eye loupe with which to view the data.

Rudi pinched the bridge of his nose and rubbed the dried salt from around his eyes as he surveyed his environment properly for the first time. With the ocean at his back, he looked east at the steep rise of dunes, whilst the terrain to the north and south appeared to offer the same promise of a slow, agonising death. He trudged to the top of the nearest sand dune in the hope that he would see something else, something that was not mile upon mile of hot, unforgiving desert.

Rudi had no way of knowing where he was along the hundreds of miles of coast. He could only assume that this was German Southwest Afrika, where the shore ran north to south and the ocean was to his west, with the desert to the east. Walking inland was suicide, so he had a choice between north or south. He brought out the silk map and realised that without any prominent features, the map could not really help him.

Then his eyes fell upon the city of Windhoek, his planned destination. It was highly likely, he thought, that his error was singular, one digit in the co-ordinates, one digit in the line of longitude. He brushed away the salt and ran a finger from Windhoek directly west to the settlement of Swakopmund. It was as though the colonial settlers had landed there and marched directly east in a perfectly straight line for two-hundred miles, before founding the town of Windhoek. So, with his planned destination to the south of the town, he adjusted his marker to the south of Swakopmund. It was a fair assumption. He could walk north in the hope of finding Swakopmund in the same amount of time it should have taken him to find Windhoek. What did he have to lose? His life, the fate of the world, Olga? Rudi Kessler had plenty to lose.

Taking a glob of petroleum jelly, he reached inside his clothing and applied it liberally to his pits and inner thighs to guard against salt rash. This done, he took another sip from his canteen and marched north in the direction of Swakopmund, he hoped. The going was hard, the skin of his feet was raw, and the leather of his boots had shrunk, but this only served as a distraction from the crushing heat and dehydration. Rudi had emptied his stomach onto the sand and now it growled, imploring him to feed it. He trudged on through the deep sand, making poor progress. He had resolved to count his paces, but his heat-addled mind lost count somewhere in the thirties each time he tried.

A fog descended, surrounding Rudi and reducing visibility to ten or twenty metres. He had read about this, but the experience was very different. He'd read that the locals called it "the land God made in anger," and sailors called it "the gates of hell". No one, however – not in this time anyway – called it the Skeleton Coast, that name would come later. He agreed with these descriptive names, but it was more than that now. Rudi had known hunger, known torture even, but this submersion into hell caused a visceral rejection of everything but water and shade. He'd been fighting an internal battle not to dive back into the surf, into the cool ocean. He knew that it would make things worse, make his journey harder, but the instant gratification of that cool water would surely be worth it? He concentrated on lifting one leg after the other whilst fighting the urge to drink, the urge to sleep, the urge to swim, the urge to give up and die right there on the molten sand.

Such was his confusion that when he finally noticed the bulge in his trouser pocket, he had already spent three hours in the burning heat under the African sun. Shaking his head at his stupidity, he finally thought to don his slouch hat. The hat was trimmed with the white of the Schuttztruppe of German East Afrika, as were his trousers and tunic. Rudi's sister Carla had found a Junker named Leutnant Horst Buchholz on the passenger manifest of the DAL Bundesrath, a steamer last seen at Cape Town and later wrecked

15

with all hands lost. Buchholz, an orphan with a modest fortune, was on his way home to Wilhelmshaven after completing his national service as an officer of the Schuttztruppe.

"He's perfect," she'd said. "No living family, but his parents left behind plenty of money and influential friends. None of whom will have seen Horst's face for years, so you'll be able to steam back into Bremerhaven, seek the patronage of a few of these men and head for Berlin, an unblemished service record behind you."

If Rudi had been able to think straight at all, he would have realised that his new situation fitted his story far better than appearing suddenly two-hundred miles inland at Windhoek, wearing a clean uniform and a tan acquired over a few weeks of using 1950s sun lamps. Now he would collapse at the door of the local station and let his appearance tell his story. They would telegram Dar es Salaam, to find that Leutnant Buchholz had left on a steamer some weeks ago and assume the rest from the evidence available.

As he glugged at his canteen, all discipline gone by the board, some of this did occur to him during a brief moment of clarity. He racked his brains over what he was carrying. Was any of it incriminating? He had never counted on being searched and he would collapse soon. He could only hope that it would be in Swakopmund and not in this arid wasteland that would certainly kill him if he lingered for too long.

"The map," he croaked as he staggered onwards. He took one last look at it, desperately trying to absorb the information it contained. He then held it aloft and touched his lighter to the corner. It shrank away from the flame and he choked on the stench of burned hair as it curled towards his hand, until the whole thing was black, crispy ashes in the sand.

Shadows seemed to form just beyond clear vison in the fog. Perhaps they were wrecked ships or perhaps they were mirages, but Rudi's fevered brain was barely capable of controlling his legs at this stage. He pressed on, not bothering to check his compass now, only offering perfunctory glances in the direction of the crashing waves without breaking his stride.

"Boss, Boss!"

"Ja! What?"

"You better come see."

Rudi lay staring up at the concerned face of a uniformed native whose eyes were moving furtively between his prostrate form and the door of the outpost. Presumably, this was where 'Boss' was? A fat, moustachioed Wachtmeister waddled over the threshold towards his junior NCO and Rudi. Ostensibly an officer of the Schuttztruppe, worse for wear after a night in his cups.

"Ach so, Herr Leutnant?" he said conspiratorially.

Rudi blinked and began to move his cracked lips.

"A night in the brothel, was it? They kick you out when you couldn't pay your bill?"

"Heels together, Wachtmeister," Rudi croaked, "you address an officer!"

The senior NCO smirked, "Do you want my help or not?"

"I don't want anything. I demand that you move me to shelter and find me medical attention immediately!" These last words tore his shrivelled larynx as he tried to shout them.

"Listen, Herr Leutnant, you are hardly in the position to be making demands of anyone. Now ask me nicely or I'll call your CO and have you charged with drunkenness."

"Look at me, man!" Rudi rasped. "Really look!"

The Wachtmeister's eyes fell upon the white trim of his uniform, the salt patches on his boots and the livid suppurating burns to his exposed flesh. Realisation hit him like a punch in the gut, though instead of doubling over, he stood straight upright and clicked his heels together.

"Herr Leutnant," he intoned, deference harmonising with supplication as he chivvied and chided his subordinate to find help. "Please forgive my ignorance, where have you come from?"

"Dar..." he growled, "Dar es Salaam..."

~

Rudi awoke for a second time in the cool of the evening to find that his clothes had been stripped away and he lay in an empty hospital ward. His skin was soggy with ointment and the vice at his temples felt tighter than ever. As he tried to move, he felt a stiffness in his muscles that took him back to an East Berlin laboratory and a much older version of himself, a version who had died many lifetimes before. Rudi tentatively moved his head to the side, where his eye fell upon a nightstand and a glass of water. With great effort, he managed to drink some before falling into another exhausted sleep.

"Ah, Kamerad Leutnant," an impossibly old Oberarzt of the Sanitätsdienst greeted him from behind a clipboard. The parity in their ranks meant that the doctor needn't defer to nor condescend, and they could speak as equals. "You have certainly been through the wringer: dehydration, sunburn, trench foot and heat exhaustion."

"How long…"

"How long have you been here? Oh, two nights and two days. Your uniform is ruined, I understand that a tailor will be by later to measure you for a new one."

These memories came back to Rudi in fragments, but this one in the hospital was of particular significance. The last time he'd know anything like innocence, the last time he'd sleep without waking in the night drenched in sweat and screaming. This was the beginning of one of the worst periods in Rudi's life, in any of his lives. He would do things in that remote corner of Africa that would damage his very soul, alter his character, and live on in his dreams for years to come.

Unforgivable acts that would echo down through the decades, repeated in places like Dachau and Buchenwald, Bergan and Treblinka, places synonymous with bestial malevolence and wicked, weak-willed men.

~

SS Valdivia, Bay of Biscay, nearly four years later

The ship steamed ahead on a flat, calm sea in the Bay of Biscay, a rarity that he cherished. The passage so far had been vile, high seas and low deeds had plagued him as he lay in his tiny cabin staving off seasickness whilst the ghosts of emaciated tribespeople demanded justice.

Right now, though, in this peaceful moment, Rudi embraced the sights, sounds, and smells of the ocean, coal smoke permeating the otherwise fresh, salty air. The wind whipped up his scraped-back blonde hair and the sun warmed his skin now tanned and leathery. The Atlantic, an enormous blue disc, unbroken in every direction but for the wake of the ship. This feeling of freedom, of endless possibilities and an exuberance that only blessed the young lasted all of half an hour before his ghosts, his guilt and his dishonour returned to drag him back to the darkness. He knew that it would pass, it had to pass, he couldn't live like this indefinitely, he would have to just harden his heart and ride it out. In time, the images of the people he had wronged would be distorted, he would tell himself lies about them, dehumanise them and eventually feel justified in his actions during the rebellion and in those of his comrades.

After all, they were only following orders.

The SS Valdivia lumbered on at a respectable twenty knots whilst her three hundred passengers searched for ways to pass the time. Those in steerage drank and danced and sung in the bowels of the ship, whilst those that could, played accordions, concertinas, harmonicas, and flutes. This was the longest spell of time off work the majority of these wretches would ever enjoy, the voyage was a celebration of this and of the hard work that had earned them their fare. Most would look back on these weeks as some of the happiest they had known, despite the dark, foetid conditions and regular bouts of seasickness.

The forty or so first-class passengers enjoyed more comfort and fresh air, but their pastimes were suitably restricted and no man, whatever his financial means or social standing, was spared the indignity of mal de mer. Men drank and smoked, played cards or chess, and discussed politics or life in the colonies. Whilst the ladies of first class might enjoy a respectable amount of alcohol, take occasional turns on deck or quietly converse with their companion, they would be foolish to do more.

As an officer and a man of means, Rudi was able to purchase a first-class ticket. Although not all first-class tickets are created equal. His cabin resembled a cupboard more than it did a bedroom, shoehorned into a tiny misshapen gap between two much larger staterooms. The bulkheads, every one at an acute angle, were the thinnest of plywood and creaked mercilessly in dirty weather. Its saving grace was a porthole, through which he would stare, mesmerised by the rolling seas as he sat at his tiny desk, writing letters to Olga that he could not send and solving equations the like of which would not be seen on the hallowed blackboards of physics institutions for another quarter of a century.

Too long in this dreary little wardrobe would drive him to distraction, thoughts of Olga and of Carla dampened his spirits and he would become lethargic. His black dog came and went several times on that voyage from Swakopmund to Bremerhaven and for such a young man usually predisposed to indefatigable drive and determination, it was a battle. Rudi had been spared the trauma of killing Rolf Schilling and witnessing the gangrape of his mother and sister, but this life had brought with it new ordeals, new nightmares, and far greater challenges. The old nightmares remained: Hohenschönhausen and the Sippenhaft, solitary confinement and the tongueless screams of a man he barely recognised as Rudolph Kessler. New physical wounds now plagued him, a Herero bullet that had torn through his thigh and another that had grazed his scalp and taken off a small piece of his ear.

But Rudi possessed an inner strength, a strength that he had not needed so far in this life, the same strength that had seen him through decades in the GDR prison system, icy forced marches, and Olga's sudden disappearance. He drew it on now. He compelled himself to rise, to wash in cold water and to dress. He dragged himself kicking and screaming to meals and he forced himself to be congenial and to win at cards.

Gerald had shown Rudi how to win at cards.

"We don't play, boy, we win. D'you understand?" Sir Gerald Clive's words echoed from the depths of memory, as he dealt a hand for himself and one each for Henry and Rudi.

Sir Gerald was Rudi's patron and the father of Henry, the man who had brought him from the smouldering ruins of Hamburg to live in his palatial home at Broadlands. The old man had taught him everything he knew and now Rudi was something of a cardsharp, carefully only winning what he needed to get by, a lesson Gerald had learned the hard way.

"Now remember, part of winning is losing just enough to keep them off your scent, boy."

Having little else in common, the regular card sessions were one of the few times he and the xenophobic old baronet had bonded. Henry, on the other hand, had been like an older brother to him. In the detached, icy manner he always affected, he had bought Rudi his first proper drink and taught him to drive in his darling, cherry red Jaguar. They visited science fairs together and Henry had helped him find and buy the parts Rudi needed for the time machine.

22

"The old time machine built by previous versions of me was over complicated and would be impossible to build in 1952," Rudi had orated. "What I propose is essentially just a crude hole ripped in spacetime by a phased singularity."

Henry had nodded politely, assuring himself that his mastery of both modern and ancient languages meant that he was equally as clever as this boy, just in a different way. That was when he knew he'd need Bertie.

Of course, it was Olga who he missed the most and who he had found the hardest to part from. Carla had taken this well and she gave them the space they needed to do it properly.

"We will find each other," she had promised, "we always do."

Rudi smiled sadly and gazed into her wise, green eyes, the eyes of a centuries-old soul in the face of a beautiful young woman.

"I'll look for your work in the papers," he chuckled, though his heart wasn't in it and when she smiled back, revealing her pearly white, adorably uneven teeth, he almost cried.

"Horst!" Rudi was jerked from his reverie by the heavily accented voice of a Berliner named Fuchs. "Are you deaf? I have been calling your name this age and more."

"Excuse me, I was miles away."

He was Horst Buchholz again and Horst sat down to a game of Skat in his new life, with his new friends.

Oxford, 1897

Henry Clive sat in the corner of The Bear Inn, Oxford, nursing a glass of some frightful blend they'd had the nerve to call whisky. He was waiting for his father and to avoid the spectacle of looking almost exactly alike, he sported a bristling pair of moustaches, grown specially in preparation. Clive Snr. was due to attend this public house with his long-time chum and the inspiration for his son's name, Henry Bradshaw. The low ceilings and smoky air were oppressive, but the oddly familiar surroundings put Clive at ease. This was a pub he knew or had known, although perhaps it should be would know.

He'd made his mind up and tonight he would set in motion a chain of events that would change the history of the British Empire forever. He watched his father stumble into the bar with his friends, already drunk at two o'clock in the afternoon. This wasn't Clive's first day in 1897 and it wasn't his first jump through time, he was an old hand with a ruthless streak as prominent as his accent. SOE for the latter part of World War Two, he had seen and done things that would turn most men into quivering wrecks crying for home and hearth. Like Olga and Rudi, Clive had lived this life before, none knew how many times or for what reason, but all had memories or echoes, and Clive's were just as chilling.

He thought back on the train to Munich in some other version of 1961.

He knew the date because the wall had just gone up and it was all over the West German papers. The girl, Olga, he knew her well now. He knew her in the way a brother might know a sister; indeed, he had an affection for her now, but back then she was just another job. The Berlin Resident, the father of an old school chum, had called him to his private office in the SIS residence out in Grunewald.

"Listen," the old man had said, without his usual preamble, and Clive could tell straight away that something was off. George was off, he was uncomfortable, and he clearly wanted to give him this job and get him out of there as quickly as possible. George Campbell was too old, too soft, and too weak for this job. London knew it of course, but George had gone to the right school, joined the right regiment and fought in the right actions. He'd done his time with the department and now this was only his due. Members of the old school tie brigade had to have their due, the safety and efficacy of Berlin Station be damned.

Henry saw the old man's flaws and he accepted them, as he knew the same system would bestow an equally undeserving promotion upon him one day, simply because of the tie he wore and the way he pronounced words like often and scone. He wasn't going to rock the boat, men who rocked boats found themselves sweating over desks in far flung corners of the empire with little hope of return.

"This girl, Olga Felson. By all accounts she's KGB and she has something to do with that Janus business."

These vagaries were George's way of showing his disapproval. Janus was the British intelligence department concerned with highly advanced foreign technology.

"They have made some gains for the space race, I suppose, and most recently Janus has caught a whiff some very spicy quantum physics in the east. We had an informant in Berlin Station last night spilling his guts about a physicist. A good communist, according to those who cared about that sort of thing. His parents were ISK and sent coded messages to Russia in the war, but everyone said that they had been Red Orchestra when they were in the basement of Normannenstrasse."

"Indeed," Clive murmured, urging George to continue.

"He was brought in a few nights ago screaming about his friend's defection and their capitalist imperialist rhetoric. When they wouldn't let him leave, he started to blab about time like curves and quantum entanglement. They thought he was mad so they just threw him in the Daldorf, but our informant thought the fine gentlemen of the British intelligence community might know better than to dismiss this sort of thing, seems that he thought it might be worth something. The strange little man, in his boxy East German suit apparently droned on for hours in the hope he'd get a few marks more than his measly retainer. God knows what they gave him in the end."

"Where's this going, George, what's it all about?" Clive asked.

"I need you to pick up this Olga and bring her back here for a chat."

George was visibly uncomfortable now, tiny beads of sweat were forming on his high forehead as he plucked a perfectly folded pocket square from his suit jacket to dab at them delicately.

"And if she doesn't come quietly?" Clive asked, eyeing his master, searching for hidden meaning in his ambiguous sentiments.

"Then persuade her," he intoned, lighting a cigarette without offering one to Clive. "I know you have a way with the ladies, Clive, half of Berlin knows you have a way with the ladies."

Clive did not have a way with the ladies, Clive prayed on vulnerable women who needed help or protection. He was cruel and manipulative with very little regard for any of the women he coerced into bed. There were usually about four or five unattached and available women in Clive's keeping. Often daughters of high-ranking Nazi officials that were either dead or in hiding. These women had lost their status and any wealth they'd once had and were now left without the necessary skills to fend for themselves in the new Trizone. Using his seemingly endless supply of money, Clive would house and clothe the women, dropping in whenever he felt like it to torment one of his playthings. If he grew bored with one of these wretched women, he would threaten to cut them off until they gave into whatever depraved act he desired that month. Blackmail was something Clive was not going to leave himself open to and another dead prostitute in the Landwehr Kanal wasn't going to raise any eyebrows with the Wasserschutzpolizei.

"Persuade her, right?"

"Sorry, Clive? Was that a question? You're doing that awful yank affectation of pitching words up at the end."

"Care to elaborate on 'persuade'?"

"You know very well what I mean, man!" George was starting to lose his trademark cool demeanour, a strand of Brylcreemed hair had broken free from atop his balding pate and now it bounced as he orated.

"You got it, boss," Clive answered in an American accent. "I'll need written orders, of course."

"Yes, yes, yes," George waved him off with a hand, as certain as Clive was that no such orders would ever appear on departmental stationery of any kind.

"Goodbye then, Sir?"

"There! You did it again," George said accusingly, whilst limply pointing in his general direction. "I'll have Sinclair prepare a goodie bag for your trip."

"My trip?"

"Oh, yes, they've booked one-way tickets to Munich."

"That's sloppy, George, it doesn't sound at all like KGB at all."

"We can ask Olga Felsen all about her sloppy travel arrangements when you bring her to Berlin station."

"Where is she now?"

"Marienfelde Refugee Camp, she's untouchable there and you know as well as I do that the BfV would have a field day if they caught us poking around."

"That parcel of washed-up Nazis couldn't catch a –"

"Now, see here, Clive!" George's face reddened but his voice maintained the same level tone it always had. "You are to wait at Messe Nord and watch them boarding the train to Nuremburg, then when you are sure that the BfV are not following her too, you may carry out your orders."

"Who are they? Who is Felsen travelling with?" Clive had watched George light another cigarette without offering him one, so he was now smoking one of his Gauloises as he gazed about the garish study at George's ridiculous possessions.

He saw books he didn't read, fine spirits he didn't have a taste for and mementoes from trips he certainly hadn't taken. George was a simple man. He read the papers, drank middling port and spent one week in a gite near Carcassonne every August with his miserable wife and vulgar children. The Balzac was unread, the Laphroaig untasted and the game trophies carried no stories of epic African safaris or exhilarating hunts through the Black Forest. The whole room was a façade, a tribute to the life he wished he'd led.

"Gosh, mustn't forget him," he snapped his fingers by his ear trying to recall the name, "Doctor Rudolf Kessler, physicist from Humboldt University and the key to all of this." George tilted his head impatiently as he waited for Clive to give him his full attention. "He must not suspect foul play."

He raised his eyebrows as if this was some sort of explicit instruction.

"Is there anything else I've forgotten, George?"

"Very good," he said, wagging a fat finger at his subordinate, the man pegged to replace him when he finally retired. "No, that's all."

He paused but as Clive turned to leave, called after him.

"And Henry?"

"Yes, George?"

"Don't mess this up, old boy."

The man seemed genuinely concerned for his old comrade, so much so that he turned away, apparently to fiddle with some papers on his Biedermeier desk.

"Thanks, George," Clive said as he stubbed out his cigarette in the man's half-finished drink and left the room.

Sinclair was a giant of a man, an ex-guardsman from Perthshire with a thick accent to match his thick red beard. His dry sense of humour was lost on most, usually taken for a sort of hostile reminder of what might happen if you misplaced any of his wares, but he liked Clive and always made time for a chat whenever he ventured down to his basement armoury.

"Standard issue Webley Mk VI revolver," Sinclair said distractedly as he looked the weapon over with practised movements. "But we don't want to give you that, there's hardly any damn bullets left."

He reached under his counter and produced a much smaller pistol.

"Here we are, a Luger P08, takes eight rounds of the widely available 9 by 19mm parabellum."

Both men knew that the other had heard this all before, but it was the old soldier's ritual and Clive always made time for useful men – he didn't have friends.

"Off anywhere nice, Mr. Clive?"

"Here and there, you know how it is, Campbell's got me running errands again. What about you?"

Clive couldn't give a Pfennig what this tired old jock was up to, but he knew that he could be trusted and trustworthy men with access to firearms were worth their weight in gold.

"It's West Berlin, my wife's dead and the bairns are all grown up, what do you think I'm up to?"

He gave Clive a look that said, 'I'm a man about town on an island of freedom floating in a sea of communist oppression,' but Clive read his expression as, 'I drink myself into a stupor each night before staggering home with a prostitute that looks like George Formby in a wig'.

He thought it best not to answer the question and took the proffered weapon, noting the lack of serial number and knurled trigger.

"Is this…the black bag edition?"

Sinclair eyed him suspiciously for a moment before breaking into a booming laugh that echoed around the vaulted cellar.

"Why do you think I keep it in a drawer?"

"Just checking, old bean. You couldn't spare a couple of magazines?"

He was now playing the role of archetypal upper-class Englishman, staring about distractedly as if this was all such a frightful bore.

"Oh, and I'll need gloves, a garrot and some restraints, if you have them."

"Right you are. Anything else, Mr. Clive?" Sinclair's appetite for social interaction was satiated now and he was ready to resume his role as solitary armskote man.

Clive dropped the pistol, ancillaries and garrot, along with his 'goodie bag', into the battered attaché case that he always carried with him around the Station, or any other department building for that matter. You never knew when you might see something that would be better off in your possession. Be it a report that showed you in a less than favourable light, or an item of contraband that might be a useful bribe. The best thing about stealing contraband? There is no recourse for the victim.

He got petty cash from the pay office, signed for in triplicate of course, and headed back to his penthouse in Charlottenburg, where he packed a bag and had it sent ahead to a suite at the Nuremberg Grand. He laid the tools of his trade out on the dining room table, the P08 loaded with two spare magazines, the garrot and the gloves.

He unzipped the small bag and tipped out the contents. There were the usual papers that identified him as a major in the Royal Corps of Pioneers, a micro camera, a listening device disguised as a button, and a smoke grenade hidden in a bottle of indigestion pills. He looked at the sorry looking offering and curled his lip in disgust.

He could pack it all in tomorrow if he only did it for money. But the truth was that he relished his clandestine status, the lack of consequence that his foolhardy actions often led to and the absolute power he enjoyed over ninety-nine percent of the population. It wasn't like that in London, of course. If he took a desk job, he'd be just another penpusher climbing the greasy pole. He could do it, he could do it well, but he would never sink so low. As for the Berlin residency, he didn't want it, and if they offered it to him, as many thought they would on George's retirement, he would turn it down. The truth was that he would be bored, order bored him, people bored him, and safety bored him. He was happiest on a knife edge, playing cat and mouse with the KGB or the GRU, fighting for his life or taking the life of another human being.

These were all just the lies he told himself. Ever since the end of the war he had been charging down this self-destructive path to nowhere, infuriated at the praise and adoration he received for behaving like an overgrown school bully. He had developed this superiority, not the born leader-landed gentry nonsense that was drummed into him at Harrow, but a genuine sense that he and only he could see the world and those in it for what they really were: idiots, deluded wage slaves all vying for their chance to step up another rung of the invisible ladder. George wants a Knighthood, Father wants a peerage, Rolf at the docks wants to be a supervisor and Bunny Warren wants to be the next deputy director general of the SIS. It all meant nothing, none of these people, his father included, had ever wielded real power. Their power had been given to them by someone else and could be taken away just as easily. Henry Clive was going to seize it, grab onto it with both hands and claim it for his own. The seed of a plan had begun to form and as it germinated in his mind, he was starting to see how the pieces might fall into place for him.

~

Twenty-four hours later he was on a late train to Nuremburg in pursuit of the pair from the east. Olga Felsen put up a brave fight. She was well trained and had he not played every dirty trick he knew, she might have got the better of him. But she didn't. She lay bleeding to death from her femoral artery on a railway siding somewhere near Erlangen. It had been a shame he'd needed the balaclava – he relished that moment just before the life of his victim was extinguished and his victory over them was inescapable, he had a visceral need for them to see his face – but something on a subconscious level had urged caution and in this line of work, instinct is all.

Now Clive sat watching Rudi Kessler from the corner of the bar. The man was a snivelling wreck, crying into his Dunkel Bier and clutching the all-important calculations in his lap, as lights from beyond the carriage sporadically lit his strong features. He waited until Rudi was ready to pass out and stepped up to help him to the sleeper he'd arranged. When Rudi was all tucked up and dreaming about Stasi prisons and nasty Englanders, Clive began to photograph every single document in the scientist's possession. Then he went to the bar, because it was his turn to drink. Only men like Clive didn't actually get pass-out drunk, they just drank

33

and that's what he did, all the way to Nuremberg. During the train change, whilst a confused Rudi waited for his connection to Munich, Clive retrieved his bag from the Grand Hotel, where he looked longingly at the luxurious suite for a moment before heading back to the station to follow Rudi to his final destination.

Clive made sure that Rudi got to the Max Planck Institute, and he watched as the infamous Werner Heisenberg shook his hand and led him to a side room. He waited outside until a group of scientists left together, closely followed by Rudi and Werner. He photographed them and then caught the sleeper back to Berlin.

Once there, he began a series of seemingly chance encounters with men like Bunny and George, men whose job it was to come up with schemes, 'big wins' for the department as the CIA boys would say. He turned on the charm and began to plant ideas in the heads of these men, ideas that would shake things up and hopefully put him at the forefront of the whole programme.

"Say, Bunny?" Clive had cornered the controller of the German desk over from London at a party in the United States diplomatic mission in Zehlendorf. Men of Henry Clive's departmental rank would not usually be invited to such highbrow soirees, but men of Clive's social standing – the heir to a baronetcy and vast tracts of the Sussex countryside – were always on the guestlist.

"Do you remember what it was that Churchill said at the end of the war?" He feigned a gesture of memory jogging. "About the Soviets?"

"Well, Henry, I'm sure he had a great deal to say on the matter. Do you care to elaborate?" Bunny said impatiently, pushing his thick-rimmed glasses up his nose before sipping some champagne.

"He was touring Dresden, or some such city flattened by allied bombing, and he said, 'We've butchered the wrong pig.' Meaning

34

that the Russians are the real danger and perhaps they always have been."

"Ah, yes, I do recall something about that now," Bunny lied. Churchill never said that, although those sentiments were reasonably accurate, as Clive always checked his sources and never spoke untruths unless he meant to. "What's this all about, Henry?"

"Oh, I don't know, Bunny, I look at the mess we're in here and I wish we could just turn back the clock."

"And side with the bally Nazis?" Bunny nearly choked on his hors d'oeuvre.

"No, Bunny, of course not. What I meant was, it's a shame we can't end the socialist millennium before it even began."

"That's all well and good, Henry, but we don't have a time machine now, do we? Look, there's Sergey Filippovna, I must catch him before he leaves. Good seeing you, old chap, and you must give me the name of your tailor."

With that, Bunny was off, weaving his way through the throng, champagne flute aloft and a dozen apologies on his lips.

Clive knocked back his champagne and helped himself to another before making a quiet exit. Outside, Berlin was warm, the linden trees rustled in the twilight and there was an atmosphere of gratitude in the air. With the wall going up overnight, Berliners were reminded of how badly off they might have been, and whilst they pitied their neighbours in the east, they felt the need to have a drink on their behalf. And as Clive drove north towards his office at SIS Berlin Station, he saw more evidence of this determination by Berliners to enjoy what it was they had, and that was freedom.

"This one," he fingered a photograph of Doctor Winfried Schroeder, engineer and retired Nazi, "there's leverage in the lost

35

uranium mines and apparent weakness of character from his activity during the war."

"My sentiments exactly, Mister Clive," the analyst assigned to Clive said. One of the handful of Baker Street Irregulars that had been absorbed along with Clive at the end of the war. Harriet Beatie was in the middle of the weekly night duty that all junior staff were required to perform, and Clive was taking advantage of the empty office to expedite his off-the-books Munich operation. "If you're going to make one of this lot your agent, then I recommend Schroeder, hands down."

"Thank you, Harriet. Now, please remember this is strictly between us for the time being, I'm still waiting for George to make his mind up about it."

The staff permanently assigned to Berlin Station had an unwavering respect for George, but Clive had surreptitiously eroded their perception of his competence as a leader. In this way he was able to push things through without his signature, supported by the widely held assumption that Clive would replace him in the not-too-distant future.

"No problem, Mister Clive, see you in KU-Kneipe tomorrow night? We're having a little leaving party for Bunty."

The Kurfürstendamm Kneipe or KU-Kneipe was a grubby little pub off the Kurfürstendamm that the more social staff members had adopted as their unofficial mess.

"I'm headed there now, actually," Clive said, expertly avoiding the question. Harriet gave an exaggerated frown and a gesture that indicated she would be here all night instead.

He appraised her then. She was roughly Clive's age, perhaps just under forty, but the years had not been kind. The trials and tribulations of nearly half a decade in occupied France had left her with sunken eyes and deep crevices where most women of her age were only just starting to show lines. In her favour, he thought, that figure is the same one that parachuted down over the French Riviera in '41. Her smile was heart-warming and most people found her laugh infectious. Clive rarely laughed and when he did, he was usually the only one who found whatever it was funny.

"Perhaps I'll see you there then, Henry?" she ventured.

"Perhaps?" he said, noncommittally.

He really was going to KU-Kneipe because it was Friday, and he knew he'd find George in there having a 'post diplomatic shandy', a favourite term of his. Clive chose to walk, taking in the balmy night and enjoying a gentle breeze on his face, so he arrived shortly after midnight. The main bar was filled with most of the junior staff, all trying to fuck each other in the orgy that was the foreign service in the swinging sixties. In the gemütlich little Nebenraum to the rear, he found George and a few of his cronies, some of the army types he loved to be associated with. In Clive's opinion, they were usually men of lower intelligence, like George. Clive waited patiently whilst George finished off an anecdote about his time in Palestine before the war.

"And he must have overheard us saying that he looked too young, because when he came back from leave, he'd grown a bloody great moustache. The colonel made him there and then, a fine addition to the mess, all things considered."

"All things considered," the congregation echoed.

"Funny thing about ex-rankers," offered a rotund man in the mess dress of a colonel of the Eighth Hussars who swayed gently as he spoke. "The men will always love them, do anything for them, anything. For in that man, that holder of a Queen's commission is the message that this army is in fact a meritocracy. But what one

37

mustn't forget... what one must always remember is that they are not, nor never shall they be," he raised a fat little finger, "One. Of. Us."

This was met with nods and murmurs of approval. "It's not their fault, you see. Try as they might and by Jove, I've seen them try, affecting the accent, educating their children, and even sending their wives off to some sort of finishing school. Try as they might, they simply don't have the breeding." He looked round at all assembled, daring them to disagree, when his eyes fell on Clive. "There, a fine example of breeding right here in Henry, good military stock, isn't that right, old boy?"

"If you say so. George, could I have a moment of your time?"

"Certainly, Henry," he looked meaningfully at his acolytes, and they left the tiny room. "What can I do for you?" he hiccupped.

Clive embarked on a prepared dialogue in which he had almost perfectly predicted George's every response. By the end of the conversation, the seed was planted, the earth covered, and water had been sprinkled liberally. Now he would watch it grow.

A week or so later Clive was seconded to Munich, with a young agent called Bernard and the analyst Harriet to assist with intelligence. On deciding that he would like to have her after all, he promptly disposed of the stable of women he had until now kept in fear and comfort all over Berlin. Their systemic and callous slaughter went unremarked. Clive simply showed up unannounced, as he always did, and dispatched the women without a word. Their accommodations were rented through third parties and not in the sorts of places where people ever answered questions from the police.

For him it was simply a case off tying up a few expensive loose ends. He saw these women as his personal property to do with as he saw fit. Such was the depth of his self-delusion, of his depravity, the lives of these women who were to someone a daughter, a sister, or a friend meant little more than that of an unwanted pet.

As he sat in the Bear Inn, Oxford, plying his twenty-one-year-old father with drink, he thought of all the wrong he had done in his strange and many lives. Most recently the murder of Bertie, the obsequious little shit, but the act of luring his father down to Folly Bridge to hire a punt that day in 1897 must be one of the most despicable.

They reclined in a drunken stupor, Henry's affected and Gerald's very real. As they floated down the Thames past Boat House Island, Clive waited patiently for his moment and devoid of ceremony, he slit his father's throat with the same lack of remorse he'd shown to those women in 1961. Clive foundered the punt and ensured the corpse of his father sank with it, before finding the horse he had left for himself in the woods to the east.

A new, leaner, more mature Sir Gerald Clive rode hard for Hampshire, changing horses at every opportunity and arriving as the sun rose over Broadlands. In the treeline at the edge of his family estate, Clive trimmed his moustaches to match the stubble on the rest of his face. Before retiring to bed, he gave the staff their notice and ordered that the house be shut up and protected against dust. That afternoon he made preparations to attend the Royal Military College at Sandhurst, his entry exams completed some time ago, and the offer of a place delivered to the PO box that Clive maintained. In town he accessed his father's dwindling funds and repurposed them into stocks and other financial vehicles that he knew would do very well for him, enjoying hindsight a broker would kill his own mother for.

Over the course of a few days Clive had acquired land, title, a growing fortune and the means to cover himself in the kind of glory one must have to propel oneself from obscurity into the upper echelons of the most powerful government in the world.

Paris, 1912

Olga Felsen drew deep on the frigid February air and exhaled slowly as the sights of her Russian-made Mosin Nagant lowered naturally onto the target. She watched in detached horror as the head of Raymond Poincaré exploded, covering the cadets around him in pieces of brain and fragments of skull. With deft movements, she removed the specially made sight and wiped down the rifle, leaving it to be discovered later. Using tweezers, Carla took a Russian made cigarette end from a small bag and dropped it where the rifle now lay. The lifeless body of the French prime minister, who would have been president within the year, was now surrounded by the new graduates of the École Militaire, their early morning ceremony interrupted first by the explosion of their Prime Minister's head and fractions of a second later by the sound of Olga's rifle.

With a few undetectable adjustments, Olga and Carla were clothed in the fine but impractical dresses expected of upper-class ladies in 1912. By the time the soldiers on the parade ground had figured out where the shooter must have been and sent a runner the six hundred meters to alert the officials at the base of the Eifel tower, the assassins had abseiled from their firing point on the midlevel down to the first level. They waited for their assailants to board the lift before descending the staircase at a leisurely pace, sauntering away, twirling their parasols, and giggling at men on their way to work. The risk was that respectable young women would not be out walking so early in the day, but that was hardly a crime and better to be a helpless, weak, and incapable woman than a suspect in the assassination of the Prime Minister of France.

They crossed the Pont D'léna to the north bank of the Seine where a coach and two horses waited to take them far from the scene.

"So, let me just get this straight in my mind," Olga said, "Poincaré was a Germaphobe and a right-wing nationalist who—"

"Who will change the alliance with Russia into one that will force their hand when Austria declares war on Serbia. He increases the size of France's army, which spooks the Germans, and he was just about to root out all of his opponents in the assembly, effectively removing the democratic process in the house," interrupted Carla as the coach rumbled east through the increasingly busy streets.

"Okay then, and by 1914 when Franz Ferdinand gets it, Poincaré's not PM, he's President?"

"Right, and as the newly elected President, he travels to Saint Petersburg and promises Russia that they will back each other and enjoy the spoils when the war is won, encouraging the Tsar to mobilise."

"Why is that so bad?" Olga asked.

"Because first of all, it's not his job to deal with foreign policy and second, politicians are supposed to avoid war at all costs, not encourage it. The mobilisation of Russian troops led to the mobilisation of German troops, which started the war. He lied to Britain about Russia mobilising first and blamed it on the Austrians. He played tricks to draw Britain into the war and was publicly pleased when war was declared."

"What a bastard!"

"He won't do any of that now, he's a dead bastard."

"What will happen?" Olga asked.

Carla explained.

"Well, by leaving the Russian rifle and Russian cigarette stub, we hope to damage the alliance between the two countries, removing Germany's legitimacy for invading France. In Paris, all indicators point to a surge from the left and a raft of anti-war and pro-German foreign policy. What if France wants revenge, you ask? Well, we are going to give it to them at the same time as removing one of the nastiest men in the Russian Duma."

"What if our actions provoke war between Russia and France?" Olga countered.

"They share no borders and the space between is filled with nations that hold sympathy for neither. Perhaps they can fight a proxy war in the colonies, but who knows, we've already changed history forever," Carla warned.

"Alright, easy on the dread, please. What time is our train?"

"It's later on this afternoon," Carla said, leafing through her sheaf of notes, "seven."

"Well then, we've got some time to kill. Shall we go shopping?" Olga produced a wad of paper francs from her own bag and fanned herself with it.

These women, Olga from a utilitarian future of dirndl skirts and crown plaits and Carla from the era of make do and mend and ersatz coffee, had not known abundance like this, nor could they have imagined it in the late forties and early fifties. For this was Paris in the Belle Époque: the beautiful era. It was the height of the grands magasins, department stores like the world famous Le Bon Marché and Galeries Lafayette. It was the era of impressionism, of architectural wonders like the Eifel Tower and the Grand Palais.

Renault Frères' taxis buzzed around the Place de l'Étoile transporting Parisians from arrondissement to arrondissement in style. These taxis were to play an important role in the defence of France, ferrying troops to the front in time to meet the invading German army, but not if Olga and Carla had anything to do with it.

As Carla browsed the aisles of Le Bon Marché, fingering the luxurious fabrics and smelling the fine perfumes, she promised herself that she would do everything she could to keep her countrymen from marching into this beautiful city.

They spent the day savouring the culture and indulging in the fashion, sipping chocolate and devouring pastries. They found 'practical' clothing in the women's sports sections and struggled to see how anyone could roller skate, cycle, or horse ride in these full-length dresses. Inspiration struck as they wandered into an entire department devoted to furs and they both spent an hour stroking, hugging, and modelling the dead animal skins, until they selected a pair of heavy overcoats with matching hat and muff.

"Perfect for the Russian winter," remarked Olga.

Both Olga and Carla had learned to sew during their childhood and had prepared their attire very carefully. Instead of the restrictive corsets of the day, they wore a sort of form-hugging, stab-proof vest with a ceramic plate over the heart, both front and rear. Carefully hidden under layers of overlapping fabric, their dresses, and skirts split to the waist and could be quickly fastened up out of the way to make movement easier. The high collars of their outfits were reinforced to protect their necks. Their parasols sported a poisoned tip and a dagger in the handle.

Both women carried .25 Baby Brownings in their clutches and wore hardened steel pins in their hats. By way of luggage, they carried a large trunk and two small valises, all three lined with bank notes, bonds, and gold.

They carried the same microfilms as Rudi, containing Carla's exhaustive research into the political events leading up to the Great War, what she called her Sarajevo hypothesis.

The trunk contained the weapons they planned to use for each assassination, for the procurement of such things was almost impossible for women and would certainly arouse suspicion. In 1912, letters from the government were used by travellers instead of passports and they had one in every language they could speak. When Olga and Carla finally emerged from Eifel's beautifully built department store, the sun was in the west, and they had one hour to fetch their things from the left luggage at the Gare de l'Est and board the Nord Express for Saint Petersburg.

The Nord Express would carry them from Paris to Saint Petersburg in less than two days, changing at the Russian border for another train with a different gauge of track. The compartment was opulence on a scale unseen by these women, even at Broadlands: teak, marble, Egyptian cotton, and rich, supple leather.

"We pass through Berlin," remarked Carla.

"Great, I had such fun last time I visited."

"No, Olga, listen." She leaned in closer. "I want to see it before... I mean before it was destroyed, before swastikas adorned every façade, before the yellow stars and the antisemitic slogans, before the shame and the horror."

She looked away for a moment steeling herself, "I spent night after night on top of Zoo Tower manning those guns and staring down at a city in ruins, a ruination of its own making, a nation duped by that nasty little Austrian."

"I can't wait to kill him," Olga cut in.

"I'm serious, Olga, I want to take a look on our way back from Saint Petersburg. I'm going to plan in a few days to look around before Vienna. Okay?"

"Okay, as long as you don't think it'll make a difference?"

"I'll have a good think about it."

That night they dined on moules marinières with a white Burgundy, followed by chocolate soufflé. Their first night in 1912 was a restful one, but as usual, Carla's dreams were plagued with images and feelings she did not understand. Helplessness and fear dominated, followed by worthlessness and dread. Slowly, in the years since she had first seen the images, Carla had pieced together what might have happened and as she read about the aftermath of the Battle of Berlin, realisation washed over her like an icy rain. She knew then what she owed Olga and of course Rudi, for in some convoluted way, he had brought her to them in their hour of need.

Every morning in the moments between sleep and awareness she felt an overwhelming sense of uncleanliness, like she needed to wash but she could not, and would not be able to for a painful amount of time. The scent of all those men, and their filth inside her, she couldn't bear it. All this came and passed in a matter of seconds, but the urge to wash did not and every morning without fail, she would shower or bath. The English servants thought it highly irregular, verging on decadent, but they could never truly understand the depth of her trauma. Up to the day Carla died, she didn't meet a soul that she would wish that on, not one.

Olga used the limited space to train, tearing Carla away from her books to join her. Carla had come a long way since that apartment in Prenzlauer Berg. She wasn't the fastest or the toughest of Olga's students, but she was a match for anyone in this time period. She understood and had made it her business to master the technical side of the art, tying most – including Olga on occasion – in knots, leaving them scratching their heads and wondering how they'd ended up on the ground begging for mercy. Suitably sweaty, they took turns washing and took a light lunch in the dining car. As they finished their salade niçoise, the train pulled into Berlin's Ostbahnhof. The enormous station rose up with its barrel-vaulted steel ceiling as the train panted to a halt, and plumes of thick white steam filled the concourse.

The clouds cleared to reveal porters with trolleys, families with children, and soldiers with sweethearts. The efficiency of the guards, conductors and porters brought Carla home. Elsewhere in Europe, staff bumbled around, fussing over their charges and worrying that they would displease them. Here they carried out their task with a curt nod and a click of the heels, efficient to the last.

As those from the west were replaced with those heading east the platform emptied, and the guard blew his whistle. The train lurched forward and pulled clear of the station, steaming through Kreuzberg with the Spree to the south. Carla strained to catch a glimpse of her hometown and although she recognised it, she did not feel the way she had hoped to. She supposed that Broadlands was her home now, which was fine, but it made her long for the life she had not led, a life as a German, a Berliner. Despite her youth she'd fought for this place, and she was doing it again now, so why didn't it feel like home? She resolved to try again on the return trip and set her mind instead to the complex geopolitical spider's web that she was trying to navigate, reminding herself of the innumerable lives she could help save by snuffing out but a few choice chess pieces.

Dining that evening was a somewhat more indulgent affair, with oysters, filet mignon, poached salmon, foie gras, roasted pigeon, and lamb. Olga and Carla, who had been subjected to rationing for over a decade, could only eat a bite or two of each course but when they looked about at the other diners, their habits were just as wasteful. A great deal of wine was poured between courses and subsequently consumed by Olga and Carla.

For some men, an apparently vulnerable woman well into her cups was an opportunity too good to pass up. Gottlieb Scholz was just such a man and his wildly erratic moral compass had never steered him wrong.

"Good evening, ladies," he said in German, slithering into the empty seat across the aisle from a slightly worse for wear Olga and Carla.

"Good evening," Olga said.

"Good evening." Carla was somewhat less discerning in her current state and began a thorough appraisal of the young man.

"Where are you two travelling all on your own?" he asked.

"Moscow," Olga lied, apparently with more of her wits about her than she had given herself credit for. "Where are you bound?"

"Königsberg," he said, affecting a modest gesture with his hand.

"Do you have work there?" Carla demanded.

"A sick relative." His favourite reason for travelling.

"Oh dear," Carla gave an exaggerated frown and turned her head to one side, a look she imagined conveyed genuine sympathy.

"Would you care to join me in the bar for a drink?"

"Yes," Carla said before Olga had opened her mouth to speak.

"Looks like I don't have a choice," Olga muttered as she rose.

"What was that?" Gottlieb leaned towards her to better hear, inflicting his breath on her.

"Oh, nothing," Olga said, fighting the urge to recoil in disgust.

Olga fell in line behind Carla and Gottlieb, and she imagined a combination of drink, the events of the day, and homesickness had led to her friend's strange behaviour. When they had lived together in Oxford Carla had enjoyed several relationships and Olga thought that she'd approached them with a level head. The intellectuals she'd dated were tall, dark types proudly sporting a Blue for rowing and the body to prove it. This guy was all suit and she doubted he could even pick up the bill, let alone a pair of six-foot oars. Conversely, Carla was a fit, lean, history machine with a brown belt in Jujitsu and a 3mm grouping.

Gottlieb must have felt Olga's laser vision burning at the back of his neck, for he rubbed it with his hand as they crossed into the bar carriage.

"Drei Schnaps, bitte," Olga said, before Gottlieb had gathered his thoughts. "Prosit."

"Prosit," the other two echoed.

"Noch einmal?" suggested Gottlieb.

"Bitte," Carla replied, Olga nodding her tacit assent and wondering how much they would regret this at the Prussian border tomorrow morning when they were changing trains in the bitter cold.

"Drei mehr, bitte," Gottlieb requested. "Danke."

He distributed the glasses and they drank again.

"Prosit."

"Prosit."

"We really should be going," insisted Olga.

"Very good, I will escort you back to your compartment."

"Oh, really, there's no need."

"I insist," Gottlieb said, his tone dropping an octave. The last man who insisted Olga do anything ended up with a broken arm and an empty dojo. She looked up and to the side of the rat-faced interloper and exhaled.

Lose your cool now, Olga, and blow the mission. What's the mission? Saving the whole fucking world from two massive wars and two genocidal regimes.

She realised that she was nodding to herself and turned red, abruptly spinning on her heel and forcing a ladylike walk in the direction of their compartment.

Gottlieb belied Olga's assumptions and left without lingering too long at all.

"See," Carla said, "a perfect gentleman."

"Fine, now get some sleep. Changing trains in the Russian winter will be bad enough without a hangover."

Olga woke as the train jolted to a stop. It took her a moment to get her bearings, and when she had them, she groaned loudly enough to provoke a response from Carla.

"Why did you let me drink so much?"

"Get up, we have to change trains and the porters will be here for our luggage any minute."

Carla was pleased to find she was already dressed and the slow realisation that for the first time in over a decade, she had woken without feeling unclean almost cured her hangover. Carnage ensued as both women scrambled to pack their things away before the porters came, and before they knew it, they were shuffling across the platform, their heavy fur coats wrapped tightly against the biting cold.

They settled in their new compartment and ordered coffee. Neither wanted to remove their furs as the train was almost as cold as the platform. At breakfast there was no sign of Gottlieb, and Olga reasoned that as Königsberg was behind them now, he must have alighted whilst they slept. They skipped training and Carla decided to go through the details of their mission.

"Vladimir Purishkevich, a Russian right-wing politician, a really quite revolting little man. He organised pogroms of Russian Jews, driving them west with a vigour that Himmler might have envied. He has since been described as the first fascist and in 1916 he is part of the plot to murder Rasputin."

"Is that a bad thing?" Olga asked. "Killing Rasputin, I mean."

"Rasputin had his faults, but for our purposes we want him to be alive and urging the Tsar to stay out of the war. Now, whilst this certainly makes him despicable, does it warrant our journey all the way to Saint Petersburg? Remember, we plan to turn the Russians and the French against each other? Well, we need a Russian to assassinate, and he seems the most deserving. Obviously, we need make it look like a Frenchman did it."

"Whilst we're here, can we get Stalin too?" Olga mused.

"From what I can find out about this period in his life, he was in exile in Vologda, but there's some reference to his repeated escape." Carla was examining the microfilm with an eye loupe. "He edited the first edition of the Pravda, – Russian for truth – which came out on April twenty-second of this year." She looked up with a satisfied grin on her face.

"Pleased with yourself? That degree pay off, did it?" Olga teased.

"I mean, I am facilitating the assassination of a man responsible for the deaths of tens of millions of innocent human beings, so yeah, I am."

51

"I'm not exactly excited about spending three months in Saint Petersburg in winter," Olga complained, folding her arms against the cold, psychosomatic or otherwise.

"It'll be more like three weeks and remember that we don't have the same information we had on the prime minister of France about this Purishkevich character, so we'll have to stake him out and work out how to kill him cleanly."

"Fine, but I want a suite at the Astoria." Olga tried to keep a straight face, but she cracked after a few seconds and burst out laughing.

"You had me going there."

"I do want to stay at the Astoria, though," she said as her face dropped.

"Where else, darling, where else?" Carla threw her hair back like a movie star and fluttered her eyelashes.

That evening the train steamed into Vitebsky station. The architectural masterpiece was reminiscent of, though far more impressive than, the OstBahnhof in Berlin. The lavish art nouveau interior complemented the wide central staircase and stained-glass windows. The history of Russia's railways was told in panels on the station walls and rising stone arches supported a glass roof. Outside Olga turned to see a beautifully decorated façade with floral reliefs and huge windows. On Zagorodny Prospect Carla hailed a carriage, and a porter loaded their luggage for them, too deferent to comment on the excessive weight. As the driver pulled away in the direction of the Astoria hotel, a rat-like man rushed onto the street and hailed a cab of his own to follow them.

Huddled against the cold night in their furs, Olga and Carla watched the city pass by the windows. The streets were busy, the sound of hooves on cobbles, men and women in evening dress converging on the opera and the occasional foghorn from the harbour. They drove over the Blue Bridge and into Saint Isaacs's Square, where the cab pulled up right under the monument to Nicholas I on horseback. As Carla climbed down she was faced with the intimidating edifice of the Hotel Astoria on one side and the Maryanski Palace on the other. Again, their bags were moved for them to the opulent marble foyer and when they had secured a modest suite of rooms, they ascended the magnificent sweeping staircase followed by a heavily burdened bell hop.

Olga tipped the boy, Gregory generously and collapsed on the settee breathing a sigh of exhaustion and relief. Travelling was a privilege, travelling in time was an unimaginable gift, but she was glad she was going to be in one place for a few weeks. She thought about the men she would need to kill in cold blood to succeed in her task, and she thought of those whose lives she had already taken. Nearly every one of them had died before she was born, but did that make it any better? She didn't know, but so far, she was sure that she had never killed a man who didn't deserve it.

Olga knew the faces of every single one, and when she shut her eyes, they were there, they lived with her now, they were part of her and always would be. She wondered if there was a limit, because she knew that a piece of her soul fell away every time she extinguished a life. But she felt like the size of that piece depended on the character of the victim. She felt that killing an innocent child might destroy her, make her soulless and she would never be whole again, but that the men she had killed were for the most part evil, perhaps not the boy in the alley in Kreuzberg, but he certainly would have raped her or let his friends rape her, so he'd had to die. The person she thought of most was Carla's mother Emma, a mercy killing of course, but still a monstrously difficult thing to come to terms with and Olga had only been eighteen.

Emma had known her, had told her that she had killed her before, she'd wanted to die and had told her how to do it. Emma Kessler's peaceful face was often the last thing she saw at night and Olga felt that in some twisted way she shared something with Carla, her closest friend, and the sister of her soulmate. Did she know? She had never discussed it, but she was scared that Carla did. Rudi had worked it out that night and had more or less consented to it, but Carla would probably never know that Olga had euthanised her mother in 1945.

At the rear of the hotel a German man bribed a porter, they shared a cigarette in the alley by the kitchen door and spoke of attractive female tourists.

Bremerhaven, 1907

Bremerhaven in 1907 was a sight to behold and for Rudi this was his first time back on home soil for nearly a decade. In stark contrast to the devastation wrought by allied bombing on Berlin and Hamburg, the port city was a shining example of Germany's prosperity in the early days of the twentieth century.

As the SS Valdivia steamed through the Wattenmeer and into the mouth of the Wesse River, Rudi grew anxious. Tomorrow he would need to begin his impersonation of Horst Buchholz properly. Until now he had spoken the words and answered to the name when called, but he had never received the scrutiny of former acquaintances, of public officials and even old school friends. Tomorrow he would have to become Horst Buchholz and remain in character for at least the next eight years.

As his re-entry into Germany was made a matter of record, Horst Buchholz was officially resurrected from the dead and his first order of business was to find his family home and move back in for a time, to prepare for his journey to Berlin. The knot in Rudi's guts grew heavy as he thought of the servants at the house.

Would there be any? What had happened when his parents died, and the real Horst was in Africa? Wasn't it strange that he didn't return for the funeral?

These questions fought for space in his head as he paced the streets of Bremen in his gleaming uniform. Hauptmann Buchholz caught his reflection in a shop front and paused to admire it. For a moment he could have sworn the image of the man staring back at him was changed, aged and haggard – a toothless old man in a dayglow tracksuit. Rudi spun around to see if a passer-by had noticed this brightly coloured anachronism, but no one was there. When he looked back, the Hauptmann had returned, resplendent in khaki trimmed with cornflower blue.

He left the squalor of the docks and the wide boulevards of the Altstadt for the tree-lined streets and cobbled Platzes of the Ostertor. It was there, in an imposing four-storey townhouse that Horst's parents had lived. As he stared up at the white façade, his anxieties were first piqued, then washed away when he began to notice the subtle signs of neglect. A dirty window here and an unkempt vine there were all it took to set Rudi at ease as he began to search for a way into the house. He made his way around to the alley at the rear into a fenced yard. It was a large space with nothing to fill it but a couple of ageing apple trees, some dustbins, and a rusting mangle. He looked up at the windows, hoping not to see the twitch of a curtain or a silhouette. He was hefting a good-sized rock and staring hard at the glass in the kitchen door when he was interrupted by the leathery voice of an elderly lady.

"Horst?" she croaked. "Horst, is that you?" He turned to face her and found that age had caused her to stoop so low that he almost missed her.

"I am so sorry about your parents, my dear boy," she crooned, taking one of his rough, tanned hands is both of hers. Noticing the ungentlemanly coarseness of his skin, she looked up with sad, cloudy, blue eyes and placed a hand on his cheek. Rudi watched as she learned the secrets of his soul, and he could almost see the scenes of his lives unfolding in her eyes. She looked confused for a moment and then frowned, her thin, wrinkled lips twisting in spite.

"Who are you?" she demanded, and her voice carried the note of anger without increasing in volume. "Where is Horst?"

Her arthritic fingers curled around his wrist, and she drew him closer before whispering in his ear,

"You don't belong here, Rudolf Kessler."

He jumped back at the sound of his name, breathing heavily and staring down at the old woman, whose eyes had come alive now and were a vivid cobalt blue.

"Eindringling!" she shouted, slowly raising her arm to point at him, "Eindringling!"

She now stood at her full height and seemed to have lost ten years in her rage. Leaves began to susurrate as a cold wind whipped up around her, lifting the thin white hair of her head and causing her shawl to fly off behind. Clouds descended and the day grew dark, still she called out over the now howling wind.

"Get thee behind me, Satan!" she shouted, repeating it, "Geh dich hinter mich, Satan!" growing taller and louder as she did, "Geh dich hinter mich, Satan!"

Terrified, Rudi began to back away when his hand brushed against a gatepost, and he looked down to see that the rock was still in his grasp. He looked at the screaming banshee, and up to the closing storm, then around him at the violently shaking trees. Without thinking too hard, he drew back his arm and hurled the rock at the shrieking old hag. It hit her on the left temple, and she crumpled to the ground in a heap, blood pooling beneath her head. As quickly as it had begun, the clouds receded, and the wind died down. Rudi felt the sun on his face as temperature rose noticeably. He strode over to the gate and closed it with a furtive glance up and down the alley. Had anyone seen him? Surely no one could have missed that seemingly supernatural display. Or perhaps it had

57

been imagined, a manifestation of his anxiety, a projection of the guilt he harboured over this stolen life? The dead woman at his feet though, remained very real.

He smashed a pane in the kitchen door and reached inside to unlock it. The door creaked open slowly and he stepped over the threshold. Casting about for something to wrap the old witch in, he noticed dust sheets on all the furniture in the next room. Whipping a cloth off the large dining table, he bundled it up in his arms as he rushed back to the yard. The old lady lay still where he had left her, but she was light, and he was able to wrap and move her with ease, propping her up in the kitchen whilst he began searching for the door to the basement. The house was large and beautifully appointed, which meant that Horst's parents – Horst himself now – must be as rich as Carla had said they were.

'As rich as creases' is what she'd called them. Rudi found a door leading down to the cellar and an old oil lamp hanging from a hook on the bare brick wall. He descended the staircase as he deftly opened his breast pocket with his free hand and produced his lighter. The lamp spluttered to life and threw a pool of yellow light onto the ground at Rudi's feet.

He wandered through the catacomb-like cellar rooms until he reached an enormous stove, full of ash and cold as the grave. When his eyes fell upon the pile of coal in one corner, he knew what he would have to do. Rudi removed his jacket and found an apron before emptying the ash and lighting a small fire in the grate. He returned with the body and considered the task that lay before him. At first, he had thought just to hide the body down here and head off to Berlin, but even if it took years, someone would find her and questions would be asked, details taken, and all of his hard work could be ruined. When he saw the furnace, he thought he could burn the body and any evidence, but now he knew that it would not fit, not in one piece anyway. With a shovel, Rudi moved a small pile of coal to the front of the furnace and began to build up the fire, aware that it would need to be upwards of 700°C for this task.

First, he burned her clothes, then he wrapped the old woman's naked body in the sheet and left to find some overalls. He returned with the bellows and brass companion set from a fireplace upstairs, a meat cleaver and a small saw. The elderly have brittle bones, and Rudi found that he did not need the saw after his first few hacks with the cleaver. He fought back thoughts of Africa and the Herrero people he had helped to massacre and shame over his equal lack of emotion in this grievous task. He had murdered an old lady, for what? For shouting at him and for apparently causing some weather? Now he was nonchalantly hacking her still warm corpse into manageable chunks for the furnace.

He wondered if he was broken, like the men he'd met during his childhood, veterans of the Great War, friends of his grandfather, all shadows of the men they'd been before. He thought of the repulsive Ordnungspolizei men that were going to rape his sister. They weren't men, not anymore, not after what they had done in the east. Was he like them now? Or was there redemption out there for him? Ice cold fear struck him as he realised that Olga would know. If they ever found each other, she would touch him and she would see it, see all of it, the emaciated children, the systematic genocide, and Rudi's active role in the whole despicable business. Now he felt some emotion and he wept hot, selfish tears at thought of being found out, tears that had been unwarranted for the murder of this poor old lady, who he was at that very moment hacking to pieces in a basement belonging to a dead man whose life he had stolen.

Now that he had a pile of body parts laid out on the blood-soaked dust cloth, Rudi opened the furnace and added more coal, mixing it in with the poker. Then he took the bellows and began to pump, so that the additional oxygen would accelerate the burn. The coals began to glow brighter, and Rudi began to sweat.

He tossed in a foot and the skin immediately shrank and turned black, fat from beneath it igniting briefly, and within a minute the foot was an unrecognisable chunk of organic matter. Rudi added more pieces and continued to work the bellows. The smell was awful, but what bothered him more was that it was familiar. He turned to find that all he had left now was the torso and head. He wasn't prepared to hack that up, so he added more coals and put the whole thing in. When her sparse hair caught fire, he finally vomited.

The brass nozzle on the bellows melted at 700°C and he was forced to stop pumping. The heat from the open door was unbearable and the body was now only bone, so Rudi added the cloth and the apron and finally his overalls and looking at his coal-blackened hands, he realised that he could not continue like this.

He couldn't enter politics and fear murky hell in the eyes every of hand he shook. Perhaps he could wear gloves, certainly in dress uniform, but not every day. He couldn't allow people to think he was strange. He looked at the glowing coals in the furnace and back to his hands.

I don't need to hurt myself badly, I just need superficial scars, enough to justify the wearing of gloves.

He went to the kitchen and carefully washed his hands. Filling a large kettle, he carried it back to the basement and thrust it into the furnace, surrounding it with the hot coals. When it boiled, he retrieved it and after a few very deep breaths, he plunged both hands into the boiling water.

"One, two, three!" he whimpered. Withdrawing them, Rudi ran back upstairs and held his hands under cold water for what seemed like an age whilst he stared unseeing out of the window until he noticed the storm outside.

He emerged from the kitchen to find a thick, heavy rain pelting the city and the blood in the yard was all but gone. It certainly wasn't suspicious anymore. He stood in his underclothes and let the rain soak him. As the all-consuming noise shut out the on-slaught of guilt, pain, and regret, he imagined that the rain was washing away his sins. He bound his hands in strips of wet cloth and the rain continued whilst he bathed. Afterwards, Rudi col-lapsed in the first bedroom he found.

In those first moments before he was truly awake, Rudi imagined he was back at Broadlands in 1952 with Olga holding him in her strong arms. He was a normal nineteen-year-old boy with his entire life ahead of him and a beautiful, fearless woman who loved him. A woman who had crossed continents and oceans to be with him. In fact, Olga had travelled through space and time via an Einstein-Rosen Bridge to rescue him, then exercised saintly patience whilst she waited for him to grow from the twelve-year-old he had been into the man he was now.

Reality plunged him into a dizzying low. The knowledge of his current situation, the immeasurable distance between him and Olga and the enormity of the task ahead was too much. He thought of Olga's reaction when she discovered what he had done in Africa and he wept.

His black dog had returned.

I deserve to feel this way, I'm a terrible human who does awful things without remorse.

He remained in bed for a while, beating himself up, but a tiny part of him, a whisper of a voice in his head willed him up and out of bed. He ignored it for hours as he reviewed every misdeed, every life taken and every lie uttered. The self-torture was merely a part of it. He would neglect himself in every way possible, the only necessity of life he would take care of was filling of his chamber pot. The burns on his hands were a constant source of discomfort and pain, but he welcomed it, revelled in it, in the suffering that he felt was only his due.

Hours became days which became weeks. He had entered a sort of pseudo existence, eating the tired apples from the yard, drinking only when absolutely necessary and sleeping for most of the day. His hair and beard grew into a lank and greasy hedge, festering on his face. The burns to his hands slowly healed, but through his neglect the scars were far worse. The rounded collar of his shirt was dark with filth, as were the cuffs and the rest of his stinking body. Purple ringed his eyes and the tan he had acquired over four years in Africa had become a sickly pallor. Rudi moved around the old house under a cloud of self-hate and stoic refusal to do anything but survive. Instead of emptying them when they filled, he had taken to searching the house for another empty chamber pot, until one night he found himself with a full bladder and nowhere in which to relieve himself. He ventured into the yard, anxiously eying the empty apple trees as his stomach growled. Defiantly, he used the trunk of the fruitless tree, and he knew deep down that he would have to force himself to leave the house. The hoot of an owl made him look up and he saw its silhouette pass in front of a full moon.

He closed his eyes and was met with an image of Olga smiling encouragement. Her beauty and strength warmed him and for the first time in weeks, the burden of his crimes seemed to lift a little. He inhaled deeply on the crisp night air and as he exhaled and allowed his shoulders to relax.

Come on Rudi, light the furnace, run a bath and tomorrow you can start living again!

He knew that he had a long way to go, and he still felt that he deserved to suffer for his part in the Herrero massacre, but he could not afford to wallow in self-pity any longer, the fate of the twentieth century depended on his success in Berlin and he hadn't even got there yet. Rudi looked down at his scarred hands, the skin taught and shiny with irregular ridges.

As he entered the cellar, he realised that he was afraid, and he understood that this fear had been a barrier to his recovery. When he lit the furnace, he realised that he wanted a bath, he wanted to feel clean and to dress well and to succeed. He refused to acknowledge the chunks of bone amongst the ashes and forged on, rushing from the basement and the scene of his latest crime.

Maybe I am better, maybe I'll leave this dark period of my life behind me and move on for good?

After his bath, he washed his clothes and in the search for a clean shirt, discovered what must have been Horst's wardrobe. Well-cut, fashionable clothes of every kind and in every conservative colour available. Surely this was too good to be true, they couldn't possibly fit him? But he found that they did, and he had before him a perfect, if slightly outdated, wardrobe for a man of his assumed class.

He would be safe from embarrassing fashion faux pas, and he wouldn't have to go shopping, a thought that delighted him. He changed back into his filthy clothes and began the unenviable task of emptying three weeks' worth of chamber pots.

At nine o'clock that Tuesday morning he stepped out of the front door of his house a new man, a little unkempt up top, but the spring in his step was unmistakable. He bought several pairs of fine kid leather gloves in different colours and a medicated ointment. After a visit to the barbers, he took breakfast at a café on the square that would one day be known as Ulrichsplatz. Then, as Horst Buchholz, he walked into the foyer of Bremer Bank, where he looked, felt and moved like a monied Junker.

"Guten Morgen, mein Herr," a uniformed bank employee said, clicking his heels as he spoke. "How may we assist you today?"

Rudi simply inclined his head by way of a greeting.

"I wish to speak with a senior clerk, a man who can handle large sums," he said curtly, doing his utmost to affect a superior manner. He was directed to a comfortable waiting area, where he sat and listened to the footsteps of the uniformed man echo around the silent bank.

Inside the large but practically appointed office of the senior clerk, Rudi said, "I would like to make a withdrawal and transfer the remainder of my funds to your affiliate branch in Berlin."

"I am sorry to hear that, Herr Buchholz, how much would you like to withdraw?" the fastidious clerk replied, a diminutive man in the early years of middle age.

Rudi had worked this out with Carla and decided upon a sum that would get him to Berlin in comfort with any luggage he might have, as well as accommodate him for a few months when he arrived. He gave this figure to the clerk, whose eyes widened as he read the written amount.

"Certainly, Sir," he said, consulting a ledger, "ach so, that won't even dent your considerable fortune."

Rudi had lived in relative poverty until the age of twelve, knowing what it is was to starve and to feel the icy wind bite through inadequate clothing, to play with broken toys and to spend Christmas in a U-Bahn station hiding from the Terrorflieger. He wondered now what it was like for this man, a lowly clerk on just enough to house and clothe his family, who was probably only one bad illness away from financial ruin, to sit here all day discussing the unearned fortunes of men like Horst Buchholz.

He stepped into the sunshine of that wintery morning with a pocket filled with more money than he had ever seen in his life, the address of his new bank and a sense that anything was possible. Rudi spent the afternoon at leisure, browsing in shops and stopping to admire interesting architecture or an increasingly rare example of a square-rigged ship. He stood mesmerised by one now, a barquentine with deep red sails and a black hull accented just above the waterline with a thick white stripe. The crew swarmed the rigging making repairs and singing as they worked.

When this is all over, he thought, I'm going to sail around the world with Olga on one of these great ships.

Rudi stared for some time, watching the sailors and carpenters work, longing for a simpler life, one in which he could be with Olga and use his own name, one that didn't take place before he was born and where the stakes weren't so dizzyingly high.

Sandhurst, 1897

Henry Clive had everything it took to be the top student in his training platoon at Sandhurst, but he was too old and too experienced to take any of it seriously enough. His instructors, battle-hardened Colour Sergeants with over a decade and a half of experience, probably guessed this wasn't his first rodeo, but if they did, they never let on. Clive was fit and robust, intelligent and capable of functioning on very little sleep. He ran rings around his fellow cadets, but he was bored, and he had eight more months of this.

What's the point in having a bloody time machine if I have to suffer though all of this drudgery?

The tactics taught were laughable, harking back to the sort of thing Wellington was doing on the peninsular. Didn't these idiots know that forming square to receive cavalry only worked when the horsemen weren't armed with semiautomatic carbines? He knew that the entire doctrine would be changed after the Boer War, but that would be too late for a lot of these wretches, mostly boys barely out of school, unaware of the horrors they would soon be facing in places like Kimberly and Spion Kop. Charging madly at guns the way it had been done in Crimea would only bring them the same fate as the five hundred.

Clive knew how to survive and how to keep his men in one piece and moreover, knew that this knowledge would see him through the war to come. His men would think him lucky, for that was the way of the common soldier, who would rather attribute luck to a man, especially an officer, than give him his due or acknowledge any particular skill.

Often, men from nearby regiments would be marched onto the training area for the cadets to practise the art of tactical manoeuvres. Hundreds of men, dragged from their warm beds to play tin soldiers for a handful of yet-to-be commissioned boys. It rather amused Clive, for whom empathy was a tool to be picked up and used only when necessary.

The other cadets looked up to him and often sought his advice on matters both military and personal. One boy of no more than seventeen asked in a laughably coy way about 'the birds and the bees.' The things that Clive told him that day started the boy down a path of womanising and chauvinism that meant he never married and that he would die a lonely old man, cursing the advice that Clive had given him.

He had fenced at school and later at Oxford, encouraging Carla to take up the sport too. He'd even put it to some practical use one night in a French Château, when he had run through a Waffen SS Sturmbannführer. The old soldier had served in the first war, he wore pilots' wings and the coveted Blue Max at his neck, so what he was doing in the combat arm of the Schutzstaffel, he would never guess. Now Clive fenced daily and in keeping with the requirements of a potential cavalry officer, he practised with both sabre and rapier, favouring the Mameluke pattern.

"Second Lieutenant Sir Gerald Clive, may I be the first to congratulate you and give you joy of your commission," Colour Sergeant Grant gushed in such an obsequious manner that Clive almost forgot the snarling beast he had known him to be for the last year. For a fleeting moment, Clive wished he hadn't killed his father.

He would have enjoyed this, he mused.

The passing-out parade was spectacular, with rich, brightly coloured uniforms, lashings of gold braid with gleaming silver and steel. The ridiculous sight of a horse and rider in full ceremonial dress ascending the steps of the old college.

He admired his reflection, a man of thirty-four masquerading as a man of twenty-three in full ceremonial dress only blemished by the slight ptosis in his left eyelid, a feature earned in battle and now easily blamed for his older appearance. The uniform and accessories had cost him a small fortune, but his vanity told him it was worth every penny as he swaggered up and down the square, basking in the pomp and ceremony of Queen Victoria's army. Clive bought the entire mess a round of drinks and stayed until the very end of the revelry, steadily drinking whilst his new messmates dropped like flies about him.

After a tough period spent learning horsemanship and cavalry tactics from more old soldiers, it was with thighs of steel and a new appreciation for cavalrymen that Clive set off to join his regiment.

The Tenth Royal Hussars had just returned from six years of policing duties in Ireland, and after a spot of ceremonial for Queen Victoria's Diamond Jubilee, the regiment joined the summer manoeuvres on Salisbury Plain. Clive first travelled to Canterbury to take his room in the mess there and collect the horse he had arranged for himself – a fine bay gelding of about seventeen hands with a soft bit and a solid temperament. He spent a week in the regimental lines getting to know Reisender and arranging his affairs before joining the regiment on the Plain.

He was met at regimental headquarters by his new squadron commander, one Major Cholmondeley.

"A word of advice, old boy," his new squadron commander said conspiratorially as he walked Clive through the perfectly straight lines of crisp white tents to meet his troop. "Your man Dolby has been running the troop in the absence of a subaltern this last six months, he's a capital fellow and if handled correctly could be a powerful ally, what?" The air was thick with horse, straw and the smoke and hammer of the farrier's furnace.

"Indeed, Sir, thank you for the advice." Clive was deferent and he planned to remain that way, because the approval of this man and men like him would make or break his political career in those crucial early days. When the time came for selection for a seat in the House of Commons, the party chairman would seek these men out, meet them at their club and one cross word, one hesitation to recommend Clive, would finish him.

"Ah, here we are. Second Lieutenant Sir Gerald Clive, meet Sergeant Dolby," the major said genially as Dolby sprang to attention and saluted beautifully, a compliment returned smartly by Clive. The thirty-year-old man before Clive wore the blue tunic of Hussars with a gold braided front, three thick stripes adorned one arm and atop his head he wore the fez-like pillbox hat, the strap of which ran under Dolby's extraordinarily prominent chin. He was clean shaven but for a fine pair of moustaches. "Right, I'll leave you to get to know each other and I expect to see you in the mess tent later, what?"

"Jolly good, Sir," Clive said, throwing up a salute which was returned in the typical field officer fashion.

"Welcome to First Troop, A Squadron of the Tenth Royal Hussars, Sir," greeted the impossibly still troop sergeant.

"Oh, relax, Dolby. Thank you, how do you do?" Clive offered a hand, an unconventional mark of profound respect and a move that no other young troop commander would risk.

"Very well, I thank you, Sir," Dolby said, taking the hand and shaking it firmly.

"Jolly good. Now, should we get the men formed up in say…" he looked about him at the troop lines, men set to tasks in every corner, grooming horses, cleaning weapons and polishing tack. His eyes fell back to Dolby and lingered.

"Evening meal is at seventeen hundred, Sir."

"Excellent, sixteen thirty will do splendidly," Clive beamed. "Now, let's you and I have a chat about our troop in the command tent, old boy."

"As you wish, Sir, this way," Dolby said, leading Clive to a generous tent containing a map table, an easel, some comfortable chairs, and a writing desk.

"Wonderful, do tell me how you've been getting on with the day-to-day running of the troop?"

"Well, Sir, I've done the best I can, and my junior NCOs are for the most part solid, reliable men. We don't have any issues with discipline and, in general, horsemanship is very good. Incidentally, your mount, Rice-sender, he's stabled with the other officers' mounts, and I can send for your groom, Trooper Naseby, whenever it suits, to show you where that is, Sir."

The pair conversed at length about tactics and training, the fitness of the troop, their marksmanship and morale. With each question Clive asked, each answer he gave his full attention to, he won more of Dolby's respect and loyalty.

"The troop will form up for inspection in the open order, right dress!" Dolby bawled at the thirty or so men under his command. "Eye-yes front," Dolby drew out the first word and affected a high-pitched squeak on the second in keeping with the traditions of the service.

The troop was now spread out in three equi-spaced ranks to allow Clive to stroll up and down between them, looking for faults or chatting briefly with his men.

The front righthand marker was necessarily the tallest in the troop and always the first to be inspected.

"This is Barnes, Sir. He plays for the regimental polo team and acts as the farrier's assistant."

"Very good, glad to meet you, Trooper Barnes," Clive said convivially, and this went on until Clive had met every man under his command and learnt a piece of trivia about them.

"All in all, a jolly good show," Clive said, addressing the troop as a whole after Dolby had bid them return to the close order. "Enjoy your scoff and I'll see you bright and early tomorrow for a mounted inspection."

"Officer on parade!" Dolby bawled. "The troop will turn to the right in threes, dismissed!"

The troop fell out by turning to the right in unison, saluting and marching three paces.

"It seems that you've done a fine job here, Dolby and I should like to involve you as much as possible in the running of the platoon. And whilst I find my feet, I would appreciate your guidance in all things. Let's try to stop this new Coronet from dropping a clanger, eh?" Clive said conspiratorially. This sealed it for Dolby,

71

who had never before received this level of respect from an officer, and he knew that he'd bagged himself a good 'un in Mr. Clive.

"Right you are, Sir, anything you need, you know where to find me," Dolby beamed.

"Naseby," Clive said, turning to his groom who waited patiently out of sight, "kindly show me to the stables. I'd like to check on Reisender."

"Yessir, right this way, Sir," the boy said, saluting awkwardly before directing Clive to a shaded pen near the troop lines.

"Reisender, hello, old boy," Clive fussed, producing a lump of sugar that was inhaled as Clive patted his flank.

"May I ask, Sir, what does Reisender mean?" Naseby asked in a high-pitched home counties accent.

"Certainly, it's German."

"Like the regimental motto, Sir?"

"Ich Dien, indeed, I serve," Clive mused. "The name means traveller,"

"A fitting name, Sir, and a fine horse, if I may."

"Thank you, Naseby. Now, take good care of him and I will take care of you."

"Oh, don't you worry about that, Sir, I will." Naseby enthused, for a good performance in this role would earn the patronage of the officer.

~

The sophisticated, charming, and affable side of Henry Clive was on form in the mess that night. He was placed next to his squadron commander and they conversed at length on horse flesh, politics and Empire. Clive was careful to read his companion's own opinions before disagreeing too drastically, but he certainly didn't bore him with the usual sycophantic yessiry that most Coronets felt bound to spout.

"You know, Clive, I think you'll do well here, despite your age," Cholmondeley confided after the loyal toast was made, the cloth had been drawn and the port came out.

"Sir?"

"C'mon now, Clive, it's quite obvious you ain't three and twenty years. Gods man, you'd pass for my age if you wasn't just out of Sandhurst."

"I dare not comment, Sir," Clive declared, smiling with false apprehension.

"Let me just say this, keep going the way you are, and you'll be celebrating the new century with a couple of pips and some more braiding on your sleeves." The major winked as he raised a glass to Clive.

That evening in the mess, when the field officers had retired, the subalterns played mess games. Tug of war with a broom handle, mess rugby¬ played with cushions, high cockalorum – a game of leapfrog whereby one team rides the other and the first to collapse loses. Topped off with recently invented bicycle jousting, when two mounted mess members with mops ride toward one another. This last game was eminently popular with cavalry units.

Clive, transported back to his days at Harrow, got well and truly stuck in, because he wanted to be popular, and this was how you won the adoration of these overgrown children. He jousted, he tugged, he flailed about atop a perfect stranger's back and he scored more tries than anyone else with cushions that must have cost more than he would earn in a year. By the end of the night, everyone in the mess knew him to be the right sort of chap, a jolly good rave who could hold his wine.

Hangovers are for people who foolishly allow themselves to become sober and Henry Clive was no fool. When the following morning's mounted inspection arrived, he rode back into troop lines and received the salute on the back of a sweaty, well exercised Reisender. The horse was contented and behaved impeccably during the tedious review. Some of the younger troopers struggled with restless mounts, whilst others sweated out last night's beer from their own mess activity, but on the whole, the professional soldiers of yesterday seemed equally adept on horseback.

"Let's go for a ride, Gentlemen," announced Clive at the end of his inspection. And they set off in formation for a hard, sticky ride over the Plain.

For the first few miles he led the troop from the front, but later, he allowed Dolby to take over so that he could assess the men from a distance. In five years' time, General Baden Powell would open the Army's cavalry school at Netherhaven, but Clive had to make do with what he'd picked up at Sandhurst, the horsemanship school and what he'd gleaned from books over the last year of preparation. He had orchestrated quite a few resistance operations, but they were a far cry from mounted manoeuvres on the veldt that could involve any number of different tasks, from protection of infantry to shock attack. But what he did have was a troop of thoroughpaced horsemen with the right attitude. These men could make his life very easy or very hard, they could cover him in glory or cause him to be cashiered and sent home in disgrace. Training them well now would pay dividends when they arrived in the Cape.

The troop rode hard at targets, dismounting and firing with their Martini Henry carbines. They practised a vast array of drills with the sabre and lance, riding in formation as a troop, as a squadron, and as a regiment. Clive spent many hours in the saddle and came to know Reisender intimately, and when Naseby was promoted, Clive did not ask for a replacement groom, choosing instead to perform the work himself. He had time, after all, as Dolby practically ran the Troop for him. Clive found the smell of the urine-soaked straw, old leather, and saddle soap a comfort, the act of brushing Reisender's coat, cleaning down his tack and picking the accumulation of filth from his hooves to be therapeutic. He wasn't the only officer who saw to his own horse, but they were few and far between.

By the spring of 1899 Clive commanded the finest troop of Hussars in the British army, sabre-wielding, hard-riding, bone crushers to a man. The troop won the annual tournament by an embarrassing margin. Dolby entered and won the Victoria Cross race. He rode against five others, galloping over obstacles under blank fire, and shooting dismounted at targets before rescuing a dummy and bringing them back to the start line.

True to his word Cholmondeley had seen Clive promoted to Lieutenant, earning him the right to wear a small silver star called a pip on his gold-braided epaulettes, and yet more gold braid was added to his uniform sleeve. Although he supressed Dolby's prospects for promotion in order to keep a capable and loyal second-in-command. Clive had maintained his reputation amongst his peers as a jolly fine chap to have around and as such enjoyed an active social life, often venturing into London from their Canterbury lines.

"Kruger's not going to budge on these reforms," Clive remarked one morning over a breakfast of kippers, bacon, eggs, pork chops, toast, and coffee. His nose was in the London Gazette as he absent-mindedly shovelled in half a kipper.

"Those damned money-grubbing Boers need a good thrashing," Notting called from the far end of the table to murmurs of assent and a few cries of, "hear him, hear him."

"They're tough old brutes, sir, those Boers," said a Highland steward called Fraser as he poured coffee for Clive.

"That's right, Fraser. Weren't you at Laing's Nek?" asked Wormsley, an older member hoping hard for major and a squadron of his own.

"Aye, Sir, and Majuba Hill. They are, as I say, tough old brutes and their sharpshooters put us to shame. We lost nearly a third of our boys that day."

Fraser stared off into the distance whilst coffee overflowed from Clive's cup. Clive was livid but saw this as yet another chance to curry favour.

"I say, Fraser," Clive said, gently taking the jug and placing it down, "why don't you take the morning off, there's a good chap, and send someone else in to clear away this coffee."

"Aye, Sir, thankee kindly," he said, still distracted.

"That was mighty good of you, Clive, mighty good," Notting said, another subaltern with a hereditary title, though his father still lived. "I say, you wouldn't fancy coming up to Greymoor for Easter weekend and a spot of shooting? The season's just beginning for roebuck," he added, feigning disinterest.

"That's frightfully kind, old chap, I'd love to, but are you sure it wouldn't be any trouble?"

"None at all, I shall wire Father this morning. Would you need a pair of guns?"

"I do have a pair, Martinis, but I'd have to fetch them from Broadlands and I've closed the place down since joining up."

"That's no bother at all, you can use a pair of ours."

During the first part of his Easter leave, Clive spent a squalid week at the home of a widow who he often saw romantically, and despite his primary reasons for visiting Notting's being to broaden his network of connections, he found himself looking forward to the trip. He boarded the Flying Scotsman at King's Cross and sped north at seventy miles per hour, alighting on a clear and bright March afternoon at the great iron-vaulted behemoth of York station, the largest railway station in the world.

He found acceptable whisky in the York Grand Hotel and drank it there until his train to Darlington where John Notting was waiting with a gig to take them to Greymoor Hall. He drove that gig hard, tearing along country lanes with little regard for anything but speed, speaking to the horses who responded in kind, never needing the whip, just running for all they were worth. Clive found the experience almost as exhilarating as parachuting into France all those years ago. He'd been terrified then too.

As they rounded the lane onto the sweeping gravel drive, a great old pile of imposing grey stone pulled into sight and the name Greymoor Hall finally made sense. Clive had read about its demolition in 1952, an action designed to absolve the heir of the crippling inheritance levy. The place had been stripped bare, every heirloom sold at auction. Eventually the house itself, built nearly four-hundred years earlier, had been reduced to rubble with copper piping and electrical wire torn from the carcass for scrap.

In contrast, now Clive saw a thriving family home supporting dozens of staff and two magnificent shooting brakes, with room for four hunters to sit comfortably and enjoy a day of civilised sport.

The horses, a matching pair of skewbald Clydesdale mares, stood patiently in the tracers.

"Here we are then, Clive, don't mind the old place, a bit run down but we've a fine cellar and a bally good spread laid on for this Easter, what?"

Notting affected the typical, misplaced modesty of the Victorian gentlemen as he jumped down from the gig and stretched his arms above his head. "We should probably change, Henry old boy?" Notting wore a heavy woollen coat, full length and buttoned to the neck against the unseasonable cold.

"Capital, should I just follow your man here to my room?" Clive suggested, as a footman hefted his case.

"I say, have you brought your valet?" Notting asked, as if expecting him to be following in some sort of peasant transport.

"When I closed Broadlands down, I let all my staff go. I haven't the need for a valet, and besides, where should I keep him during regimental duties?" Clive laughed, joined enthusiastically by Notting.

"Yes," he said, still laughing," I don't suppose there's space in your trunk now, is there?" More laughter. "I imagine you'll have a batman before too long, the Colonel and old Cholmondeley seem very taken with you, old boy."

"Well, Naseby was doing a fine job but strictly, he should have only been looking after Reisender and not me, but his attentions prevented me from seeking out a valet and now that he's gone..."

"Groom is a fine opportunity for bright young men to get noticed, and Naseby made the most of it and earned a well-deserved step."

"I'd better catch that footman," Clive said, watching the liveried young man disappear through the heavy oak doors.

"He'll be taking the back stairs, I'll walk with you, I'm on the same floor."

The entrance hall, whilst not as graceful as that of Broadlands, still had its charms and thick rays from the equinoctial sun hung in the cool stonewalled space, giving a true sense of the halcyon age his father had often lamented. This feeling was exaggerated by the suits of armour and a frieze depicting the battle of Agincourt that adorned one wall.

"Here we are. Don't waste your time unpacking, I'll send my man round to get you set up whilst we're out shooting."

"I really must thank you, old boy, I feel like quite the flat, turning up to this sort of thing without a valet."

"Nonsense! As you say, it doesn't make any sort of sense for you to have one whilst we've been so busy on manoeuvres. My man Braithwaite was positively climbing the walls when we were in Ireland. Still, we can relax a bit now."

"I don't know about that, old chap. I think we could be quite busy with these damned Boers."

"Oh, surely not, a few thousand farmers with shotguns are no match for the might of the Empire."

~

"I say, you're a damned good shot, Clive, something of a dark horse," his shooting partner called over the din of rifle fire and the flapping of wings. "We could've used a man of your parts in the Sudan."

"I must say that I'm bally sorry to have missed out," Clive called. Churchill gave him a knowing look as they climbed back into the brake.

"You seem to me like a man that's seen a few scraps?" Churchill said, leaning close to be heard.

"Well, I can't..."

"And modest too. Did you say you were with the tenth?" To this Clive nodded mutely.

"From what I hear, you chaps will be headed off to the Cape if Kruger can't come to terms with Milner over these Uitlanders."

The brake lurched forward, and the pair were able to resume a more conversational volume.

"The Uitlanders, now they're the settlers that turned up after all the gold was discovered?"

"That's right and despite the Boers being as rich as Croesus, they are outnumbered two to one there by the newcomers."

"So they tax them outlandishly to deter them?" Clive bellowed.

"Ha, ha! A most excellent witticism, Clive, I shall have to borrow that one," Churchill laughed, producing a handkerchief to dab the tears at his eyes. "But in all seriousness, they pay tax but have no political rights, and this is the crux of the issue. If neither Kruger nor Steyn will make the concessions, our man in the Cape, Milner—do you know Lord Milner?"

"I can't say that I've had the pleasure."

"One couldn't ask for a better man for High Commissioner. Do you know that he's taught himself Dutch and Afrikaans to further his attempts at diplomacy. Alas, it doesn't appear to be working," Churchill lamented, shaking his head.

"So, it's war with the Burghers then?"

"I can't see that peace is a viable course of action, and their treatment of the blacks down there is nothing short of abhorrent, little more than slavery and you know what else? The black man in the Transvaal cannot even walk on the pavement. If nothing else, we could put a stop to those brutal, archaic ways. Saying that, I'd like to see the Boers treated fairly, with generosity and tolerance, two wrongs don't make a right and all that."

"Indeed." Clive had read all about Kitchener's concentration camps and he knew that despite the views of this young idealistic Winston Churchill, the Boer people were about to suffer some terrible hardships. "I hope you're right, old boy."

"Don't think it's going to be easy either, they've spent all that money from gold and diamonds on the very best German and French guns."

"Oh, don't worry, old chap, I know the Burghers aren't to be underestimated."

This chance encounter with a man who, if managed adroitly, could become a powerful ally, was a masterstroke of fate. Clive knew Churchill's views on every important subject, what political history student of the 1950s didn't?

Clive spent the remainder of the Easter weekend expertly schmoozing the aristocracy whilst taking care not to neglect Notting or waste the opportunity for him and Churchill to forge a lasting acquaintance. He even contrived to be on the same train back to London as the would-be prime minister and continued to espouse exactly the sort of rhetoric that old Winnie loved to hear.

Saint Petersburg, 1912

Olga Felson was bored. The suite she'd rented at the Astoria was a far cry from the squalid tenement she now occupied. She knew what she must do, knew that she needed to be here at this window watching the Tauride Palace in shifts with Carla, but it drove her mad. The same bare, paper-thin walls, the cold, the inactivity, and the lack of any entertainment. She realised quickly that this was worse, in fact, than her life in the Reich, for at least there she had something to do.

Reconnaissance was not her thing, and she knew to avoid it at all costs, but her lifetimes of tactical training told her that bad recon got you killed and if she died, millions would die as a result. The pressure of this should have kept her motivated, but instead she just resented it.

Carla had found the place by accident one day in the first week of their stay in Saint Petersburg.

"It's perfect," she'd said.

"It's far from perfect," Olga answered, looking around at the small, damp room with its two tiny windows and rat shit everywhere.

"It's a corner room, we'll be able to watch Purishkevich come and go from Duma sessions and begin to figure out his routine," Carla said.

"Why don't I just follow him home one evening and shoot him in the back of the head? I'll leave a note on the body that says a Frenchman did it."

"Olga, you know far better than I do that this is how it's done. Hard work, long hours, and fastidious attention to detail. Besides, we only have a French rifle, not a French pistol."

"That's an issue, but why can't we just hire a hansom cab and follow him about for a few days?" Olga suggested.

"Because that would mean hiring a hansom cab, and the driver could be anyone. What if they reported us to the Okhrana?"

"You can just say secret police. In fact, saying secret police in English instead of German to me would probably be safer."

"That's the only sensible point you've made since we got here. Now, I've arranged for two weeks' occupation via a fourth party. How do eight-hour shifts sound? That way, every other day we'll have time to get other things done," Carla said with finality.

"Fine, but I want a comfortable chair and a heater."

"There's a stove," Carla said, gesturing towards a small metal object in one corner.

"I genuinely thought that was a rubbish bin."

Both women laughed.

~

"This is getting us nowhere," Olga moaned when Carla arrived for her shift. "He hardly ever attends, and when he does it's only for a few hours at most."

"Well, you've got plenty of time to think of something else," Carla said with a shrug, settling down and placing her things on the small table between the windows.

"I don't think we should stay past the time you've already paid for."

"It's only been seven days, Olga…"

"Yes, so we've seen a week in the life of Vladimir Purishkevich and it's got us nowhere," she interrupted. "I'm supposed be the expert here, we've done it your way, now let's do it mine."

"And what do you suggest?" Carla mocked.

"What do all Russian aristocrats love?"

"Oppressing peasants?"

"The ballet, you oaf!"

"The ballet, or the theatre, or the opera," Carla offered, beginning to see where Olga was going.

"We have his address, right?"

"Right," she nodded.

"Then every evening we dress for the opera and make several passes by his house, and maybe we can use different cabs on the pretence of forgetting things."

"Even better," Carla said, looking at a microfiche map of Saint Petersburg though her eye loupe. "He lives across from Mikhailovsky Garden, we can walk there from the Astoria and take a turn around the promenade."

"How far is that from the potential venues?"

"Ha, the Mikhailovsky is right there, but I can't see that he would want to go there if it's right around the corner. Then there's the Maryanski Theatre, which is just south of the Astoria, and the Conservatoire across the road from that," Carla said, looking up with the eye loupe comically enlarging one eye.

Olga threw her head back and barked a laugh.

"You look beautiful, darling!"

Carla winked her unmodified eye.

"Can we get out of here and never come back then?"

"Umm, yes, let's go dress shopping," Carla said, raising her eyebrows.

"To the Passage," they cried in unison.

At the Passage they spent an inordinate amount of money on three complete outfits suitable for the opera, ballet, or theatre.

"Bonjour," Carla called obnoxiously, as they entered a boutique.

Carla spoke fluent French, German, English, and passable Latin, but her Russian was inadequate. Besides, French was the language of the Russian aristocracy and of European politics. "This is my German cousin, Frieda."

"Guten Tag," Olga said through gritted teeth, inclining her head.

Why fucking Frieda? Of all the names in the damned Reich!

"We are impossibly rich, and we'd like three gowns each with all the usual accoutrements," Carla instructed in French.

"Oui, madame," the hostess replied with an exaggerated bow, expertly masking the disgust she felt for this product of undeserved wealth and privilege. "Please, take a seat and wait whilst one of our dressers can see to your every wish. Champagne?"

"Oui."

They sat in upholstered chairs and drank vintage champagne whilst shopgirls tried the dresses on and modelled them. When they had decided on three elegant gowns, they were measured and fitted.

"Thank you, Madame, we will have the dresses sent to your suite by tomorrow lunch time."

"Thank you," Carla said, tipping the girl generously.

Gottlieb Scholz stood in the tenement, looking from the comfortable chair to the window and the pile of coal by the tiny stove. He sniffed. They had been here, their scent was all over the chair, although he sniffed the seat to be sure. At the window he watched the members of the Duma come and go for a while and mused. He was an opened-minded man, and he could believe that two women might be carrying out a surveillance operation on a Russian Politian, but who and why were far more important and difficult questions to answer.

Despite his considerable efforts, he could not gain clandestine access to their suite. It wasn't that the staff at the Astoria were too scrupulous, it was more the case that Olga and Carla had already bought their loyalty for themselves. One could only linger amongst the hansom cabs on Saint Isaac's Square for so long without arousing suspicion and Gottlieb was running out of options. These women were good, and their tradecraft meant that he'd struggled to follow them, but the brunette drank and today she'd been sloppy.

Olga had planned it all out in the bath that morning. She and Carla would take tea in the Gardens and watch the Purishkevich residence.

"Then we can return to the Astoria to change into evening wear and take a turn in the gardens before supper at the Grand, where between courses we can take walks up and down Sadovaya street."

"I have a plan too. We do all of that, but we find ourselves someone who would be sure to hate Purishkevich and have them wait around to see where he goes."

"And how will we know that they hate him?" Olga asked.

"The pogroms," Carla said sheepishly. The guilt and shame she felt over her part in the Nazi regime was very much alive and the idea of using a Jewish man or woman to further her own ends, no matter how noble the cause, did not sit well with her.

"Genius, but you don't seem keen?" said Olga, but Carla just shrugged in reply.

"Oh yeah, well you were a kid, and your contribution to that was to shoot down bombers, the men who were trying and succeeding, I might add to..." Olga stopped herself from saying to kill your mother. "Anyway, Yael and the whole of Israel are the only reason we are here right now instead of living out our own dictatorial nightmares."

"That's a very good point." Carla attempted a smile and got up from the elbow chair in the lounge, "I'm just going to the loo."

"Loo? Nazis don't say loo," Olga called after her. Inside, Carla carefully removed the bottle of vodka from its hiding place and took a long drink. It tasted vile, but she needed the feeling it gave her.

"That's better," she said, sitting back down.

"Don't you flush?"

"Not every time."

"Fine. Did you have someone in mind?"

"What?"

"Did you have a Jewish person in mind," Olga asked irritably. She was used to being one step behind Carla, not the other way around.

"Oh, one of the bellhops, or we could go to a newspaper like Pravda on the pretence of giving an interview?" Carla suggested.

"Stalin's rag?"

"He's not the editor yet and for our purposes, it's a leftist paper and Purishkevich is exactly the kind of chap they want to see gone."

"So we bring them in? Full disclosure?" asked Olga, sceptically.

"No, not at all, we just sound out the journalist and see if they are the type of person that could help us?"

"It seems like this might be the job of a street urchin, one we can deny or shove onto a train to Moscow with a pocketful of hush money?"

"I like your idea better, middle ground. Could you shove that tall bell hop onto a train?"

"Gregory? Sure, he's skinny, I could fold him up and put him in a suitcase," Olga said, straight-faced.

"Oh, the irony," Carla said, laughing far too hard.

"Are you okay?"

"Yeah, let's get Gregory up here."

"I might deal with Gregory on my own," Olga said, looking hard at her friend.

"Suit yourself, how long do we have until tea?"

"Four hours," Olga said, checking her pocket watch.

~

Olga found Gregory smoking a cigarette in the alley behind the kitchens. He was a tall, narrow-shouldered youth of about seventeen, though his swarthy features and intelligent eyes made him seem older.

"Hi," Olga said, stepping out into the cool air.

"Fräu Felsen," Gregory said, dropping his cigarette and adjusting his uniform.

"Oh, please, you didn't need to do that and its Fräulein."

"I did, I would lose my job if the boss saw me smoking and speaking to a guest at the same time."

"Your German is very good, Gregory," Olga gushed. Gently tapping an earring in the shape of a teardrop, she turned her head to the side and moved her eyes to look at him again, smiling coyly.

"Thank you, my babushka is from Dresden," he said, trying not to look at Olga.

"Do you speak any other language? Yiddish perhaps?"

"I do, zeyer gut," he smiled, revealing some white teeth.

"Oh, good, you've made me very happy, Gregory. I wonder if you would help me with something?"

"Anything, Fräulein Felsen," Gregory smiled even wider.

"Come up to my suite when you have the opportunity? Should I call the desk with an excuse?"

"Yes, say that your toilet is broken, they always send me for that." Gregory's face dropped, mortified at what he had said.

"I am not going to say that, Gregory," Olga said, frowning for as long as she could before she burst out laughing, "but seriously, what should I say?"

"Ah, say that you want your trunks from the storage room," he said.

"Very good, I'll see you later," Olga said, risking a wink as Gregory floated away.

Olga returned to find the bathroom locked and Carla could be heard singing loudly from behind the door.

"Carla," she called, knocking, "Carla, are you alright? You never sing."

"I'm fine, leave me to bathe in peace, you mithering old woman," Carla called back.

"Fine," she laughed, walking to the phone and winding it up with the handle on the side.

"Front desk."

"Hello, could you send someone up to bring my trunks out of the store, please?"

"Certainly, Madame, which room?"

"The Kamchatka Suite."

She hung up the phone and hurriedly changed into nightwear with a long, flowing, silk dressing gown carefully tied so that a very slight hint of skin could be seen at her chest. She stood for a moment admiring the three-foot bronze bear on the coffee table and wondered what the significance was. It was one o'clock, so she ate an apple and poured herself some water from the ornate jug that never seemed to empty.

A knock at the door and a Gregory hidden behind six large, brightly coloured boxes, each tied with a bow, and bearing a note from the dressmaker.

"These were at the front desk," he explained.

"Thank you, just put them on the bed in my room, please."

When Olga turned, she found he was standing in the doorway shifting his feet and looking anywhere but at her.

"Sit down, Gregory," Olga instructed, motioning to the couch and sitting across from him with a good few inches of ankle on display. "Water?"

"No, thank you," he croaked, waving a hand, and realising he didn't remember what he normally did with his limbs, he began to move them about until they felt normal. It didn't work, though.

"Does your family live in Saint Petersburg, Gregory?"

"Not anymore, my uncle was driven out of Minsk in a pogrom a few years ago. He was lucky to escape with his life, let alone the money from his business. He started again in Dresden, where he was born, and when he had the means he sent for my mother – his sister and our family. I did not want to go, because I hoped for a place at the conservatoire, but when I failed to get in, I could not bring myself to tell my family. They were so against my remaining here and we had such heated arguments about it, so here I am."

He gestured sorrowfully at his surroundings.

"What instrument do you play?" Olga asked, leaning in to show she was genuinely interested.

"I used to play the violin."

He stared down at his hands as if they might be incapable of playing now.

"Used to?" she asked, concern in her tone and in her eyes.

"I sold it, I needed the money."

Olga was quiet for a long minute, allowing Gregory to wallow in the wretchedness of a life that had once held so much promise.

"Do you know who Vladimir Purishkevich is?"

"Yes," Gregory said flatly, his face darkening. "He is an evil hater of Jews and he will be the end of Russia as we know it."

"I agree. Do you really feel that strongly about him?" she asked, gazing at him and trying to read his face.

"I do, I really do, he is a, a bastard! Oh, oh gosh, I am sorry, Fräulein Felsen, please…"

"Fucking hell, Gregory, I didn't know you had it in you, and now that I've sworn too, it makes it okay," she said with a wink.

"Okay," he croaked, flushing red and staring at the bear.

"Why do we have a bear in here, Gregory?"

"The Kamchatka suite," he said, as if that explained it in full.

"Kamchatka…" she nodded, urging him to say more on the subject.

"Kamchatka is a type of bear found in Russia."

"Oh, thank you." She shifted her position on the settee and leaned forward to look Gregory in the eye. "I plan to kill Purishkevich… Will you help me?"

"Yes," he said without hesitation, "yes I will."

"Oh, I'm so glad to hear that," she chuckled. "Because if you had said no…" she made a throat-cutting motion with her hand and Gregory laughed. "What time do you finish?"

"Six," he said eagerly.

"I don't suppose you have evening clothes?" she asked him, cringing at her thoughtlessness.

"I do, I had them for my recitals, and I could not pawn them because of my 'strange shape'," he said, rolling his eyes.

"I shall take you to the… I'm not sure," she admitted. "We must find out where Purishkevich is going first."

The company of a male would add legitimacy to her reconnaissance and give her greater access.

"I need a French-made weapon, a pistol or even a knife, a bayonet perhaps."

"Hmm. Well, as you can imagine, Napoleon's retreating army left a lot behind them and most of it has found its way into the pawn shops of Petersburg and Moscow. I'll take a look on my way home to change."

"Here are some roubles, be back by seven thirty," she said with a warm smile and the subtlest glimpse of skin.

When Gregory had left, Olga knocked again on the bathroom door.

"What!"

"I need a wee," Olga called through the locked door.

"Oh, Gott im Himmel, Olga!"

Splashing ensued and she flung open the door and stood on the tiled floor dripping wet and completely naked. Olga noticed that Carla was very different to her. Where Olga was fair, tall, and slender, gazelle-like, Carla was darker, broader, and more voluptuous, with fuller breasts and wider hips. Olga knew herself to be beautiful, but she found herself envying Carla's body and she realised that she was staring. When she looked up to meet Carla's eye, she found a vacant expression on her face and a gentle sway to her stance.

"Had a good look?" she slurred, pushing past, and walking straight to her room.

Olga trod carefully on the wet floor and still managed to stub her toe on something – an empty vodka bottle. She picked it up and turned it over in her hands whilst using the toilet. When Olga returned to the lounge, she could hear Carla snoring through the door to her room. It was two thirty, time to dress for tea, alone.

When Carla woke, the sun had set over the Neva Bay and a vale of darkness was engulfing the city. Lamplighters plied their trade whilst prostitutes painted their tired faces. Carla did not remember going to sleep, she'd had a bath and… it came back to her, she flew out of bed, paused to appreciate the gravity of her headache, and ran to the bathroom where she found the empty vodka bottle in the bin. She sighed, she shrugged, she hung her head.

"Front desk?"

"Yes, can you send a bottle of Perrier-Jouët to the Kamchatka Suite? Make it two." Carla hung up the receiver.

Champagne was sophisticated, it didn't count in the same way vodka did.

Carla drank some water and when she felt slightly better, she thought she'd better dress. She found a robe, wrapping it tightly around her before collapsing onto the settee, where she leant forward, head in hands and breathed deeply. She had not woken feeling dirty, she had not thought about it for the entire day, not for days in fact. This feeling of–what was it, really? A headache and some nausea, it was worth it not to wake feeling filthy and worthless every morning, to remember all those men pawing at her. On the worst days she could smell them, she could hear her mother whimpering beside her, and she could feel their leavings running from her and it made her want to vomit, want to dig her nails into the skin of her face and scream.

The door rapped politely. Carla rushed to open it, revealing a smiling bell hop bearing two bottles of glistening Perrier-Jouët and two glasses.

"Thank you, let me find you something."

She found a few roubles and tipped the boy, short and broad in contrast to Gregory.

"Would Madam like me to open the champagne?" he asked.

"No, no thank you," she sighed.

"Very good, Madam," he said, closing the door behind him.

Carla hurriedly tore at the foil and untwisted the muselet, allowing both to fall to the floor. She pointed the bottle away from her and pushed the cork with her thumb.

"Whoop!" she exclaimed at the satisfying pop. She hoovered up the foam, coughing on the bubbles, and poured the golden liquid into a wide, shallow coupe, apparently modelled on the shape of Marie Antoinette's breast. The capacity of the glass was frustrating and after her first mouthful drained it, Carla filled a tumbler with the vintage champagne, quaffing it without relish.

"Right," she said aloud, her eyes falling upon the pile of opened boxes on Olga's bed. "She didn't?"

When it finally occurred to her check the time, Carla found that it was already eight thirty and she had missed half of the operation. She found the three boxes that bore her name and carried them into her room, unwrapping them and admiring the rich fabrics and intricate lace. She unfolded a burnt orange empire with chocolate trim, and after donning her specially made tactical corset, she stepped into the dress. It fitted loosely from the breasts down allowing her to conceal objects beneath, suspended from the array of useful loops sewn into the corset. Her hair was cut into a practical bob, not fashionable yet, but it meant she only need brush it.

Out on Saint Isaac's Square she pulled her sable coat tightly around her against the biting Siberian wind and decided that it had been a good idea to open the second bottle and indeed, to finish it. Hailing a cab, she climbed in. At Mikhailovsky Garden, her watch told her that it was nine thirty.

Gottlieb Scholz knew about the two bottles of Perrier-Jouët, he knew that they had been drunk and he knew that Carla was alone. Now he too hailed a cab and followed Carla to the Mikhailovsky Garden.

Carla, intelligent, level-headed Carla who always had a plan, stepped down from the cab and paid her driver. She gazed about at the lamplit gardens, at the onion domes and vibrant friezes of the Saviour on the Spilled Blood and at the gondolas on the Griboyedov canal. She had no plan, and suddenly the gardens seemed to grow darker, the cathedral towered above her and the canal widened, making Carla feel quite small.

Right, it's nine forty-five, Olga will be having dinner at the Grand, I'll go there.

She took a deep breath and set off in the direction of the Grand Hotel. Every one of the people she passed in the gardens seemed like a potential threat, carriages appeared out of nowhere, narrowly missing her, and she quickened her pace, for she had never felt more like she was being followed than she did now.

If you think you have a tail, find a safe, well-lit public space and wait there for a long time. If they're amateurs, they'll get bored and leave and if they're professionals you don't stand a chance, dear girl.

Henry's words came to her in that moment as she threw a furtive glance about her, almost losing her balance in the process.

Gottlieb Scholz thought he might have spooked his quarry in the gardens, but the girl never made him, for he was a pro, an officer of the Geheimpolizei. But when she sat alone in a brightly lit, highly visible section of a busy restaurant and remained there uninterrupted for hours, he realised that she had him beat, for now.

Berlin, 1907

Rudi Kessler stared out of the window of his private compartment of the first-class section of the Royal Prussian State Railways train to Berlin. He watched the rolling fields and shining rivers, wondering at the simple lives these people led and longing for such an existence.

A hard life no doubt, but a life free of deception, a life where a man could work all day without the constant fear of discovery. Then he thought of what he was fighting to prevent, of the 1933 Enabling Act and the wretched souls who lived under the threat of resettlement in the east for over ten years. The unending fear of denouncement by friends, neighbours or even family members. He thought of the camps, camps like the ones in Africa that he had helped to build and operate, of the human beings that he had allowed to be tortured, starved, and murdered before being dumped ignominiously in a mass grave. For what? Land to grow turnips, Lebensraum.

Every time he thought like this he cried, and he had always told himself that he would rather die than have been a prison camp guard. But this was about more than him, more than his conscience, it was about the people he could save if he could make it back to Germany.

To get here he'd had to sell his soul to a devil in Khaki riding breeches named von Trotha. The man had been hell bent on the systematic destruction of the Herero, Namaqua, and San peoples and the acquisition of their native lands. He had succeeded at the cost of over one hundred thousand lives.

There had been fighting too, for the tribespeople were fierce and they had outnumbered the German forces four to one, but they were no match for the modern weapons at von Trotha's disposal. A bungled pincer movement allowed most of the warriors to escape into the desert along with their families. This, however, was their undoing. Rudi and his men pursued them relentlessly for weeks and they starved to death in the desert whilst running for their lives.

Then came the camps. Rudi had been ordered to sweep the bush and scour the veldt, bringing in any and all he found. He eventually followed them to Shark Island as second-in-command of the camp, now Oberleutnant Buchholz, mentioned in despatches and rumoured to be in line for a medal for bravery no less. He had wanted to throw the bauble into the sea, but he knew what it meant for his advancement and what his advancement meant to the population of Europe.

He often thought of Henry Clive, complicit in a similarly heinous campaign during the Boer war. He hoped that he had not been directly responsible for the images he'd seen of Boer families, emaciated beyond recognition and begging for the lives of their children.

Every morning he looked in the mirror and asked himself, Am I a monster? What could I have done short of suicide to prevent the horrific suffering of those people? And how would my suicide have benefited them?

The truth, he knew, was that it would not have helped anyone but himself, his absence one morning at roll call would have made no difference and a week later another officer would have arrived to replace him.

This reason, this cold, heartless logic changed nothing for the people whose suffering he oversaw, and it did nothing for his conscience. He would live with the images of those wretched families engraved on the inside of his skull for the rest of his life and to make it worse, Rudi was to all intents and purposes, immortal.

Rudi's contemplations brought him all the way to Berlin Potsdamer Bahnhof, where he stepped onto the platform and found a porter to bring his luggage and hail him a cab. He gawked in amazement at the city his home had once been and the disparity between the bombed-out wreck he had left in 1945 and this shining example of imperial might, Baroque architecture, and German engineering.

When he reached Unter den Linden, memories assailed him of a time before the war, before the Terrorflieger, and before he lost everything. He recalled the Sunday trip via Pariser Platz and under the Brandenburg Gate to enjoy a picnic in the Tiergarten. The monuments had made him feel so small, but at the same time he had felt part of something big. These were the finite days within his mental grasp, his earliest memories, before the uniforms and the brutality of the Hitler Youth, and the songs describing vividly the violence these little boys would inflict on their Jewish neighbours and former friends. He sometimes heard himself in the high-pitched voice of his youth singing the words and it made him sick. How could one man have so little shame and consider himself decent?

It was with mixed feelings of nostalgia, national pride, and unabated shame that he entered the lobby of the newly opened Hotel Adlon. Richly detailed rugs adorned Italian marble floors polished so highly they reflected the intricate plasterwork of the vaulted ceilings.

"Guten tag, mein Herr, do you have a reservation?" the desk clerk asked, a moustachioed man in his late forties.

"Ja, natürlich. Buchholz, Horst Buchholz," Rudi replied, so used to the name after four years, it would have felt strange to use his own.

"Ah, so," he said, running his finger down the page of a ledger. "Here, Hauptmann Horst Buchholz. You are very welcome at the Hotel Adlon, Herr Hauptmann. Here is some post for you and would you like some help with your luggage?"

"Nein, danke," Rudi said, taking the proffered key.

"Please sign here and here, Herr Hauptmann," the clerk said, pointing at the paperwork, "Wilhelm!" he called, handing over the letters. "Show the Hauptmann to his room."

Once alone, Rudi took the opportunity to remove his gloves and let his hands breath. Then he turned his attention to the letters.

Dear Horst,

I hope that this letter finds you well and that your journey from Bremerhaven was pleasant. Now, we only met a handful of times when you were very small. I am sure that we would not recognise each other were we to pass in the Potsdamer Platz, but your father and I have been the closest of friends since our days at Lichterfelde all the way until the end.

It saddened me deeply to hear of his death, as did your mother's subsequent passing and for both I offer my deepest, most heartfelt sympathy. I hope that I can do for you that which I would like to have been able do for my own son, had he survived into adulthood.

I hear that you distinguished yourself in the colonies and won both promotion and decoration. These achievements only make my job easier. I have found an excellent position for you, and I

should like to discuss it with you as soon as you are able. Time is
of the essence, my boy, and the world is at your feet.

   Sincerely

   Theobald von Albrecht

The letter left Rudi feeling the loss of another man's parents having never discovered what became of his own father. He had always assumed that he'd died in World War Two alongside millions of others, but he had never seen proof of this. Henry and Gerald had done their best which was more that he'd had in any other life, and for that he was grateful. He found himself looking forward to meeting with Henry again one day, perhaps on some diplomatic trip to London, or even a holiday. Henry would be forty by now, playing the role of a thirty-two-year-old Gerald. As he wondered how he was doing his thoughts ran to the other unopened letters on the desk in his room.

My Dear Horst,

   I trust I find you well. How was Africa? Did you win? I did pretty well down there myself, you know, and I am doing quite well now that I am back here too.

   All my best.

   Your old pal

   Heinrich

   P.S Keep an eye out for me next May!

Rudi didn't know a Heinrich and the letter used such strange German, almost as though a foreigner had... "Ah, Henry," he said aloud and in English. Rudi produced a lighter and carefully ran the flame along the underside of the paper to reveal more text.

Glad you cottoned on, old boy– burn after reading and all that. I am doing well and I have agents already operating in Berlin, but they will not make themselves known to you for your own safety. I have taken a civil service post in Whitehall, and I am back in the intelligence game, but next year I hope to be elected to the House of Commons, where I will begin my climb into a position of influence.

I have made overtures to Grey about working for him, he is yet to become foreign sec. but it's never too early to make the right friends.

That is what you should be doing, my boy. Why has it taken you so long to arrive in Berlin? The only thing we don't have is time, so don't waste it. I hear you are to be a junior diplomat in some embassy, though I've not heard where yet. Congratulations and remember to act surprised. Old Albrecht has really pulled some strings to get you this position and he will have used up all of his influence in that regard. Don't waste this opportunity.

Well done on the promotions and the medal, they will come in handy and be sure to maintain that reserve commission!

Good luck and God speed.

H

Rudi read the letter through a few more times before burning it as instructed and looking to the next. This letter was different from the others, the paper was coarser and felt cheap.

I KNOW WHO YOU ARE.

Rudi fell back into a chair as his pulse quickened and his head grew light. The words were written in such a way that it disguised the handwriting, perhaps even with the nondominant hand. He looked around as if the solution lay amongst the luxurious furnishings and Egyptian cotton of his room, and his gaze fell to Theobald's letter. He snatched it up. As soon as you are able, it said and he remembered that this was for a foreign posting, which meant he could run from his problems without abandoning his cause. He read the address at the top, Charlottenburg, minutes away, so he could send a boy from the hotel to deliver his reply.

Dear Theobald,

Thank you so much for your letter, your kind words, and all you have done for me.

I have just this afternoon arrived in Berlin and would be happy to call upon you at your earliest convenience.

The boy will wait for your reply.

Sincerely

Horst

Rudi delivered the note to the front desk and paid the boy three times the going rate for messages, then rushed back upstairs. The time according to his battered pocket watch told him it was one fifteen. He decided to bathe and change his clothes in case he was summoned immediately. As he undressed, he realised that he had forgotten to put his gloves back on. After considering this lapse, he thought that it was, in fact, a positive thing if a few people saw his scarred hands, then he wouldn't need to explain his always wearing gloves. It had, of course, occurred to him that to prevent those touching him from seeing his past, he could have just lied about the burns and worn gloves anyway, but if he was caught in a lie, it could ruin his reputation. A reputation forged in the embers of his burning soul.

He received a note inviting him for drinks with Albrecht at his club on the Kurfürstendamm and then a dinner at his home in Charlottenburg. Rudi arranged for his evening clothes to be pressed and stepped out onto Pariser Platz in a cool November afternoon to find a gift for this man who was doing so much for him. He found a pair of gold cufflinks with a blue enamel setting of the imperial eagle and had them wrapped.

~

That evening the lobby, bar, and restaurant of the Adlon were all filled with men in dark evening dress and women in long, flowing gowns of rich, vibrant fabrics. The Schutztruppe did not wear a mess uniform and neither did his counterparts in the army, so Rudi wore simple civilian evening dress with his campaign miniatures at his left breast and his pour le Mérite at his throat. Despite the connotations these trinkets held for him personally, he enjoyed the impression they gave to others, and he knew that Albrecht would have invited some influential people to his house in order to help him make connections.

The Bengal Club was a collection of dark, smoky barrooms with comfortable leather chairs and too many rules. He drank Schnaps without relish, for drink had never appealed to Rudi as the loss of control made him anxious, and he had yet to find a drink that he enjoyed the taste of.

"So, Horst, my boy, a man, in fact, as you sit here before me. I cannot get over it," Albrecht chuckled, smiling warmly with an appraising eye. "Tall and strapping like your father and oh, with your mother's eyes. I cannot wait for you to meet Renate, she will be so pleased to see you, and our daughters, Liselotte and Margot," Albrecht gushed and smiled his most charming smile.

"How are you?" Rudi asked, looking into the man's eyes before saying his name, "Theo."

"Oh, you know, I am old and I have an old man's problems, problems that should not concern a man of such a young age. Now, tell me of Africa and of the rebellion?" Rudi had dreaded this. Would this well-informed man expect a candid account of the horrors of colonial rule or was he testing his loyalty, his zeal for the Reich?

"Theo," he sighed, "it was war, it was terrible, and I would sooner forget it."

"Of course," Albrecht said placatingly. "Naturally I have read your record, your mentions in despatches and your medal citation. I know the official story and let me tell you, it casts you in a brilliant light. However you feel about it, what you did down there sets you head and shoulders above the other young men of your age with law degrees and aspirations towards ambassador one day."

"Thank you, Onkel. May I call you that?" Rudi asked.

"Yes, yes, I should like that very much. Now the men I have invited to dinner this evening are men who can offer you patronage. If," he said holding up a finger, "if you do well in Vienna."

"Vienna?"

"Ah, yes, you will be posted to the embassy in Vienna in a very junior position, the idea being that you go there for a year or so, and when you return you can take the diplomatic exams. You don't have any difficulty with exams, do you, Horst?"

"No, Onkel, no problem at all," he replied, supressing a smile at the thought of Rudi Kessler struggling with anything academic.

"It's just, at school... Well, there's a reason you joined the army, my boy, and I must say that I'm surprised that you don't stick with it. You could have gone far, you know?"

"I know, Onkel, but I want do more for the fatherland and I don't relish the thought of sleeping in a tent for the rest of my working life."

It was the first time he'd thought of Horst as a man of lesser parts.

"Well, you remain a Hauptmann of reserves and if the Kaiser gets the war he has been trying for since he dismissed Bismarck, then you can expect to be back in that tent."

"War? With whom?"

"Oh," Albrecht said dismissively, "the French, the British, the Russians. He keeps stirring it up in Morocco to try to get France to declare war, but the British navy stepped in last time and he had to back down."

"Why doesn't he just declare war himself?"

"Why indeed? The volk don't want a war so he would need to generate a fervour about the foreign enemy and encirclement, which he has been trying to do unsuccessfully for years. On top of that, our allies would not support us in a war of aggression, so we must be seen as the reactors," he said knowingly, before waving a hand for more drinks.

"I see you don't like a drink, boy? That's an excellent habit, especially in the diplomatic service, but take my advice, always finish the first drink, that way you won't seem impolite."

Albrecht proceeded to run Rudi through the guest list for dinner and how to answer certain questions when asked.

"A great deal hangs on your conduct this evening, Horst, and if you get it right, which I'm sure you will, then you'll be foreign minister before you're forty, ha ha," he said, erupting in joyous laughter. The old man's eyes glistened with a mixture of joy at the good turn he was able to do and grief that he could not have done the same for his own son.

Theobald von Albrecht's social stature and influence were palpable that evening. His twelve guests provided a glittering example of Berlin's great and good at the height its industrial and military might. To Renate von Albrecht's left sat a Bavarian prince, tall and elegant in evening dress with full royal accoutrement. Across the table from her there was the bespectacled second secretary to the Austrian ambassador, charming and witty despite his grating Vienna accent. Dominating the soup course with tales of gold mining and gun fights in the Transvaal was a Rhinelander with hands like shovels and eyebrows that threatened to crawl off into a chrysalis at any moment. Listening with wide-eyed glee was a Graf, an attractive youth with a pencil moustache who'd inherited acres of land in Silesia that he'd never visited and was wealthy from chemical works in Saxony that he didn't understand and the sale of products he could not name.

The women were as impressive as the men and just as interesting. The Bavarian princess had toured the world on her father's merchant ships as a girl and had learnt to say Tuesday – the day of her birth – in forty-eight languages. The goldminer's English wife had gone on safari and sketched the plethora of wildlife along the way. The book she had published on the subject was endorsed by The Royal Society, and the wife of the diplomat had been a lady-in-waiting to the late Empress Elizabeth of Austria.

Albrecht had designed the dining room to complement such esteemed company, with fine art, linen, crystal and silver. The food and wines were exceptional. Horst Buchholz would have been able to hold his own admirably in such eminent company, but Rudolf Kessler was in his element. A highly educated, widely travelled war hero with the wisdom of ages behind the bright blue eyes of a man in his early twenties. The demons had departed, and he was transported back to the dining halls of Broadlands and Christ Church College. He even ventured to remove the white gloves he'd worn during the introductions, his disfigured hands only serving to confirm his status as a grizzled veteran. He spoke of Africa only in intriguing vagaries, expertly steering the subject back to safer ground. He told amusing stories to the princess and discussed life on the Veldt with the goldminer. He listened intently as the diplomat's wife talked of Vienna and the royal court. When the cloth was drawn, and the sexes parted company, Albrecht sought out his best friend's son.

"Horst, my boy, that went as well as I could have wished for you. You have made some valuable allies this evening, but the night is young," he said, guiding him to a quiet corner, "and I'd like you to meet Gottlieb von Jagow, the secretary to the Reichskanzler. Gottlieb this is Horst Buchholz, a young man in whose future I take a particular interest."

"How do you do?" von Jagow said, offering a hand. Rudi, who had been fighting with his gloves for the last forty-five seconds, extended his right arm as the tips of his fingers found their target and he supressed a sigh of relief.

"How do you do, mein Herr?"

Von Jagow was a bald man with a tidy, unobtrusive moustache and severe countenance.

"Very well. I see that you have been busy in the colonies?" he said, with a barely perceptible nod at Rudi's tin necktie and the array of only slightly less impressive medals. "I hope that your appetite for glory and recognition has been sated, because in the diplomatic service we toil for the glory of others."

"Oh, yes, mein Herr, I was only saying to Onkel Theo earlier that I hope to do this for the good of the Fatherland."

"Well, I'm glad to hear that. Tell me, Horst, what is our current political position in Europe as you see it?" he asked kindly.

Rudi shot a look at his patron, who nodded for him to go on.

"Well, we have an alliance with Austria-Hungary and Italy. Austria-Hungary are at odds with their Balkan neighbours and some of them are allied with Russia. Russia is our biggest threat on land, but they will take another decade to recover from their defeat in Manchuria and the 1905 revolution. But the Russians are allied with France, which means that if we were to attack France, Russia could be at our undefended rear. Britain, who could, with some concessions become a great and powerful ally, is currently locked in a naval arms race with us, a race that will take us years to win. Industrially, socially, and militarily we are the strongest empire in the world. But we are geographically encircled by our enemies and if we wait, we will lose our military advantage over Russia."

"So why not attack now, enact the Schlieffen plan and take continental Europe whilst the odds are in our favour?" von Jagow asked.

"Firstly, we can't be seen to start a war of aggression, the volk won't stand for it and neither will our allies. Secondly, we need to finish the expansion of the Kiel Canal and build a few more of these dreadnoughts if we intend to invoke the wrath of the Royal Navy." When Rudi had finished speaking, von Jagow smiled at him, turned to Albrecht, and nodded his approval.

"One last question for you, Horst. What would you do to fix it, without H G Wells' time machine, of course?"

To this Rudi stifled a nervous laugh.

"Cosy up to Russia whilst driving a wedge between her and France. Cosy up to Britain and take Franz Joseph in hand, tell him to stop messing about in the Balkans and give the Slavs the autonomy they are so desperate for. Help clear out the Ottomans and reach stability in the region. Then, once Germany and Britain have reached an accord, we might annex a small piece, just a sliver of eastern France to placate the Kaiser."

Rudi was not at all sure that what he had said was what von Jagow was looking for, but he thought it was a good strategy. He watched the man's face change shape as he processed the information until he produced a beaming smile.

"If only it were that simple, young Buchholz, but I think you'll make a fine addition to our embassy in Vienna, and I'd like to be the first to welcome you to the Prussian diplomatic service."

⁓

The following day Rudi called in at the foreign office and filled out some paperwork, then he received his orders and signed in triplicate for his travel warrant and new diplomatic passport. He met

Albrecht at the Bengal, who took Rudi to buy the clothing and stationery required of a Prussian diplomat.

"Listen, Horst," Albrecht said over a beer when they were finished, "you said some fine things last night and I don't doubt that you gave old Jagow a lot to think about, but don't go saying that stuff to just anyone. It's brilliant, visionary, it really is, but not everyone sees it that way and you might find yourself in a tight spot if the wrong person hears it. I shouldn't worry though, that'll be the last time anyone important asks for your opinion in a good long while."

SS Issmore, 1899

The leaders of the Transvaal and the Orange Free state could not reach an accord with Milner, and a state of war was declared with the British Empire. The Burghers rode their ponies over the border into Natal and sieged the towns of Kimberly and Ladysmith. They fired indiscriminately, killing women and children with impunity. It was the Boers' deeply held belief that the British hoped to use the Uitlander issue to annex the Transvaal and the Orange Free State and take their God-given, gold-ridden lands.

The Tenth Hussars were issued khaki uniforms, putties, and pith helmets. They were given their marching orders and made sure to pack enough champagne and polo equipment to stave off boredom when the fighting was over. On a foul November day in 1899, Lieutenant Sir Gerald Clive boarded the SS Issmore at Liverpool with his Squadron and three hundred horses, including his treasured Reisender. Sailing was delayed because some of the hands refused to sail on a Friday.

"I'll tell you a story of naval superstition, shall I, Lieutenant?" the first officer of the Issmore offered in a strong West Country accent that carried a slight lisp.

"Please do," Notting said. The officers of both the army units and the ship were dining together in their shared mess and because they were alongside, the victuals were of the highest standard. They ate soused hog's face, followed by a sea pie, halibut with anchovy sauce, codlings, partridge and figgy dowdy, all washed down with a '75 Chambolle-Musigny. The Hussars' contribution to the meal was a case of the finest '25 Perrier-Jouët.

"So, the superstition goes that it's unlucky for a ship to set sail on a Friday. Fine, I hear you say." The first officer was a middle-aged man with a shining bald pate who seemed to be making up for it with his magnificent side whiskers.

"I have heard that, aye," agreed a Lowland artillery captain.

"Well, them at the Admiralty found this to be very inconvenient. Imagine that you couldn't put to sea at a moment's notice? Making all haste to pursue an enemy frigate or worse, a privateer, just because it happened to be Friday?"

"I wouldn't stand for it," Cholmondeley offered.

"No sir, I don't expect you would. So, the first sea lord at the time, I forget whether it was one of the Melvilles or Old Jarvie..."

"You don't know because it isn't true, Nevil," the captain said, younger than his first mate, with a full head of long, blonde hair.

"Don't give me that, Sir."

"Come on now, don't let the truth get in the way of a good story," Clive laughed, "let's hear it."

"Alright, alright, so they hatched a scheme to commission a ship, only a corvette mind, and name her the HMS Friday. She had her keel laid down on a Friday, she was run off stocks on a Friday, and she put to sea on her maiden voyage on Friday the 13th, under the command of a Captain James Friday." Nevil looked about, enjoying the attention of all present except the captain, who had heard this ditty a few too many times.

"And?" several diners said in unison.

"And she was never seen nor heard from again," Nevil said glibly, supressing a laugh.

113

"And you know what they say about shit dits?" asked the captain, looking around the table. "They sink ships!"

The weather proved so vile that the captain was forced to seek shelter off Anglesey. Pressing on, she only made it to south Wales before the seasick horses forced him to put in again. Clive was no seaman, so he spent most of the journey to the Canary Islands locked away in his cabin, battling with seasickness and plagued by the memories of a cocaine-fuelled passage across the North Sea.

At Tenerife he longed to tread the solid volcanic ground whilst the stokers hurriedly replenished the ship's coal stores, but no sooner had they begun to change course than a signal came in to press on for Cape Town and the Issmore was back at it, pitching and rolling in the Atlantic swell. When Clive did eventually find his sea legs, he found Reisender in a pathetic state. Many of the mounts had died and the troopers had been frantically working to keep the remainder heathy. A batch of rotten meat had led to sickness among the men and consequently a reduction in rations, so this lack of manpower had made caring for the horses even harder.

The men had been instructed to massage the muscles of the beasts to keep them fit, but a bout of distemper called the strangles had weakened the animals further still. Clive fought back tears at the sight of Reisender in a sling, his legs too weak to support him. He just swayed with the motion of the ship, dull-eyed and despondent.

Clive felt compelled to join his estranged messmates for a game of cards, melancholy though he was at the state of his beloved mount.

"Whisky, Clive?"

"Dare he?" quipped the stout form of Captain Fulmar, his moustaches quivering as he laughed along with all gathered.

"I'd better not, you know," Clive said, a hand on his belly. And it occurred to him that a lifetime – many lifetimes – of alcohol dependency had been left onshore in Birkenhead and the case of Royal Lochnagar lay untouched in his cabin. He imagined the withdrawal had been masked by the mal de mer and as his spirits momentarily lifted, he stifled a chuckle. This did not go unnoticed.

"I have him, chaps," Fulmar called, pointing at Clive, "I have him pegged, by Jove."

Clive beamed, clearheaded and surrounded by men he had a genuine liking for, who seemed devoted to him, both as friend and brother officer.

He looked around: Fulmar the squadron second-in-command was a jovial man but cool and exacting under pressure. Major Cholmondeley, elegant and tall, the true bachelor of the world, with whom he could not put a foot wrong. Notting, his longstanding accomplice by now, and a Yeoman named Smyth, a veteran of Afghanistan and the only troop commander to have known action on the scale they expected to see with the Boers. Long did he orate about his experiences at Kandahar and the Sherpur Cantonment, the need for extra care for the mounts in arid theatres and moreover, the nature of guerrilla warfare that he expected the Burghers to employ. Clive silently gave thanks for his bout of seasickness, now doubly beneficial.

The outsider was an officer from B squadron, seconded along with his troop to travel with A squadron on the Issmore. His name was Pettyfer and the mess loathed him. Clive had yet to form an opinion, but he got the impression that the dislike was not entirely unfounded.

"I say... I say, Clive, is it?" whined Pettyfer, his voice grating and nasal.

"Your servant, Sir," Clive said with an inclination of the head.

"How do you do? Pettyfer, I am come from B Squadron with my troop, just for the voyage mind, just for the voyage, then I shall re-join them at the Cape."

"Indeed, glad to meet you, I'm sure," Clive said, noncommittally, desperately casting about for one of the smirking idiots he called friends to rescue him.

"I say, it's nice to see you out of your cabin for once, what?" Pettyfer appeared to be making a joke, a jibe at Clive's expense, and now he looked about with a ridiculous grin, hoping that someone, anyone, might laugh at his pale imitation of Fulmar's earlier banter. The faces of the men turned down or out of a porthole.

"Oh, yes, I see, very good," Clive laughed out of pity more than anything else, as though throwing table scraps to a dog. "Now, who's for a game of piquet?" he said, looking at anyone else.

"Capital," Notting said and made to join him. It was widely known, even to Clive, that Pettyfer had already lost all of his ready cash playing cards and now he would be forced to watch from another table or retire altogether. It was cruel but Clive was at heart a cruel man; cold and unfeeling.

Clive was Gerald's son in many ways and his proclivity for winning was certainly one. He cleaned up, because his absence over the past weeks meant that he could win as much as he wanted, if only for this evening. He didn't need the money, his man of business – his very happy, newly rich man of business – had written to him with a summary of his fortune and Clive could now afford to run both the London house and Broadlands with a full staff indefinitely. He watched in wonder at Fulmar's port as it slid across the table towards him. The night had been calm thus far. He made to catch the glass in one hand before it fell to the deck, but the ship lurched violently in the opposite direction and an almighty grinding noise filling the night. The lights flickered, bottles smashed, and men lost their balance falling painfully to the deck. Shouts rose up outside with confused hails up and down the ship. Clive stood and pocketed his winnings, looking at the others for an answer, but they looked back with frowns and shrugs.

"All hands there! All hands on deck there!" a boatswain's call whistled, piercing all other sound to be joined a moment later by a trumpet call to muster.

"Sirs, I do beg pardon, but we must abandon ship at once."

The man did not hang around for an answer.

"The horses!" Clive cried. "We must give them the chance to swim ashore."

On deck a black spumy sea boiled about them, spraying and soaking all hands. Clive saw, despite the darkness of the night, that the boats were already being put over the side. He rushed to help, thrown about by a three-thousand-ton ship precariously balanced on unseen rocks. Men hurriedly prepared boats whilst others were sent below to gather vital equipment.

"There's still a war to be fought if we get ashore, and for that we need our kit, lads."

The voice in the dark was the familiar bellow of the squadron sergeant major.

Clive fought through the crowds of panicking men, calm sailors, and frightened boys to the hold, where the horses were stowed.

"Reisender!" Clive yelled, rushing towards him, fearing the worst. He hung limp in his sling, not quite lifeless but he would never make it over the side, let alone swim to shore. Clive put his arms around Reisender's neck, rubbing his coat gently.

"Shh, shh, shh, there's a good boy," he continued to comfort him in this way as his right hand fell away and found the white leather pouch that contained his Webley service revolver.

Better a skull full of lead than a lungful of seawater.

He drew back the hammer and placed the muzzle in between Reisender's ears. Clive breathed deeply and screwed his own eyes tight shut. Reisender's head dropped the last few inches as the shot rang out, reverberating around the steel bowels of the ship. He returned his pistol to the pouch and without looking back, walked quickly away.

He would always maintain that Reisender's was the most difficult life he ever took.

Clive made his way back on deck and found Dolby who, as usual, had everything under control, so he found the other officers on the quarterdeck.

"Where's the OC?" Clive asked no one in particular.

"He's poking about below with the captain and the engineer to see how bad it all is," came a voice from the darkness.

"Perhaps we could do that in the cold light of day, when the men are safely ashore?" Clive suggested, irritably.

"Here they are now," Notting said.

"Evening, gentlemen. The engineer has said we have time to gather all personal equipment and space in the boats to carry it. That's the men, but obviously, we officers have brought a deal more than them. So, pass the word to your NCOs and then collect what you think is reasonable from your cabins."

With a modest collection of his belongings, Clive emerged to see the first traces of dawn in the eastern sky. In the eerie spray-soaked half-light, the order was given to encourage the horses into the water via a large door in the ship's side. Few went voluntarily, and many had to be forced, dragged or even roped into the sea. The sight of those horses, floundering on hidden rocks or drowning in the rough sea was too much for some; these horses had been with them for years, a huge part of their daily life in the regiment and now they were forced to push them overboard in the vain hope that they might swim ashore. The land appeared with the sun, and it seemed far too far for a horse to make it.

Men emerged with saddles and tack, rifles and sabres, boxes of ammunition and other stores to be lowered into the waiting boats. This done, Clive saw his men over the side and remained with the other officers until every enlisted man was accounted for. Clive then joined his troop and in three boats they pulled hard for the shore. Unseen rocks littered the most direct route and they had to pick their way carefully. When the troop found a white sandy beach to land on, the surf turned Clive's boat over. He thrashed about in the shallow water, pulling injured men to their feet whilst his possessions were lost, pulled back out to sea by the undertow. The other two boats landed safely and returned for more kit and equipment.

"What's that, Sir?"

"Oh God, it looks like a horse," Clive cried as he stripped off and waded into the surf. A grey mare coughed and spluttered, thrashing its head about and panicking.

"Okay, girl, look at me," Clive panted, gently taking the mare's bridle, "this way, that's it."

It seemed as though she'd make it when a freak wave frightened her and she jerked her head so violently that Clive lost his grip and the weary horse, only a dozen yards from the shallows, was swept out to sea, exhausted, and resigned to her fate. Clive continued trying to guide horses in, until the bay was peppered with them, and he knew that barely half of the mounts loaded at Birkenhead had even made it into the water. Finally, he waded up the beach drained, with a belly full of seawater and an insatiable thirst.

He found Dolby and gave instructions for the men to rest in the shade and share out any drinking water. The march that night wasn't far or fast, but it was gruelling, nonetheless. A farmer had let them use his well, and ox carts carried the equipment, but the men were fit to break. Half drowned, traumatised by the fate of their mounts, and lamenting photographs of loved ones and other treasured possessions lost forever beneath the waves. While no men had died, behind them limped the paltry twenty-two horses that had survived the wreck.

The HMS Niobe, HMS Doris, and SS Columbian picked up the bedraggled remains of Clive's party. He was surprised to find that the boat that carried them to Cape Town was the same SS Columbian that had brought the remainder of the Tenth Hussars from England.

"One man from each section will report to the quartermaster for a tin of Khaki paint and two brushes," Sergeant Dolby called in a parade ground voice. "You are then to take turns painting your white pouches, belts, scabbards and straps so that you do not stand out like a spare prick at a wedding for the Burgher sharpshooters, who by all accounts are very, very good at killing Tommies."

There was a Kraal at the remount camp in Stellenbosch and Clive stood at the edge staring at the half-broken ponies, pining after Reisender. Finally, he spotted a dappled bay that reminded him of the camouflage that had come in towards the end of World War Two and he thought of his men painting their webbing with boot polish.

"That one, Corporal," Clive ordered, pointing at the horse.

"The dappled bay? He's a right bugger, Sir, good luck to you."

The Corporal rode in and lassoed the gelding with practised skill, bringing him out as he bucked and pulled. "We've been calling him Biter, Sir, I leave the rest up to you."

"Thank you, Corporal," Clive said, springing up onto the bare back of the horse and gripping tightly with his legs. "Just like training," he muttered.

The horse made to lower his head, a sure sign that he might buck, but Clive fought it and led the beast on, talking to him, trying to build a rapport. He quickly learned why they called him Biter and continued to ride him hard in a sweat-soaked fervour of stubborn determination for the rest of the day. The next day he introduced a saddle and took the unruly bugger out for a ride with rest of the troop.

"Why Tarnung sir?" asked Dolby as he fought with his own mount.

"Ah, I seem to be making habit of naming my beasts in German, it means camofl—" Clive stopped himself, remembering the term wouldn't be coined until the Great War, "—disguise, as found in nature. The way the leopards' spots allow it to blend into the background unseen."

"Very good, Sir," Dolby frowned. "though Biter is a fine name for a warhorse, I do see your point."

Not one troop horse had made it ashore at Saint Helena Bay and now the finest, most able troop in the division looked farcical. Misbehaving, ill-tempered mounts to a man, ridden by half-starved, dehydrated troopers used to English weather. As the sun beat down on the bedraggled body of horse soldiers, they rode steadily onwards, slowly building an affinity with their ponies and the work grew marginally easier. By midday the troop reached a wide, shallow stream and by way of example, Clive stripped off and began to bathe. The troop followed and they relaxed for an hour or so, splashing about and playing games. Some of the horses joined them and others had to be tied up for fear that they might bolt.

When the troop returned to the entrainment camp, two thirds were steady in the saddle, but the rest needed some more time to break their mounts in. Although it was clear that no other could ride him safely, Tarnung had capitulated and now he was Clive's for better or for worse.

Clive had read the Tenth Hussars' regimental history, but he'd found no mention of the Issmore or its ill-fated voyage to the Cape. Now he began to question the other events that he'd expected to happen. He stared out of the window of the train to Colesberg, where he believed there would be a battle and his friend Notting would win a Victoria Cross for bravery under fire. He watched the kopjes, the small hills, roll by, searching for the Burghers with rifles who were supposed to attack this train as they were unloading at Arundel. Clive had hoped to distinguish himself with the miracle of hindsight.

Having spent six of the last eight years in Ireland, the Tenth Hussars had a distinct advantage over other regiments who were used to fighting native peoples with no modern weapons and little notion of insurgency. This respect for the Irish rebel was conferred onto the Burghers who had a brigade of republican soldiers supporting them. The Highland Brigade did not, and they paid a high price for this refusal to take the twenty thousand Boers seriously. They marched in quarter column, at night and neglected to use scouts. At the foot of Magersfontein Hill, the British force stumbled into the Boer line, entrenched and ready. Seven hundred were killed in the first five minutes and those that fought through the line and up the hill were killed by their own artillery. The fight went on all day until a truce was finally called.

Anxiety, the anticipation of the coming action besieged him, churned in his guts and played tricks on his mind. This was all the worse because his fellow officers continued to laugh and joke as they had always done. He could not reveal his fear, his knowledge of the impending attack during the vulnerable detraining, because it could ever only sound like cowardice.

"Sir?" Clive said, interrupting Major Cholmondeley whilst he read a copy of the London Gazette dated three weeks earlier.

"Clive," he beamed, "what can I do for you, old chap?"

"I'd like to volunteer to be the first out."

"Out?"

"On patrol, Sir."

"Indeed, I know you're keen for a taste of action, my boy, but from what I've been told, the Boers are miles from Arundel."

"Let me reconnoitre the area, Sir, before we expose ourselves by detraining the entire force?"

"What you suggest is prudent, Clive," Cholmondeley contemplated for a moment, gazing at the harsh landscape, hot and dry with low hills and large rocks. Perfect for guerrillas and sharpshooters. "Very well, take a section, leave Dolby here to run the troop. And Clive?"

"Yes, Sir?"

"Be careful, troop commanders don't grow on trees, what?"

"Very good, Sir."

Clive found and briefed the men he'd chosen, men he trusted and whose respect and loyalty he knew to be unwavering. Their horses came off the train in marching order having been saddled inside and loaded with the bare necessities of double water, ammunition, and iron rations. Clive led his men away from the sidings. His section included Barnes, the first Trooper he'd met, Sykes, his batman, and Lance Corporal Naseby, his former groom.

The heat of the sun was oppressive, dulling the senses as it beat on Clive's exposed skin. Tarnung cooked him from below and he encouraged his men to drink as they pushed out a mile or so beyond the watchtowers, using the kopjes as cover. Clive would sketch the ground, noting any features of interest and returning until the camp was in sight, repeating this in a flower petal pattern until they had scouted in every direction.

Each time they returned, more of the horses had been unloaded and the squadron seemed more vulnerable. Then came the screaming of artillery whining overhead. The shells landed well short of the siding, but it did spook the horses.

The section was pushing out for the final time when the ground around Clive's men began to explode with tiny puffs of dust as they took small-arms fire, he wheeled round in search of cover only to watch the lower part of Trooper Barnes' face disintegrate before him. The tallest man in the troop looked at his commander as blood sprayed from what was left of his neck, oddly calm, upright in the saddle for a long moment before falling hard into the dust. His left foot caught in the stirrup as his terrified mount bolted, dragging the man and pitching up a great dust cloud that drew the Boer fire away.

"On me!" Clive roared, riding hard for the cover of some large rocks, where he dismounted and drew his field glasses. Scouring the landscape for something, anything to just give him a clue, and there it was: the powder smoke of an old Martini-Henry. No sooner had he seen the puff of smoke than he heard the shot ring out and felt it bending the air next to his face.

"Section! Four hundred." The men adjusted their sights to the maximum range and Clive talked them onto the target, moving position before he popped back up for another look. The men opened fire, raining lead on the Burgher sharpshooter. Clive watched him stand to run, twist violently and fall back to the ground.

"Mount up, we're going to rout these buggers out!" Clive ordered. They cantered forward, the men with swords drawn and Clive with his Webley. Avoiding total exposure was hard and when it was necessary, they galloped. They reached the shooter's position and Naseby searched the man, finding a map among his papers which he passed to Clive, and some personal effects which he trousered. Clive noted a rocky promontory and decided that would be his limit of exploitation. Having reached it, the seven riders rested briefly in the shade of the promontory as insects beleaguered their faces and hands, swarming the horses' eyes and muzzles.

"Right, drink up, we're going to head back in."

Clive screwed on the lid to his canteen and passed it to Sykes, a wiry youth, strong, handsome, and well liked by all. They were forced to cross back over the open ground, again at the gallop. This time the hidden Burghers opened up. The fast-moving horses were difficult targets and it looked like they might make it to the relative safety of the rocks, when from behind Clive came a howl of agony and the change in hoofbeat that accompanies a fallen rider. He turned to see Sykes struggle to remain mounted, with an ominous spreading patch of dark on his tunic.

"Ride on to those rocks and cover us," Clive screamed in Naseby's ear, as he wheeled round with his men riding hard past him, the resulting dust offering some cover. He manoeuvred alongside Sykes and took his horse's reins, encouraging the chestnut Arab to speed up, but Sykes couldn't manage more than a trot. Clive was twisted in the saddle, both mounts' reins in one hand and Sykes' blood-soaked webbing strap in the other. The rocks and his section grew closer, and the Burghers' heads seemed to be down, only the odd shot landing nearby.

Sykes was wrenched from his grip as the horse twisted away from Tarnung and whinnied, crashing hard into the dusty earth. Clive rode clear and wheeled round once more to see that Sykes was struggling under the weight of his horse and desperately trying to push himself free as the chestnut gelding was filled with lead from the enemy rifles. Clive made a pass, reaching down to grab the youth. His first attempt pulled him clear, and Sykes lay flat on the ground using the horse as cover until the moment before Clive rode by again to grab his webbing. With the last of Sykes' strength, he was over the front of Clive's saddle and they rode hard for the cover, not stopping when they reached the section.

"Follow on!" Clive called as he left them behind. They soon caught up and the section cantered back towards the sidings.

"Ride ahead and fetch the doctor, tell him Sykes is gut shot," Clive shouted to Reynolds, an old sweat called up from reserve service back to his old regiment. He looked down at the boy's back, to see a blackened hole in his tunic where the bullet had gone straight through, "and tell him that the bullet went clean through."

"What about you, Sir?" Reynolds nodded.

"What about me, damn it?" Clive's eyes widening in rage.

"Your shoulder, Sir, that's a gunshot wound if I ever saw one."

The pain was instant, the moment he saw it from the corner of his eye.

"Mention that too, now go!"

Sykes died on a hospital ship back to England. The cloth from his tunic had festered in his guts to cause an infection, and with no penicillin to fight it, he died in the foetid bowels of the HMHS Avoca. The men still on campaign did not need to be told, and they still believed he'd caught a Blighty and was living it up back in Canterbury with his pick of the local women.

Clive gave the map Naseby found to Cholmondeley who passed it to army intelligence where it turned out to be a vital tool in the battle of Colesberg. With his patrol justified, his actions that day earned him the Regiment's first Victoria Cross, one of the three won on that campaign. The following week, Notting performed an equally daring rescue, and by the spring, both received promotion to Captain. The fact that Clive had effectively stolen his friend's VC was not something he gave more than a moment's thought to.

The Mikhailovsky, 1912

"Is it French?" Olga demanded as she took the dagger from Gregory.

"That's what the old man said. And look at the inscription, Je prends villes et canons."

"I take towns and guns? That's the motto of a French Dragoon regiment," Olga said, unsure of where the knowledge had come from, but used to these little nuggets of information popping up unexpectedly by now. She hefted it for balance and curled her fingers around the handle. The inscription ran along a thin hand guard and the blade bore a coat of arms that she did not recognise.

"This will do nicely. I'll leave it sticking out of his heart," she whispered.

The private dining room she had paid for at the Grand Hotel afforded just that, but one could never be too careful.

"Why does it have to be a French weapon?" Gregory asked, absentmindedly turning the leather scabbard over in his hands.

"There will be a war," Olga said, leaning in to fix his gaze, "a war to end all wars, except it won't, it will lead to more war, more fighting and more death until millions are slaughtered."

"Won't this antagonise two of the most powerful nations in the world?"

"France and Russia are allies, and their alliance is one of the things that will help other countries decide to go to war." Olga was struggling to verbalise the complex geopolitical situation that led to the Great War, and she realised how much she had relied on Carla for this sort of thing.

"How can you know this?" Gregory asked as the okroshka was served.

"You know Carla?" she asked, spooning in the fish soup. "Oh, it's cold."

"Of course."

"She's a genius and she…" Olga sighed, "I'm not going to lie to you, Gregory, we know the future because that's where we came from."

"Like H.G. Wells?"

"Yes, except we only have one chance and no way back to our time, so the stakes are pretty high, and I really hope that I've done the right thing in trusting you," she blurted out.

"Does it get any better for my people, you know the pogroms and the persecution?" Gregory asked, pleading with his eyes.

"No, it gets so much worse for a long time, but have you heard of the Zionists?"

"Of course I have."

"Well, it works, and in 1917 the British agree to give you Palestine, but it takes thirty years for it to become the state of Israel and many millions stay in Europe. It is those who suffer. But we will fix it, what we hope to achieve will stop the suffering and…"

"How can you know all this? Where are you really from? Did you have me buy that knife so that a French Jew is blamed for the assassination?" Gregory cried, fear behind the tears in his eyes.

"No, no, Gregory." She took him by the hand and looked directly at him. "No, and if you think that this dagger will incriminate you, then I won't use it. Okay?"

She watched as the horrors of the twentieth century played out in Gregory's mind as myriad expressions passed across his young face.

"It won't, it cannot be linked to me," he said, dazed.

"It's all true," she said quietly, desperate to fill the silence. "Everything you saw just now will happen. Russia goes to war because Serbia offends Austria-Hungary and Germany goads them. Germany invades France via Belgium, which brings the British in too. But Russia would not have risked war without knowing that Germany would invade France and…" she sighed again, "I don't know if I've got this right, but Carla understands it so much better than me."

"Did you kill Poincaré?" Gregory whispered accusingly. Olga's silence answered for her as she looked regretfully at the dagger.

"Listen," he sighed, "I don't care what you did, I will help you do this because I hate Purishkevich and his pogroms, I hate his vile rhetoric and I hate this new idea of his, this fascism. For me that is enough."

"It doesn't have to be."

"What?"

"I have every intention of paying you for helping me with this. You could join your family in Dresden or buy back your violin and have enough to practise for a while without working. I also have some financial information, should you wish to invest the money?"

"I don't do this for money, but I'd be lying if I said my life was not miserable for want of it."

He looked down at his untouched soup and exhaled loudly. "What do we do now?"

"Now we watch the bastard's house and follow him to his chosen entertainment."

Gottlieb walked home dejected, outwitted by a girl and with nothing to show for his efforts, efforts that he had exerted whilst on leave and at his own expense. His instincts had been right, this had proved it, but he had nothing on them. All that was left to do now was to pay the bell hop to wire him when the pair left Saint Petersburg and invent a reason to pull them off the train at the Prussian border. He'd have them, it would just take time. As Gottlieb rounded the corner to head south on Mikhaylovskaya Street, he wondered at the lives these aristocrats led, the carriages they kept and the fine establishments they frequented. Most obvious was the juxtaposition between the ordinary Russian and the ruling elite, the line between squalor and luxury so fine that it blurred in some cases. He watched as a girl of no more than twelve years old sold herself on the street outside the window of a restaurant where a wealthy couple was ordering bottles of wine that cost more than she could make in ten years. As he gazed in awe at the façade of the Grand Hotel, he was jerked from his reverie by the sight of the scrupulous bell hop he had been unable to buy. He was wearing evening dress and on his arm was Felsen. Without making any sudden moves, he shrank backwards into the throng and behind a cab. Adrenaline accelerated his pulse and sharpened his senses as he danced effortlessly among the carriages, inconspicuously observing the pair as they walked north towards Arts Square.

Olga and Gregory strolled with apparent indifference into the square and paused to enjoy the atmosphere of the gardens, as each fought to control their anxiety over the task at hand: the public murder of a powerful political figure.

Carla stumbled from the Restaurant on Italyanskya Street wondering where she might catch up with Olga. The cool night air assaulted her drink-addled mind and sent the world around her into a momentary spin. When she regained her composure, she decided that Arts Square would be the obvious place to begin and headed west in search of her friend. As she stood at the edge of the square, poised to enter the swarm of revellers and horse-drawn cabs between her and the gardens, she saw Olga with Gregory apparently taking the air in a most companiable way. They stepped off along the treelined path in the direction of Purishkevich's house and she watched in confusion, not party to Olga's early discussion or their updated plan. Her slow brain kept her feet planted firmly where they were. During this period of indecision and the resulting inaction, Carla watched whilst a tall, rodent-like man, out of place in a lounge suit, danced through the traffic to follow her friend. She made a bee-line for him, disregarding the danger from the iron-shod hooves and the heavy cartwheels. As she drew closer, the lethargic synapses finally fired and the words Gottlieb Scholz rang out in her befuddled mind.

A sick relative in Konigsberg?

That's what he'd said and now he was here, apparently following Olga.

Was he following me?

When Gottlieb stopped abruptly, Carla did the same. She could see her friend sitting with the bell hop on a bench that gave an excellent view of Purishkevich's front door, but between her and them was this stranger from the train, a liar and someone who followed people.

A policeman? A spy?

Olga's heart raced as she watched Purishkevich step out onto the square, alone and in well-tailored evening dress. He turned right and made for the Mikhailovsky Theatre. After forcing herself to wait, she and Gregory followed him, stopping just short of the box office.

"How much do you have?" Gregory asked quietly. Olga shoved a bundle of notes into his hand. "This is only enough for a couple of seats in the third circle," he told her.

"What is that?" Olga hissed impatiently.

"Up high, the cheap seats, nowhere near where Purishkevich would likely sit. I bet he has a box."

"Fine, we'll have a good view then, right?"

"I suppose," he said, taking the money to the box office. "Two for Le Corsaire, third circle."

Olga was right, from the third circle they could see everything. They walked the entire horseshoe of seats, scanning for Purishkevich's bald head and distinctive goatee.

"I knew it was too good to be true," Olga sighed. "Look, he's with his wife."

"Or mistress," Gregory suggested. They had taken a couple of seats with a vantage point from which Purishkevich would not see them without lowering himself to the ground.

"Either way, she's a witness and as far as we know, entirely innocent."

Olga had picked up a pair of opera glasses discarded in the lobby and now, like most of her fellow patrons, used them to look at the rich, fabulously dressed occupants of the boxes.

"I have a plan," Gregory whispered. The theatre was filling up now and the single row of seats that made up the third circle was packed tight. "We slip away when the ballet has begun and we find a disguise. A mask would do."

"Do you know the way?" Olga murmured.

"I have performed here many times. I was the third violin of this production in 1908," he lamented.

"So you know it well enough to time the ending?" Olga asked, the beginnings of a smile at the corners of her mouth.

"Certainly, what are you thinking?" asked Gregory.

"We slip away to grab these masks, then just as the final act comes to a close, we lock Purishkevich's box, wedge the door, whatever it takes. In the ensuing crowd we can hide in the box next door and put on our disguises. When we step unrecognisable into Purishkevich's box, the stalls will have emptied and there will be no witnesses except his lady friend, who you will keep quiet whilst I work."

All this Olga conveyed in a hoarse whisper, barely audible to Gregory, let alone their neighbours.

The first act began, and Olga watched entranced as the curtain rose to reveal a middle eastern bazaar, vibrantly dressed Arabians, wretched slave girls and Medora, a coquettish ballerina in a white tutu. She pranced and twirled around the stage, teasing the men, attracting a train of followers at one point, and paying particular attention to a piratical man named Conrad, known as Le Corsaire. Medora and Le Corsaire were in love.

Olga stared, mesmerised by the perfection of the choreography, the beauty of the dancers and the magnificent music. Gregory knew this ballet, had seen it many times, and his pleasure came from seeing Olga's first experience of it.

He understood the transactional nature of their relationship. She was paying him to help her assassinate an evil man, a man he too wanted to see dead. But her beauty, the amazement in her eyes at this spectacle, and the strength and confidence she had shown in the short time since he'd met her were too much for him. As Seyd Pasha convinced Medora's guardian to sell her, Gregory realised that he was in love with Olga.

By the time Conrad was rescuing Medora from Seyd Pasha, Olga had to be torn away to go to the costume department in search of a disguise.

"Tell me what happens, do they live happily ever after?" Olga pleaded as they ascended the stairs.

"Yes," he said, "they escape to sea and after a storm and a failed mutiny, they live happily ever after. Here, this is it."

The costume department was a large room, filled with rack after rack of colourful costumes detailed with the finest gold lace, sequins and gemstones. Olga saw endless tutus in every colour, nutcracker uniforms, rat costumes, pirates, Arabian princes, swan princes, Pharaohs, Spaniards and, suspended from the ceiling was Cinderella's pumpkin carriage.

"Here," Gregory whispered as he held out a tulle headdress with a detachable veil. For himself he had found an enormous beard.

"It's beautiful, just like Medora's. What are they?" she asked, pointing at the two cloaks under his arm.

"To hide our clothes, or if there is blood perhaps?" he said sheepishly. Olga nodded and as they left, she plucked a wedge from under the door and gave it to Gregory.

They caught glimpses of the ships in a storm as they made their way to Purishkevich's box, the music matching their mood of high suspense.

"There's an usher right there," Olga whispered, "I'll talk to him whilst you kick the wedge under the door."

Olga advanced on the man, arming herself with a smile that would bring Seyd Pasha himself to his knees.

"Excuse me," she said in French, fluttering her eyelashes and taking him by the arm, turning his back to Gregory, who in time with each crescendo, kicked the wedge hard so that the door to Purishkevich box was stuck fast in the frame.

"Help me balance," Olga demanded as she stood on one leg to remove her shoe, pretending to empty it and winking at the usher as she slipped it back on and walked away, following Gregory around corner.

"This is the Birbanto, Les Corsaires, it's only about a minute long, then the final bow," he whispered as they stood awkwardly in an alcove. The music stopped and the crowd erupted in a round of applause which seemed to go on forever.

"People are presenting bouquets to the dancers and the director," Gregory told Olga. Finally, voices rose from the stalls and people began to file out. They stepped into the crowd and watched the two doors anxiously, the one in which they hoped to linger and change, the other that probably contained an angry, confused Purishkevich.

At the last possible moment, the occupants of Purishkevich's neighbouring box stepped out and Olga and Gregory slipped in.

136

They could hear the muffled shouts of Purishkevich, but the noise made by the patrons filing out was enough to mask it. Keeping well back from the edge, they changed into the blue hooded cloaks, Olga with her Arabian veil and Gregory with his great, bushy beard.

"The coast is clear," Gregory said with a meaningful look at Olga, one that said here we go then, our first assassination.

The difference was disturbing, silence but for the rattling of the door, with not a soul remaining behind. To Purishkevich's credit, he'd managed to loosen the wedge and Olga braced the door as Gregory stooped to remove it.

"Who is there?" a voice demanded. "What is…" Gregory stepped through fast as Olga opened the door, pushing through Purishkevich to silence his wife by stuffing a rag into her mouth and forcing her to the ground. Purishkevich turned to stop Gregory, and Olga stepped in, dagger in hand. He gasped as the razor-sharp blade was drawn expertly across his throat, spraying the wall of the box with thick, red jets of hot, sticky blood. Gregory's cloak was soaked, as was the face of Irena, Purishkevich's companion. Muffled screams came as she watched her man fall to the ground and Olga drove the dagger into his back, the French inscription clear for all to see.

Olga backed out, removing her disguise at the last possible moment. Gregory made to follow but Irena grabbed at his clothes as he struggled to remove the blood-soaked cloak. She stood and he flailed about wildly as she pulled desperately at the cloak. As Gregory wriggled free of the garment, Irena, still pulling on it, stumbled backwards and over the low balcony. The sound of her body hitting the stalls below was sickening and the unnatural position of her neck told him all he needed to know. Olga dragged him out of the box and into the lobby where they collected their coats.

"You get lost?" the coat check girl asked.

"Something like that," Olga said, smiling lasciviously. The girl frowned disapprovingly and handed them their coats, two of the four that remained. They walked calmly towards the entrance.

"Murder! Murder at the Mikhailovsky!"

They heard the cry as they passed through the outer doors and did not stop or turn to look. Olga rounded on Gregory and with a few furtive glances, tore his beard painfully from his face, tossing it into a shrubbery before hailing a cab for the Astoria.

~

Carla watched as Gottlieb was first denied entry for being incorrectly dressed and then when he realised that he could not pay the ticket price, she watched him walk around the outside to the stage door and followed.

"Who are you, why are you following us?" she demanded, producing the Baby Browning from her clutch bag.

"I do no such thing, why are you wandering the streets unaccompanied like a common prostitute?" Gottlieb countered.

"You couldn't afford me; you can't even pay for the ballet."

"Remind me, who is following who?" he sneered.

"What happened to Königsberg? To your sick relative?"

"They had to wait. I found a couple of spies on the train and I had to follow my suspicions."

"Turn around," Carla demanded, gesturing with the pistol.

"Have you ever shot anyone, girly?" he mocked.

"Hundreds, maybe thousands," she said, thinking of that anticraft gun on Zoo Tower and the hundreds of British airmen she'd sent hurtling to their deaths every night.

"Sure," he laughed, "up close? Ever watched a man die?"

"Yes," she sighed, thinking of the dozens throughout the war and the soldiers on that boat in 1945, the man who would have raped her. Who had died on top of her. "Turn around!"

"Alright, alright, alles ist in Ordnung," he said, laughing as he turned. Carla let the sleeve of her fur coat cover the pistol and hailed a cab. As it pulled up, she encouraged Gottlieb in, giving him a prod with the pistol as she did so.

"Vitebsky station," she called to the driver. "Let's get you on a train back to Berlin, Herr Scholz."

Gottlieb smiled.

"If I make it back there, you can never show your faces in Prussia again, you know that?"

Carla was silent for a long time, wishing she had her full wits about her as she racked her brain for the answer to this nightmare. She knew she had about twenty minutes to figure it out before they were at the station, but how long before he realised that she wouldn't shoot him in public like this?

"We have to leave Petersburg, tonight," Olga panted as they raced up the back stairs of the Hotel Astoria.

"Where will I go?" Gregory asked, suddenly sounding a lot younger and less independent.

"Come to Berlin with us and there, if you want, you can catch a train to Dresden. I'll pay for your ticket and make sure you have enough to live on until you find a job," Olga said, pausing on the landing to give his arm a reassuring squeeze.

"Thank you, Olga," he said, opening the door from the sparse stairwell to the luxuriant corridor with its deep red carpets, and gilt-framed art.

"Do you... is that blood?" Olga said, stooping to look more closely.

"There's more and it leads to your suite," Gregory gulped, pointing despondently at the bloodied door handle.

"Carla!"

Olga stifled a shout and drawing her pistol, she chambered a round, handing Gregory a small knife and the room key. "If you're not sure how to use it, ditch the knife, that way it can't be used against you, okay?"

"Okay," Gregory squeaked.

Olga stood back, took aim and nodded to Gregory who, finding the door unlocked, threw it open and moved clear. Olga strode through the doorway, poised for action and casting her eyes, head and weapon as one, in every direction until she saw Carla slouched in a chair pointing her gun at a familiar face.

"Gottlieb, I knew you were a rat!" Olga said, taking in the scene and noticing the blood slowly oozing from Gottlieb's thigh. "You shot him?"

"He called my bluff just as a great coach and six rumbled past, so I let him have it," Carla said with a shrug.

"He won't do that again, will you, rat boy?" Olga asked, tilting her head to get the dejected spy's attention.

"I need a Doktor or I will bleed to death," he pleaded.

"Gregory, I don't suppose that you committed the ultimate sin of wearing a belt with evening dress?" Olga asked. He smiled nervously and removed the cracked and worn belt, handing it to Olga, who applied the tourniquet to Gottlieb's thigh.

"Argh, be careful," he moaned.

"Olga, can I see you in the next room?" Carla asked through gritted teeth.

"Gregory, this is a Colt 1908. Here," she ran a finger along the rear of the grip, "this is the grip safety, you squeeze this first to allow you to fire, then just point it at his groin and gently squeeze the trigger."

But one look at Gregory's face told her to just tie the rat up. She bound his hands with the skill of a master mariner and shoved a balled-up napkin into his mouth.

"We can't leave him alive," Carla muttered, looking Olga hard in the face but swaying gently.

"No, you're right, so why bring him here?" she demanded.

"Originally, I was taking him to the station, but I thought better of it. I figured that if I came here and waited for you, we could work it out together."

"You mean I could kill him for you?" Olga spat, accusingly.

"No–"

Olga cut her off and called to Gregory.

"Gregory, can you start packing up our things, we're leaving!"

"Okay."

"Listen," she said, turning back to Carla. "Purishkevich is dead and so is his mistress. Gregory helped me."

"Oh," was all she said, her eyes widening as she mulled over the implications. "The French connection?"

"An old Napoleonic cavalry dagger, with an inscription on the hand guard."

"That should do it, but you're right, we need to get gone and he needs to die. Not here though." Carla's betrunken mind worked overtime, trying to access her trademark ingenuity.

"Why don't we just throw him off the roof?" Olga sighed. "It'll look like suicide."

"It's all the blood," Carla said, gesturing at the lounge. "Surely, they'll put two and two together and get four? Especially with a gunshot wound."

"Carla, this is imperial Russia, the authorities aren't going to care about some nobody in a scruffy foreign lounge suit, and the Astoria certainly won't want this kind of publicity. Gregory?" Olga called, "Get someone you trust from housekeeping to make this room fit for the Tsar. Tell her we'll pay her rent for a year."

"I know just the girl," he said, rushing from the suite.

"Finish packing and leave enough money out to pay the maid," Olga snapped, starting to see that this was all down to Carla's being drunk and not wanting to miss out on the evening's activities.

"You!" she said to Gottlieb, "up!"

She waved the pistol at him and he shuffled across the room.

"Carla, wrap his leg in something, we can't have him bleeding all over the hotel again." Carla obliged and saw them through the door.

Olga pressed the barrel of the Colt hard into his bony spine, forcing him up the corridor to the service stairs. The Kamchatka suite was just below the penthouse, so two agonisingly slow flights got them out onto the roof and into the bitterly cold Saint Petersburg night.

"You don't have to do this," he pleaded, "I'll disappear, you'll never see me again, please."

"Don't die like this," Olga sneered, "die with some dignity."

She chivvied him along a trough between two gables to the low stone parapet and felt in his pockets, pulling out an empty billfold and some dogeared identity papers.

"Any last words?"

"Plea—argh!"

With practised speed, Olga placed a kick squarely into his chest. He seemed to fall for a long time before finally landing in the alley behind the hotel with a sickening crunch. Olga, who had stepped back from the edge and out of sight, looked through his papers to see that he was a Hauptleute of the Prussian Secret Police.

"Hans Gruber?" she said aloud with a tentative peak over the parapet before heading back downstairs.

Olga found Gregory's friend had finished the corridor and was hard at work in the lounge of their suite. Carla stood impatiently by their luggage as Gregory wheeled in a trolley.

"Have you paid this fine woman?" Olga asked.

"Yes, she's highly motivated," Carla said, almost ruefully.

"I've got a cab waiting, the last train leaves in thirty minutes," Gregory announced, slightly out of breath.

The three of them left via the service elevator, climbed into a cab to the station and with minutes to spare, onto the Nord Express Paris-bound train.

Vienna, 1908

The first six months of Rudi's posting were a whirlwind of dinners, functions, soirees, luncheons, galas, balls, and the occasional diplomatic meeting. Usually, Rudi would be assigned to take notes or deliver important messages. Not just any messages, though. He was no footman – these were the kinds of messages that one would only trust to a former Hauptmann in the diplomatic service of the Kaiser. His job in Vienna's German embassy was simply to do as he was asked and remain affable. He was to dance with the wives of men too old, too busy, or too tired to do it themselves. He was to charm guests at the ambassador's lavish dinners and provide stimulating conversation when none could be found amongst the others in attendance.

Rudi considered one day that if someone had taken him aside and explained what the life of a junior diplomat was really like, he should have dropped science there and then and pursued the law, in the hope that he might find a way into this vocation. The downside for him was the inactivity, the hours alone with his thoughts and the ghosts that had followed him home from Africa, from the GDR, and from the Second World War. He only harboured the feelings of crippling guilt from the former and he found, with a mixture of relief and disapprobation that he had learned to accept what he had done on some level.

He told himself that the Herrero people could have surrendered, that Germany and von Trotha had only wanted to help them become civilised. At first the obvious lies had sickened him, but now he could feel himself giving into the notions of superiority and he found that he was able to empathise with von Trotha. It was easier to tell himself that whilst deeply saddening, what happened in Africa was unavoidable. That was just how it was in the colonies and if Germany was to compete on the world stage, then all of this was necessary for the good of the German volk and of the empire. It took months for these affirmations to assuage the guilt he felt, the near debilitating shame that what he had done, what he had ordered others to do, had caused so much suffering and so much death.

Now, when asked about his time in Africa, instead of the ever-increasing knot of anxiety and the white-hot flush of guilt, Rudi would smile and tell of the day he earned his Blue Max. He would touch the blue and gold cross at his neck as if absentmindedly and stare off into the distance before putting in a performance worthy of the stage.

~

German South-West Afrika, 1905.

Leutnant Horst Buchholz was supernumerary. He did not have a platoon to lead, he did not have a general to aid and he did not have a real purpose in this campaign. For this he was grateful, because he was a charlatan, an imposter, and given the command of any number of men, he would have been disastrously out of his depth. The plan had always been to hang around for a few weeks until a ship could carry him on to Europe, using Horst's good but unremarkable service record from his time in German East Africa as a platform from which to launch his career.

Such was the lack of coverage of this dark period in Germany's colonial history that Carla could not have planned for this and as such, Rudi was woefully underprepared. So, surplus to requirements though he was, when the doctor had deemed him fit, the local commander had issued him a horse and rifle and told him to get on the train to Waterberg.

There was no train to Waterberg, the train tracks stopped one hundred kilometres short of the Herero position and Rudi had been assigned to supervise the caravans of ox carts used to transport the men, guns, troops, and supplies to the staging ground of the battle. It was hot, heavy work, hours in the saddle interspersed with moments of high stress or difficult problems, with everyone looking to him for the solution. Often he had one, for he was sharp-witted and highly intelligent, but he was not used to this kind of work and it exhausted him. He was not an accomplished horseman, and his body was not accustomed to the deprivations of labour.

For three months he did this, being the only spare and apparently competent officer in von Trotha's army. He grew to know and love his palomino Arab, a mare called Strudel. She was an uncomplaining veteran cavalry mount who seemed to understand that Rudi was barely capable and took it easy on him. By the time the two thousand men were encamped, the hundreds of guns emplaced, and the latrines sited and dug, Rudi could ride, and ride well. He and Strudel trusted one another and the knowledge that he would have her to guide him in the coming battle was a comfort.

Rudi found himself in the retinue of General Adrian Dietrich Lothar von Trotha, still without official appointment, but at least now he was acclimatised and able to ride.

"This will be a standard pincer," von Trotha said, his Prussian whiskers remaining impossibly still as he orated. "The Schwarzer, roughly sixty thousand of them, are on this plateau and we will surround them and compel them to surrender. Terms will be met, and peace will be restored."

He looked around at the assembled troops.

"If, however, they choose to make their stand in this place, then this day will be the last day that the Herero people will exist. The Empire will not stand for dissent, and I will be without mercy!"

The plan was straight out of a Lichterfelde textbook. Vast columns of men marched or rode in unison, wheeling around like the great ships of another age. From every direction the blocking columns came.

"What on earth is von Kessel doing?" roared von Trotha. "Where is my signaller?" He looked around for the soldier whose job it was to operate the semaphore.

"He's gone down with dysentery, Herr General," offered an aide. Von Trotha cast about for a solution. "You, Buchholz, ride down there and find out why he hasn't stepped off yet!"

"Ja, Herr General!" Rudi wheeled around and spurred Strudel onwards to the southeast. The column was not moving and the enormous gap that was starting to appear would allow the Herero to escape. It was over a mile and Rudi pushed Strudel to her limit, ever aware of Trotha's withering eye at his back. Every second would permit hundreds of rebels to escape, allowing them to counter at the expense of German lives.

As he came closer, he drew his Reichsrevolver and fired three shots into the air that gained the attention of the Oberst von Kessel and his column. Rudi turned to see that the Herero, who had noticed the gap in the encirclement, were advancing on his position.

147

He slowed, head spinning back and forth between the advancing native forces and the stationary Germans. He fumbled in his pocket for three more rounds before remembering he would need the piece of wood provided to eject the three empty cases.

As he performed this task whilst mounted and with the thundering of the Herero forces bearing down upon him, he began to panic. Repeated, hopeful looks to the left told him that von Kessel's column still had not moved.

But von Kessel had sent a rider, one man to face sixty thousand.

Rudi heard the crack and thump of enemy fire as dust exploded at Strudel's feet. She whinnied but stood firm and resolute as fear gripped Rudi and twisted his insides.

"Herr Leutnant, do you have a message for the Oberst?" the trooper panted, a swarthy youth with oversized features that glistened with sweat. He winced each time a round landed near their entirely exposed position between two armies.

"Ja! Advance! He's late and he's making a Schlamassel of the whole operation!"

The youth produced a bugle and sounded the advance. Rudi watched the sound reach the ears of the colonel and heard it echoed by other buglers. He turned back to see the ever-advancing mass of Herero. Looking to his rear for the first time, Rudi saw that the western column had not stopped, and they were approaching the Herero left flank. He watched as the westernmost soldiers turned east and the ripple caused each file to turn to run from the advancing column. Soon the men to his front, the men he feared he would be facing with his army of one bugler, were running eastwards into the Kalahari Desert.

"Order the column to left wheel!" Rudi demanded and the bugler obliged. The colonel must also have seen what was going on, because the bugle call was echoed once more and the column wheeled, making to cut the fleeing troops off with their superior speed. As the calls died down and Rudi's heart began to beat normally, the staccato rattle of the maxim gun started up. In the chaos, a unit of Herrero mounted infantry had managed to take the military station and were holding it. The belt-fed machine gun tore through bone and flesh to devastating effect, both into the backs of the retreating mass and the now defenders of the station. The bugler, now Rudi's shadow, nearly fell from his horse when the artillery began firing. They watched as the supplies he'd spent three months assembling were destroyed by the men they were supposed to feed and arm. Strudel bristled and he realised his thighs were clamping down on the saddle so hard with his anguish that he was upsetting his mount.

The Herero mostly escaped, although nearly all those occupying the station were killed, and the rearmost section of the retreating force suffered heavy casualties. What followed was a pursuit through the Kalahari Desert, but with the German supplies all but destroyed, von Trotha was forced to wait for more.

The Herero people died out there in the desert of thirst and starvation as they fled the guns and bayonets of the pursuing troops. After his actions on the first day, Rudi was finally given a command of his own. He went on to tell of his weeks in the desert, his hardships and those of his men, ¬ the deprivation they faced, and the subsequent death of Strudel.

What he glossed over, what his mind had begun to repress, were the stark and horrifying truths of the matter. Samuel Maharero had assembled tens of thousands of his people on that plateau, many women and children, as well as their livestock. They were there to negotiate for peace, but when they found themselves beset on all sides, the Herero knew that they had been deceived. Some fought bravely while most chose to get their families to safety. They had waited on that sparse ground for two months and were already low on water and rations, but the desert was worse, and the unrelenting pursuit meant they could not find grazing for their cattle or water to stay alive. The Herero people were chased to near extinction in that unyielding desert, driven like cattle by the colonial soldiers at their backs. Von Trotha then ordered for a two-hundred-mile fence to be built and gave the annihilation order:

"I, the great General of the German troops, send this letter to the Herero people. The Herero people are no longer German subjects. The Herero people must leave the country. If the nation does not do this, I will force them with the cannon. Within the German borders, every Herero, with or without gun, with or without cattle, will be shot. I will no longer accept women or children. I will drive them back to their people or I will let them be shot."

Trapped in the desert, mothers watched as their children starved or died of thirst, emaciated animals dropped dead, and the remnants of this once great people were rounded up and sent to camps. Only one thousand escaped over the border. They were forced to work as slaves and build ports so that more Germans could arrive and more of their land's resources could be shipped away for profit.

Rudi found himself at Shark Island, "Arbeit Macht Frei," may not have been written over the gates but nevertheless, this was the prototype for the Nazi death camps. Eight-thousand Herero were murdered there, and Rudi had held a position of responsibility. He had chased these people from their home, harried them through the desert and corralled them for extermination. He had looked on without protest, as men like Eugen Fischer, father of Nazi eugenic policy, had conducted his medical experiments.

But he was only following orders.

Rudi saw these people as the cause of his suffering, as the cause of the deaths of his men, and the reason he was still here at what he saw as the ends of the earth. In this colonial echo chamber his resentment grew into hatred, and from watching his victims grow weak from meagre rations and hard labour, the narrative of superiority was affirmed. By the time he left, though wracked with guilt over what he had done, what he had condoned, he felt sure that there was something in this eugenics theory.

Why were they so weak and stooped, when he and his fellow Germans were so strong? Had he forgotten the bravery of the towering Herero warriors who had borne down upon him in Waterberg? Their speed on foot and their prowess on horse? Had He forgotten how scared he had been? Such was the twisted absurdity of this logic, Rudi might have pulled the wings from a bee and chastised it for not being able to fly.

Now, back in Germany, the camps had been decried by the Volk and closed down, the fifteen-thousand remaining prisoners sold as slaves to German farmers. The Herero people had been one-hundred thousand a few years earlier, but Rudi's notions that the Germanic people were better, stronger, more capable, were only bolstered by the national narrative. The Kaiser believed it to be true, as did many others. These concepts were not new to him. Rudi had grown up believing it, singing Hitlerjugend songs and berating Jewish neighbours in the street. He remembered the day his friend Morty was taken away for resettlement in the east. He had thought it was a great idea, he was jealous that Morty would live on a farm and not in an apartment like he had to. He knew the truth now though, he found out in the late forties during an argument with Olga, when he'd been fifteen years old and the realisation of what his countrymen had done had hit him hard. He shut himself away for days, he refused to speak with Carla when she returned from Oxford, saying that she must have known something at her age. Must have been in some way complicit.

Then a cruel twist of fate had placed him in the very position of the men he'd spent so long despising and lifetimes trying to thwart. But he was only following orders, just like they were, just like the men under him. He knew that if he didn't comply, if he didn't come home with a glowing record, then his part in this great cause was over and he would have failed. Failed Olga, failed the Volk and failed every other wretched victim of the Reich over the coming half century. He twisted and turned his mind into justifying the despicable treatment of these innocent people. He told himself that their sacrifice was necessary, that it had happened already, and he was only really filling the shoes of another German officer who had obviously complied. And slowly, over the months and years, the justification of saving the world slipped away and he grew, like his peers, to hate his prisoners. He knew it was wrong, but it was only seven years since he'd been a vehement Nazi, so this was not such a leap for him when everyone he lived with, ate with and socialised with, believed it too.

"After that, I aways carried my own bugle," Rudi, the soldier turned diplomat, said to his fellow diner's delight.

152

Shortly afterwards in the bathroom, Rudi stared in the mirror at Host Buchholz, but before the negative thoughts could creep back in, he splashed his face with cold water, dried himself with a soft, fluffy towel and returned to the fine dining and exquisite wines.

Wealthy and valuing his privacy, Rudi had taken spacious rooms in between the embassy and the opera house. As a diplomat he moved in the highest of social circles, but as a young, erudite Berliner, filled with ideas and dreams, he went in search of like-minded individuals with whom to discuss them.

He met August Kubizek, a young musician in Volksgarten, one fine July afternoon in 1908.

"Beautiful, is it not?" Rudi mused as he joined him gazing contemplatively at the Empress Elizabeth Monument.

"It is," the young man replied distantly, and then checking himself, he turned to offer a hand.

"August Kubizek, pleased to meet you." He smiled warmly, inclining his head.

"Horst Buchholz, delighted to meet you." Rudi shook the hand and returned the smile.

"What brings you to Austria, Herr Buchholz?" he asked, ignoring Rudi's gloves.

"Is it that obvious?" he chuckled. "I work at the embassy."

"Ah, diplomacy, the art of…" he trailed of, realising that this was a stranger. "If you're new in the city and don't know anyone, I was going to meet some friends of mine for coffee, would you care to join me?"

"If you promise to finish that quotation at some point?"

"Of course, as soon as I know you a little better. Oh, and my friends call me Gustl."

"Gustl it is," Rudi laughed.

They strolled through the streets of Vienna speaking amicably of art and the theatre, of Freud and Wagner, until they reached a coffee house overlooking a picturesque Platz.

"Friends, this is Horst, he's from Berlin, but don't hold that against him," Gustl announced to a table of long-haired, flamboyantly dressed young men with brightly coloured cravats and waistcoats.

Conversely, Rudi was dressed conservatively in a dark suit and plain tie. Nevertheless, he felt welcome and enjoyed the relaxed atmosphere and intelligent conversation. Something he'd learned quickly at the embassy, was that class, breeding and title did not necessarily mean intellect, common sense, or depth.

"Good afternoon, Gustl."

The voice came from behind Rudi and contrasted greatly with the carefree chatter that had made up the afternoon so far. He turned to see the speaker and standing before him was a well-dressed man of about his age with dark, lank hair, deathly pale skin, and the beginnings of a broad moustache.

"Adolf, I'm so glad you could join us."

Rudi's stomach turned, and rising bile flooded his mouth, causing his head to spin. This was his childhood idol, the man whose face had adorned the wall of every public building, home, and office in the Fatherland for the first twelve years of his life. This man was the former hero, arbiter of doom and the focus of Rudi's deep and burning hatred for immeasurable lifetimes. He stood to leave, but Gustl placed a hand on his arm.

"Please, he doesn't have many friends," he implored.

Rudi looked from Gustl to Adolf and back. He experienced a magnetic curiosity, compelling him to remain, just for a short while, just to meet the man who was capable of such evil. His curiosity prompted him to weigh this young Adolf against others he'd met and truly get the measure of a man who would become infamous the world over.

Minutes became hours as the men spoke of art, philosophy, and architecture. It would seem that the history books were wrong, Adolf was in fact enrolled in the prestigious Vienna school of art. Gustl was a fine musician who hoped to one day be a conductor and he attributed his success so far to Adolf's influence, his strict and somewhat overbearing insistence that he practise for hours each day.

When Rudi went home that evening, they parted friends and he had no idea how the man he had devoted countless lives to stopping, hating from afar, had won him over so easily. Everything he said made so much sense, there was no doubt in Rudi's mind that the man was a genius. There was no antisemitism, no racial superiority, just brilliant ideas about society and government. There wasn't a problem he couldn't solve, and Rudi had spent the evening enraptured.

He awoke the next day disgusted with himself. He should have taken the opportunity to kill the man, saving the lives of millions in the process.

He went about his work at the embassy and tried to put the evening out of his mind, but he felt unclean, unfaithful, and unworthy. Weeks went by without seeing the pair again and he had begun to put the shameful encounter from his mind, until one September evening on his way home from the opera.

"Horst, Horst is that you, my good fellow?" Gustl called from across Krugerstrasse, but Rudi walked hurriedly on, pretending not to hear. Kind-hearted Gustl, though, could not believe that his good friend Horst would snub him like that, so he persisted, forcing Rudi to turn and greet the two inseparable chums.

"Gustl, Adolf, how good to see you both, did you see the show?" he asked, hoping that he had struck the perfect balance between polite and unencouraging – something the English had developed into an artform. Both men shook his hand vigorously and railroaded him into a fashionable café.

"Horst," Adolf said, staring into his eyes and making Rudi uncomfortable, "where have you been? I have missed you."

"Oh, you know, life as a diplomat is all parties and extravagant dinners, I barely have time to do any of my actual work this time of year," he joked.

"Indeed... I have a book for you." He slid a copy of Nietzsche's On The Genealogy of Morality across the table to him. Rudi ran his hands over the deep blue leather and the embossed gold letters.

"Thank you, what is it about?"

"Germany! My dear Horst, it contains all the answers for a prosperous Germany."

Rudi's pulse quickened, because he knew where this was going, and he had no desire to tread that path or encourage others along either.

"There is nothing about Germany that is not prosperous," he said flatly.

"So it would seem," Adolf fixed him with those cold grey-blue eyes for a long moment.

"Please, read the book and then speak to me of how it made you feel," he intoned, grabbing at the air in front of his face and pulling it down to slam the table in front of him. Several patrons eyed him with disdain at the disturbance. Adolf Hitler simply stuck out his chin and, closing his eyes, drew in a deep breath through his nose.

"Horst, the world is changing and men like us will be faced with a decision. We must choose to be on the right side of history."

Sweat soaked Rudi's dress shirt and when he lifted his hand from the book, he saw that it trembled. Without speaking, he rose to leave, his eyes darting from one man to the other in tacit farewell.

"Horst," Gustl called after him, "you forgot your gift." He caught up with him outside and pressed the book into his hands. "Dolph is very fond of you, Horst, he would be very hurt if you didn't accept this."

Rudi looked at the man who would be a great composer and nothing more, not a mass murderer or despot, but a stoic friend to the most hated man of the twentieth century. Rudi knew that if Adolf had chased after him, Rudi would not have taken the book, but because it was Gustl, sweet, kind Gustl, he simply nodded, clicked his heels and strode out into the night.

In bed he could not sleep, as each time he closed his eyes he saw an assortment of images from both his current life and others, unable to differentiate between the things he had done in Africa and the things he saw on the news reels after the Second World War.

The right side of history.

By one in the morning, he relented and lit his bedside lamp and fumbled around under his bed for the book. He propped himself up and began to read.

"We are unknown to ourselves, we men of knowledge: and for good reason. We have never sought ourselves – how then should it happen that we find ourselves one day?"

157

Unbeknownst to anyone at the time, least of all men of science such as Rudi, the work of Nietzsche had been seized by his antisemitic sister and her husband when Nietzsche went mad. She had doctored it and filled his prose with anti-Jewish sentiment and hate. The words burrowed into Rudi's already beleaguered brain and took hold. They found his innate weakness, his shame over the evil he had already committed and the resentment he felt towards his victims. He was a scared, broken young man with a brilliant mind, but he had been brainwashed before with the same sick ideologies and they found their old grooves with ease. He read long past sunrise and on into the evening without food or drink, waking the following morning desperate to discuss these ideas with Adolf and Gustl. He felt he could temper the man, guide him to a less extreme path and perhaps, save millions of innocent lives.

If I don't succeed, I can always kill him... I'm quite good at killing these days.

Over the autumn and winter of 1908, they discussed Nietzsche, Hegel, Fichte, Treitschke and the Englishman, Houston Stewart Chamberlain. Rudi did his best to offer new, more conservative interpretations that weren't fuelled by hate and the othering of everyone outside mythical ideals of what constitutes a German. It was an uphill struggle and despite Adolf's obvious awkwardness, his powers of persuasion and fiery temper were too much for Rudi's arguments for restraint. Instead, Rudi found himself coming around to the idea of a strong, prosperous Germany, despite the fact that one already existed and the evidence all around him. He began to see behaviours that weren't there in the groups of people that Adolf despised.

When his posting back to Berlin came in February of 1909 with a promotion, he saw his opportunity slipping away from him. He still told himself that his plan was on track and his efforts to calm his close friend and steer him away from extremism were working. But like a poison, Hitler's hatred and unwavering belief in the superiority of the Germanic people was slowly filling Rudi's subconscious.

"Dolph?" he said over coffee in their favourite café one frigid afternoon, "I have been called back to Berlin to sit my exams and take up a new position in the Foreign Ministry."

"I see," he replied without emotion. "Will you go?"

"Of course I will go, Dolph, it is in service to the Fatherland that glory lies."

"Certainly, but what about your friends here? Gustl will miss you terribly."

"I had thought about that, actually." Rudi knew from Carla's research nestled secretly in his pocket watch, that Hitler would soon run to Munich to avoid conscription into the Austrian army. "Your conscription must be due soon, Dolph?"

"Nonsense, students are exempt conscription, Horst, do you know nothing of Austria? Of course not, you are but a tourist, here one moment and gone the next."

"Dolph, I'm not a fool." His words hung in the air between them for a painfully long time before Hitler finally spoke.

"You can't go to Berlin on your own, I will have to postpone my studies and accompany you," he announced. "No, no, don't thank me. Despite the tremendous imposition, I alone understand what duty to one's friends truly means."

"Oh Dolph, nothing would give me greater pleasure."

Berlin, 1912

The Berlin morning papers of March fourth, 1912, all bore the same shocking headline: Murder at the Mikhailovsky!

Some added the tagline: French dagger found in heart of Russian Member for Kursk!

Parks, cafes, and trams all buzzed with the news. The collapse of the Russo-French alliance, what did it mean?

But for Olga, Carla, and Gregory, this was not news. This was the result of months of work, weeks of painstaking surveillance and many sleepless nights.

"What are we going to do with him?" Carla demanded as the train sped west and rhythmic vibrations faded into the background from hours of repetition.

"I promised him money to go to Dresden," Olga said.

"How much?"

"We didn't discuss an amount, but I said I'd help him with some investments," Olga confessed, wincing in apprehension of Carla's reproachful tirade, but none came.

"Fine, a one-way train ticket to Dresden, a month's rent and board, seed money for a portfolio and extra for a few suits."

She counted them off on her fingers and scribbled in a notebook. Her mouth moved and she stared at the ceiling whilst she did her sums.

"We are going to need to cash in one of the gold bars."

There was no emotion, no chiding or disapproval to her tone, just a flat recital of fact.

"It was bound to happen at some point," Olga added, unnecessarily.

"Maybe I'll just give him a bar and a train ticket, that way he'll be on the train with no liquid funds and out of our hair."

"Why do you want to be rid of him so badly?"

"Well," she stumbled, "he knows, he's..."

"Just as guilty as me or you!" Olga cut in.

"I suppose, but he's one more mouth to feed and he's Russian, which is odd and he's all, all—"

"You don't like him because he's Jewish?" Olga hurled the accusation, lip curled with incredulous disgust. "Are you fucking joking? After all you've seen, after having it all dragged up again at Nuremburg?" Olga stood over her friend, her sister to all intents.

"I, I... it's hard for me..."

"Hard for you? You've seen the photographs? Studied it all at college? Dissected the egregious nature of the Holocaust. Death. Factories. Carla, that's what they were. Do you know that they shaved those poor people, made piles of their hair and wove it into slippers for U-boat crews? We passed one, a death factory. In Brandenburg, it was a prototype for the bigger ones in the east. I—"

"I remember. I'm sorry, but it is ingrained in me. I was two years old when the enablement act was passed and seven at Kristallnacht."

"The night of the broken glass?"

"Yes. Thousands of Jewish businesses and homes were smashed, leaving glass strewn all over Berlin. You have to understand that when you are told repeatedly that something or someone is evil, then it becomes part of you. I can't shake it, I don't hate Gregory or any other Jew, I just can't be near him. Perhaps it's guilt, perhaps I can't stand to think about what we did as a country to his people?"

"Believe me, Carla, I had the same rhetoric fed to me as a child and I was eighteen before the wool was pulled from my eyes."

"Yes, Olga, but you were rescued by Jews, and you owe them your life. They kept you safe and told you everything was okay, that it wasn't your fault. What I got was the eyes of the world upon me and my countrymen, accusing, hating, gloating. I was fourteen!"

Tears streamed down Carla's face and Olga moved to comfort her.

"No, I'm fine, this is a manifestation of my guilt, nothing more."

Carla stood and stepped to the window to watch the Prussian countryside, shimmering lakes and verdant forests topped with snow. A crane rose tall from the reeds onto long elegant legs and spreading its wings, it took flight in a flurry of movement followed by a serene glide. Flapping occasionally to keep pace with the train, it seemed to look at Carla and see into her very soul.

Gregory was sad to leave Olga, but he took the bar and the ticket with a grateful smile, boarding the very next train south.

Safely ensconced in the hotel Adlon, Carla began to study her microfiche in an effort to plan their next move.

"I need to go to a library," she announced. "Something isn't right."

Carla stood and called louder so that Olga could hear her from the bath.

"Okay, bring me a book about women who do more than fucking and needlepoint," she called back, expecting nothing.

Carla had wanted to wander the city freely, taking in the atmosphere with an unburdened mind, but to do that, she would need to finish her work, to plan their next act. Their next assassination.

She walked with purpose along Franz Strasse, east through the Gendarmenmarkt, looking up at the domed spire of the Deutscher Dom and it hit her like a blast of hot air. This place somehow evoked a memory of another life, events buried deep in her subconscious by layers of shame and denial.

Icy fingers gripped her heart as sweat ran in rivulets down her spine. About her in the busy square, her mind overlayed the stalls and carts with two great scaffolds. Her mother was there with a man she felt sure she should know. In the middle a woman turned her head to look in Carla's direction.

The woman was Carla. Older, careworn and underfed, but there was no mistaking it.

Each held ropes, her eyes followed them through a system of pulleys overhead and what she saw forced the breath from her lungs. She fought to inhale, and the breath was instantly expelled. It happened again and again, until she realised that she was screaming. The impossible, grotesque sight was her brother, Rudi.

Again, he was older, gaunt and ravaged by time and circumstance, but the wretched figure was Rudolph Kessler. Her brain took a moment to process the scene before her. Eventually seeing it for what it was: Sippenhaft. Rudi screamed as another version of her family slowly lowered him into a barrel of acid. He seemed to be looking directly into her eyes, into her soul, puss dribbling from his mouth, mingling with sweat and blood and tears.

She felt hands on her back, gentle and consolatory, concerned voices and questioning looks as the scene faded. She rushed from the market over the Kupfergraben and into the library on Breite

163

Strasse. Inside she found a quiet corner and cried silently until she was able to calm down. Carla slowly realised something with such gravity that she could see neither over nor around it, it was as a wall to a child, the ocean to a cat, or the vastness of the heavens to mortal men.

The concept she now groped at in the dark was difficult for her to verbalise, though she would try later with Olga and maybe Rudi someday. She realised that what had happened to her in the Gendarmenmarkt, in Sonnenallee, or out on a yacht on Plauer See would stay with her forever. Not in the usual use of this word, but in the eternal, unending, immortal sense. These three horrors and more belike would visit her or other Carla Kesslers until the Götterdämmerung. She didn't know if she believed in the rapture, the end time or judgement day, but the promise of an ending to her relentless torment was too enticing to dismiss.

In search of some literary solace, Carla found among the shelves a copy of Goethe's Faust. She knew the story if not the actual text and pondered on the plot.

Perhaps Rudi is like Faust? Would that make Olga Gretchen?

She put the book away and turned her mind to the task she'd left the hotel for.

Thirty minutes later she confirmed her suspicions. Emperor Franz Joseph was indeed dead, and Franz Ferdinand now ruled Austria-Hungary. With the addition of a third, Slavic crown, the Serbian people are content, and a large European war is less likely. Carla wondered if killing Dragutin Dimitrijević and his black-hand organisation would be necessary now.

"We need to go to London."

"Okay," Olga said with a shrug. She was inspecting her toes very carefully and Carla thought she hadn't heard what she was saying.

"Olga! Franz Joseph is dead! We need to speak to Henry and find out what we should do."

She sat down heavily and sighed.

"Where will Rudi be? I've been waiting to see him. I'm not leaving Berlin if he's here. Not until I've seen him."

"I don't know, he could be in any one of the German embassies, they have them all over the world, except Mexico," Carla said, having just found that out. "It's strange because Germany always supported Mexico. Remember the Zimmermann telegraph?"

"No, will it tell me where Rudi is?"

"I'll bet Henry would know?" Carla sighed.

A knock at the door of their suite turned out to be a bell hop with a note for each of the women.

"It's from Henry," Carla said.

"How can you tell?"

"Listen. Dearest Carla, I trust this brief note finds you well?" she read. "Well done in Paris and Saint Petersburg, excellent show. I need you to pop over to London for a catch-up, a lot has transpired since last we met."

"That all?"

"Yes."

"My one says, Dearest Olga, are you in good health? Splendid work recently, drop by the old place one weekend so I can bring you up to speed on the latest gossip."

"That's definitely Henry," Carla said, reading her note through once more.

"I assume he means Broadlands?"

"Where else? It's Tuesday now, shall we get a sleeper on Thursday night?"

"Where to? Le Havre? Hoek of Holland?" Olga stretched, catlike before rising to pace the room.

"The train is much faster than the boat, we could eat breakfast in Paris and be at Broadlands for tea."

"I like it, and I'll have a few days to wander the streets of my old hometown," Carla said without thinking. It had been what she'd wanted to do before, but now she feared the ghosts of her many lives would be waiting for her on every Platz down every Allee. She would not hide; she would face it down.

"I missed the ballet the other night and I'd like to make up for that. I'd like to see our old apartment building and I have a strange notion that I'd like to visit Aldershof. I want to go to the Tiergarten and the Romanisches café."

"Anything else? Perhaps a ride in a hot air balloon?" Olga suggested.

"That would be fantastic," she said, the sarcasm lost as she became excited again. "I could see my old emplacement atop Zoo tower and experience Berlin as the Terrorflieger did."

"I was joking, but it does sound fun. Maybe I'll spot Rudi if he's here?" she said as the veneer of bravado melted away and she felt the pull of the man she loved from deep within her.

As they strolled the banks of the Spree, drank coffee at the edge of a bustling Platz or roamed amongst the statues in the Tiergarten, Olga absentmindedly searched for the one thing she wanted in this world: Rudolf Kessler. The feeling of hope and prosperity amongst

166

the Berliners was palpable, and it affected Carla far more as this was a grotesque parody of the Berlin she had known: starving children playing in the rubble of their future, colourless but for the dark rings at their sunken eyes. Ragged mothers, prematurely aged and brainwashed into feverish optimism – or too scared to speak to the contrary. Uniforms were still de rigueur, but they weren't draped over children or old men, they adorned the healthy and the young, limbs intact, smiling, and full of energy. Most noticeably, there wasn't a swastika in sight.

Carla had seen thousands of planes; bombers, fighters and scouts most nights for over two years, as they rained indiscriminate hell upon her dying city, but had never actually flown before. The limp, silk bladder was inflated with hydrogen and took the shape of an upturned pear, as a small crowd watched from behind rope stanchions. The tickets had cost a small fortune, but Carla had reasoned away her doubts as humans would.

Olga peevishly shook off the aeronaut as he tried to help her into the basket. He didn't offer any to Carla after that. All three donned a warm, padded flying helmet and with due ceremony, the ropes were cast off and the balloon lurched skyward. Butterflies danced in the pit of Carla's stomach, rising in intensity with the basket, which creaked and moaned with the stress of opposing forces. The aeronaut had one role: to operate the flap atop the envelope of silk that would allow hydrogen to escape and cause the balloon to descend. They remained tethered to the ground via a long manila rope.

From the ground and from the balloon, Carla found the number of wide-open spaces delighted her, as did the freedom enjoyed by all to roam the streets free of brownshirts, checkpoints, and barbed wire. Beautifully crafted carriages and motor cars made steady progress across squares and along treelined boulevards. She smiled down on her fellow Berliners as they grew small and more distant. Only from the air could Carla appreciate the true majesty of the parade route from the Charlottenburger Torr along the Charlottenburger Chaussee, through the Brandenburger Torr and onto Unter den Linden, a near straight line all the way from the Spree to the Havel. She remembered the parades and the scarlet banners of her childhood and for the first time noticed that the Siegessäule was not in the Tiergarten but in Königsplatz and it seemed to have shrunk.

"Do you remember when you thought the Wannsee was a sea we could escape over?" Carla asked, as both women looked out over the western expanse of green and shimmering silver that was the Havel basin.

"Simpler times, though terrifying," Olga mused.

"You miss Rudi badly, don't you?"

She gave her friend a one-armed squeeze and was reminded of her solidity and physical strength.

"I do, I've spent most of my life missing him. Sometimes I wish we could have just had our six months in 1961 and be done with it. Every other moment of my life, my lives outside that golden time has been torture. Some of it literal, mostly the pain of separation, of longing for someone that you cannot have. I need him, Carla, don't you see? Not the little boy I found down there in 1945, but my Rudi."

Tears threatened as a rogue gust shook the basket.

"We'll find him, Olga, I promise," Carla said, placing a hand on her shoulder. The words felt empty, insufficient, and even lazy, but what else could she say? Olga said nothing, her gaze resting on a microscopic boat with dark red sails as it beat steadily upward.

She thought of that boat and compared it to her life, never really heading in the direction she wanted, merely following a theory that, if she kept on in this way, would eventually get her to where she intended to be.

Berlin's ballet dancers weren't a patch on the Russians, but Olga didn't feel the need to point that out. The performance was just spellbinding and this time she was free to simply enjoy it and she gave herself over to it entirely. The beauty of youth, the vibrant colours and music enveloped her as she relished the distraction it offered. As they filed out into the lobby a voice rose from the crowd.

"I love your gown. You simply have to tell me where you found such a wonder," demanded a tall, winnowing Englishwoman wearing the latest Paris had to offer.

"Oh, I had them imported from Petersburg," Olga replied in English. "I have a girl that's rather splendid who alters them for me."

"Marvellous. Say, do you fine ladies have plans this evening? We're off to a reception with the French ambassador. Why not come along and you can tell me all about your Petersburg connections?"

They went, radiating youth and sophistication. Both able to converse in multiple languages on a range of topics that, for the time, were deemed complex issues and not for the likes of women. Many minds were opened that cold spring night in 1912. Olga excused herself from a rigorous conversation about women's suffrage to take some air. As she returned to the din of the salon, their eyes met.

He was older, weather beaten and with the countenance of a statesman and not a physicist, but there was no mistaking those cobalt eyes. He wore a black tie with a medal at his neck, a blue cross very much like the one her mother had worn, a medal of the Reich. They weaved through the throng towards one another, frantic to feel, hear, smell and taste. She was no older and in only a few months, time had reversed its cruel trick and now they were both in their mid-twenties with years of happiness ahead of them. Silently, they embraced and Olga felt her entire being relax, shedding a weight she had not known she'd borne.

"Your hands?"

"I didn't think I would see you so soon, this is a wonderful surprise."

"Carla wanted to see Berlin before…"

She looked about for Carla, to see her holding court in the corner, a retinue of young men enraptured, hanging on her every word. Olga caught her eye and she waved, giving her a look that said, I know he's my brother, but I'll wait.

"Before the Nazis?"

Olga made to shush him and realised that the concept of the word was nothing to these people and the multitude of languages in use at this party would mask any strange word one cared to utter.

She looked up at him. He was only a few inches taller but still, she did not wish to talk to his chin.

"Dance with me, Rudi."

She led him to a miniature ballroom and to the sound of a string quartet they danced as they had done for what seemed eternity. This could have been Paris, or Munich, London, or Prague. Neither had catalogued the many places and ways that they had loved one another and neither needed to. This moment, here and now, whenever, wherever that was, singularly counted above any that had come before it.

"Let's go somewhere else," Rudi whispered in her ear after both were near exhaustion.

She eyed him wryly as she moved away and smiled, bearing her wonderfully imperfect teeth. "Where?"

"I know a place."

He led Olga away from the salon and down a corridor, up a backstair and suddenly she was back at Grunewald, back with Frieda Altstötter. Rudi opened a door onto a hall lit by gas lamps, and she was back in Berlin, back with the man she loved, the only person she could ever be with.

They fell into a huge luxurious bed, slowly kissing, touching, and rediscovering. There was no urgency, each knew the other with an intimacy most lovers never reached. He covered her with soft kisses, exploring her. She took one of his hands in hers, running her fingers gently over the ridges and contours, feeling the smooth skin plateaus left by his burns.

"Did you touch someone?"

She turned her head to see his face and he nodded silently, hoping she had not been assailed with images of the eight years since they had last met. If she had, she gave no sign and he realised that this was not the first time they had reconnected in this timeline. The knowing, the assault of memories, feelings and revelations must be for that first meeting alone. He had not burned his hands for naught, but he needn't worry about Olga, Carla, Henry or any other from his past or future.

As they made love, Rudi could not shake the images of his misdeeds, or of the old woman in Bremen, her hair in the wind and her eyes as the light left them. Olga, delighted at his new-found stamina, revelled as wave after wave of ecstasy rolled over her, until finally, she asked if he was okay.

"I…, I think I have had too much Schnaps," he said as he rolled away, gasping for breath as he faced the ceiling. Olga rested her head on his chest. He was more muscular than she remembered, and she found that he was covered with small scars. She fingered one softly.

"Tell me about Africa, Rudi? Was it terrible?"

When Carla had decided to send him, she had not known of the horrors that befell the native peoples of West Africa in the name of expansion, but Olga was not stupid and junior officers did not win medals in peace time, nor did they become so scarred.

"I would rather leave it for another time."

He gently shook her off and rose to sit at the edge of the bed where he began to dress.

"Something is different about you, Rudi," she said, failing to remove the accusation from her tone.

Dropping a shoe to the floor pointedly, he rounded on her.

"Everything is different, Olga, I have travelled through time, fought a war, seen unspeakable cruelty and in Vienna…" he stopped for a moment, turning his head away. "In Vienna I met a man who has opened my eyes to the truth of things. I see now what I was too young to understand. Too naïve to appreciate and too self-righteous to accept."

"What are you talking about, Rudi?" Olga demanded, uncomfortable for the first time in the presence of the man she loved.

"I knew you wouldn't understand, you had it and you took it for granted. You took the sacrifice of millions and threw it away because you…" he stopped, knowing that what he was about to say would cause an irreparable rift between them.

"We should find your sister. She'll begin to worry."

"Of course, I should like to see her again after all this time," he said without emotion. She knelt behind him and placed an arm around each shoulder, clasping her hands at his chest, and she kissed him lightly on the neck.

"I have missed you terribly, Rudi. I know it's only been a few months for me and nearly a decade for you, but I'm the same woman you left behind. You can still talk to me about anything… I just wanted you to know that."

Before leaving the room, they stood opposite one another, correcting minor faults with their attire and, kissing once more, they headed downstairs.

"Oh, Rudi," Carla exclaimed and immediately realising her mistake she looked straight past her brother and feigned recognition of another man who she painfully accused of being 'Rudi,' for long enough to allay any suspicion.

"Horst, my dear friend, how are you? You look well, that is a fine medal."

She pecked his cheek, and they embraced in the manner friends might in mixed company. Instead of asking the questions that burned in her mind, she continued the talk of the politics that Olga and Rudi had interrupted until enough time had passed for her to politely excuse herself and her friends from the conversation.

"Now," Carla said when they were alone on the street outside the party, "we have a suite at the Adlon and I so want to speak with you, but I assume you have rooms here in Berlin and more pressing matters to attended to?"

She shot questioning a look at Olga.

"Actually, those matters have been pressed already, let's all go to the Adlon. Rudi?"

"That suits me, it's closer than my house and I share it with a fellow I met in Vienna."

"Oh, you'll have to tell me all about him, but first I want to know all about Africa and the diplomatic service, have you met the Kaiser?" Carla asked excitedly.

"Why don't you accompany us to London," Olga suggested, changing the subject and giving Rudi time to gather his thoughts.

"I do have some leave to take, and yes, that would be lovely. Are you going to see Clive?"

"Henry? Yes, since when do you call him Clive?" Carla asked.

"He…" Rudi looked furtively around him before continuing, "he's not all we once thought, he's a ruthless bastard who doesn't take no for an answer."

~

It was a lonely journey for Carla, who was by now used to Olga's constant presence. She spent hours reading or staring out of the window as the moon danced on the surface of the rivers and lakes of northern Germany. Always though, her mind went back to Rudi's words about Clive.

What had passed between then in the last eight years to change his opinion of the man? And how had Clive known that they were in Berlin? The train rattled on and Carla tried to read Faust but finding it too heavy going, she crawled into bed as the feelings of dread washed over her. This night like every other would be plagued by nightmares, so sliding back down from her bunk, she rummaged in her valise for solace in a bottle of Schnaps, which was finished before her head hit the pillow.

Breakfast in Paris became a croissant and coffee in the dining car of the latest possible boat train. The crossing was rough and even Olga felt the need to lie down when they reached the chops of the channel. At Portsmouth they found a sign bearing the word Broadlands held by a liveried driver who showed them to a Daimler 57 Limousine. With all three seated comfortably in the back, they motored north to Broadlands.

Forty minutes later the magnificent sweeping drive lay before them. The house was forty years younger and all the better for it. The lawns and box trees showed the kind of care that one old man could simply never have rendered. The windows gleamed and smoke billowed from every stack. As the tires crunched to a halt on the gravel, a man in the uniform of a butler appeared in the grand entrance. He lacked the quintessential demeanour of a butler and both Rudi and Olga felt that he was more likely some sort of intelligence lacky.

Curtly and without ceremony or introduction, he led the trio to the drawing room.

"Yes, we know the way, thank you," Carla said, impatiently.

"Carla, you can't let on that you lived here for seven years, it belies any explanation you might care to give," Olga hissed when they believed the butler was gone.

"She's right, Carla, and remarks like that will get straight back to Clive..."

"Clive? Why do you call him that? Three months ago, it was Henry this and Henry that, Henry let me drive the Jag and..."

"Okay Carla, I think he gets it, let him answer."

"Forget it, why has no one offered us a drink?" she said, standing meercat-fashion and walking over to the drinks trolley.

"Brother? Olga?" she waved a decanter of brown liquid at them both.

"Is that scotch? No, thank you, it tastes like soil, what else is there?" asked Rudi.

"I'll have a very small brandy, please."

"Oh yes, I'll have the same as Olga," Rudi said.

Carla poured herself a dram and finished it whilst she poured and delivered the brandies, then returned to pour herself a second before sitting again.

"Do you remember when we first met Gerald, right here in this room?" Carla recalled.

"Carla!" Rudi hissed. "Please just stop talking like that."

"Suit yourself," Carla said, finishing her whisky and grimacing at the unpleasant taste as Clive walked into the room.

The disparity between the warmth Clive showed to the women and the cool, almost disdainful manner in which he greeted Rudi was palpable.

"Herr Buchholz, welcome to Broadlands. How strange that you should accompany these ladies on such a long journey."

Clive was so much older than Olga remembered and looked far older than the forty-five that he should roughly be. She perceived a note of vanity about his appearance that had not been there before. His suit was of the same high quality it had always been, but his shoes and the accessories he wore spoke volumes, buffed to a high shine and selected to complement the ensemble, and he even carried himself differently. He surveyed them now from a minor height advantage, his withering gaze transforming inches into feet.

"Please, Horst is fine," Rudi replied, apparently unphased by his frigid reception.

"Ah, ladies, forgive me, Horst and I know one another from the diplomatic circuit. You know how it is, champagne and hors d'œuvres until one feels they might go pop."

Clive laughed; his cold grey eyes boring into Rudi with a contempt Olga didn't think him capable of. "I suppose you'd like to rest a while before changing for dinner?"

"Actually, I was hoping for a quick chat over tea. It is four, after all," Olga insisted.

"Of course, where are my manners?" Clive said, reaching for a bell pull without looking and summoning a servant.

"Tea for four," he said dismissively and the young girl, who had not received so much as a nod, curtseyed, and backed out of the room.

Tea arrived rapidly.

"I'll be mother," Clive sighed, taking the pot and delicately pouring four cups of Darjeeling.

"Now, I should say that this room has been sanitised and we may speak freely, but one can never be too careful, eh, Horst?"

"That's right, Sir Gerald, one cannot." Rudi showed no emotion, no hurt was evident in his voice nor was there any discomfort in the way he sat.

"The reason I called you two here this weekend was to bring you in from the cold. There are no more assignments, your mission such as it was, is now complete."

The finality with which he said this brooked no discussion, but he waited nonetheless, daring them to argue, but they simply sipped their tea, glancing to their neighbours. Finally, Olga broke the silence.

"There was a list as long as my arm of targ—"

"Olga, dear, please don't go on and on about it, you can be rather dreary. Now, we had tea and a chat, let's all meet for dinner around six." Clive began to inspect his fingernails as he waited for them to leave. "Baxter will show you to your rooms, and Horst? Just hang on a moment, would you?" Clive called after his forlorn guests and Rudi stepped back into the drawing room.

"What the devil are you doing?" Clive hissed, when he felt they were alone.

"Escorting my sister and my, my Olga on a trip to see a former acquaintance," he said flatly.

"The invitation was for two, Horst, old man, you impose on my hospitality," Clive said through gritted teeth.

"I always felt so welcome here, Clive, old boy. Almost like it was a second home for me."

"You go too far, Herr Buchholz," Clive snarled, refusing to use his one-time ward's real name.

"I went too far years ago and now I feel there can be no going back."

"Look, you did some important work in Vienna and since, but make no mistake, boy, I owe you nothing. You have no claim to any of this and you never did."

"Ha, I don't want your money, Clive, nor do I want the contempt you so readily dole out to your lackies. I loved you like a brother, a father even. What changed, Henry? Why did you cast me aside so heartlessly? When will you invite me in from the cold?"

Finally, Rudi's emotion showed and to Clive's discomfort, his display of it was gratifying.

"This really isn't cricket, Horst. You don't show up at a man's house uninvited and start demanding... what? To be loved? Didn't daddy give you enough when you were a boy?"

"Mine or yours?" Rudi shot back.

"Mine? Don't presume to know my father, boy, you barely know me."

"Clearly, although I thought I did... once."

"You don't know the first thing about me, only that which I choose for you to know," Clive said triumphantly.

"I know more than you imagine, Herr Major Felsen."

The words hung in the air like a poison gas that Clive dared not inhale.

"Ha, is that supposed to mean something to me?"

"It should, it was your name for three years," Rudi spat.

"Tread very carefully, Herr Buchholz, enemy aliens are easily detained in the current climate."

It was Rudi's turn to laugh.

"I arrived officially on diplomatic papers and any mistreatment of me would give my emperor the justification to start the war he so is desperate for."

"Can I quote you on that?"

"Listen, Clive, war between our two nations is not unavoidable, but we two need to reach an understanding before things get out of hand, or I won't be held responsible for the consequences."

"You're nothing, a second secretary with no influence and a closet filled with enough skeletons to ruin you thrice over."

"Think what you like, Henry, and as for dirt, I could bury this house with what I have on you."

"Just tell me what you want," Clive spat.

That was it, Rudi had had him on the ropes, Clive was acceding to demands.

"Call off your goons, let me alone and don't treat my sister and the woman I love like they're your personal death squad. They are done when they say they are done."

"And if I don't?"

"Let's just say, I know where the bodies are buried," Rudi said, eying Clive's unreadable face for even the ghost of a reaction.

"Fine, you've outlived your usefulness anyway."

Rudi smiled, for he was not the boy Clive had left in 1952 and he would not rise to the bait.

"Have you quite finished?"

"Not quite," Clive said with a smile, "Baxter!"

The hood came down and Rudi's world went dark. Rough hands took hold of him, and someone hit him hard in the kidneys.

"You know, Rudi, I haven't had you followed in years. I don't know where you live anymore, and if you'd stayed away, this wouldn't be necessary."

"Olga won't let you get away with this! She'll find me and expose you for the fraud you are. There are documents, papers that prove it all! Major Felsen and his atom bomb!"

Rudi shouted hysterically as they dragged him from the room.

Cellar, 1912

Time lost all meaning to Rudi. Night and day were indefinable and meals were never at the same time. His cell was lined with black padded tiles, they absorbed his bodily fluids and returned them with an unceasing stench. At first, he'd shouted himself hoarse, hoping to alert Olga or Carla of his presence, so they beat him.

When he continued, they cut off a toe and another until finally, fearing he'd never walk again, he capitulated and was rewarded with a thin gruel. On the fourth day as he shivered uncontrollably in neck high water, he realised what Clive had done. This was the prison of his nightmares, an echo of another life, a life he'd poured from his heart into Clive's waiting maw. He'd clung to the information, kept it safe and when the opportunity arose, had had it carefully reconstructed in the cellar at Broadlands.

He was left there in the absolute darkness until his mind was soft. Weeks, months, years, all were one. Occasionally guards would burst in, pin him down, trim his nails and shave his beard, just to keep him ignorant of the passage of time. He imagined Dolph, alone in Berlin and wondering where his friend had gone. He thought of Africa and of his sins there, of Vienna and of his sins there, of Berlin and of his sins. Was there a city on earth he had visited without he sinned before departing? He began in his fevered rantings to recite the names of his victims, those whom he knew.

Rolf Schilling? Had he killed him, or had he stopped? The red army man on Sonnenallee, was that an echo or something he'd done in this life? The soldier on the boat, he definitely killed him, and for that he felt no remorse. Then years of innocence, of clean living right here in this house. Africa, and the bodies piled high in his mind's eye, nameless and legion. The old lady in Bremen, that had been regrettable but necessary. Vienna and the old man, the emperor, which was his first time for Clive, the beginning of the end, his true descent into the mire he now trod. Many more times for Clive, as he counted them off, until he found sleep. The following night he did the same, until it became ritual.

When Clive first visited Rudi flew at him, savagely clawing at the air between them as guards restrained him. He feigned submission and tried again, each time receiving a savage beating. The torture began after that, thumbscrews, electrodes and fake executions.

After suffering this carousel of misery for an immeasurable time, the door burst open and his guards rushed in, hooded him and dragged him from the cell. The dim light from the hood was more than he'd known since the water chamber in the first few days of his ordeal and when it came off, he was strapped to a wheeled bed. A matronly woman with a kind voice and green eyes washed, shaved, and trimmed him, her plunging neckline revealing far more cleavage than society considered decent.

"There, there, my dear, we'll get you looking respectable," she said in the unique brogue of the Yorkshire Dales.

"What for?" Rudi croaked.

"It's best you don't ask questions," she said as she sponged the thick layers of grime from one thigh. He made to speak, his mouth forming the words, but none came, and he lay there mutely as she washed him, handling his genitals suggestively and winking when they made eye contact. When he became aroused, she moved on to clean the rest of his filthy body, no mean feat, and Rudi found himself drifting in and out of sleep. Finally clean, she towelled him off and stepped back to appraise her work.

With a satisfied nod she began to remove her uniform. It was not a performance, nor was it brisk. After she unbuttoned the tunic and folded it carefully over a chair, she stood before him, in her chemise, the line of her plump figure visible beneath. She'd maintained eye contact throughout this, but now she broke it to pull the silky garment over her head.

She was not a beautiful woman, but she was the only human being he had seen for an inestimable amount of time. Her body was well fed and her underwear unflattering. Still, her piercing green eyes never left his as she let her bra fall to the ground. The removal of a pin caused her long auburn hair to fall tousled about her shoulders and pendulous breasts. She moved towards him unblinking as a wicked grin spread across her thin lips. He was aroused, there was no denying the evidence before him, and he started to believe that this was something he wanted. The gentle caress of another living thing had been sublime, the sponge bath was a place of comfort he would retreat to in his mind when all else was lost to him. But this, did he really want this old woman with her resolute advance and her licentious grin?

His lip curled as she bent over him, and a nipple then a breast pressed again his emaciated, scarred body. He felt the sting of a needle and the icy fingers of a foreign liquid reach out into his bloodstream.

Panic set in briefly before he closed his eyes and let it happen, let her kiss his mouth as he inhaled stale breath, heavy with cigarette smoke and despair. When he did try to fight, restrained though he was, chubby fingers gripped his jaw and a rough tongue tasting like an ashtray was forced into his mouth, causing him to gag. His head thrashed about a few times before he finally passed out.

Light blinded him and he found that he was in his bedroom room in the upstairs of the house and no longer alone. Clive looked on from the doorway in disgust and with him were Olga and Carla, who both wept and looked at him with a disdain that crushed his very soul. He could hear heavy breathing from the bed next to him, but Clive's voice from beyond the door rang loud with scorn.

"He turned up while you two were in the Balkans, I had no idea he was entertaining company, or I would not have brought up here to witness this... this depravity."

Rudi tried to move, to protest, but only his eyes seemed able. Forcing them to the right he could see the rise and fall of an unknown bedfellow, presumably the reason for the looks he was receiving from the doorway. The scene must be one of fallout after a night of debauchery and infidelity.

Had he been able to look down Rudi would see the restraints were gone and all about the floor were his clothes¬ clothes he'd not seen since that day in the drawing room.

There were the signs of a party. Glasses and drinks bottles lay empty, the remnants of cocaine and other party drugs littered the table and German bank notes protruded from a woman's handbag.

"How could you?" Olga cried as Carla tried to comfort her, staring at her brother in disgust.

He fought to speak, but the paralysis gripped him still. His three spectators stood watching in silence, horrified, or amused but unwilling to leave. When Rudi failed to move, he saw it in Olga's eyes as her heart was cleaved in two and he knew that in that moment he had lost her forever.

"Ye gods, man, I'd thought better of you. Come on, ladies, once again I am sorry you had to see this."

Clive led the women from the room and from Rudi's life. The creature beside him rolled over and snored loudly as Rudi drifted from consciousness.

When he awoke, the smell of sex mingled with the smoke from the fire and harsh electric lighting showed the scene for what it truly was, while he took it in, she stood staring at him, her face devoid of expression. He found he was able to sit up and he vomited the thin gruel and stomach acid that was his lot and wept whilst the woman remained at the foot of the bed unmoving and silent, but for her laboured breath.

After some minutes he stood and she moved closer to him, her rank breath hot on his cheek. She made to embrace him and when he did not fight, she pressed her soft body, cold with sweat against his and knotted her fingers in his hair. They remained this way for some minutes, and Rudi sensed from her a genuine empathy for what she had done to him and what it meant. Eventually, when he did not pull away, she encouraged him to lie down again and kissing his forehead, began to prepare another sponge bath. Exhausted and completely devoid of any emotion, he drifted off to sleep.

When he awoke, the restraints had returned and once again bound him to the bed. He was moving slowly through the cellar with no hood, and it was the nurse, now dressed, who pushed him. Without a word, she wheeled him into a room divided by bars, which had the look of a kitchen with a stove, a sink, and a comfortable chair. Beyond the bars there was a toilet and washbasin.

"Now, love, you should call me Mrs Braithwaite, and I'm going to take care of you for Sir Gerald. I'm to make sure you're fit and strong," she said.

"What for? I want to die," he croaked.

"Now then, we'll have less of that talk." She wheeled him through a gap in the bars and closed the door to his new cell. Reaching through, she freed one arm and stepped back. He was able to free the other and sit up to release his ankles himself. He looked at her. She'd obviously showered and changed, for now she wore a floral dress and an apron. He noticed her cleavage and to his shame felt a stirring.

"What now?" he demanded.

"Now, you will start speaking to me with a little bit of respect. I can make your life very easy in here or very hard."

Noticing the shadow of fear that crossed his face, she said, "If you behave, you won't ever need to see the guards again."

"And what? I just live here with you and eat hotpot and fuck?"

"I knew you liked it, but no, there'll be no more of that. Not ever, do you understand?"

"Yes," he said, disgusted at the pang of disappointment he felt.

"And I hate hotpot, that's what those buggers on t'other side o't Pennines eat."

Soon afterwards, sleep reclaimed him and he awoke to the smell of cooking.

"C'mon, rouse and bit, show a leg there, sailor," Mrs Braithwaite said as she laid a table that had not been in the room before.

"You might remember our friend here," she motioned to the door with her head.

"He's going to make sure you behave, and if you do, soon it'll be just us two for tea."

"Tea?"

"Tea is the evening meal up north. We aren't at leisure to take it at four like our betters. Although since I took this job..." she trailed off and unlocked Rudi's cage. He sat up on his bed and the guard took a few steps inside the room. Instead of escape, he found himself thinking about what Mrs Braithwaite might have done that led to this.

She let the door swing inward and stepped back behind the table, watching him and occasionally glancing at the guard. He didn't stand a chance and they knew it, so resigned to his fate, he sat and allowed Mrs Braithwaite to serve him a ladle of what looked suspiciously like hotpot, although he was no expert. The guard retreated a pace or two and she sat in the armchair, watching him eat for a while before taking up some knitting. The wool was a vile green and the resulting garment unclear, but Rudi was not interested. This was the first hot food he'd eaten since the sleeper train from Berlin to Paris what felt like a lifetime ago.

"Slowly now, you'll only bring it back up if you wolf it down."

When he'd finished, she ushered him back into his cell and having locked him inside, dismissed the guard. Filling a kettle, she put it to boil and resumed her knitting. Rudi sat on the edge of his hospital bed and stared at the woman who had ruined his life on the orders of a man he'd called brother. Her swine-like nostrils flared each time she breathed, in time with the incessant clicking of her knitting needles, gripped in fat fingers like bratwurst with tooth-bitten nails.

A tiny window at the top of his cell wall showed him that it was becoming night. He lay staring at it, despairing at his new low. Was this some kind of cosmic rebalancing? Deep down, he knew that he deserved far worse.

Each morning at five he would be removed from his cell and taken to the water chamber, where he would stand on tiptoes for hours, desperately trying to keep his mouth above the water, this submersion left his skin soft and easily damaged. Afterwards, usually around lunchtime, Mrs Braithwaite would be waiting outside with a soft, warm towel to lead him back to his cell. Days passed and became a full week. She was a competent cook, and he ate well under her supervision.

Everything he did was strictly controlled. When she left at night, a generator would fire up in a nearby room and the guards would sporadically switch the light on and off, leaving him exhausted for the following day's torture. But always, when she was with him, he was warm, comfortable, and seemingly safe. She closely controlled his every moment, how long he brushed his teeth, how much he ate, and he was not permitted to speak unbidden.

On the evening of the eighth day the guard did not enter, and Mrs Braithwaite served herself in a dish opposite his. The following morning, he woke to find it was light and he'd not been dragged from his bed. Mrs Braithwaite wheeled in a gramophone and played a calisthenics instruction record. She watched him perform the exercises and gave him a breakfast of watery porridge. Afterwards, a guard led him out of the cell and into a room with a grating in the floor, where they put the cold hose on him for fifteen seconds. Sucking in air, he flinched and tried to dodge the icy barrage. When the water stopped, Mrs Braithwaite stepped up and began to wash him, lathering soap all over his arms, torso, legs, and genitals. Stepping back, she nodded, and the frozen tirade resumed.

"It won't stop until you're rinsed, so get on with it," she called over the sound of splashing water. He turned slowly and rinsed quickly. "And your nethers." He rinsed his 'nethers' and she signalled for it to stop, approaching with a towel.

He returned to find that the hospital bed had been replaced by a comfortable queen-sized bed with a blanket and pillows.

"I'll expect it made every morning, hospital corners," Mrs Braithwaite said. "Now then, read this."

He'd seen it before, it was Clive's old SOE field guide, 'How to be an Agent in Occupied Europe,' but the title had been redacted, he assumed because those words would raise too many questions.

Mrs Braithwaite knitted and Rudi read until a lunch of soup and freshly baked bread. In the afternoon he was given paper and pen and instructed to write down everything he could remember from his morning of reading. He wrote for an hour and handed her an essay on the rudiments of tradecraft. She took it and smiled.

"Well done, now get back in your cell whilst I read it through."

He found himself obeying without question. She studied his work and made notes for about an hour. During that time Rudi was idle, comfortable and without fear.

"Now then," she said, standing from her chair without taking her eyes from the notes she'd been making. "There are twenty-five inaccuracies, errors or omissions."

"Well," he smiled, "it has been¬—"

"Don't interrupt me," she said, cutting him off. "As I was saying, twenty-five."

She knocked on the outer door and a guard opened it.

"Twenty-five," she repeated. The guard nodded and, followed by a colleague, he strode across the room towards Rudi's cell door. As he was dragged from the room, he looked to Mrs Braithwaite for some clue as to his fate, but she had turned from him, busying herself at the stove. He was back in the room where he had washed earlier that day. Over the grating, a crude horse had been constructed and he knew his lot. His hands were bound and his shirt lifted over his head, then he felt the men retreat.

"Hello, old chap." The voice was Clive's. "I hear you're making splendid progress, it's a shame we have to employ these corrective measures, but I'm sure you'll learn soon enough."

With that, he or one of his men began the flogging. A multi-tailed leather whip struck the water-damaged flesh of his back and flayed it mercilessly. A voice he did not recognise counted each stroke. The second was far worse and caused him to cry out with pain. The third saw skin fall from his back to the floor and the fourth caused him to lose consciousness.

He awoke face down on his bed, his hands bound to a ring in the wall, and Mrs Braithwaite was treating his wounds.

"Ah, you're awake. I'd meant to say, any more than five marks against you and you'll be flogged. Once for every five after that," she said casually.

The following morning, he woke to the sound of the record player and found that his hands were still bound. He made to rise, but was reminded immediately of last night's flagellation, and he groaned at the recollection. The skin of his back was tight and even the slightest movement caused him excruciating pain. Using every ounce of strength he possessed, he turned his head to see that Mrs Braithwaite was carrying a bowl towards him, the cell door open.

"Don't move, lad, just lie still, that's it," she said, setting the bowl down. It contained a poultice that she began to apply with care to his wounded back. He lay like that for the rest of the day and the following night, but in the morning, Mrs Braithwaite instructed him to rise and carry out his calisthenics. With considerable effort and great pain, he heaved himself from the bed and began to follow the voice on the record as before. Mrs Braithwaite looked on, arms folded and a satisfied smile on her jowly face.

Afterwards she cleaned his wounds and applied a fresh poultice. For the rest of the day, she read to him from the manual, stopping every so often to ask a question or make a cup of tea. This went on, days became weeks and Rudi's back began to heal. Eventually, under Mrs Braithwaite's care and strict supervision, Rudi emerged without any permanent loss of function. Nevertheless, his back, like his hands, bore horrible scars.

She eased him back into the calisthenics and showering returned to the usual hosing down. His world had shrunk from the vastness of space and eternity offered to a time-travelling diplomat, down to the four walls of this room and the shower block, with Mrs Braithwaite at the epicentre. She continued to control his every waking moment, what he ate, when he slept and how frequently he used the toilet. She did this with changes to his diet and water intake, and if he stood, she looked up from her knitting and eyed him questioningly until he explained himself. Eventually, to avoid this he simply waited to receive instruction, which always came.

"You haven't had a bowel movement today, try it now. There's a good lad," or "It's been hours since you've passed water, go on, off you go." And he would sit, or stand and use the toilet whilst she knitted, occasionally passing comment on the sound or duration.

One evening, at the time she would usually leave, she approached the bars and threw him a bundle of clothes. He caught it and realised with horror that he held a straightjacket.

"If you put that on, I'll come and give you a cuddle, maybe even stay until the morning."

Her voice was casual, like she could take it or leave it, when in fact, she had already put her coat on and changed her slippers for shoes. Rudi stared at the floor for a moment and looked up at his jailer, this plump middle-aged woman with blotched skin and a pig-like nose. She fixed him with those green eyes as if daring him to turn her down, to deny himself the comfort that this would bring.

Miserably, he stood and struggled into the contraption, and she stepped inside the cage. With his buckles tight she left the door open and tethered him to the ring on the wall and he lay there waiting for her to join him. To his surprise, she stripped naked and wriggled under the blanket next to him.

"I sleep naked, always have."

She put her arm around him and pressed her soft, warm body against his. He lay still and felt the heat of shame wash over him as he became aroused. If Mrs Braithwaite noticed, she did nothing to show it and soon he fell asleep. As always, the parade of echoes marched through his subconscious, giving him a vivid reminder of the most horrific events ever to befall him. New to the ranks was the night he'd first met Mrs Braithwaite, and tonight for the first time he relived the whole ordeal as if it were happening again. The mixed feelings of shame, worthlessness and arousal, of pleasure even.

A brief flicker of light and the smell of smoke woke him and told him she had lit a cigarette. He breathed in the smoke, a welcome respite from the breath and body odour of his new bedfellow.

The next smell he encountered was that of frying bacon.

"Special treat for you this morning," she called from outside his locked cell. She never used his name. Indeed, it was as if she didn't even care to know it. His straps had been loosened and the tether removed, so he stood and wiggled free of the garment.

"I'll give that a wash, it might be a bit sweaty," she said with a wink and a smile that showed a set of crooked yellowing teeth. He shuddered and began to weep.

"Now then, lad, less of that. I was told you're a war hero, war heroes don't blub like bairns."

"Anyone who has fought in a war knows what it is to weep," he said coldly.

"I suppose, I wouldn't know," she said absentmindedly as she wound the record player. He stood mechanically and began his exercises to the instruction. He knew them by heart, but he never moved before the word of command. This was his life now, wake, exercise, cold shower, breakfast then study all day until supper. Every night he would fall asleep next to his jailor and every morning she would be awake and making breakfast on the other side of the bars. The routine continued for months with little variation, bar the book he studied. He came to associate Mrs Braithwaite with safety and comfort, understanding only that displeasing her meant pain, and this slowly broke him and bent him to her will. To Clive's will.

As usual, after his calisthenics, Rudi was led to the wet room for his daily shower. There he found a woman kneeling over the grating where he knew he was supposed to stand. In panic, he looked to Mrs Braithwaite, who twisted her thin lips into a smile and produced a revolver from her apron. With a deft movement, she flicked open the cylinder and loaded a single round before handing it to Rudi.

"Kill her," she said flatly. The woman looked up into Rudi's eyes, shaking her head and pleading silently, he stared back into the face of his sister. Rudi began to cry silently as his arm rose to aim at Carla, at his own flesh and blood. The pistol was British and felt strange in his hand. Somewhere a deeply buried part of him beseeched him to turn the gun on Braithwaite and to end it all now. But so much more powerful, so much louder were the words, "kill her."

His finger curled around the trigger and he drew in a deep breath, raising the weapon high. As he exhaled, he let his arm fall slowly, pulling the trigger as his sister's head appeared in his sights. The bullet entered through her left eye and exited at the base of her skull. Blood, skull fragments and pieces of her brain spread out behind her. He turned silently and returned the empty pistol to Mrs Braithwaite.

"Drag her out of the way, you still need to take your shower," she instructed without emotion.

He picked up Carla's ankles and dragged her, smearing the floor with the same blood that ran through his own veins, until he was told to stop. He undressed and stood barefoot over the grate as his sister's life blood drained into it. As what little was left of his soul after nine years in the past shrivelled to nothing, Rudi washed himself in the cold water.

He stood in the barn at Broadlands waiting to be told what to do. Aside from breathing, he had not performed an autonomous act for over a year.

"Now then," his master's voice, Mrs Braithwaite said. He winced inwardly, terrified to react and desperate to please. "Sir Gerald has ordered that you build him a contraption, here are the particulars," she said, waving a thick file at him.

Rudi opened his mouth to speak, but fear of reprisal stayed his tongue.

"Out with it, lad," she snapped, and again Rudi flinched without moving.

"I don't know if I can," he said feebly.

"That's alright, lad, because I know that you can."

She thrust the file into his chest. He wasn't physically weak anymore, a year of her cooking and enforced PT had seen to that, but his mental resilience was paper-thin. On Clive's orders, Mrs Braithwaite had taken the broken, malleable wreckage of Rudolf Kessler and transformed him into a creature all her own.

"Go on then," she demanded, arms folded, waiting impatiently for him to begin.

Something close to positive emotion dared to surface as he realised that for the first time, he had been given the agency to perform a task more complex than memorising field manuals. In his new, bleak existence the only comfort, warmth or pleasure he was allowed to know came directly from Mrs Braithwaite. He had been conditioned to understand that without her assent he would know only cold and discomfort. He focused his mind, drawing on knowledge he hadn't used for nearly a decade.

Eventually he said, "I need a writing desk, a blackboard and a workbench. I'll make a list of tools." The idea of noncompliance hadn't crossed his mind, his captors had been thorough.

"Aye, follow me," Mrs Braithwaite sighed, leading him to a work area at the far end of the barn, a near perfect reconstruction of his workshop from 1952. Without speaking, she sat down in a comfortable chair and began to knit, in no doubt that Rudi would begin work without further prompting.

That night they slept in the apartment above and as with every other night for the last thirteen months, she held him and he inhaled her rancid breath.

Rudi enjoyed the clarity of absolute submission. He had no notion of ethics, morality, or the intended use of this time machine, only obedience and the avoidance of punishment. This allowed him to focus entirely on the task, beginning with some mental exercises to re-establish long dormant synapses. He used the blackboard to write out some equations and let his mind take them in, blowing away years of mental cobwebs.

After a few days becoming reacquainted with the theory, he set about building his machine. He looked around the shop at the anachronistic equipment and parts. It seemed that Clive had simply carried the necessary technology with him to 1897 and stored it here for this moment, it was the only explanation. These components simply could not exist in 1914. His first dissentious thought crept in, but his addled frontal lobe, the property of Mrs Braithwaite, dismissed it and he set about his work – following orders was and always would be all.

With his own plans and all the necessary parts, it only took a week to begin trials and by March 1914, he had a working singularity generator. He had been ordered to train one of Clive's men to operate the machine and now this man fired it up. The space before him began to wobble like the heat haze he knew so well from his months of hunting other human beings in the Kalahari Desert. Soon the haze seemed to part, like the universe was tearing open before his very eyes. Rudi felt a soft hand at his back and he was shoved through the tear. He stumbled and fell face-first onto soft carpet.

Was he free? He began to feel lost and alone, a falling sensation came over him as he became untethered from the safety of the new life he had learned to accept. Sweat coated him and his breathing grew shallow. Looking back in desperation, he saw a silhouette block the light from 1914, and they stepped through clutching something at chest height.

"Get up, Lad! We've got work to do," Mrs Braithwaite chided.

~

Olga watched in horror as the grotesque woman lay naked and snoring beside the man she loved, the only man she had ever slept with, the man she had crossed space and time to be with. She couldn't take her eyes from the scene. Why would he do this? She was right here with him for the first time in years and he chose to betray her in this way. She tore her eyes away from the unashamed lovers to survey the scene before her, the drugs and the booze, their clothes strewn about the floor, and was he looking at her? Rudi was staring right at her. It was too much and finally she found the strength to run from the room.

"Olga, dear," Clive called after her woodenly as Carla followed her adopted sister from the room.

Olga took the stairs two at a time, not stopping until she reached her own room. There she locked herself in and dived into the bed. Her head spun as her world, her future, past, and present came crashing down around her. She began to fumble in the darkness for allies, for people she could trust. Nothing was as it had been: her closest friend was his sister, she always would be, but Olga could not reconcile with that right now¬¬ – Carla was out. Clive and Olga were close, she trusted him, he'd rescued her and the then children from Germany, given them a home, a family, and an education when the entire world was against them.

She had left at short notice with Carla to deal with the Black Hand in the Balkans, and the work had taken months. Painstakingly seeking each member out and waiting for the right moment to kill them, then onto the next. Fifteen more blemishes on Olga's soul, fifteen more faces to haunt her dreams. Without Carla, the mission would have gone nowhere, it was all down to her research – the knowledge she had brought with her on those tiny slides – and what she called her Sarajevo Hypothesis. Carla's drinking had continued to be a problem and if she was honest, Olga was glad for an excuse to distance herself from it.

As she slept, she dreamt of Rudi and his whore, every fond memory soured by that one betrayal. How many more had there been in the eight years he'd been gone? Why did he have to do it with her so close?

She woke with one thought at the forefront of her mind: get away and stay busy. She saw herself in the employ of the British government, killing without remorse, from one city to the next in luxurious hotel rooms as the bodies stacked up along with her bank balance. Clive could certainly arrange this, and she felt sure he would have a list of enemies in need of despatch.

"Is he gone?" she asked. Clive looked up from his kedgeree and set down his fork. Carla was nowhere to be seen.

"In his room, if the maids are to be trusted, and they are," he lied, smiling sympathetically. "Don't be too hard on him, Olga dear, he's had rather a rough time of it."

"Haven't we all?" she said, turning on her heel to seek him out.

The door to his room was locked.

"Rudi, Rudi!" she called. "This is your one and only chance to explain this to me. If I leave, you will never see me again." She waited outside the empty room for another minute, for her pride would allow no more before marching back downstairs and into the breakfast room.

"I have a proposition for you," Olga said, when the maid who had poured her coffee was gone.

"What's that?" Clive asked, a faint smile on his face.

"Give me a job with the British government. I need to get far away from here and I need something to focus on."

"Doing what? You can't imagine that His Majesty's government employs assassins of any ilk, let alone girls," he said.

Easy, old boy, make her work for it. Make her think you're doing her a favour.

"You know very well that I know you would do just about anything to ensure the success of whatever scheme you have cooking."

She paused, watching his unreadable face as he chewed his toast.

"You also know that there is no man alive today more capable than me at this kind of work."

"You're about thirty years too early, my girl, it would never wash with the men at Whitehall."

"Don't do this, it's tiresome," she sighed.

"Do what?"

"This whole reluctant act. I know that you value my skills and that you have the power to do as you bloody well like."

"Fine, but there are some ground rules."

"Such as?" she asked.

"You cannot see Rudi again. As a British agent, it won't do for you to be romantically involved with a German diplomat."

"Ha! Fine by me," she said sardonically. "What else?"

"You will be deniable. Do you understand what that means?" he said gravely.

"If I fuck up, get caught or stranded, the government will denounce me publicly and I will receive no assistance."

"No official assistance, although I will always do what I can to help you, Olga, you know that. Speaking of your name, you'll need something a bit less foreign. Have a think about what you'd like to be called."

"My mother's name was Nadine Lynch."

"Irish is about to be very unpopular, what was your grandmother's name?"

"Kath, Kathleen, I like that," she beamed.

"I knew a Kathleen Lynch once, a firebrand and about as ruthless as they come. Couldn't possibly be your grandmother, of course, this was long before your time, before my time in fact."

"It's an old family name, all the way back from before the occupation."

"As I live and breathe, what a small world. Could it be that before me and for all these years I have been rubbing shoulders with a descendent of the great Kath 'Boudicca' Lynch?"

"Boudicca?"

"The ancient British warrior queen, it means bringer of victory. She led a band of female resistance fighters called the Iceni. They were fierce and the Germans were terrified of them."

"She sounds like my kind of woman!"

"Indeed, now back to this job. As you so astutely assume, I do have a list of targets for you."

Clive drained the last of his coffee and stood, feeling his breast pocket for the cigarettes he no longer kept there. "Help yourself to breakfast, then I want you to spend the day with Baxter. He'll put you through your paces and perhaps even teach you a thing or two."

With that, he smiled paternally and left the room.

Olga wasn't hungry, but those months at sea and in the desert had taught her to eat when the opportunity arose, regardless of appetite, as she never knew where her next meal would come from.

"Kath?" asked an unassuming man of average height with an upper-class accent and the kind of face one could easily forget. Olga stared at him blankly for a moment, her cup halfway to her mouth.

"Oh, we've started that, have we? Yes, I'm Kath."

"A pleasure, Ma'am, I'm Baxter."

He produced a sheaf of papers and took a seat next to her at the breakfast table.

"I have taken the liberty of drawing you up some British papers, and officially you will be entered on the staff at Whitehall as a clerk typist or some other innocuous position. I have a woman of the right age briefed to claim she is your mother, a servant at a remote country house."

He checked his notes.

"A Mrs Braithwaite at Greymoor Hall, it's likely that you'll never meet her, but you should know that much, at least."

"Kathleen Braithwaite, it'll do," she said with a shrug, trying it on for size and disliking it for no reason she could identify.

"This is your pay book," he showed her a document naming a Captain K Brathwaite of the Royal Engineers. It stated her gender as male, the age was correct, and he was listed as married. "If you happen to need to access your pay, you can use this, the marriage certificate, and your other documents to show that you are this man's wife."

"That's fucking ridiculous," she said flatly.

"It's improbable that you'll need to use it, but if you're stranded in a British colony, it could be very useful. Have you eaten your fill?"

Olga looked at her empty plate and eyed the man contemptuously.

"Right," he said standing, "if you'd like to follow me, we'll get started."

Olga already wore the practical clothing she preferred when not keeping up appearances, and Baxter appraised her with a nod.

"We can kit you out later," he said as he led her to a barn in the grounds, the same building that had been Rudi's workshop. She had rarely ventured down there. It didn't interest her and she had avoided Bertie his didactic and pompous little friend as much as possible during that last summer. For a moment, it did sadden her to think of him as he had been, as he would never be again, not in her eyes.

Next to the workshop, Olga's old gymnasium had been reconstructed, with rings, horses, and a large, matted area. Baxter removed his suit jacket and tie and began to roll up his sleeves. After hooking a thumb under each of his braces and letting them fall about his waist, he started to loosen off, cracking his neck and throwing a few loose-fisted punches. Olga smirked, cracking her own neck and kicking off her beige pumps.

"Are we going to fight?" she said haughtily.

"I thought we should go a few rounds, just so I can understand what I'm dealing with."

"Why don't you ask H–Sir Gerald, I've put him on his arse enough times."

"He's a bit older than me, Ma'am," he said, rolling his shoulders and eying her sceptically.

They met at the centre of the mats, two practised killers from entirely different worlds. Each nodded and stepped back. At this point Olga was curious to see what Baxter could do. He was trim with toned forearms and a way about him that that said he wasn't accustomed to losing physical contests, although the barely notice-able crook to his nose said that he had done so at least once.

She stood neutrally, arms by her side and allowed him to show his hand. He was a boxer, and this was how he came at her, dancing, fists up, never breaking eye contact. Still, she remained passive, she wasn't going to give him anything. When he jabbed with his left, she stepped to the side, grabbing the meaty paw in both hands. Barely dodging a powerful straight right, she stepped to his left and struck with a palm behind his ear, throwing him off balance and leaning forward to wrap her arms around his waist, grabbing him behind the thighs. The strength in her own legs powering forward and forcing him to the ground, she landed on him with a knee in his guts. Baxter fought desperately to block multiple blows to the face with his forearms, bucking his hips impotently as Olga watched his left arm try for a jab and let it come. She took control of his wrist as she backed outside his reach with ease, bringing her right leg around to clamp Baxter's skull to the matt. Falling back to straighten her body, she felt the satisfying crack as she nearly dislocated his elbow.

When she caught the look of astonishment in his eyes, she smiled and stood, backing away lest he try to sweep her feet from under her.

"What the fuck?" he screamed in disbelief, clutching his forearm and standing with surprising agility for a man who had just had his arm all but broken by a lighter, weaker, not to mention female opponent.

"Why not see how to cope with two attackers?" a voice behind her said. Olga spun around, to find a second faceless man in shirtsleeves bearing down on her with violence in his eyes.

"Allow me to introduce our colleague, Mr Quartermain," Baxter panted.

"Charmed, I'm sure," Quartermain growled.

She moved left, putting both men to her front, waiting to see how they might proceed. She was reminded of an alley in Berlin nearly ten years before. They had been skinny boys, but one had had a rifle trained on her. These might be well-fed, well-practised men, but she felt confident that she was a match for them too.

She pounced, flying at Baxter with a foot into his solar plexus that winded him a second time, forcing him to sit down hard. Turning on Quartermain, who was much closer, she brought both arms above her head, but as she swung them down in an arc for his neck, he punched her hard in the guts. Olga bent double, exaggerating the effect of the painful blow and hoping to invite a kick to her downturned face – the obvious move. It came and she grabbed his foot, securing it under her right armpit, while she swept his remaining foot from beneath him.

Baxter punched her so hard in the side of the head that she saw stars, and when her vision returned, she was on the ground with Baxter looming over her whilst Quartermain was struggling to stand. Shaking off the fug she rolled effortlessly to her feet, dodging Baxter to kick his friend in the face as he rose. He fell onto his back and she put some distance between them, concentrating on Baxter once more. His successful blow had given him back the confidence she had taken earlier, and he charged, his left arm flailing flaccidly at his side. She sidestepped again and pushed him sideways to the ground, falling upon him, but this time the ringing in her ear told her it was just fine to continue.

She hammered him with blows to the face as blood flowed from his nose, cheeks and brow. She finally rolled off him to face Quartermain, who was standing once more, and out for vengeance.

Olga cracked her neck and bounced into a fighting stance, ready to make good her promise. He was Rudi and she was going to punish him for Rudi's transgressions. He was angry and careless, and he still thought that pugilism would win out. He was wrong. His first jab glanced, cutting her cheek, but he over committed and she used his momentum to turn him, wrapping a leg around his and climbing him like a small tree to fell him like a sequoia. They hit the ground together and she placed him in a rear naked choke until he passed out – stubborn bastard, she thought. Extricating herself, she turned to see Baxter sitting at the edge of the mats, dabbing at his face with his functioning hand and feeling sorry for himself.

"Right," she asked, "anyone else want a shot at the title? Challengers form an orderly queue to my left."

"What? Shut up, you stupid girl," Baxter sneered.

"Oh, I see, you wanted to knock me down a peg or two this morning and this isn't how you'd planned for it to play out?"

"I told you to shut the bloody hell up!"

"Gosh, do you kiss you mother with that mouth?" she laughed.

"I'm warning you, girl!"

"Ha, ha, ha," she giggled, "what is it you think you can do to me?"

"I suppose we'll find out, won't we," he said, with the conviction of someone who believed retribution would be simple. "Who do you think you'll be working for? Who do you think plans your assignments? Your hubris today has cost you more than you will ever know."

"Stop," she said with a finality that could halt an armoured column.

"As you lay dying, weeks or months from now, or languishing in some ignominious hole, suffering untold misery, I hope you'll think of me and of this day. The day you built your own gallows, tied your own noose and while finding the whole thing frightfully amusing, slipped that exquisite neck through and pulled the lever. I don't doubt that as you dance the hangman's jig and your eyes begin bulge, even then you won't truly understand that this was all your own doing."

"A word of advice," she said as she walked slowly towards her new master, "when you want to ruin someone, don't tell them about it first."

She fell upon him for a third time and after beating him unconscious, she stood and with carefully measured movements, she sat him up and rested his limp form on her knees. A quick look at Quartermain showed he was still out cold, so she cradled Baxter's chin and with one swift movement, she snapped his neck.

"Bravo, bravo!" Clive called as he emerged from the shadows, clapping slowly and grinning widely.

"What?" Olga demanded coolly.

"That was your job interview, my dear girl, and I am pleased to tell you that you passed with flying colours."

"You had me kill a man in cold blood…" She paused midway through her outrage to consider the job she had asked for and what it entailed. "So did he know he was going to die?"

"He knew that it was a possibility, but I doubt that he ever imagined you would succeed. His instructions were to fight until you called for quarry."

He looked down at the other man and his lip curled in disgust.

"Quartermain will be… reassigned. I don't want his hard feelings to get in the way of your success in the field."

"I could just…"

"No, no, the loss of one highly trained agent is enough for today. Anyway, Captain Brathwaite, welcome aboard."

Clive shook her hand, smiling warmly as men appeared to remove Baxter's bloodied corpse and to help Quartermain to his feet. "Now, I have appearances to maintain, and we must not be seen together by anyone from outside my inner circle, so I would like you to remain here."

He pointed to an apartment in the roof in the barn.

Olga furrowed her brow, taking in the unseen space, before eying Clive sceptically.

"I assure you it's rather cosy, with every modern convenience."

"H—Sir Gerald, I don't want to sleep in your barn."

"You'll have to be careful with that. Another reason we need to distance ourselves from one another, and as for my barn," he gestured around, "it's rather more than that, wouldn't you agree?"

"That remains to be seen."

The apartment was acceptable, as promised, with all the amenities she'd expect. She felt as though she could be comfortable for a few days, maybe a week.

"What's my first assignment?" she asked, by way of capitulation.

Clive produced a file from inside his coat and dropped it onto Olga's writing desk, switching on the green-shaded desk lamp. Olga flicked it open casually and read the name before studying the picture.

"The German dictator? The one everyone was talking about after the war?"

"The very same. He'll be visiting his brother in Liverpool next month and I want you to see that he never leaves."

"Any particular way you want him to go?" she asked.

Olga had found it increasingly easy to speak casually about death and killing. She thought of Baxter briefly and although she knew his face would join the dozens that paraded through her mind each night, she felt no remorse and it didn't occur to her that he might have a family or a mother who would mourn him. She found that now, as she spoke to Clive of killing this man in Liverpool, it excited her. She wasn't ready to admit it to herself, but she found that the thought of killing, the extinguishing of another human life, aroused her.

As Clive strode across his expansive lawns back to the Palladian mansion his family had lived in for generations, he watched regretfully as Baxter's body was wheeled down to the incinerator. He thought of how useful the man had been and thought about their single most important achievement together.

In the spring of 1910 Clive, with a small, discreet retinue, visited Mexico City. Baxter had been Clive's man in the Spanish embassy, spoke the language fluently, and he'd had diplomatic training and experience before moving into intelligence work. Clement was an assassin, cold blooded and eminently biddable, his swarthy complexion and language skills allowing him to blend in and move unnoticed through the capital. Rogers, a Canadian diplomat and loyal imperial subject was there to deal with the interfering Americans and their frankly amateurish intelligence outfits. The four men flew themselves in stages via Madrid, Casablanca, and São Paulo. The operation was off the books and completely unsanctioned.

"So, Señor Felsen, what is it you think you can do for Mexico?" Clive was using his old alias and speaking with future president and current mine owner Francisco Madero. Future General Pascual Orozco, General Bernardo Reyes, General Pancho Villa, and revolutionary leader Emiliano Zapata joined him. Clive appraised the five Mexican legends and began his prepared speech in Spanish.

"Forgive my ignorance, gentlemen, I have learned this by rote as I do not speak Spanish. However, my colleague here does, and we will be happy to answer any questions when I have finished… A great and bloody revolution is coming to your fine country. Diaz will renege on his promise and run in the election later this year."

He allowed that to sink in for a moment as the men around noticeably changed the atmosphere with their considerable force of character.

"Millions will die on both sides. What I offer is a solution to this catastrophe, and when a stable government is in place, British arms and money to regain the territories you lost to the United States."

Clive spoke perfect Spanish, he'd studied languages at Oxford and spent months in the Pyrenees with local guides, helping to extricate downed airmen during World War Two. This was a ploy to buy time as Baxter needlessly translated for him or offered cultural advice and insights.

"What will that do for the landless peasants, starving because we grow coffee instead of wheat?" Orozco asked.

"All those who take up arms will have lands in the north after the fighting, those who don't will not. We would work to help you expel any unwanted foreign entities too," Clive said after waiting for a translation.

"Like the Germans?" Reyes asked.

"Among others."

"What do you propose to do about Diaz, Corral, and Mondragon?" asked Madero.

Clive checked his watch.

"They are already dead," he said in Spanish, to a collective gasp.

"Who do you think you are, coming to our country and assassinating our president?" Reyes demanded. He was older than the others, maybe sixty, a long-serving politician and soldier. Clive inclined his head.

"I've probably saved half a million Mexican lives this evening. Now to save the rest, you fine gentlemen need to form a new government. In this room, tonight."

Baxter placed an attaché case on the low table at the centre of the group.

"Here are forged documents that show each of the murdered men and any other possible opponents to be traitors of some kind.

Here is a big bag of money to get you started and here is a list of things you must do if you would like to receive more money."

"Universal suffrage? You cannot be serious. You don't even have that in Britain," Pancho Villa sneered as he scanned the list.

"Oh, but we will, and Mexico can lead the way. Just think about this. You will immediately gain the support of fifty percent of your voting population as well as the undying support of all the men that cannot vote right now."

"There are many factions we must unite under one cause. How do you suggest we do this?" Madero asked calmly.

"The enemy to the north, the bogie man that hides beyond the Rio Grande?" Clive offered. "It's simple and easy for all Mexicans to get behind. Take back the land the Yankees stole in 1848."

"Intern all American and German Citizens?" Pancho read aloud. "And cause an international incident? This is too much."

"Very soon there will be a war. A war to end all wars." Clive paused to let that sink in. "You men, the new leaders of the Republic of Mexico must pick a side and I'll tell you now, the British Empire, with our four hundred million subjects, world-leading weapons technology and an unmatched navy, will emerge victorious."

"Okay," said Madero carefully, "who else will be in this alliance?"

Clive drew a deep breath, for this was the bitter pill and he was nanny.

"As you know, in 1904 we signed the Entente Cordiale with France and they are our closest neighbours…" All five men began to talk at once of the French interventions and invasion of 1864.

"Gentlemen, please." Clive gave a tacit command to Baxter, who unfurled a map of the world.

"If you would look here," he said, flicking a hand towards the map, "in red are the British colonial possessions and in blue are the French. If France were to side against us in a war, the consequences could be devastating, and we would be in no position to help you."

Baxter laid a sheet of film over the map. It covered the current Mexican territory with green and the USA with yellow. Baxter laid another film over that, and the states of California, Nevada, Arizona, New Mexico and Texas became yellow also. Territory from the Dakotas to the Pacific, as well as Alaska, became red. Land from Louisiana to the Atlantic now blue, the major rivers acting as both border and buffer resulting in a USA a quarter of the size it had been.

"These, my friends, are our North American war aims," Clive said, grinning widely.

"You promise a great deal, Señor Felsen, but how do you suppose to deliver this victory? The American army is a match for us in size, well trained and proven in combat, so we need to tip the scales in our favour. We need a bigger army," Reyes said, leaning forward to look Clive in the eye.

"And for that you will need arms, equipment and money?" suggested Clive.

"Sí."

"It's no secret that the American marksman lost us the war back in 1776, but that lesson did not go unlearned, we came home with our tails between our legs and we made damned sure it could never happen again. By the time we faced Old Boney, we had whole regiments of riflemen, and we still do. Over the next year I will send you highly skilled officers, veterans of the Boer war, men who can mentor your new class of Mexican leaders. I'll send NCOs to train you in the use of the very latest weapons and equipment, I'll send artificers to help you learn to fix it and best of all, I'll send engineers to help you build factories to produce your own arms and equipment."

As Clive finished his speech in fluent Spanish, Baxter passed around xtabentún and the seven men drank to Mexico's bright and shiny future.

Adolf, 1912

Rudi breathed a sigh of relief. He was safe again. He let the feeling wash over him as he rose to his feet obediently and waited for instructions as items of luggage were passed through the tear. One look from his captor told him to take the luggage from 1914 and place it carefully on the floor in this time. It did not occur to him to ask when this was, that part of his brain no longer demanded answers as it once had.

The tear closed and Rudi looked vacantly at the room and its furnishings: two drab settees and a cheap coffee table, a desk in the corner and some standard lamps. Light from a window flooded the room, but he had no interest in what lay beyond it, he simply stood amongst the bags.

"Now then," she announced, pointing at a small suitcase, "this is yours, take it to that room and come back and take these to that room." She indicated where with a slight jerk of her head, he did as he was told and returned to the sitting room.

"Sit. This is Berlin in March of 1912."

~

Rudi Kessler reported for work at the foreign office as though the last two years had been a dream. Clive had sent them back to the final evening of the leave he had taken for his visit to Broadlands with Carla and Olga. That morning over breakfast, Mrs Braithwaite gave him freedom to take lunch and toilet breaks as and when required, then went on to relay Clive's instructions. Rudi was to absorb all around him, surreptitiously gleaning information, day in, day out until someone realised that he wasn't quite right. Then phase two would begin.

He hadn't forgotten how to be a diplomatic secretary, but now he had no free will to exercise and his masters weren't sure how long he would be able pull it off. What they did know was that they could take him back to Broadlands at any time to reset the entire mission. That morning, his colleagues just assumed he was hungover, no unusual concept, and left him to recover in his tiny enclave of the large office. This continued for the rest of the week, during which Rudi would come and go in a trance, completing all tasks with a level of professionalism he had not displayed before, and he would listen. Listen at meetings, listen to phone calls, and listen to colleagues' banal chatter.

Every evening he would recount everything verbatim to Mrs Braithwaite and every night he would fall asleep in her arms, to the unpleasant but comforting sound and smell of her breathing. On Friday his colleagues invited him for lunch, and he accepted. When they offered him his first drink in two years he assented and when lunch became a boozy afternoon, because the first secretary was celebrating his latest posting to Samoa, Rudi got very drunk.

Too drunk to find his own way home, so his friends took him directly to the house he shared with Adolf, who had expected him six days earlier, but simply assumed he was spending more time with the girl he always talked about, the one who had just come back into his life.

"Horst, my dear friend, did you spend the entire journey in the buffet car?" Adolf asked, concerned to see Rudi drunk for the first time since they had met.

"Dolph, you're my best friend. I've missed you terribly."

Rudi hugged him, which neither man enjoyed.

"What a mess you're in, let's get you to bed."

~

"What do you mean, you lost track of him?" Mrs Braithwaite demanded coldly, her thin lips peeling back across her yellow teeth.

"Well, Ma'am, he was out to lunch, you see, and there was a great deal of them, and they all piled into a couple of hansom cabs and... we think we followed the wrong one."

The man wasn't a giant, but he had the air of someone accustomed to violence and using it to instil fear into others, but around Mrs Braithwaite, he and his friends behaved as errant children trying desperately to avoid the birch.

"I can't for the life of me understand what you're doing here. Now get out into that stinking swamp of a city and find my asset."

She didn't shout, but spoke calmly, and the men jumped frantically into action.

~

The following morning Rudi woke at the same time he had every morning for the last year. He mechanically rose from his familiar, yet unfamiliar bed and stood ready for his calisthenics. When the record did not play, he stood forlornly in his bedroom, unsure of what to do and terrified of the consequences. Eventually Adolf entered and led him by the arm to the breakfast table where they ate some fruit and rye bread with coffee.

"What happened in England, Horst?" he asked after a long time.

"I lost Olga," he said without emotion.

"Lost? Can she be found again?"

"No, never. I belong to, to—"

Before he could finish his sentence, he vomited onto the floor at his left side.

"Who? Horst, who do you belong to?" Adolf demanded, ignoring the mess.

"To her," he said, his lip curled in disgust.

"Not Olga?"

"No, never Olga, I have lost her for all eternity."

Tears streamed down his cheeks as he sat limply, staring into space.

"What is her name, Horst?" he asked, snapping his fingers in an attempt bring him out of what he was beginning to believe was not a drunken stupor. When Rudi failed to answer he telephoned the foreign office to excuse Rudi from work. Then he made another call, this time to a friend of his, a Doctor of Psychology who shared Hitler's ideology and had his own extreme views surrounding eugenics. Doctor Alfred Hoche arrived within the hour, enough time for Rudi to take his first warm shower in over a year and a half and for Adolf to clean up the mess in the kitchen.

"He appears to have gone through some sort of prolonged ordeal, yet you say he has only been away for one week?" said Hoche, stoking his grey goatee as he appraised the young man before him.

"That is correct, Herr Doktor. He also mentioned losing his woman and being owned by someone, and he vomited when he tried to say their name."

He thought for a moment before speaking again.

"I have something I would like to try. Will you allow it, Horst?"

Rudi just nodded as saliva ran from the corner of his mouth. It had been so long since he had received an instruction from Mrs Braithwaite and he was reeling from the absence of the rigid structure provided to him for so long. As Hoche rummaged in his doctor's bag, Rudi soiled himself and a puddle of urine pooled at his feet.

"Never mind that," Hoche said, waving Adolf away as he produced a large card. Printed on it was a black and white spiral pattern which he held in front of Rudi's face.

"Listen to my voice, Horst, and look at the picture I have for you."

Hoche spoke softly and rhythmically, slowly gaining Rudi's attention. He counted back from twenty and his gentle voice in the language of Rudi's birth reached down through the layers of indoctrination to something deeper.

"Listen to me, Horst. You are a free man, a hero of the Reich. You are a shining example of the master race and you cannot be owned by anyone."

Hoche continued like this for some time, with the rhetoric typical of men like Wagner and Nietzsche and more recently Hitler and Rudi himself. The message was clear, Horst Buchholz was Übermensch, strong and fearless, all he needed to do was to remember that and he could be free once again.

218

It took weeks, but the slow process of recovery played out on Rudi's face as slowly, he realised what he had done to Carla and what he had done with Mrs Braithwaite. Shortly after lunch one day in the third week, he began blinking rapidly and the intelligence seemed to return to his face as he recognised Adolf and looked questioningly at Hoche.

"My name is Hoche, Doktor Alfred Hoche," he said, shaking Rudi's hand.

"Clive must die, but first there's an old hag in a stinking tenement over in Friedrichshain who must be taken alive," Rudi said in a quiet, purposeful tone without standing from his chair.

"I recommend that you rest, my dear boy," Hoche suggested.

"I slept better last night than I have in nearly two years. Dolph, you saved me. You have my eternal gratitude and friendship."

Now he stood and hugged the man who would be Führer, the man destined to order the deaths of so many millions of innocents.

"Tell me, Horst, what do you need me to do?" Hitler asked gravely.

"I need some of those rough men that hang around at your meetings, say five, and a horse and cart with a tarpaulin?"

"Okay, I'll see who I can find." Adolf saw Hoche out and walked down to the café where his unemployed friends hung out. Rudi went to his bedroom and pulled his trunk out from under the bed. It was filled with uniform tunics and trousers, belts, and pouches. In one such pouch he found his old Reichsrevolver and in another he found some rounds and a cleaning kit. He carried them over to his desk where he sat to strip, clean, and oil the weapon before loading it.

"Thank you for coming gentlemen. I won't waste any more of your time with pleasantries. Tonight, I need to abduct someone who has harmed me and the only family I had left alive, but in order to do that, I must first be abducted myself. I know that sounds counterintuitive, but you will need to trust me. Watch me closely and follow the men who will take me from outside the foreign office. In that house is the target. If I don't come back for you after five minutes, force your way in. I will have them tied up and ready, it is imperative that we take this person alive. Then it's back here with the horse and cart before I take you all for drinks at the Bürgerbräu Keller. Any questions?"

The men were all thick set and looked like they shared a solitary brain cell between them; exactly the sort of blunt instruments that Hitler first recruited to his Sturmabteilung in another timeline. They murmured assent and looked to Adolf for guidance.

"Don't look at me, this is Hauptmann Horst Buchholz and for you, his word is law! Let's go," Adolf said.

Rudi travelled under the tarp to his place of work and snuck in through the service entrance, emerging from the front door around five in the evening. He was immediately aware of Clive's men following him. They wouldn't take him right in front of the government buildings and if he stayed on busy streets, he could avoid capture altogether, especially if they thought he was heading to Friedrichshain.

With some residual apprehension, Rudi entered the tenement to confront Braithwaite. In the hall he rushed past the staircase and waited in the shadows at the back, as his pursuers followed shortly behind. He allowed them to climb to the first floor, then he opened the front door and beckoned his men inside the house. Rudi ran up the stairs two at a time, his pistol drawn.

"Sit down with your hands on your head," he ordered as he stepped into the sitting room. Braithwaite was already seated, holding court, as her two jesters tried to explain that they thought Rudi would be up here already.

"What the bloody hell do you think you're doing, lad? Put that thing down and get to your room this instant," she spat as the clamour of heavy boots reverberated around the building.

Rudi laughed loudly and cried silently without taking his eyes of his prey for a second.

"I said sit, hands on heads." His goons arrived and lined the walls. "Kill that one and tie those two up, hurt them if they don't comply," he snarled.

Each of the would-be Nazi's seemed to relish the opportunity to inflict pain on the orders of another and a bald man with beady eyes and a small, pointed nose punched Braithwaite hard in the face, knocking her unconscious. Others set about Clive's men with clubs, following Rudi's instructions and tying two up before killing the lucky one.

Once it was dark they moved the two prisoners and the body to the cart. With Adolf driving and Rudi riding shotgun, the would-be SA thugs followed in a parody of a funeral procession.

In the alley at the rear of Rudi's house they unloaded their human cargo and moved it into the basement. Rudi caught sight of the furnace and with déjà vu, he realised what must be done with his dead adversary. Their prisoners were tied to chairs in separate rooms and gagged.

"No, no, this doesn't work," Rudi said, untying the gag on Braithwaite's mouth, pouring in some water and stuffing a filthy rag in there before retying it.

"What is the water for?" asked the bald goon.

"I want her to piss herself," he said. "Now, replace his gag next door like I showed you."

He stepped back from Braithwaite to look her over, her green eyes boring into him with a hatred he'd always known was there, bubbling beneath the surface. He met her eye for long enough to acknowledge his victory, before leaving the room and locking the door.

"One more job before beer, my good men. Who wants to break that island monkey's fat fingers and toes?"

Rudi supervised the breaking of his prisoner's fingers, hands, and feet and remembering his own severed toes, he took immense pleasure in the pain that it caused the old woman and looked forward to spending more time with her over the coming months. A goon passed him a bag containing Braithwaite's personal effects and Rudi realised he hadn't been wearing his gloves and that he hadn't thought about them since his first days in Clive's dungeon.

Did this bitch know all of his secrets? What had she told Clive?

I had better make it known that I don't like to be touched, that will be easier than wearing gloves all the time.

"Right, that should keep them from causing any trouble. One man to volunteer to stay for the first hour, then we take turns," Rudi ordered. Baldy nodded and took a chair down to the cellar whilst the rest of the group left to hear Adolf speak at the beer hall down the street.

Adolf Hitler's intoxicating speeches were full of rousing notions of nationalism and Germanic pride set against hatred for those he saw as the enemy, with a smattering of social Darwinism mixed in. The crowds of men willing to listen were far fewer than there would be after Germany had lost a war, a monarch and several million sons, but the few dozen in attendance on that night were regulars and their number had grown slowly over the last three years. They weren't much to look at, from intellectuals like Hoche to unemployed labourers, and they all inhabited the fringes of their respective social groups. Often they were unmarried loners with traumatic pasts, though some seemed normal enough, but when the beer was in full flow and Hitler's oration had brought their blood up, hatred flowed from their mouths with shocking enthusiasm. One sympathetic publican was all it took for these would-be monsters to emerge from the shadows to worship their idol.

Rudi was still torn, because he saw the direction Germany was headed, he saw their war-mongering Kaiser and the sycophants in the Kanzlei for what they were, but he also knew what lay down the road these men wanted to tread. Rudi's reality now, however, was but for the protection this group offered him, he was alone in this world, hunted by a powerful British spymaster no doubt with his eye on Downing Street. For now, he needed Hitler and his acolytes, but the more time he spent in their company, the more he saw them as human beings, the more he slowly came around to their point of view.

If he had to choose between this and life as a zombie with Braithwaite, he would choose the Bierhalle filled with friendly fascists without missing a beat.

After coming to terms with this, he decided to throw himself into party work, to surround himself with a burgeoning movement that could protect him from Clive and his henchmen.

"What are we going to do about these Verdammt communists?" he called over the din.

"Smash them!" came the replies of more than one man.

"I have a better idea," Rudi said, gesturing for silence. "We are few, they are many, let us get others to do the work for us. We will show the centrists what these spineless commies are capable of and grow our membership whilst dealing a blow to their credibility."

Rudi paused as he looked around the room at the misfits and zealots; law abiding men, waiting for an opportunity to do the evil that lay dormant in their hearts.

"Let us burn down the Reichstag building and frame Karl Liebknecht or that Schlampe Luxemburg."

The briefest of silences followed, then murmurs of approval.

Later that evening, Rudi stood in an alley across from the Prenzlauer Burg branch of the Social Democratic Party of Germany, as he watched a man stumble from the building a little worse for wear through drink. Earlier that year the SDP had won nearly thirty-five percent of the federal vote and the most seats in the house. Other parties were unwilling to form an alliance with such a radical faction though, so with division in the house, the conservative Kanzler and his government were left to do as they pleased. The red tide, however, was rising and many feared the outcome. Tonight would give those sitting astride the fence a shove into the Nazi camp.

"Okay, this is it. Wessel, Gruber, follow him up the road and wait until I pull alongside with the cart, then grab him. Winter and Stuber, pull him into the back."

They nodded and set off to follow, as Rudi and the other two men climbed aboard. Rudi clicked his tongue, urging the horse forward and out of the alley. The abduction went smoothly and when Rudi had checked his wallet to make sure he was a card-carrying member of the SDP when Friedrich Wieland was subdued in the cart, they turned west onto Marienburger Strasse and headed towards the centre of the city.

Outside the Reichstag, Wessel and Gruber dragged their victim down from the cart as Winter forced the door. Stuber had already jogged ahead to silence the nightwatchman.

In the main chamber, Rudi punched Wieland hard in the temple to avoid marking him and poured petrol onto the sleeves of his coat. Wessel untied him and wrapped the lengths of rope around a smashed chair leg to make a torch. Wieland lay on the ground unmoving, but his breathing was steady, and Rudi was sure that he would wake soon. He looked around him as his goons splashed gallons of petrol about the chamber with childlike glee, before dragging Wieland to the lobby. Winter solemnly handed a torch to Rudi, who indicated with a jerk of his head that they should leave. He walked with some ceremony to the doors of the chamber, lighting his torch at the threshold and bending to touch his flame to a puddle of fuel.

The fire spread with a speed and ferocity that shocked Rudi as he tossed the torch into the house and backed away. Passing Wieland, he knelt beside him and slapped his face gently to bring him round. The man looked up at him with terrified eyes widening at the smell of smoke.

"What have you done?" he whispered as smoke billowed from the doors into the lobby.

"No, comrade, what have you done?" Rudi said, standing and walking to the doors. The other men let him out and shut the door behind him, leaving Wieland inside.

"What about the nightwatchman?" asked Gruber.

"Hier rein," Rudi ordered, pointing at the door he'd just walked through. They tossed the man inside, and this time thick clouds of smoke spilled onto the street, causing all five men to turn away.

"Better let our arsonist out, he needs to be alive to stand trial."

The doors opened again and Wieland fell out into the street in a fit of coughing, his face and hands blackened with soot.

"Wessel, Winter? Do you remember what to do?"

"We wait here with Karl Marx for the police and tell them that we saw him running from the building and shouting "death to the Kaiser"?"

"Genau," Rudi nodded, "give me your matches."

He held out his palm, and when Winter dropped his match book into Rudi's hand, they touched. Rudi snatched it back and watched the man's eyes as he struggled to comprehend what he was seeing in his mind.

"On second thoughts," Rudi said quickly, "Gruber, you stay with Wessel. Stuber, I need you to run back to give Adolf the news."

Stuber was a wiry youth of low intelligence and undying loyalty. He set off at a run, glad of the chance to tell his idol something positive.

"Winter, we will return the horse and cart."

Winter seemed unconcerned by the change of plan, staring off into the distance unable to speak. All four men flinched as the glass-domed roof of the Reichstag shattered and flames licked at the night sky whilst smoke tracked across the roof tops of Berlin, two decades before they were supposed to. Rudi let Winter take the reins and they drove off as the bells of fire engines grew nearer.

When they were alone, driving slowly along a quiet alley, Winter asked, "Who are you really, Horst?"

"Who am I really? What kind of question is that?" he replied with a nervous chuckle.

"I think you are an imposter. I think that your real name is Rudolf Kessler and you are pretending to be Horst Buchholz because he is a war hero."

"I am Horst Buchholz, I went to Afrika and I did those terrible things," Rudi insisted, his fingers curled around the grip of his Reichsrevolver as the wind increased, causing litter to lift and swirl around them as the horse snorted and grew nervous.

"Eindringling," he whispered, then he said it again louder, "Eindringling!"

His eyes wild with fear and anger, he lifted accusatory finger and levelled it.

"Eindringling!"

Rudi pressed the barrel into Winter's ribs and reached for the reins.

"No, my friend, it is you who does not belong. You are the interloper."

He squeezed the trigger and Winter recoiled away, falling from the cart into the alley as the pistol's report echoed from the high walls. He seemed to fall in slow motion, his hands reaching out to Rudi and his eyes beseeching him, but the damage was done, the act committed, and Rudi's soul was finally beyond redemption.

He knew it and he accepted it. The ideals for which he had struggled, fought and even died for, had been left behind him on Shark Island, in Emperor Franz Joseph's study, down the drain of the wet room, and in Mrs Braithwaite's clammy embrace.

Two notions struck Rudi as he paced the alley. First, he thought of his sister, whom he had not yet executed, this followed swiftly by

227

the realisation of the good that could come of the heinous but entirely necessary act of Winter's murder. He sprang into action knowing that the gunshot would bring more trouble. Grabbing a piece of scrap wood from the alley, he plunged his fingers into Winters open wound, causing him to groan with agony. Rudi hesitated, for he was not as familiar with Communist rhetoric as he had been in other lives, so he wrote "bourgeois" and considered again, adding the words "boot licker," Speichellecker. Taking a hammer and nail from the cart, he placed the plank on Winter's chest and drove it through, and into the flesh and bone beneath, but Winter did not have the energy to cry out. Rudi stepped up to the wall of the alley and closed his eyes. Inhaling deeply, he drew back his head. He felt the cartilage in his nose crunch on impact and without wasting another minute, he jumped back onto the cart and drove away.

⁓

"I have to find my sister!" Rudi shouted, grabbing Hitler by the lapels.

"I sympathise with you, my dear friend, but how?" Rudi had burst into the house they shared covered in blood, cursing the communists, and lamenting the loss of Winter. No one questioned the integrity of Horst, the only war hero they knew.

"She was in England two weeks ago. We must start there!"

"England is not safe for you, but we could send a man?" Hitler offered.

"A man? A man! There's a man in the basement!" Rudi exclaimed, rushing down the stairs. He checked his pace at the door to the makeshift cell and took a moment to compose himself. Placing a hand on the doorknob, he slid the bolt and stepped inside. He was immediately assailed by a man on his knees hurling mangled fists into his midsection. It was like being attacked by a small child, as the man wailed with pain upon each ineffectual blow. Rudi lifted one foot and without much force, pushed the man over and stood on one of his broken hands.

"When are you from?" he demanded in English. The man spoke German but the question would sound so strange to anyone listening that he thought it best avoided. The man tried a defiant stare, so Rudi applied more pressure and he howled with pain.

"Fuck you!"

"I have already had your hands and feet broken with hammers, old fruit, simply because I thought it was quicker than binding you, and I did rather fancy a pint."

His English accent was an almost perfect reflection of his formative years spent at Broadlands.

"How far do you do you think I'll go to save the life of my sister and to keep the love of my woman?"

The man looked at him. He was an experienced operator, he knew the cold eyes of a killer when he saw them, and in Rudi Kessler's eyes he could see the bodies piled high.

"Just kill me and be done with it, I won't be saying a word."

"Ha," Rudi barked, "you will live a long time yet, my friend, perhaps not into old age, but many years to come. It's a case of whether you choose to spend them in my basement or not?"

Again, the man saw the evil in Rudi's eyes and he knew he was beaten. It might not have been his hand that inflicted nearly two years of torture on Rudi, but Rudi knew that this man could be made to pay for it in spades.

"1914," he replied in English.

"Good. If you help me find my sister, I will let you live, and if you help me destroy Clive, I will set you free."

"She's dead, you–"

"Not yet," Rudi cut in, "not for some time yet."

The man nodded, realising the truth of what he heard.

"Where is she in April 1912?"

"Sir Gerald sent her and the other one to the Balkans, they were there for months," he said, clutching his hands to his chest.

"Where in the Balkans?"

"All over, they were... are, routing out the Black Hand."

"Good, good," Rudi said, nodding encouragement, "can you remember the date of one of the assassinations?"

His voice was calm, almost friendly now. Those books he'd been forced to study on pain of flogging had sunk in.

"Water," Rudi called to the open door.

"Err," he mumbled, the panic evident in his unceasing eye movement. "Dragutin Dimitrijević," he said triumphantly. "It was all over the news, they pinned it on a Russian and it destroyed the alliance between Serbia and Russia. Sir Gerald was very pleased."

"Go on," Rudi said patiently, "tell me everything you know about the assassination of Dragutin Dimitrijević."

The man talked and Rudi wrote, then he clarified each point and arranged for hot food, water, and a bed to be brought to him.

"Thank you, I am a man of my word. If this information helps me to save my family, you will not die on my orders. Think about my offer of freedom carefully," Rudi said as he shut the door.

America, 1913

Olga, now travelling as Kathleen Brathwaite, had spent the last three weeks in a draughty garret room overlooking one hundred and two Upper Stanhope Street in Toxteth, Liverpool. Clive's file had told her that the target would be living at this address for months. So far, she had only identified his brother Alios, sister in-law Bridget, and their infant son William. This was not what she'd had in mind, she'd wanted to be kept busy, not to have endless hours to ruminate on Rudi's betrayal and what that meant for her.

After successive reports that Hitler was not in evidence, Clive had her recalled to Broadlands and reassigned to Mexico. Here she worked with the new government, training their special forces. This initiative was Clive's as he wanted someone to carry out black bag operations in central America on his behalf. Olga found post-revolutionary Mexico to be a progressive country with universal suffrage and women serving in the armed forces.

After a year in Mexico City, Olga was sent to Washington, where her orders were to identify useful individuals with British sympathies. These ambiguous instructions left her somewhat forlorn, until she found her expense account bulging with dollars and she understood. She took herself to Woodward & Lothrop, bought herself a wardrobe to suit any occasion and had it all delivered to a suite at the Willard on Pennsylvania Avenue. Her beautifully appointed sitting room overlooked the south lawn of the White House, though she never caught a glimpse of Woodrow Wilson or his wife Edith.

The lobby took her back to the opulence of Petersburg, reminding her of Carla, whom she had begun to allow herself to miss, but this in turn reminded her of Rudi and the pain she still felt over his betrayal, so she pushed both from her mind.

"Champagne," she said to the baby-faced barman as she sat down.

"Ma'am, I'm sorry but women aren't permitted to sit at the bar. If you would sit down over there, I can bring your champagne over."

Olga fought to remain composed as her knuckles grew white and her fingernails dug into the palm of her hand.

"Fine," she managed to say through gritted teeth as she turned and strode purposefully across the bar.

The champagne, vintage though it was, had lost all appeal as she quietly seething in her booth, imagining ways that she would like to teach the barman some manners. Then she reminded herself that he was only trying not to lose his job. Carla would have known that and guided her to a seat saving Olga the embarrassment. She wondered now where her friend might be, because she had not been at Broadlands before Olga left for Mexico last year, so perhaps she was back in Berlin?

She took a sip of the champagne and began to think about her assignment in Washington. She had learned these aspects of trade craft from Yael and relearned them with Clive, both recently and back in the 1950s, but still, she felt rusty. Gregory had been easy to handle   low income, failed dreams and separated from his family in a city hostile to his people. This time, however, she was in a prosperous land that still celebrated its successful rebellion against Britain nearly one hundred and fifty years earlier.

Right now, she needed someone to help her make connections, to introduce her to influential people and to show her what was what and who was who in this pokey old town. As she finished her second glass, she realised that a man at the bar had been looking at her for a few minutes, and now that he had caught her eye, he was heading over. He was handsome and athletic, maybe it was time to get over Rudi once and for all?

"Hello, my name is Chester Dickey. Join you for a drink?" he said laconically.

"What if I said no?"

"Well, I guess I'd do what any man does when a beautiful girl shoots him down. Head on back to the bar the most dejected man in all of DC," he chuckled, placing a hand on his heart.

"That seems like an overreaction for a woman whose name you don't even know," she said coolly.

"You could change that?"

"I could. Why don't you sit down first?"

She gestured for him to join her, and he pulled out a chair.

"Is that a British accent I hear? My mother was British and so was my paternal grandfather."

"So was mine," she said with a wry smile.

"You Brits and your sardonic ways, you crack me up," he laughed. "Are you going to tell me your name, or should I start guessing?"

"Please don't do that, Chester, it would be awful. My name is Kathy Philips, how do you do?"

"How do you do? Sure is swell to meet you Kathy, what's that short for? Katherine?"

"Sure is," she mocked.

"You're a live one, Kathy. Say, would you want to have dinner with me tonight?"

"That would be lovely, we can have it sent up to my suite afterwards. Naturally I'm buying," she said nonchalantly.

He looked at her, unsure of what she meant until realisation slowly spread across his face.

"Have, have you done this sort of thing before, Kathy?"

"Never."

"Why now?"

"If your next question isn't about my room number, I shall change my mind."

"What's your room number?" he asked with a nervous chuckle.

"It's the Jenny Lind Suite. Finish your drink, I'll leave the door unlocked," she said, standing and plucking her bottle from the ice bucket.

When Olga was out of earshot she sighed heavily, and by the time she was on the stairs, the panic had set in. What was she doing? Ladies did not behave this way in 1912.

So fucking what, I'm not from 1912, I've given him a fake name and I can do what I like, I'm a time travelling assassin descended from Boudicca herself.

By the time she reached her room, Olga had talked herself back into it and she was excited by the idea. For the first time in all of her lives she was going to have sex with a man who was not Rudi Kessler.

Inside, she stripped off and put on a silk wrap before making herself comfortable on the sofa with another glass. Then she picked up the phone.

"Hello, this is Kathleen Braithwaite in the Jenny Lind Suite, I'd like two steaks, rare, another bottle of champagne and some ice cream brought up in three quarters of an hour."

"Yes, Ma'am, I thought it was just you in the Jenny Lind?"

"I shouldn't think it's any of your business how much steak I order. Now, forty-five minutes, not a moment before."

She hung up the phone as Chester knocked, waited and entered. He seemed to have regained some of his composure and he held a fresh drink.

"Hello, Kath," he said, "don't you look beautiful?"

"Hi Chester, you already said that."

She stood to greet him and let the wrap fall open, exposing her toned body, tanned from her year in Mexico. The wrap clung to her nipples, leaving her breasts seductively covered. She placed a strong hand behind his head and pulled it down to meet hers, kissing him forcefully, before retreating to the bedroom, where she turned at the door and let the wrap fall to the floor. Chester followed, discarding items of clothing as he walked, and when he reached the bed, he too was naked.

"You're in good shape, do you play a sport?" Olga asked from the bed, where she lay propped up on her elbows."

"I rowed crew in college and I've kept it up since moving here to work for Mr Wilson. What do you do to have a body like that?" he said, as he joined her on the enormous bed.

"Oh, nothing, just a bit of calisthenics and some ju-jitsu," she said dismissively.

"Juju–what?"

"Never mind," she said, first looming over him, then devouring him whole.

Olga soon found that whilst sex with a stranger could be great fun, she learned that without the emotional connection that she and Rudi shared, it was a very different experience.

Over steak and champagne, Olga decided to see if she could salvage anything productive from an evening paid for by His Majesty's government.

"Who did you say you worked for, Chester?"

"Oh, err, Woodrow Wilson," he replied bashfully. She hadn't made the connection before, but Mr Wilson was, of course, the President of these United States.

"How silly of me, I heard you say Mr Wilson, but I didn't realise you meant that Mr. Wilson." She sipped some champagne and continued. "What's it like working for the President?"

"Oh, it's just swell, he's a real nice guy... for a southerner," he replied.

"For a southerner?"

"Yeah, he's a goddamn racist and it can be hard to hold my tongue sometimes."

"Really?"

"You only have to look at the segregation and mass firings of black staff right after he assumed office."

"Sounds like you work for a man who you can't agree with on important matters of principle?"

"I guess you're right," he admitted, running his fingers through his dark hair. "But what can I do, I work at the White House, what would I be walking away from if I quit?"

"Well, what did you study at...?" she asked, encouraging him to finish the sentence.

"Yale, and I read law. My father runs a pretty successful law firm back in Connecticut."

"Does he share Wilson's views?"

"No, of course not, my dad's a good man. A little old fashioned, but he raised me to take the declaration at face value when it says that all men are created equal and have the right to life, liberty, and the pursuit of happiness," Chester said animatedly.

"I think you'd make a good lawyer, but is resigning enough?"

"How so?"

"Of course, you're a solid chap with plenty to recommend you, but you aren't arrogant enough to assume that your leaving will bring down the administration?"

"Oh, sure. I see what you're saying. But what can I do? I'm just an overpaid gofer."

"I don't know, Chester, just don't go rushing in tomorrow morning shouting I quit, alright?"

"You bet, I'm the kind of guy who needs a plan before I turn my life upside down like that. Listen," he said, checking the silver hunter he'd set on the coffee table, "If I do want to keep my job, I'll have to be going."

"Maybe you can stay a little bit longer?" she said, stretching out a long, tanned leg to stroke his thigh."

"You've twisted my arm," he laughed, and it was his turn to loom.

After Chester left, Olga began to make notes on their conversation for the morning when she would be sober enough to form a plan.

Brownshirt, 1912

The morning after the Reichstag fire, the papers were filled with anti-communist outrage and right-wing sympathy. The events of that night marked the start of a new age in Germany; an age of fear and anger. Citizens were encouraged to fear the red tide of communism and the fear they felt manifested as violence towards party members and party premises. The Reichstag was relocated to the Kroll Opera House and SDP members were attacked and even killed on their way to work, whilst the perpetrators never saw the inside of a prison cell.

The German Workers Party was formed on the Twentieth of April 1912, three years after Rudi had brought Adolf Hitler to Berlin, in an effort to prevent his radicalisation, and now the new chairman of the DAP enjoyed a membership of hundreds. By May, numbers had swelled into their thousands and Rudi had left the diplomatic service to run in one of the dozens of empty SDP seats.

Much as they had done before, conservative politicians ignored the more outlandish views of men like Horst Buchholz and Adolf Hitler, concentrating on what might be done to further their own aims. Whilst Rudi waited for the date when his sister and Olga would kill Apis, the leader of The Black Hand, he trained a team of men to accompany him on the mission. It wasn't a rescue operation because they were destined to return safely to Broadlands after their work was complete. It would either be a meeting to warn the women he loved or an abduction, he still wasn't sure which, so he planned for both.

He knew that there had been time to prevent the worst of his torture, but somehow the pain and scars felt part of him now. He didn't know what would happen if he changed things so drastically, nor what he might remember. He discovered something else one evening as he watched his men waterboarding Braithwaite, the sound of her drowning soothing him like a lullaby. It was this:

I want my revenge more than I want my toes back, more than I want to undo this dark and horrific chapter in my life. If I did go to Broadlands to stop it, then this bitch would be free again and I just can't live with that.

By August, the DAP had twenty seats in the Reichstag and membership was in the tens of thousands, political uniforms had become normal in Berlin, khaki for the DAP and overalls with a red scarf for the SDP. On thirteenth August 1912, Rosa Luxemburg was beaten to death in the street by brown-shirted men. The following day, both sides took to the streets and marched towards one another in their thousands. The Chancellor ordered the army in to assist the brownshirts and a massacre ensued. Machine guns and rifles rattled as lead tore through the soft flesh of the crowd, killing and wounding hundreds. SDP losses were so high that Hitler's cronies were able to waltz into union-controlled factories and take over. They had the remaining communists sacked and placed their own men in charge of the workforce. The owners only saw the potential gains as their most vehement opponents to profit was marched from the premises for them.

After The Battle of Bendlerstrasse, the communists fought back with the same tactics as the fascists but enjoyed none of the same sympathies. Hitler held enormous rallies and more German citizens flocked to his new way of thinking.

"What do you think of this fellow Hitler?" asked Kaiser Wilhelm as he gazed from his palace window at a small group of brownshirts loitering and spitting on the street.

"Well, your Imperial Highness, they are dealing with the communists for us, but they are also gaining a worryingly large following," his aide said, careful not to commit.

"But they are..." the kaiser paused to think for a moment as he stroked his large moustaches, "on our side?"

"Oh, yes, Your Majesty, Herr Hitler has spoken many times of his devotion to you and to the Reich."

"Yes, but isn't he an Austrian?"

"He was born Austrian but became a naturalised German a year or so ago."

"Indeed, so we like him, then?"

"We like him, Your Majesty?"

"Will he be Kanzler one day?"

"Oh, I highly doubt that, Your Majesty."

"Very good, have my horse readied, I wish to ride before lunch."

A warm summer breeze blew through Rudi's blonde hair as his Daimler TE20 bumped along the country road from Novi Sad to Belgrade. Olga and Carla's safe house was little more than a shack, but during the Indian summer of 1912, they could have comfortably slept outside. The primary reason for choosing this location was the commanding view it gave out over the valley. Olga was not expecting him, nor was Carla, but neither had been betrayed by him in this timeline, so Rudi strolled up to the door and knocked confidently.

"Rudi," Olga exclaimed, throwing her arms around him before looking past him to see an open-top Daimler filled with uniformed men.

"Who are they, Rudi?" she asked, her tone flat and serious.

"Oh, they're with me," he said with a smile.

"They look like brownshirts," Carla said with a confused frown. Olga stepped back to let Rudi into their hovel. Rudi saw Carla and beamed at the sister he had thought to be dead for so long. He wrapped her in a bear hug and fought back tears.

"What was that for?"

"I missed you sister, that is all," Rudi croaked.

"What are brownshirts?" Olga demanded.

"Nazis," Carla said flatly, stepping back from Rudi.

"They are not Nazis, Nazis don't exist in this timeline," Rudi countered.

"They certainly look like Nazis," Carla said.

"Rudi, what's going on?"

"Remember that night in April when I disappeared at Broadlands?"

"Yeah, you were called away on urgent business, something to do with the embassy," Olga replied, having no reason to mistrust Clive.

"Who told you that?"

"Clive did," Carla offered.

"Clive lied."

He let that sink in whilst he watched both women's reactions. Carla appeared to accept that Clive could mislead them, but Olga looked unsure.

"He took me prisoner and kept me in his basement," he said eventually.

"That's not funny, Rudi, he's been so good to us," Olga said.

"It was all an act. He wanted the time machine and for us to do his dirty work, and when you're done here, he'll be done with both of you, too."

"How can you know that?" Olga demanded.

"He took me prisoner, Olga," Rudi said flatly, "for two years. Then, when I was completely brainwashed, he made me build him a time machine and when it was done, he sent me back to 1912 to spy on Germany for him."

"Oh, mein Gott," Carla exclaimed. "That would explain his strange behaviour in April."

"If you've been brainwashed, how have you managed to be here?" Olga asked incredulously.

"Olga, why do you doubt me over Clive?"

"Because you showed up here with a parcel of Nazis, Rudi, that's why!"

"He tortured me for nearly two years," Rudi cried, tears flowing freely down his face. Inspiration struck him and he sat down to pull off his hessian boots. "Look Olga, he had them cut off my toes, one by one."

"What did you do?"

"Rudi broke down, resting his face in his hands as both women tried to comfort him.

"Just come back to Berlin with me, I'll explain everything on the way."

"Okay, but those Nazi-looking fuckers out there are going to take a good deal of explaining, Rudolf Kessler!" Olga warned. "And

I have to make a stop on the way to the station. In fact, drop me off and I'll meet you on the platform for Prague."

"Remember to call me Horst Buchholz," he said quietly, as he strode across the one-room shack to a wash bowl and splashed water into his face.

"What did you have to do?" Rudi asked as they boarded the train.

"Finish my mission," she whispered into his ear, "Apis."

"You didn't?"

"I did," she said indignantly.

"If Clive wanted him gone, and Clive is our enemy, then why would you help him?" Rudi growled.

"Carla explained to me in great detail why, and if you want to spend the entire journey back to Berlin hearing about it, you can ask her yourself, but the long and the short of it is this: The end of the Black Hand, and Russia's implication that ending will help to prevent the Great War," she said matter of factly.

"Fine, just stop doing things for that bastard," he said, pulling the sliding door across to shut them inside their lavish compartment.

"Is this marble?" Olga asked, absentmindedly rapping the sink with her knuckles.

"Yes, this is the Orient Express, darling," he sang, but his heart wasn't in it. He felt wretched that Olga could doubt him.

"Come on then," Olga said, "explain these brown shorts."

"Brownshirts," Rudi corrected.

"So, they are Nazis?"

"Ah, yes, I see what you did there. No, there is no such organisation. They are employees of the DAP."

"What's the DAP."

"The German Workers Party," he said in German.

"Are you a member?"

"Yes, I represent them in the Reichstag," he said solemnly.

"Who is their leader?"

"Ah," Rudi said.

"Who?" she said forcefully.

"Adolf Hitler," he whispered.

Olga didn't speak, she just stood from the leather elbow chair and left the compartment in silence, closing the door behind her with measured force.

Some time later, Carla appeared at the door and let herself in.

"Is it true? Did you join the Nazi party?"

"No, it's called the DAP!"

"Mein Gott, Rudi! The DAP became the NSDAP, which was the Nazis. I can't believe for one second that you forgot that?"

"It's different this time."

"How?"

"I've been steering him away from antisemitism and all of that other stuff," he said petulantly.

"Is it working?"

"I think so, we've been focusing on communists and of course he hates Clive because of what he did to me."

"Do you truly believe that you can change Adolf Hitler and create a Germany that is great and fair to all?"

"I think I can with your help," he pleaded.

"What about Clive?"

"Clive wants you dead!"

"How can you know that?" she demanded.

Rudi just looked away, tears in eyes as he struggled to maintain his composure, just as Olga burst in.

"You joined the fucking Nazi's, Rudi! Adolf Fucking Hitler and the SDAP, I don't have the words... I, I need some time. Carla? Are you coming?"

Carla said nothing, she simply stared out of the window, turning her back on her sister.

With tears in her eyes, Olga hefted her luggage and stormed from the compartment in silence, slamming the door closed behind her. Rudi simply looked after her forlornly as his cried his silent tears.

"Hey, brother?" Carla whispered, without taking her eye's from the window. "I believe you, and now it looks like I've got nowhere else to go, have you got room for your sister?"

Had Rudi turned at that moment to look out of the window too, he might have seen a blur of blonde and khaki rolling down the embankment and into the treeline.

For the second time, Rudi lost Olga on a train. When he finally shook off the shock of her loss, he and his men searched the train from engine to caboose and back again, but found no trace of her.

Olga had seen his total emersion into the fascism they had both spent their many lives fighting, as a betrayal the equal of anything she might have seen him doing with Braithwaite in another timeline. As such, she believed nothing he had told her about Clive, whom she trusted and admired for helping them so much. Olga didn't know what she would say to him about Rudi and his political activities.

Perhaps I'll see what he knows first and keep an eye out for anything suspicious.

Rudi dealt with his loss as he had done before, by throwing himself headlong into his work, but this time he was building and empire instead of a time machine.

"Listen, I know it's risky, but if we don't take risks, we'll be forever on the outside looking in. You have to ask yourself, Dolph, how badly do I want this?"

"I want it very much, Horst, you know that."

"How much, enough to go through with this?" Rudi paced the drawing room of their new, much larger house in Moabit.

"Come to the dungeon and I'll walk you through the plan," Rudi insisted.

Over the last year as tensions rose between France and Germany over the Kaiser's perceived encirclement, the DAP had grown from a minor faction to mainstream notoriety. Carla had been forced to guide Rudi from the shadows, as the men of 1914 Berlin would not entertain the ramblings of a girl, no matter how pleasing she was to look at. She planned to change that too, but first she needed Rudi, by now Hitler's second in command, to have real power, and that meant getting the party real power.

If Carla remembered one thing from previous lives, it was that she hated the Soviet Union, she hated Walter Albrecht and she hated communism. The first step in her plan involved the wiry little man in the basement of their house on Waldstrasse.

"Dolph, meet Peter," Rudi announced, pointing at a bearded little man with large spectacles, hunched over in the corner of his cell and refusing to make eye contact.

"Last year, I paid Peter a lot of money to join the SDP, and now he's a bone fide, card-carrying communist, aren't you Peter?"

"Ja, Herr Buchholz," he said timidly, shuffling across the cell to meet his captor. Rudi slammed the door in his face and took Hitler to the other end of the cellar.

"This is Peter's wife," he whispered. The woman in the cell was in much better shape, but still pale from lack of sunlight, with dark rings beneath her eyes. Her quarters were far more comfortable and she had some small luxuries like soap and chocolate on a solitary, rough wooden shelf.

"If Peter doesn't do as he's told tomorrow, Maria here will find herself in a world of pain, won't you?" he nodded to her.

"Ja, Herr Buchholz," she said defiantly. She was not a beautiful woman, but something in the combination of her large nose and piecing, almost black eyes made her striking and Rudi could see that Adolf found himself attracted to her.

As he walked along the basement corridor with Carla briskly leading the way, he paused at one of the heavy wooden doors.

"I'll catch you two up in a moment," he called after them.

When they were out of sight, he rested his head against the rough wood of the door and inhaled deeply. She still had a hold over him and he hated her for that more than anything else. Producing a set of keys, he selected a large, black, iron mortice key and thrust it into the lock. The noise of the mechanism tumbling into place echoed off the stone walls and the sturdy hinges groaned for want of oil as Rudi let the door swing inwards.

Ignoring the occupant, Rudi picked up the latrine bucket by the handle and turning his face away, he set it outside before closing the door. He looked at the emaciated woman who lay on the straw mattress staring at him with keen, undefeated eyes. He hadn't really known what to do with her at first, so he'd placed her on starvation rations and a routine of cold showers and enforced exercise. Then he just tried to put her out of his mind – easy for a busy man during the day, but near impossible during the dark hours before dawn, when the ghosts of all haunted men were at their most pernicious.

"You've lost weight," he said coolly, with a slight nod. She looked like she had more to say, but all that came in reply was a bark of humourless laughter.

"Are you ready to talk?"

"No."

She shook her head causing the once auburn hair to move as one; matted and foul. She looked pathetic, her formerly plump face and neck now jowly, and where her complexion had been ruddy, it was now almost translucent. The truth was, that whilst he wanted to punish this woman for the evil she had visited upon him, he had neither the time nor the energy to carry out a soul-breaking campaign of torture and reward. Nor did he want to delegate it. Frustration and anger overtook him and he clenched his fists, breathing hard whilst staring into her sunken eyes. The spark that was still so evident there pushed him over the edge and drawing back one jackbooted leg, he kicked her hard in the stomach, tearing the ragged clothing that hung about her. She rolled sideways off the mattress and sobbed into the cold, stone floor.

"I'm going to increase your rations and have a chair bought in here for you," he said, walking from the cell and nearly kicking over the bucket outside, and as it shook, a turd floated briefly to the surface.

"Braithwaite?" he called. She rolled painfully onto her side and looked at him standing in the doorway poised to throw the bucket of stale piss and shit over her. It seemed to travel in slow motion across the cell to cover the wretched woman in her own waste.

"Guard, Frau Brathwaite will need another cold shower!" he called as he walked away without closing the door.

Upstairs bustled with social activity. Drinks, animated discussion, and political fervour filled every room. His sister held three men captive with robust, eloquent arguments for her vision of the new Germany. This was Hitler's going away party. Determined to serve Germany and find glory in the coming war, he had enlisted in some Bavarian reserve regiment. Rudi had the influence to have him commissioned into a good Prussian line regiment, but Hitler had balked at the idea of spending months in officer training and missing the war.

"Tell me, Carla dear, why is it you think we are at war with France?" asked a stocky leutnant in the uniform of the Bavarian infantry.

"The Kaiser has made a connection between the communists and the French, however tenuous, and it has given him his war. Those assassinations a few years ago, remember Poincaré and that Duma member? Well, they destroyed the Franco-Russian alliance and the Kaiser swept in and shored up relations with his cousin Nicholas, allowing him to attack France with impunity. All he needed was a reason and the SDP gave him one when they torched the Reichstag."

"An excellent summary, my dear," Hitler gushed. "I also think that the rise of fascism in Russia could strengthen an alliance. But we must remember that the Slav is not Aryan and can never be our equal!"

Carla and Adolf's affair had been going on for months and whilst Rudi wasn't exactly happy about it, he knew that the hold she had over him would certainly come in useful. He thought of the lovers Adolf had taken last time around and realised that Carla was far from his type, aside from his niece, Geli Raubal, both British aristocrat Unity Mitford and Eva Braun had blonde hair and blue eyes. The most disturbing fact surrounding these women was that they had all died by their own hand.

She'll probably die of cirrhosis anyway, Rudi mused as Carla knocked back another glass of Krug.

Figures from the Nazi Party's history were beginning to emerge during this new DAP rise to power and with Carla stood Herman Göring, the head of operations in Bavaria and an infantry subaltern. With Göring was a man Rudi knew from Africa, Hauptman Franz Epp. This man would distinguish himself in the Great War, winning a Blue Max and a Knighthood, but later he would commit atrocities in the name of the NSDAP and serve as Reichsleiter in Hitler's government. These men would soon find themselves in France, fighting their red-trousered foe and witnessing the horror of trench warfare for themselves.

Flashes of the past like this reminded him of his promise to moderate Hitler and ensure Germany stayed true to the dreams of its youth. If he lost his grip of events or let the goal slide out of view, the enabling act, the camps, and millions of deaths would be on his disfigured hands.

The Choice, 1914

Clive had certainly given Olga what she'd asked for. The bodies were piling up, as were the miles.

It had made sense when travelling throughout the United States to learn to fly the planes that she was ferried about in, and she had discovered in herself an increasing need for excitement. The adrenaline rush of killing was still there, it still beckoned to her in the night, but she wasn't that kind of killer. Olga knew she needed some form of justification to take the lives she did.

But the barrel rolls, flat spins, and hammerheads she performed in her Curtiss Model D, gave her that rush and got her from city to city without leaving a trail.

As much as she loved it, she was forced to leave her biplane stateside for this mission, but after docking at Southampton she was able to acquire a brand new Sopwith Tabloid. This type of travel made the carriage of weapons far easier, especially as hostilities between France and Germany were ready to boil over, and she could be alone, something she wanted increasingly these days. Although Britain was neutral, Hitler's influence in the Reichstag was making it hard to enter the country at the main ports.

Frustratingly, she would have to stop in Belgium as the range of the biplane was just over eight hundred kilometres, and the flight to Nuremberg was nine hundred and two.

Olga loaded the side-by-side seats with supplies, strapped her covered Springfield 1903 to the axle and climbed into the cockpit. Bundled up against the remains of a Hampshire winter, she leaned out and signalled to the mechanic, who pulled down hard on the prop to fire up the French rotary engine. It spluttered briefly, then roared into life, vibrating the flimsy crate and filling Olga with that all too familiar mixture of excitement and fear – her addiction.

The mechanic nodded to Olga and she rolled her shoulders, gripped the yoke, and placed her feet squarely on the rudder pedals, craning her neck around to watch each component respond as it should. This done, she ran her eye over the instruments and with her arm extended out of the cockpit, gave the mechanic a thumbs-up. He tugged sharply on a length of rope, removing chocks from the front wheels and allowing the plane to surge forward. Olga was unable to stop the broad grin spreading across her face.

The wooden plane bumped along the taxiway, occasionally buffeted by a crosswind as Olga followed the curved route to the runway, using her feet to operate the rudder at the rear of the tail and getting a feel for how this most modern of aircraft might handle in the air. Lining up with the main runway, she began to slowly open the throttle, feeding the thirsty engine and propelling herself along the airstrip. As she pulled back on the yoke, the cables caused the wing to warp, providing lift, and the nose began to rise beyond the horizon as she climbed steadily over the rich and fertile farmland of southern England and the sprawling New Forest. When Olga eased the yoke forward again, levelling out at five-thousand feet, she gently moved it to the south, causing the wings to warp in opposing directions and initiating a gentle roll. Pulling back gave more lift and put the plane on a south-easterly heading for Belgium, where she planned to refuel.

Relaxing slightly for the first time since take-off, she rummaged for a pork pie and adjusted her clothing against the bitter cold of the open cockpit. She gazed all the while in wonder at the beauty of England with its green, rolling hills and sheer, white cliffs, the patchwork of fields bordered by hedgerows and winding country lanes. Herds of tiny cattle seemed to watch her as she flew past the distinctive round kells of Kentish oasthouses. The hop gardens were fallow this time of year, but the orchards were in full blossom, covering vast swathes of the countryside in shades of white and pink. To the north she could see the town where she had grown up, unrecognisable under the ominous shadow of smog from a million coal fires.

~

In Berlin, Peter Jacobson pushed his way through the crowd towards the dais. He was small and quick, despite his age and the effects of confinement, but the crowd was large, filled with grey-clad soldiers destined for France, so it might take him an hour or more to reach the front. In the right pocket of his jacket the Luger felt heavy, but heavier still were the two bombs rolling about in his left. The ten-second fuse would burn slowly and kill him quickly after he had completed his task.

~

Olga's numb hands gripped the yoke as her numb backside bounced along the Saint-Ghislain Airstrip just outside Mons, Belgium. She taxied towards the fuel store, taking care to point the nose back towards the runway and pausing a moment at low idle before killing the engine completely.

The sound of silence assaulted her and she sat in the cockpit composing herself, summoning the motivation to clamber down from the plane with stiff, disobliging limbs. Pulling off her oil-soaked sheepskin mittens, first with her teeth then her free hand, she rubbed her hands together and blew on her fingers. The taste of castor oil from the engine, foul on her lips, would linger there for the coming days and if she was very unlucky, it would turn her guts to liquid. As she unwound her scarf, Olga felt the spring sunshine on her face and basked in its warmth for a moment, until finally, she removed her flying helmet and shook out her long, blond hair.

Retrieving a Smith and Wesson police special from her bag on the seat, she thrust it into the pocket of her leather flying jacket, found bolt cutters, and climbed down from the cockpit. After a cursory inspection of the Saturday morning quiet at the rural aerodrome, she proceeded to cut the lock off the fuel store and help herself to the petroleum within.

Suitably refuelled, Olga found a pair of sturdy chocks with a long rope and placed one under the left wheel and the other in the cockpit.

With everything in place and wearing all of her flying gear, she draped the rope over one wing and approached the propeller. Grabbing one of the two blades in both hands, she pulled down hard, using all of her weight, and the still-warm engine fired right up, causing the plane to twist slowly against the single chock. She sprang up into the cockpit rope in hand, deftly yanking it and pulling the chock clear of the wheel. Once again, the bird surged forward and Olga took to the skies on a south-easterly heading. If her route had taken her further south, over the Alsace–Lorraine or the Black Forest, she might have seen the millions of troops massing at the Franco-German border. As it was, she saw the convoys filling every road from east to west with the terrible machinations of modern warfare.

~

Peter Jacobson's bony fingers curled around the knurled grip of his Luger, coating it in sweat. He was at the front now, vying for a clear view of the dais and the man everyone was here to see. As he, too craned his neck for a glimpse, the fingers of his left hand played with the firing cap of his bomb. Like many philanderers, he was a broken man, incapable of real love, which is why he had started families and then abandoned them all over Germany.

Christina in Sassnitz was struggling to raise his eldest sons Peter and Paul from the table scraps he sent at irregular intervals. He had begun to fear the boys now that they had reached post-adolescent strength, and he often imagined the day they would seek him out looking for answers to awkward questions and retribution for his crimes against their mother. He secretly hoped that this war would take them, and they would no longer be his problem. Then there was Liselotte in Rheindahlen with young Janik and Johanna, but they had only been small when this new woman had turned his head and he had pursued her here to Berlin. Peter knew that she would be the last, she would be the one woman who could make him truly happy and he would never stray again. The truth was that Peter was getting old, and the charm that had once come so easily was fading, along with his hair.

Over Germany, Olga climbed to seven thousand feet, the Tabloid's operational ceiling. Planes were a rare sight over the skies of Nord-Rhine Westphalia in 1914 but not unheard of, and when she reached the outskirts of Nuremberg she throttled right back, because the engine was still loud and she didn't need to court unnecessary attention.

She found her airstrip, a forest firebreak to the east of the city, just as the last of the sun disappeared behind the horizon at her back. Bumping down in the dying light of dusk was perfect and she let herself believe that she'd planned it this way. At the bottom edge of the clearing where it returned to a wide-spaced forestry block, she stamped on the rudder pedal to spin the plane about as she killed the engine. Pushing the whole thing back into the treeline and using branches, she concealed the wings and nacelle. Under her flying suit Olga wore the sensible clothes of the German middle classes, with one of Carla's ingenious trouser skirts allowing normal movement whilst maintaining the illusion of patriarchal compliance.

As twilight descended into the darkness of a clear, but as yet moonless night, Olga retrieved her thirty-ought-six from its place strapped to the axle and slung it before donning her ankle-length coat and her rucksack. She checked her compass briefly before setting off westwards through the Kleinschwarzenlohe forest to Zeppelin Field.

"And now I would ask those who today call us agitators: 'what then have you to give to the people as a faith to which it might cling?'" Hitler exclaimed, his arms moving animatedly with each syllable. The small crowd roared with applause, stamping their feet and banging steins of beer on the long wooden tables, adding to the river of amber on the flagstone floor.

"This war with France will show Europe and the world that Germany is a force to be reckoned with and as our brave sons march into Paris, I intend to be there, for I have here my enlistment papers for Bavarian Reserve Infantry Regiment Sixteen!"

He held the papers aloft and again, those assembled erupted with cheers and applause.

"They love him, I can't believe how much they love him," Rudi whispered incredulously to his sister.

"Really? I can," she said without taking her eyes off the young man at the lectern, sweating profusely after his impassioned speech.

"I'm just glad he's leaving the Jews alone. I'm definitely making headway there."

"I don't know why you waste your time, what do you owe a Jew?" Carla sneered.

"They are human beings, sister, and you'd do well to remember the unimaginable tragedy that befalls them should we stray back to that path of hatred and evil."

"Okay, brother, relax," she said, "we will leave your precious Jews alone," and to herself she added for now.

"Listen," Rudi told her. "My regiment, the one Albrecht got me a reserve commission with, it's been mobilised. Now as a member of the Reichstag, I don't have to go, but I wonder how it will look if I don't?"

"You will need to be in Berlin to run the party, Horst. You have already served Germany with distinction, and you have the scars and medals to prove it," Carla said with finality, as Hitler strode over and kissed her lightly on the cheek, before smiling pleasantly at Rudi, his closest friend.

"Come, we have an early start tomorrow, my friends," he said, beckoning his inner circle to walk with him back to the hotel they had booked out for the occasion.

"Russia has joined the war!" shouted a boy of no more than seventeen standing in a doorway with his schoolfriends. He clutched enlistment papers in one hand and a bottle of cheap schnapps in the other, the grin he wore spread wide across his face.

~

Olga stood at ground zero, gazing about her for one kilometre in every direction – the effective range of her rifle. She had done this sort of thing so many times now, in so many ways that she knew instinctively what would work, where would offer the best vantage point and how best to plan her exfiltration. Ground zero was Zeppelin Field, so named because Ferdinand Graf von Zeppelin landed his airship LZ6 on this spot in 1909.

Olga's eyes fell upon a tall, flat-roofed building with crenelations running along the eaves.

Perfect, she thought.

On closer investigation it appeared to be commercial, empty until at least Monday morning, by which time she'd be tucking into a champagne breakfast at the Hotel National in Zürich. Olga let herself in via the service entrance and as she made her way up through the building, she planned her extraction, noting alternative routes and exits. On the roof she produced a custom-made scope from her rucksack and used it to look back at where she had been standing on Zeppelin Field. When she had chosen several viable fire positions, she returned to a small, lockable storeroom and entered a state of pseudo sleep that Yael had trained her to use back in Libya.

At breakfast the atmosphere in the packed dining room was palpable, and Rudi knew better than anyone, except maybe Carla, that days like today were what solidified the people's belief in national socialism and in Hitler. When the man stood from his black bread and poached eggs that morning, the room stood with him, and they followed him into the foyer and out onto the cobbled streets. Hitler, Göring, Rohm, Carla, and Rudi led an impromptu procession through the streets, singing the old songs and chanting the new slogans.

It was nearly time, Peter Jacobson could see his entourage approaching the dais and the man himself, with his famous moustache. He wasn't sure why Herr Buchholz wanted him dead, but he knew the price of failure and it wasn't about Maria or the unborn child, it was the horrific torture that he'd heard every night since his capture. He knew there were prisoners down there only kept alive to prolong their suffering, because they had displeased him. And more than anything, Peter feared that pain.

He'd contemplated just using the Luger on himself in a quiet alley, but he knew he wouldn't be able to go through with it. So, as he soiled himself with fear, he dropped his wallet to the ground, primed the bombs in his pocket and drew his pistol. Stepping forward, he emptied all eight rounds into his target, the slugs tearing through flesh and bone, jerking the dying man in a new direction with each percussive shot. The unlucky men who wrestled Peter to the ground were blown to pieces as his bombs exploded, and Kaiser Wilhelm II was pronounced dead at the scene.

~

Olga exhaled slowly as the animated man at the lectern spewed his hate-filled bile, which travelled to her in a distorted electrical rasp via the loudspeakers.

"Gentlemen, for many years we have fought at home against the idea of international Marxist solidarity. We perceived in this supposed international solidarity only the enemy of a truly national attitude, a phantom which drew men away from the only reasonable solidarity there can be: from the solidarity eternally rooted in the blood."

She could see Rudi and Carla standing behind him, clapping and smiling, being good little Nazis. She shed a tear for the friends she'd lost as she squeezed the trigger, causing a small red circle to appear between Hitler's eyes. Fractions of a second later, Rudi and Carla were covered with blood and brains.

Rudi seemed to look at her then. Right at her.

Olga had already chambered a second round and found the second pressure on the trigger, but she couldn't follow Clive's orders and take Rudi's life too. In that moment's hesitation, he was gone. The thousands-strong crowd was dispersing, and Olga was away. She ran down the stairs and threw her rifle into the storeroom, locking the door. The building was empty, and the street outside had filled with terrified would-be national socialists. She fell into goosestep alongside them and aimed for the forest and her primary means of escape.

Clive would be angry about Rudi but it would be a while before he found out, and she could be far away by then. She realised in that moment, in the impossibly loud throng of the fleeing crowd, that she had resigned herself to leaving Clive and the safety of his protection, to fending for herself and putting this life of death behind her. In contrast to the physical press of bodies, she felt free, unburdened, and capable of just about anything.

~

Rudi paced the carpet of his hotel room, still covered in pieces of one of the most evil minds in history. Despite shaking with the physical manifestation of his horror, he experienced mental clarity that was free of the fervour and palpable presence of the man who now lay cold on the coroner's slab.

"You know, Carla, this could work in our favour."

"How? Our leader is dead and the rally is a disaster," she said calmly, as she wiped her face with a lace handkerchief.

"The Kaiser has just been slain in the street by a communist, Hitler has just been shot dead…"

"By a communist," she said, picking up the thread with her sharp mind.

"Exactly, so now is the time to finish the job. We need to stir up enough ardour in our supporters that they go out tonight and kill every communist they see. Instead of a war with Jews, we can direct them to the real enemy, the Bolsheviks."

Rudi's eyes gleamed with the same passion he'd channelled into his time machine, into stopping this now dead despot, whose party and rhetoric were very much alive.

"And the French," Carla added.

The hatred both Carla and Rudi felt towards communists of any ilk was derived mainly from their lives in post-war Germany, known to them as the DDR. A soviet puppet state and western flagship for communism. Conversely, the Nazis had never op-pressed them, never persecuted them. Both felt sure that they could use fascism as a tool for good, for the liberation of the Volk, whilst avoiding the atrocities perpetrated by Hitler's iteration of national socialism.

Ascent, 1914

Olga flew west from a country on the brink of war to a country that never warred. She lay low in the Hotel National as planned and cashed in the last of her gold bars in a Swiss bank in exchange for US dollars. She sold the Tabloid and caught a train to La Rochelle, from there taking a ship to New York. As the French coast disappeared over the horizon, turning her entire world into a great blue disc, she realised that there was no one left in the whole of Europe who she could call friend and now she was headed to a continent filled with people she'd spent over a year grooming for an invasion that she no longer believed in.

As she thought about Clive and the man he really was, the despicable things he had ordered her to do, chief among these being the murder of the only man she would ever love, she realised that she was finally free of him. A great weight seemed to lift from her shoulders and she breathed deeply on the salty air, the same air she'd breathed all those years before on the Herev.

She resolved to find Chester Dickey, to use him for a scratching post, and when she was done, convince him to warn Wilson of the invasion.

The rest of 1914 passed Rudi by in a blur of putsches and elections, power grabs, and coronations. By Christmas he was the wartime Kanzler of Germany and a close, personal friend of the new Kaiser.

Some had argued that at thirty-one he was too young to lead a country, but others had cited his war record and the way he'd dealt with the rising tide of communism, but Wilhelm loved him, he coveted the medal at his throat and sat rapt as Rudi told war stories whilst they drank together.

In the tradition of Bismarck, Rudi held the title of both President and Kanzler. He courted the Princes of the Bundesrat and commanded the votes of the Reichstag with its heavy DAP majority. Those long discussions with Mirabelle and Eder left Rudi in no doubt how to go about winning this war and whilst normally the political leader of Germany would advise against the monarch marching to war with his men, Rudi saw it as an opportunity to rule with impunity.

With the late Kaiser Wilhelm's parting gift of the alliance with Russia, he began planning with industrialist Walther Rathenau to begin mutually beneficial trading between the two empires. Rudi wanted cotton, camphor, pyrites, and saltpetre for weapons production. Russia needed Germany's production capabilities and superior technology; chiefly weapons, for there were not enough rifles to equip the millions of reservists she could call upon.

Rudi sent engineers to eastern Russian cities to overhaul their production lines and modernise their processes. The two empires worked out a standardised calibre for weapons and artillery and built vehicles to the same specification. Because the Russian railways used a different gauge of track, he built a new railroad purely for shipping war materials. He also arranged for exchange programs, Russian officers were seconded to German regiments and invited to attend Prussian staff colleges, whilst German officers assisted with training Russia's five million reservists. Rudi had seen the Russian aristocrat's contempt for the peasant and the low value they placed on human life, although in his experience the aristocrats called themselves party members in a grotesque pantomime of class solidarity and social parity. With that in mind, he allowed Russian citizens to join German regiments, and whilst these weren't mixed units, the German officers in charge appreciated the sanctity of human life and were drawn to the lower echelons of society.

Wilhelm III set off to war, his head filled with Rudi's sage advice for swift victory. Kaiser Bill had three times the men and an embarrassing technological advantage, so all he had to do was to wait patiently whilst his enormous guns reduced the fortified Meuse valley to rubble, and to sweep through with their three million, eight hundred thousand men. By the time the Kaiser was ready to advance, the million men Tsar Nicholas had sent were ready too. It was a blood bath and brave French soldiers died in their thousands before finally, the British stepped in. Apparently, Clive was waiting to clarify a point of diplomacy to do with the Middle East.

The men of the British Expeditionary Force were able only to force a stalemate and in a sick repetition of history, so began the horrors of trench warfare.

—

"It might be a long hole and you may very well call it a trench, but a hole's a hole and this one's full of piss and shit and rats. Rats what eat the bodies we can't see in the mud that sucks us down to us deaths," Rifleman Billy Young said enthusiastically as he shovelled another spoonful of bully beef into his mouth. He'd been a fussy eater once, but war had remedied that.

"Yesterday, when I was delivering that message to staff HQ, I saw a man drown in the mud." The beef still churned in his maw as he spoke. "Full battle dress plus signal wire. I ran to him, one hundred yards along those treacherous, bloody wire-bound duck-boards, but he was gone before I reached him. No sign he'd ever existed."

Billy Young was a short, stocky boy of nineteen with bright red hair cut close to his scalp at the sides but left in a long, unruly mess at the top.

"It's fucking hopeless, we're all fucked, this is it for us, you know? All you can really hope for is a clean death," Riflemen Lynch bemoaned, Billy's story pushing him over the cliff edge he'd been treading for weeks now.

"Listen, son, this is war. It's always been shit and I'll grant you that this is pretty awful, but we're here for the foreseeable, so get used to it," Serjeant Lynch told the younger of the two sons he had claimed after they were both conscripted, his soft Irish brogue calming the boy.

"Now, you put that beef away and you, find your brother, we're about to go over the top."

He placed a firm hand on his son's shoulder and looked him in the eye.

"Stay with him and keep your fucking head down. I'll find you and we'll get through this together. Who are we?"

"The chosen men, dad," his son said, his voice cracking as he fought back tears.

"Here, put this tin in your breast pocket, over your heart," he said, hurriedly unbuttoning the pocket of his son's ill-fitting uniform. "It's packed tight with wadding, and it might just save your life."

"I'm scared, Dad. I'm sorry."

"We're all scared, son, but that doesn't make you a coward. Bravery is acknowledging that fear and overcoming it, for your muckers out there and for your mum and sister back in London. Go on now, I'll see you out there, you'll be fine."

He clapped his boy on the back and they both took up their positions. Brett on the fire step and Domhnall on the duckboards, whistle at the ready. He looked at his elder son, Marc, whose back was turned to face the enemy. They had fought last night when Domhnall had stopped him from going on raid, but he'd only wanted to protect him. Now Marc wasn't speaking to him unless ordered to. Domhnall reached out a hand to say something, anything to make sure their last words weren't cross ones, but the platoon commander blew his whistle and he fell back in line, blowing his and shouting the words of encouragement required of him as platoon serjeant.

He watched his sons clamber out of the trench and into smoke and the hail of German lead that the boss had assured them couldn't be there. He made to follow, but his place was at the rear to pick up stragglers and direct the stretcher bearers. Lieutenant Davidson was leading the charge, sabre in one hand, Webley in the other, a whistle clasped between his teeth, born in anger at an unseen enemy. As Domhnall climbed the ladder, the body of a young man fell backwards into the trench. The blood gushing from his jugular and carotid arteries covered his face. Domhnall's eyes fell to the bulge at his breast and the faded scar on the back of his right hand as it clutched at the neck, fighting to stem the flow. It was Brett, there was no doubt. He scrambled back down to kneel beside him, to hold his boy and offer some comfort in his last moments.

A hand gripped his shoulder, "Serjeant Lynch, where are you going? The Hun is that way."

The voice was crisp, its pronunciation immaculate and the tone carried the weight of the man's rank.

"Major Smythe, Sir, that's my boy, he's dying," Domhnall pleaded as he shook off the hand and turned to his son. Kneeling, he felt the cold steel of Smyth's Webley pressing against the soft skin at the nape of his neck.

"Don't make young Mr Davidson have to write two letters to your wife, he's got rather enough to do as it is, Serjeant. Get out there and concentrate on the men of your platoon that you can save."

His words were cold and they brooked no compromise. Domhnall laid a hand on the boy's chest and as he stood to obey, his son reached out in desperation with blood-soaked hands. He was forty years old with twenty-four-years' service in places like Afghanistan, The Cape, Ireland, India, the Sudan, the Levant, and now France. To say this man was hard would be to grossly understate the facts. Domhnall Lynch inhaled and closed his eyes briefly before spinning on his heel and knocking the pistol from Smyth's limp hand.

A swift blow to the throat was all it took to render him passive. Whilst Smyth grasped at his neck in a grotesque parody of his dying son, Domhnall flung him bodily over the parapet where he lay cowering from the unceasing rain of lead spewing from the German guns.

"My boy," he whispered, holding Brett close to him, oblivious to the pints of blood flowing from his wounds, and the fact he might have to wear this uniform for many more months before it would be replaced. Cooing words of comfort to ease his son from this world and into the next, Domhnall wept for the first time in decades. His tears were not only for the boy he held, but for every other young man whose life he had watched drain away, every death sentence he'd had to give in the form of a legal order, and every friend he'd had to bury in an ignominious grave in some far-flung corner of an Empire he cared so little for.

When Brett was gone he closed his eyes and covered him with a greatcoat. Standing upright, he shook off the grief and steeled himself for another dance with death. Tears streaked his begrimed cheeks and he wore them with pride. He had two more sons and one of them was out there in no-man's-land waiting for his dad to find him and keep him safe, whether he knew it or not.

His mind focused now on the staccato rattle of the machine guns. He counted the bursts, turning the rigid efficiency of his foe to his advantage and when he knew the two-hundred-and-fifty-round belt was nearing its end, he ascended the ladder. He watched the dirt fly up as the last of the belt was expended and he flew over the parapet, grabbing the cowering Major Smyth as he passed. In London, Domhnall had bought three Clements trench knives and had given one to each son. His daughter, Kath had secretly taken them to be engraved, overcome by the gesture, he hadn't the heart to tell her she'd spelled Serjeant a 'G', like the bloody French.

He produced his now, almost wincing at the viciousness of the weapon as he placed his fingers through the brass rings, cut the lanyard of Smyth's Webley and introduced the tip into his back. Thrusting the pistol in one pocket, he ran forward using the man as a shield against the renewed enemy fire. Smyth was awkward on his feet and required constant cajoling and dragging upright. It wasn't long before the man was riddled with bullets and little more than dead weight, so Domhnall dropped into a shell hole using the body as a sort of sled.

"Dad?"

"My boy," he replied hoarsely. The mud-caked form of Major Smyth could have been anyone by now, even a Hun, so he offered no explanation, just crawled through the mud to his eldest son and wrapped his bear-like arms around him. They were not alone in the trench and all five men were his direct subordinates, terrified of their salty veteran of a Serjeant. They now stared in disbelief at the affection this man was capable of.

"What's the craic?" he said after he finally let go of Marc.

"Two MG oh-eights, one to our ten and the other to our two o'clock."

"Come on then, lads, we're missing all the fun!" He grabbed Billy, nicknamed Billy Wizz for his speed, and pointed him in the direction of another shell hole, "Covering fire! Move!"

"I'm up, he's seen me, I'm down," Serjeant Lynch bellowed at the boy, who threw himself to the ground in time to his Serjeant's chant, crawling to change his position before the anticipated call of, "Move."

They had all done this hundreds if not thousands of times, often to the sound of Domhnall's gravelly voice and it brought a measure of comfort to hear it now, as each man ran the gauntlet to their new position of relative safety. He timed it so that his son would run during the reload. He didn't like playing favourites, but he couldn't lose both, it would break him.

Using this method they approached the first emplacement and waited for the reload to coincide with that of the other gun. Armed with his stolen Webley in one hand and the trench knife in the other, he crawled from the hole, followed by an insistent Marc holding a Mills bomb in place of the pistol and wire-cutters in place of the knife. The three men they had left behind in the hole had the delicate task of keeping the gun crew's heads down with a constant rate of fire, synchronising reloads so it didn't give the Bosch a chance to get their gun going again.

Although it was only a matter of yards to the German trench, three layers of thick barbed wire had to be cut and traversed before they could complete their assault. The artillery had tried everything to destroy this new miracle defence, which caught men and pinned them to await their fate as target practice for the enemy snipers. All the bombs and shells succeeded to do though, was lift the stuff into the air and drop it back down again, intact, and somehow more difficult to navigate. One eye on the German gun crew, they cut frantically at the wire, taking great care not to catch themselves in its deadly embrace.

As they started on the third and final coil of wire, the fire behind them began to slow and stumble from the even rate they had so far maintained.

"They're running out of rounds," Domhnall called over the din of rifle fire and the distant rattle of machine guns. The haunting whistle of artillery was oddly absent and it made him uneasy as he watched the gun crew become braver and begin to make progress with their barrel change. He looked back to his boys in the shell hole and saw the panic in their faces as they fired as slowly as they dared and cold dread washed over him as the loader slammed closed the cover and the gunner reached forward to pull back the action.

He produced a Mills bomb and yanked out the pin. Raising himself to one knee, he bowled the grenade in a long high arc so that it exploded in the air near the heads of the gun crew and throwing a second into the trench behind. With a metallic twang the wire parted, Marc dropped his cutters in favour of a trench knife and threw his own Mills bomb. The pair, father and son, hurtled towards the blood-drenched gun and down into the trench, to find the neatly sandbagged walls plastered with the innards of the men they had bombed. Many writhed in agony amongst their fallen comrades but some still had the fight within them. Back-to-back, they struggled against fit, young farm boys from Hess and mighty steelworkers from the Rhineland, hardened by the horrors of this new war and hell bent on killing Tommies.

With blackened eyes and bloodied noses the pair fought on, stabbing and gouging, using every dirty trick in the book just to stay alive until help came. A giant of a man wielding a great hammer, black with dried blood and wet with fresh, grappled Domhnall to the duckboards. He was drowning him in the filthy mud, his weapon raised high in the air, ready to bring it down onto Domhnall's skull when Billy appeared. A shot from his Lee Enfield ended the reign of the would-be God of thunder and the hammer fell unused into the puddle. He stared down into the death-filled trench as an arc of thick, hot blood sprayed his face and he wept for the boy he had once been and all those left dead or dying behind him in the mud.

The Bill

"Mr Speaker, what the honourable gentleman fails to grasp is that war was unavoidable. Clemenceau wanted it at least as much as Kaiser Wilhelm wanted it, and despite what his ministers may say to the contrary, Tsar Nicholas wanted it."

Murmurs rose up from both sides of the house and grew to an all-pervading din.

"Order!" the Speaker demanded, "Order!" His words drawn out and skewed as tradition dictated.

"Mr Speaker, does the Prime Minister have any idea what entering this border dispute has cost the British purse?"

"I have a very good idea, Mr Speaker, and should the honourable gentleman like to see the figures, he can find them on page ninety-seven of the bill."

The man in the despatch box was calm, his voice was level and his words measured. This was his bill and passing it would be the culmination of nearly two decades of unceasing work.

"Mr Speaker, the honourable gentleman must understand that the Hun is at the gate! The French are all but defeated and soon Herr Buchholz will look to the north for yet more spoils. As for the cost, the honourable gentleman will also see that I have outlined a plan to save billions of pounds that are currently wasted in colonies that offer no benefit whatsoever to the empire."

"Mr Speaker, I would assume the Prime Minister refers to his proposed alliance with the Ottoman Empire and our withdrawal from the Levant. If that is in fact to what he refers, then I would ask him, Mr Speaker, does he understand the significance of Mesopotamian oil and how important it will become?"

The house was in turmoil by now and the Speaker struggled to restore order.

"Mr Speaker, I have one last point to deliver and it is this. Tonight we have voted on my bill. It is a brilliant piece of policy and it will enable us to do great things for both the Empire and the people of Great Britain. But from now on, I will not be wasting my valuable time standing here answering your banal questions and placating your delicate sensibilities. Go back to your constituencies and prepare them for the coming war."

As The Right Honourable Sir Gerald Clive VC stepped down from the box to uproar from both sides of the house, he knew that the bill was a certainty. The paper had been read three times by both houses and tonight had been the final stage before royal assent. King George, a firm friend and occasional hunting companion, had assured him that first thing tomorrow he would wave it through. Clive walked the five hundred yards to his residence in number ten Downing Street, having let his driver, Kath, go home for the evening.

The Defence of the Realm Act 1914 gave Clive some serious power. Ostensibly, it was a means to increase home defence and triple the regular and reserve army from seven hundred thousand to just over two million. The new laws also set aside money for ship building and arms manufacture, for the provision of a dedicated foreign secret service and to censor journalism. The bill had received wide publicity and strong protest, both on the streets and in the house, but politicians could be bribed, blackmailed, and coerced while the plebs could simply be ignored.

"What about the electorate, Sir Gerald?" the permanent private secretary had asked, his voice nagging like a rotten tooth.

"Ah, well, Montagu, you see this part of page two-hundred?" Clive flipped through and fingered an obscure, harmless sounding paragraph about national needs and prime ministers' discretion, "this gives me the power to extend the period between general elections to up to ten years."

"My god, that is sneaky, Sir Gerald, what else have you been up to?"

"Well, there's this bit about martial law and the rather juicy nugget that lets me skip parliamentary procedure and go straight to royal assent. Let's see now, this one here allows the Cabinet to pass emergency laws, and this allows me to disband parliament altogether."

He looked at Montagu now, fixing him with those cold, grey eyes.

"Got what you needed there, old chap?"

"What, what do you mean, Sir Gerald?" the old man backed away, raising his arms defensively, abject terror in his milky eyes.

"Do you take me for a fool? Did you really think I wouldn't notice all your late-night assignations with Lloyd-George? The whispers in the corridor and conveniently brief telephone calls as I enter the room?" Clive pressed a button on his desk and two immaculately dressed men entered, strode across the study and frog-marched Montague from the highest office in the empire and into the network of tunnels that ran beneath Westminster.

"You shan't get away with this Clive, I'm a fucking Etonian, I roomed with Asquith at Balliol! My mother is a personal friend of Queen Mary," Montague called as he was dragged down the corridor.

"Bloody champaign socialists," Clive said aloud as he lit a cigar and inspected the glowing tip.

Clive had been in office for just over a year, winning a leadership campaign as the Foreign Secretary who had kept Britain out of the Great War. With Clive at the helm, the Liberals had won the 1914 general election by a landslide, but tomorrow was when his reign would truly begin.

Clive's time since returning from the Cape had been filled with work, the kind of work no man in his position, with his title, lands and war record should ever need to do, and it had aged him. He was fifty years old attempting to pass for a man in his forties. His late twenties had been kind to him, but two wars, and twenty years of constantly playing parts and lying with every breath he drew, meant he could easily pass for sixty. He'd stopped smoking and laid off the booze, he exercised and ensured he slept a full eight hours every night, but still he bore the lines of age and the rot, as he called it, had begun to set in.

His goal was simply to live long enough to prevent the collapse of the British Empire before he died. For Clive, the dreams of other lives that plagued every time-traveller were merely informative, an added bonus to his restful sleep.

He secured his selection to the Liberal party as the candidate for New Forest by murdering the current incumbent, triggering a by-election, and winning by a landslide. Everybody loved a war hero. Clive then used his influential friends to move up in the Campbell-Bannerman government as a junior foreign minister. In Asquith's government he moved up again, convincing Sir Edward Grey to create a new position for him as security minister, in charge of all foreign espionage operations and absorbing the duties and staff of the Imperial Defence Committee. He began streamlining the operations and concentrating on gathering intelligence in the areas he alone knew would be a threat.

Clive placed his good friend Sir John Notting in the position of 'C', shuffling the elderly Smith-Cumming back into retirement. He managed to obtain powers of arrest at home and placed a man in every embassy, with two in Germany. He used Rudi to great effect in Vienna and oversaw several coups. His successes saw him promoted to Foreign Minister when in 1912, Sir Edward was killed in a tragic fly-fishing accident.

Clive placed a creature of his own making in his old position and began to engineer foreign policy to prevent or at least delay World War One. With Olga and Carla running about Europe for him, this should have been easy, and he had hoped to be the man who brought Europe back from the brink of war.

When Rudi Kessler had gone rogue, he'd found a young Adolf Hitler and helped him set up the Nazi party early. Clive had seen his chance and his attempt to brainwash the man he'd raised like a son had worked, but the idiots sent to watch over him had failed and lost him in Berlin. So he'd sent Olga to dispatch both Rudi and Hitler just as the Franco-German war was kicking off, but Olga had failed him too. Now Rudi was the most powerful man in Germany, Chancellor to Kaiser Wilhelm III, the son of the man he'd had assassinated only a year earlier.

With Russia supporting them, Germany would soon break the French line, and it would only be a matter of weeks before they were staring across the Channel at the white cliffs of southern England and wringing their hands with greed. Of course, he had a plan, Henry Clive always did.

Clive received royal assent for his bill and proceeded to exercise his new powers. He had once heard a CIA man by the name of Waylon Givens say that bad news should always be a shit sandwich on a silver platter. "Give 'em something good – the bread – then drop the turd and quickly follow with another slice of tasty bread. Oh, and make sure the whole damn thing looks pretty as Peggy-Sue on prom night."

That's how Clive altered the British system of government without inciting revolt. The day he introduced national service for all men and women not in reserved occupations or full-time education, he also gave the vote to all adults, regardless of age, gender or standing. The same week he declared the whole of Ireland an independent republic, he cut both alcohol duty and capital gains tax. Clive went to great lengths to ensure Britain was self-reliant when it came to food, fuel, and other basic necessities. He also encouraged emigration to Canada with incentives such as reduced national service, free passage, cheap land, and support to start farms and other businesses. Clive wanted as many fit, young men and women in Canada as possible. For a country forty times the size of Britain, it had one fifth of the population. In the likely event of a naval blockade, Clive wanted as few mouths to feed at home and as many volunteers for the new Swiss-style Canadian militia as possible.

By late 1914, Clive was the beloved hero of the working classes, savvy reformer to the middle classes and tolerated by landed gentry whom he dealt with in the shadows with either carrot or stick. They didn't seem to mind when he sent a few hundred thousand men off to die in France, but if their stock in The Anglo-Persian Oil Company took a hit, he was accosted at his club by outraged lords foaming at the mouth over the injustice. On the street, Clive could do no wrong.

"That Gerald Clive knows what he's doing, we trust our man Clive," they'd say, as the telegram boys cycled up the cobbled streets of working-class neighbourhoods delivering grief and pain in neat little envelopes.

Clive knew that India was about to become a problem for the Empire and since making his deal with the Mexicans, he had begun to grant the Indian people ever increasing autonomy. In exchange for this, he wanted fighting-age men for his war, and India had a population of two hundred and fifty million. Clive made a deal with his puppet ruler to supply them by the boatload. Only he didn't need ships to transport his new army. Clive simply used one of the many reproductions of Rudi's time machine and as the un-witting men were taken to the Thar desert by train and the engine steamed through the arid scrubland, spacetime was torn open and then when the men disembarked, they were in the West Australian Outback.

Huge farms were built to feed the ever-growing, secret army and within six months, there were two million trained men with offic-ers and NCOs to lead them. They enjoyed the latest equipment, produced for them in Australian factories and shipped round the coast instead of all the way to Europe as believed. Clive used his new Royal Marine Commando units to test the army on manoeu-vres in the unforgiving Australian bush, pushing them to the limits of physical and mental exertion, then asking for more.

Two million men of the Royal Indian Army were marched into the Outback one evening, never to be seen again. They reappeared in similar terrain on the Baja Peninsular where President Madero had built a series of fake mines, the largest in the world. The port of San Felipe began to receive shipments of grain from the enormous farms of Western Australia and a barracks the size of a town sprang up around the mining complex. It was here that the largest army in history was billeted, its inhabitants well fed, well trained and ready to fight hard on the promise of their own fertile slice of America when the war was won.

Instead of switching the Royal Navy to oil as his old pal Churchill had insisted, Clive took the man into his confidence and showed him how the time machine worked. He showed him how an entire fleet could sail through the rip and emerge on the other side of the world, thus freeing them of the mire that was middle eastern oil. He conveniently left out the time element, trusting that Winston's grasp of quantum mechanics was not sufficient to see that faster-than-light travel was all that one needed for a spot of temporal tourism. Clive himself was reluctant to use it after the fiasco with Rudi and Mrs Braithwaite.

March 1915, **Ottawa, Canada.**

His liver-spotted hands trembled and the sweat that coated his entire body stung his eyes. It ran in rivulets down his arms and dripped into the ice-filled butler's sink below. This was plan B, a backup, a last resort. It always had been. This was not how it was supposed to go.

He'd waited in that damned lay-by for hours, four nights in a row, but no one had come. He'd been forced to use the dead letter drop, forced to risk all in breaking cover like that. Three days later the reply had come in the usual way. He'd waited for dark; proper dark, the kind you only got hours after sunset on a moonless night. Only then had he chanced it. The loose brick was easier to find now, but it had been a pig at first. He'd needed to count seventeen over from the west corner of Ogilvy's department store. Then up five and right four, all this in the pitch black. His fingers found the crumbling mortar and he eased the brick free.

The note simply said: Plan B. It contained a few dollars. He knew what it was for and he was horrified.

So he went to twelve different chemists and gave twelve cover stories, wearing twelve disguises. John Watson had been forced to drug Mrs Frame, his landlady, and she now slept upstairs whilst he clung to a foot-long glass rod in the basement of her boarding house in Lower Town. The rod stood upright in a mixture of acids. John slowly stirred it, adding drops of glycerine with a pipette. He had the temperature correct, he knew that, and the bowl was good and clean, but he still felt viscerally terrified of the liquid in front of him. His pulse throbbed in his ears and his stomach lurched with every movement. He was transported back to a classroom in Fort Myer, Virginia, a lifetime ago.

"The volatility of this substance cannot be overstated," the master sergeant at the front of the class had said.

Sergeant John Watson, US Army, was long dead, he'd died somewhere between Manila and Fort Leavenworth. This was before all that, back when he'd believed in his country and what he thought it stood for. The course had taught him to make improvised explosives. He had gone to Ireland afterwards, another nation under the yoke of British colonialism. His mentorship, the skills he'd armed men with, were to be used to fight against that colonial oppression. The same oppression his great grandfather had fought against at Bunker Hill, Saratoga and Cowpens. And again, in 1812 his grandfather had fought the British on the USS Constitution, whilst a confederate bullet had taken his father from him before he was born. In the Philippines, they were the oppressor, he was the colonial foot soldier committing atrocities in the name of profit. He had been ordered to kill children for tobacco and sugar, for a foothold in Asia. It stank and he'd said so, too many times. 'Conniving wilful falsehoods.' That's what he'd been sentenced for, the stack of letters he'd mailed to journalists waved about like a smoking gun: Twenty-two years at Fort Leavenworth.

When his discharge came through, he moved next door to the civilian prison, where he escaped with a man called Frank Grigware. They ran north, over the border and into Canada, where Frank kept going north and John headed east. Last he'd heard, Frank was mayor of a small town called Spirit River.

His shirt clung to his back, transparent with sweat and he could feel his socks had become damp with it. When the ratio was correct, John carefully laid the rod down and dropped the pipette into the ice bath. He stepped back, nearly tripping over a bag of sand, and breathed in deeply. He was barely halfway through his ordeal.

He filled the sink with more ice and placed a second, larger bowl beside the first. This bowl was filled with good old Canadian water, distilled for this purpose and no less terrifying. Gingerly, he took hold of the first bowl and poured the nitro-glycerine into the water, washing it of impurities as it sank to the bottom of the bowl. With trembling hands, he gently agitated the bowl and watched carefully as the milky substance settled. Using a ladle, John removed the water, leaving only the deadly explosive. He repeated this step with soda and salt water, until the solution was clear. He added more ice to the sink and collapsed into a pile of laundry, his heart pounding against his ribcage.

The previous night John had taken an empty oil can from the back of a restaurant and carried it home. Using Mrs Frame's tin opener, he removed the whole of the top, then taking the can to the sink he cleaned it thoroughly three times. Placing it carefully into the ice-water, he let it cool down as he added sand. With an inch of sand on the bottom, he looked at the bowl of nitro-glycerine and the knot in his stomach that had begun to recede, returned with malice.

He poured a small amount into a fastidiously cleaned jug, which he decanted slowly onto the layer of sand. He repeated this process until the can was filled with a rudimentary dynamite. He added more ice and left the drum in the sink.

In a sack filled with yet more sand, the device looked fairly innocuous, and he placed it with others on a wheelbarrow and pushed it away from Mrs Frame's before she woke. John had his own place, and it was here in his small but neatly kept back yard that he left the wheelbarrow. After his meeting with the mysterious and alluring Kathleen Braithwaite, the money from the British government had started to pay his bills and John had left his job at the cement works, telling Thelma he had got a new job as a travelling salesman. It covered his disappearances and explained away almost any suspicions with an easy shrug.

She snored loudly as he stripped and climbed into bed beside her. He lay staring at the plastered ceiling and waited for the true dark to descend over Ottawa. Nudging her awake, he kissed her and to make good his alibi, he made unenthusiastic love to his wife for what could be the last time.

At four, he rose from his sleepless repose and gazed upon the woman he loved, her greying, red hair and lined face. The peace of sleep lent some beauty, serenity perhaps, to the careworn visage. In cement-stained overalls he pushed the barrow through Byward Market down to the canal, where he walked along the towpath for some time before emerging onto McLeod Street and on into Downtown. For the first time he looked out of place, and he felt it with near crippling force, until finally he entered the museum gardens, where his wheelbarrow gave him permission to exist again. At the basement door, John untied one of the sacks and produced a crowbar. Inside, he was once again conspicuous, once again a target for nightwatchmen or worse, crimson-clad Mounties.

He replayed the instructions he'd memorised in his mind, all the lefts, rights and counted paces, all the while his tattered nerves on a hair trigger. The door, as promised, was marked with chalk and mercifully unlocked. This, he was told, was directly under the House of Commons, and he locked the door behind him. John didn't care if he killed some more colonial lackies and he was even less aware of his role in yet another empire-expanding war. Anarchy was his watchword now and with the money he'd saved from this caper, he could sail off into the sunset with Thelma, like that fella Joshua Slocum.

John rummaged in the open sack and found an American-made shotgun cartridge and a drinking straw. When he set the oil-can filled with dynamite carefully on the floor, he pushed the paper straw into the sand with the least amount of pressure possible, leaving five inches proud of the surface. John tipped the powder from the cartridge into the straw, taking care to remove the shot. He checked his watch; it was seven thirty. He turned the sack upside down and enveloped the bomb with it before settling in for a long wait.

⁓

March 1915, HMS Thunderer, the west Pacific Ocean.

Clive peered through the door into the captain's dining room at the assembled men. Japanese foreign minister Katō Takaaki sat with his back to the door, whilst opposite him was Madero, nearly a half a decade into his leadership of a prosperous and unified Mexico. To his left sat the French General Maurice Sarrail and across from him General Sir John Notting, Supreme Allied Commander in the American theatre. Standing at the rear of the room were more generals, including Pancho Villa and Reyes, as well as the Indian General Dhruv Randhawa, General Sir Edwin Alderson of the Canadian Army Corps, and the Admiral of the Pacific Fleet, Richard Beatty.

"Are you ready, Sir Gerald?" Lord Kitchener asked, placing a firm hand on Clive's back.

"After you," Clive said with a sweep of his hand.

The two men entered the room and Clive took a seat at the head of the table. Kitchener stood, riding crop in hand at a map board.

"Good evening, gentlemen, I think we all know why we are here. Whilst your counterparts in Europe are dealing with the unholy alliance of Ivan and the Hun, we are Empire building, ensuring that our boys in Verdun don't run out of bully beef and Mills bombs. Our man in DC assures me that whilst they believe some sort of Mexican border skirmish is imminent, they have no notion of what is about to befall them. Now, this war won't be our fault, because tomorrow morning a series of synchronised events will take place all over the continent. These events are designed to provoke a war in which our enemies are the aggressors, and we are the noble defenders of peace. There are fifth columnists all over the USA sowing sedition and damaging infrastructure on our behalf. Now, the Americans have an army of about fifty thousand men, fine men, but that's a division or two, hardly an army in modern terms. I understand that Mexico now has three times that number, all armed with the latest Lee Enfield rifles?"

Madero nodded, as did Reyes and Villa. "And a further four divisions of militia ready to mobilise," offered Villa, who had spearheaded the program.

"Excellent. Now, General Randhawa, your one hundred divisions are raring to go somewhere near San Felipe, what?"

"Correct, your excellency," Randhawa replied with a slight nod of the head.

"The Mexican army will advance north to the Rio Grande and begin a bombardment of these US border towns," Kitchener pointed to the map, "the most important being Columbus, New Mexico."

Clive smiled knowingly at Pancho Villa as he recalled his rash actions in another life, stumbling upon a US cavalry regiment and the surrounding homes filled with armed civilians.

"Now, Randhawa, your men will be the main attacking force and will move north by night whilst the enemy's attention is to the east. As you reach the border, the Royal Navy," he nodded to Beatty, "will begin a bombardment of the US Naval base on North Island in San Diego, the home of the Pacific Fleet. We expect the governor of California to mobilise the National Guard at this point and you may face limited resistance in small numbers. Remember, most Americans exercise their Second Amendment rights and own a firearm of some description." He paused to stroke his huge moustaches and briefly closed his eyes. "Now, I'd say this this makes any male that you may encounter a likely combatant and therefore fair game, what!"

The assembled men laughed dutifully at the jest, although they knew that Kitchener could not be more serious.

The US population was well over two-hundred million and if allowed, they could raise, feed and equip a formidable army. Clive alone knew that number to be four million in the first war and sixteen million in the second, so this really was a sleeping giant they were poking, and mistakes could mean the end of the Empire.

"Kakka Takaaki," Kitchener said, nodding to the Japanese Foreign Minister, "you have your own plans, so I will say for the benefit of all assembled that you intend to invade Hawaii, the Philippines, Guam, Midway and Wake Island. With these secured, you will commence hostilities with both China and Russia, which will receive British naval and air support. The key objective in the north is the Bering Strait, because we need to control it to prevent a large-scale Russian invasion of Alaska.

"Sir Edwin," Kitchener said to the Canadian supremo, "your war will be in the west and your goal is to meet with General Randhawa somewhere near Portland, Oregon, when you will both proceed east to the banks of the Mississippi. And remember, every Yankee who crosses that river will be back one day with a gun and a score to settle."

"Now, General Sarrail."

"Oui."

"You will land along the southern coasts of Louisiana, Alabama and Florida, pushing north to the banks of the Savannah and Tennessee Rivers. Similarly, several divisions of the BEF will push south through New England to the Hudson."

He glanced around the room, looking each man in the eye.

"These great rivers will be our colonial borders. The Sabine will separate the new French territory from Texas and the others I have mentioned will keep the Yanks at bay. The rewards for our countries in this endeavour are obvious, but so is the risk. Now, Sir Gerald has a few words on policy."

Kitchener took a seat and lit a cigar, offering Clive his crop without making eye contact.

"Lord Kitchener has mentioned the threat that comes from the enormous US population, and he is absolutely right. That is why I am sanctioning the use of internment camps similar to those used in the Boer War. These have two clear advantages, the first is simply to deny fighting men to the enemy and the second is a political tool to force Wilson to capitulate. I'll expect the armies of each new territory to take care of this on a local level."

Every man in this room had something to gain personally from this war. They would govern provinces or climb higher in their current professions. Land, prestige, and treasure awaited even the lowliest of colonial foot soldiers. If any harboured images of concentration camps from earlier wars, or millions forced from their open prairie homes into crowded shanty towns, they pushed the thoughts far from their minds and focused on the spoils.

Ford, 1915

After warning Chester and taking him to her suite again, she had waited to see what Wilson's reaction would be. When nothing happened and the news had no mention of the impending invasion, she made her way to Chester's home on the upper-east side. He wasn't there, but his roommate answered.

"Hi, I'm looking for Chester Dickey, you must be Clarence?" she asked, touching her hair and fixing him with her hard, green eyes.

"I haven't seen him since breakfast yesterday. And I can tell you I'm darn ticked off with old Chester, I had a double date lined up for us and mine was a real peach."

He kissed his fingers, which made Olga want to break them.

"Say, what's all this about, lady?"

Olga thought for a moment before replying, because it was likely that this man was also a lawyer and a principled one, as Chester was. If she walked away having given a half-baked excuse, then he might well follow it up with some questions of his own. With a strength that paralysed the larger man, Olga grabbed him and dragged him through the house, closing the front door behind her. By the time he'd recovered his composure, he was sitting in a lounger in the living room he shared with Chester.

"I'm Chester's lover, he was with me last night and this morning," she said with a wicked smile at the discomfort her forwardness evoked. "But he was supposed to meet me hours ago and I'm beginning to worry. Do you have a telephone number that you can reach him on at work?"

She watched as he recovered his composure and the mask of confidence that had momentarily slipped was back in place.

"A telephone number for the White House? Sure, old Woodrow's a bosom buddy of mine. In fact, whilst you were bumping uglies with my pal Chester last night, Woody and I were down at Harry's on Tenth drinking bourbon and playing pinochle."

"Remember that you were standing at your door a moment ago and now, against your will, you sit here, mocking me," she said irritably with a hint of the threat her words carried.

Clarence adjusted his collar and made to stand, but Olga pushed him back down again with ease. She leant over him and grabbed his tie.

"Wise up, mate, I'm getting bored and when I get bored, heads roll."

"Good gravy, you aren't kidding, you got that look, I seen it before, see. I'm a defence attorney, and a guy like me's got... Sorry, I talk when I'm nervous. What do you need?"

"I need to make sure Chester's okay. I gave him some important information to pass on to his boss and I haven't seen him since."

"What kind of information?"

"Information that a defence attorney has no use for," she said coolly.

"Sure, you got it. Now let me see, his folks are a ways away in Connecticut," he rubbed the back of his neck. The man was the opposite of Chester in every way. Fair hair, quick intelligent features, and no chin to speak of. "Until I met you just now, I would a swore I'm all he's got down here in DC. The fellas he works with don't want nothing to do with him and like I said, all his people are up north."

"Okay, Clarence, write down every number and address you can think of, and I'll leave you be. Do I need to point out that if I find out you have mentioned my visit to anyone, anyone at all, I'll be back, and you can tell me all about why you think I'm a killer?"

"How can I reach you if he turns up?"

The man wasn't a coward, but he had seen that look too many times in the eyes of clients he knew to be guilty of brutal murders, and Clarence Getzinger was no idiot.

"I'm staying at the Willard, in the Jenny Lind Suite. Ask for Miss Braithwaite."

She swallowed her disgust at having to use that bloody name.

Back at the Willard Olga told the front desk to put any calls straight through, regardless of the hour, adding a tale of sick parents to cover her tracks. She took the stairs and tried to think about where she should go. If the FBI or the Secret Service – she couldn't keep up with all the different law agencies the Americans had – if they were interrogating Chester, then he would give her up eventually, so was it foolish to have come back here? She didn't feel strongly about Chester, he was just another source to be worked, that just happened to have fringe benefits.

As she stepped onto her floor, she sensed something. These were the skills Yael had promised would come with time. Instincts and ability that were earned, she'd called it reading the atmospherics and Olga was getting to appreciate it more these days and learning to use it. It could be the behaviour of an apparently normal crowd, a change in the air pressure or something even more subtle, as it was right now. The hairs on the back of her neck were like alarm bells sounding in her head and without thinking too hard, her hand worked its way beneath the layers of skirt to find the holster at her thigh. She drew the Baby Browning and quietly chambered a round.

The door to her suite was locked so she moved past it, sweeping the rest of the floor before dropping her guard to mess about with the key. Once inside, she resumed a tactical stance and began clearing the rooms one by one until she found him on the bed. Chester had been thoroughly worked over. His left eye was beginning to swell, and tissue had been stuffed into each nostril to stem the flow of blood which had stained the entire front of his shirt.

Quickly she ran through the possibilities in her head as she spun around, expecting a couple of suits to be closing in. That was the only real reason Chester could be here, they'd used him as bait at the centre of a trap built just for her.

"Wake up," she hissed. "Chester," she nudged him without taking her eyes off the door, "we have to leave, right now." The telephone rang. "Hello?"

"Good evening, Ms Braithwaite I have a Mr Getzinger for you?"

"Thank you, put him through."

"Run," came the hoarse voice down the line right before it went dead. She looked at the handset as though it might offer guidance, before letting it fall to the floor.

"Chester, get up or you're on your own!"

He struggled into an upright position and winced at what Olga imagined to be a torso riddled with deep purple bruises. She moved to the bed and offered him a shoulder before stepping away to see if he could stand.

"Good enough, follow me."

He limped after her as she swept through, gathering her meagre positions and throwing them into a bag. She picked up the police special and looked from it to the tiny weapon in her right hand and then to Chester.

"Can you shoot?"

"I was with the ROTC in college, I do alright," he groaned.

"What?"

"Reserve Officer's Training Corps."

She stifled a laugh before handing him the Baby Browning and slinging the backpack. At the threshold she checked her revolver over and glanced back at Chester.

"Where are we going?" he hissed.

"I have a car outside and there's an airstrip just outside of Gainesville with weak security."

"You can drive? Why am I not surprised by that?" Chester said with difficulty.

Chester must have been very confused, watching Olga move tactically towards the fire escape, pistol raised and pointing wherever her eyes did. But Olga understood the need for it and had no intention of dying. Hotels in 1915 did not have underground parking. In fact, Olga had parked across the street.

"Swap," she demanded, taking the tiny pistol, and thrusting the thirty-eight into Chester's suit jacket. The Browning fit into her palm and was not the red flag the Smith and Wesson would have been. Arm in arm, they walked calmly across the forecourt to the other side of the near-deserted street, whilst Chester fought to conceal his discomfort. It was a Monday evening, and most people were still recovering from their weekend activity.

She helped Chester into the passenger's seat and ran around to the driver's side of her black Ford Model T. Leaning in, she turned

293

the key, set the spark lever and emergency brake, then gave the throttle lever a slight knock. Moving to the front, she pushed in the crank handle and paused briefly to pray before giving it a turn. The engine puttered to life with a far less impressive noise than her Tabloid had given her. Glancing up and down the streets in fear of federal agents, she climbed into Thin Lizzie, as the previous owner had called it.

Now came the hard part. She placed her left foot on the gear pedal and her right on the brake, giving the engine a touch more throttle before releasing the emergency brake and depressing the gear pedal into first, causing the car to ease forward.

"You're not making that look easy, Kath."

"That's because it's not easy," she said distractedly whilst she gingerly gave it more gas and allowed the gear pedal to spring up into top gear as they sped out of the small town that would one day be considered the capital of the free world. Thin Lizzie managed forty miles per hour as she wound through the Virginia countryside towards Gainesville.

Of course, the FBI followed and of course Olga knew they would, but if she saw them at all, she wasn't ever sure. What she did know was that they would never let her fly away, they were just hanging back, hoping she'd lead them to someone else. But if there was a British intelligence command structure in North America, then Major Brathwaite was the supreme commander until someone else more important turned up. She also knew they would never believe a woman would be capable of anything like that, let alone be trusted by the British government.

"Chester? Are you feeling any better?" she asked, giving his knee a gentle shake, whilst glancing in the mirror at the headlights behind them.

"A little, why?"

"Your friends have found us and I need you to take the wheel whilst I deal with them. Can you drive?"

"No, I never learned."

"Well, the gas is set, you can slow us down if you need to with this lever," she said, grabbing the throttle, and we're in gear, so take the wheel and follow the road. That," she said, pointing at the brake pedal, "is the brake."

She took his wrist and placed his hand on the wheel, "that's it, minor adjustments, good. Watch the road not me!" she said as she climbed into the back seat and started rummaging around.

"I picked this up from an Italian general in Zürich, it fires automatically."

She produced a Villar Perosa sub-machine gun, a strange contraption with twin barrels, twin actions and twin thumb triggers. It took two twenty-five round magazines that a careless operator could discharge in seconds, so Olga made sure she had spares ready to go.

"Automatic, like you don't pull the trigger?"

"No, it means you don't have to work the action after each round," she said impatiently.

When she was satisfied the weapon was ready to fire, Olga reached forward and slowed the car.

"Whoa, hey I coulda done that," Chester protested.

"Sorry," she said watching the headlights grow larger, whilst groping around in the dark for the roof latch, "ready?"

"What for?"

"For this," Olga shouted, yanking the lever and causing the roof to fly open, then backwards, trailing behind the car for a moment before the hinges gave out and the roof took off like a kite in the direction of their assailant. The car behind swerved to avoid the huge piece of debris and Olga wedged the bipod legs in between the seat and the rear bulkhead.

"Slow right down, half throttle," she commanded over the buffeting winds.

"Half throttle," Chester repeated as the car slowed and Olga's thumbs caressed the knurled trigger paddles. The headlights grew larger, and Olga strained to make out the occupants through the glare as her hair whipped about her face. She fired the first burst low and it hit the road in front of the car, panicking the driver, the next burst hit the engine and steam billowed, causing him to slow.

"Slow down," she called, "quarter throttle."

Another three-round burst hit the passenger, who was leaning out of his window and aiming a huge revolver. He convulsed and slumped down in his seat as the driver recoiled in fear but did not slow. Olga let him have it too, sending more bursts through the steam and although the driver fell forward, the car did not slow. It must have had the same kind of throttle as Thin Lizzie. She emptied the rest of one magazine into the block and the engine finally gave out.

"Okay, stop," she said, "throttle right back, now brake and press the left pedal halfway."

The car lurched forward. "That's too far, ease off the left pedal."

Olga reached around him and hauled on the emergency brake, which both slowed the car and engaged neutral.

"Leave⌐—" the distinctive sound of lead flying past her ear cut her short, "—it running," she finished, turning to see the silhouette of a third man walking brazenly up the centre of the highway. Olga let him have the other magazine, reloading before she checked to see if he was neutralised. The Villar Perosa was too unwieldy for carriage in combat, so she reached forward and took her thirty-eight from Chester's pocket and gave him back the emasculating Browning.

"Think you can handle reverse?"

"Only one way to find out."

"That's the spirit. Foot on the brake, press the middle pedal and release the hand brake."

She manned the Villar Perosa as they drew nearer, dismounting when they passed the man in the road. Gun up, she approached him slowly. When she stood over him, she drew back her right leg and kicked the agent between the legs with all her might.

"He's dead," she called to a wincing Chester when the man failed to react. Olga searched the body and found a wallet and a badge she didn't recognise, along with a photograph of her. She turned it over to see the words hysterical woman jump out from among other details from her army paybook, along with a description. Olga's blood ran cold, because this was serious and it was time to get the hell out of Dodge, or Gainesville. She sprinted to the wrecked car and searched the bodies for her photograph, taking any weapons and ammo she found.

"Time to go," she shouted, jumping in the car. Chester deftly pulled off and sped up to forty, leaving three dead federal agents in the road for someone else to find.

"I can never go back now, can I?" Chester asked, his fear pushing his voice up an octave.

"No, you can't, but if it's any consolation, this invasion will be bad and the government is going to forget all about us whilst it deals with the largest army ever assembled."

"Would it surprise you to hear that none of that consoles me in the least bit?" he snapped, still shouting over the wind. "And if you're British, then why are you here telling me to go to the Whitehouse and rat out your own guys?"

Olga smiled nervously and Chester continued.

"Oh, I get it, they're done with you? What d'you do to make them so mad they ran you clean outta Europe?"

"As you might have noticed, I don't have a problem with killing people? It's my job, in fact. Mostly I travel around the world encouraging bad people off this mortal coil, or at least people who are bad for the Empire. Anyway, I was sent to kill someone I could not kill, I would not kill, and my boss... My boss is not the understanding type."

"I see, that's a pretty messed up thing for a broad to be doing, for anyone to be doing, for that matter. I s'pose you were grooming me for something? Don't worry, I got nobody else, I'm stuck with you and it's obvious to me that you could kick my Yankee ass six ways from Sunday, but I gotta know, Kath, is that how it is?"

"No, not at first. You approached me and we fucked, then we ate steak and I found out who you worked for. Then I started grooming you, but I never got around to exploiting you as an asset. I was going to feed you misinformation. Instead, I gave you the truth and it nearly got us both killed."

"Geeze, you got a mouth like a sailor."

"I am a sailor," she said tonelessly.

Okay, I'm a lawyer, I get lied to all the time and I have to bend the truth sometimes myself. I don't think you're lying to me, Kath, but I don't think Kath is your real name, is it?"

"No, it's not and if we get clean away, I'll tell you my real name in the air."

"The air? You're about to tell me you can fly?"

The plane hit the grass airstrip on fumes just outside of Guthrie, Kentucky, on the Tennessee border. Olga was exhausted and the taste of castor hung in her mouth, foul and pungent as ever. Chester, who had taken a severe beating, was fast asleep in his seat and Olga decided to leave him be whilst she figured out what to do. She picked up an electric flashlight and went in search of a solution. She knew this plane had taken them as far as it would when her light showed a frayed aileron cable and a disconcerting tear in the rear fuselage.

This was rural Kentucky in 1915 and no one was about at two in the morning. Their options were limited to stealing fuel, stealing anther plane, or stealing a car. Olga enjoyed flying far more than driving and they were in an airfield, not a car park. One hangar loomed large at the edge of the runway, still only large enough for two or three planes. Olga walked over and pulled on the lock, tutting at the poor standard and casting about for something heavy.

A rock made light work of the shackle and she slid the heavy door open just wide enough to slip inside. The weak beam of light produced by Olga's torch showed a Curtis Model D, a Martin Pusher biplane and something she did not recognise. Curious, she eyed the contraption for a moment before concluding that this was no time for learning a new skill and the Curtis would be the right choice.

Chester woke at the excruciating noise the hangar doors made when she slid them open, and after some exaggerated stretches, he limped over to help. Together they prepared the plane for flight, checking fuel, oil, and function. It was too dark for a full suite of checks, so they would be placing their faith in the owner of this plane, and it would serve them right if he was a lousy mechanic.

"What are we doing, Kath?"

"Stealing a plane?" she said impatiently.

"Why?"

"Because the old one is worn out and we need to keep moving."

"I mean where to?" he intoned, wiping grease from his hands.

"Oh, I haven't quite figured that out. West, obviously, but that's as specific as it gets, I'm afraid."

"And this invasion? The one that you had me ruin my life over? What about that?"

"Well," Olga said, closing the engine cowling and fastening the clips. "I plan to fight my own war, to give the American people a chance of pushing back this invasion and hopefully undo some of the terrible things I've done."

"I don't know much about that, but I'm willing to learn, and like I said before... I got no place to go."

"I know," she said, looking him up and down as she climbed into the cockpit. "I'm sure we could use a mascot."

She leant over and kissed his forehead before shooing him to the front of the plane and when she gave the signal, he started the engine by hauling on the wooden propeller. As the engine spluttered to life Olga couldn't shake the feeling that townspeople would emerge from the low-hanging mist and demand to know just what it was they thought they were doing, but they never came. The plane lurched with Chester's weight and when Olga gave him a playful nudge, he yanked on the chock and the bird surged forward.

Bumping along the dark airstrip was more than dangerous, but as Olga opened the throttle and felt the vibration of the engine, she smiled wickedly and realised that she was chasing adrenaline harder than ever, looking for it in everything she did, but she didn't care. What else was there, anyway? Rudi was dead to her, Carla was with him in Berlin, probably screwing all of his Nazi friends, and Clive had turned on her. She had Chester, but who was he really? A warm body on cold nights? Someone who she felt guilt over because she'd ruined his life? That wasn't love and she'd find out for sure soon enough when the chips were down and one of them had to make a selfless decision.

Then they would know.

The engine purred, the windspeed increased against her cheeks and the plane started to lift. Olga drew back on the stick and luxuriated in the rush of take-off, taking pleasure in Chester's obvious discomfort as he gripped the leather handhold.

~

Six months later, Olga lay on a rocky outcrop watching a heavily laden locomotive wind its way through the Beaver Valley north towards Salt Lake City. Besides the carriages crammed with colonial troops, there were flatcars sporting howitzers and pintle-mounted Lewis guns.

Olga had watched the same train twice before as it reached a remote spot in the Escalante Desert and disappeared through a tear in space time, ostensibly to supply fresh meat for the grinder that was the Columbia Valley. She cast her mind back to the painstaking work that had led up to this point.

"Not a sound from now on," Olga hissed as she motioned for the small group to stop and sink to their belt buckles amongst the rocks and shrubs. Ahead lay the iron rails and timber of the Las Vegas Salt Lake Railroad. The regular friction from the wheels of countless trains had left the upper surface pitted but polished, and it glinted now in the light of a full moon. The same moon illuminated the hands of Olga's Hunter, showing her that the next British patrol should be along any moment. Her fingers caressed the safety lever of the thirty-ought-six she'd carried since Wichita, an unconscious act of preparation, common to soldiers the world over.

She felt their presence before hearing the highly disciplined, near-silent footfalls of one section, three platoon, thirty-ninth Garhwal Rifles. Veterans of the Anglo-Indian Wars, these men had honed their already formidable skills in the Australian desert. Whilst others learned to march and hold a rifle, these soldiers were under the mentorship of the best the British army had to offer, and failure was not a notion they entertained.

Guarding a railroad might not seem like the job of an elite rifle battalion, but the havoc wrought by Olga's Guerrillas was such that the old men and reservists had to be replaced, and now it was her turn to raise the stakes.

Olga felt the eyes of the patrol combing the desert for anything abnormal, but what they really wanted to find was her. As ever, she was ready for a scrap, but she knew that on this occasion it would be her last. Outmanned, outgunned and if she was honest, outsoldiered, a firefight in the desert this evening would end with the blood of her team soaking into the warm sand.

Minutes that felt like hours passed as she watched the shadowing mass mask the shining tracks as they ghosted along their route. As with death, the last sense to function for the Garhwali would also be hearing. It was for this reason that Olga sacrificed precious seconds to allow the distance to grow between her and certain, ignominious death.

Signalling for her team to remain, she rose slowly to one knee and strained her ears for the padding of the guards. Satisfied, Olga thumbed her safety on and began to move quickly towards the tracks, followed by Sandy, a Navajo warrior deadly with both blade and rifle, who now carried the explosive charges he'd become adept at both making and placing.

Behind him was Jemima, a fierce woman of nearly six feet whose ancestors had been snatched from their home on the banks of the Gambia over one-hundred years before, by callous men who worshipped Mammon. Laden with bandoleers and Olga's old Italian machine gun, she pushed north to the limit of sight and sound, lest the Garhwali return. Limping to the south with a similar task was Braxton Bedford Lee, a seventy-year-old veteran of Shiloh, Perryville, and Chattanooga. His presence was allowed only under the solemn oath that in the event of likely capture, all involved would do their utmost to give Braxton a clean death, and that he should under no circumstances slow the team down.

Bringing up the rear was Chester, his rifle slung and in its place, a shovel. Silently he drew level with Olga, who directed him to begin digging away the sand from between the sleepers. When the holes were big enough, Sandy would place a hand on his shoulder and he would move on, allowing room to place a charge and run detonation cord. Each time Chester looked up from his task, Olga would be standing by the next identified weak point indicating where he should dig.

World War

When France and Germany went to war in March 1914, Woodrow Wilson had refused, like Sir Gerald Clive, to have any part in what the global community viewed as a border dispute. By September 1914, when Clive had given in to pressure from Francophiles in his own government and fears of an invasion of Britain, Wilson remained stoically neutral. The men at Remington, Smith and Wesson, and Browning however, decided that soon enough Wilson would make a deal with Clive to provide arms to the British, so they ramped up production on their semi-automatic rifles, side arms, and close-quarters shotguns.

When a junior aide had marched into his office one morning in January, talking of a British conspiracy to invade, he'd had the man interrogated, beaten, and released in the hope he might lead them to his source. Clive's man in the British embassy was more than helpful, assuring Wilson that this hysterical woman was the crazed wife of a British army officer attached to the diplomatic mission. He'd offered to go with the FBI agents assigned to the case and help track Mrs Kathleen Brathwaite down, he even had photographs to circulate. When all three turned up dead on the highway in Fairfax County, a nationwide manhunt began, but no one in government took the warnings seriously.

Two months later, an American terrorist blew up the government building in Ottawa, and without any diplomatic overtures or backchannelling, Britain declared war on the United States. Reports came in of huge numbers of troops at the Mexican border.

US towns were under attack from artillery and the naval installation at North Island was under bombardment from the sea. When the Canadian militia mobilised and began to march into New England, the National Guard was called upon and a state of war was declared.

"Mr President, might I implore you to meet with the German Ambassador, if only for a few minutes?" the Secretary of State, Robert Lansing risked for a third time that day..

"What for? We're at war, man! The French have just invaded Florida, goddamn it!"

"I believe they want to propose an alliance, for there are nearly two and a half million ethnic Germans in the US and they will support the move."

"What can they do? They're tied up in France."

"Well, Mr President, it's not the Germans so much as the Russians who will help us."

"Goddamn it, Lansing, we cannot align ourselves with Russia! The Jewish population will not stand for it and they're even greater in number than the German Americans."

"Okay, Sir, but a lot of those German Americans are also Jews."

"I can't do it-"

"Sorry to interrupt Mr, President," an aide whispered. "I'm getting reports that we have lost San Francisco and Seattle is under attack from the north."

"Goddamn it, tell both the German and Russian Ambassadors I'd be glad to see them," he said, and his face fell forwards into his hands.

He was right, though, and great swathes of the American Jewish population were outraged.

That was when Clive announced his treaty of Zion. He promised that if Britain emerged victorious against their former colony, he would create a Jewish sovereign state and provide military aid for as long as necessary. All that was required was the service of one adult from every family, and that would qualify up to three generations for citizenship. Hundreds of thousands crossed the battle lines, some to be shot in the back by their former comrades, whilst others were threatened into staying.

"Gentlemen, allow me to speak plainly," Wilson said when the two ambassadors were seated in the oval office. Roman Rosen sipped tea and stroked his immaculate beard whilst his German counterpart, Heinrich von Eckardt sat rigidly and refused offers of refreshment.

"I've got Mexicans and Frenchmen at my southern border, the British Indians on the west coast and the Canadians in the north. What can you do to help me, to help the American people?"

"Everything," Rosen said nonchalantly in accented English.

"We are prepared to assist you with all the means at our disposal," von Eckardt said flatly.

"Okay, look, we have all the money and natural resources we could ever want, but we need time to train an army large enough to beat back this invasion. Clive just put two million colonial soldiers in California, two million!" Wilson pinched the bridge of his nose and began pacing the room.

"We have six million men equipped with German Gewehr 98 rifles ready to cross the Bering Strait, and the Tsar's armies have been making the painstaking journey eastwards since the rumours began."

"So, if I had refused the alliance?" Wilson asked, but the Russian ambassador just shrugged and took a sip of tea. "What do you want from America in return?"

"Alaska, Yukon and the Northwest Territories."

"What am I supposed to do with the sixty-some-thousand Americans living in Alaska?"

"Whatever you like, Mr President. Remember, if we win this war, you will have the southern provinces of Canada. Relocate them?"

"Okay," Wilson said, staring at a map of the vast tracts of land for which he was responsible and the land between, which he stood to gain.

"How are you going to move six million men from the Bering Strait to Vancouver in time? It's close to three thousand miles, through some of the harshest terrain possible."

"That's where we come in. Whilst I must acknowledge the hardiness of the Russian soldier, the time it would take to march that distance would likely render our assistance pointless." Von Eckardt cleared his throat. "Have you heard of Count Zeppelin's flying machines?"

"Those balloons?" Wilson asked, his eyes widening with incredulity.

"An airship is much more than a balloon, Mr President. But the pertinent fact in this instance is that these airships have a payload of between fifteen thousand and thirty thousand kilograms."

"Sure, what's that in American?"

"It's five hundred and fifty Russian men with rifles and the German Empire has over two hundred Zeppelins," von Eckardt said with pride.

"I see where you're going with this," he said, nodding as he did the calculations, "an airborne invasion of Vancouver, wow. But that's only one hundred thousand men?"

"Indeed, we don't expect too much resistance, and we will continue to ferry troops in this way and by ship until the army is in a position to march on Washington. Now, our wider aims if you will allow me, Mr President... Russia would like more of Asia and when the time comes, it would like naval assistance in the far east."

"Of course, that can be arranged, if we still have a navy."

"Germany would like Western Europe, including Britain. Also, we plan to take most of Africa and some of South America."

"Whatever you say. When can you begin the invasion of Vancouver?" Wilson asked impatiently.

"Soon. We are ready and the Zeppelins are already making their way from Silesia. But first, I have to ask, what do you plan to do with all of the displaced Jews?"

Wilson hadn't given it any thought, but as he stared at the map, his eyes fell on Quebec and he thought of the back-stabbing French.

"I'll give them Quebec. I'll announce it tonight. Stay neutral and you shall have Quebec," he repeated.

Zeppelin, 1915

Hauptmann Otto Kessler had no idea that his grandson was Reichskanzler, but he did think that Horst Buchholz was a good leader and was pleased to have won a place last year on his new fast-track officer program. After the horrors of France and the fierce hand-to-hand nature of the fighting there, he'd felt ready for anything, as long as it was a change from the putrid squalor of the trenches. The Reich wanted experienced NCOs to train as officers and lead units of Russian peasants. The pay was the same and after the war he would leave the army anyway, so what was the difference?

They key difference was the language barrier. Otto spoke no Russian and his NCOs spoke no German, he only had a handful of translators from the ranks and was forced to trust them implicitly with his orders. In training on the Lavrentiya Bay that was fine, but when the chips were down and men's lives were at stake, Otto needed more. He'd begun testing the trustworthiness of his interpreters with subtle tricks and found most, if not all, to be honest. To his favourite, Ilya Tomchek, he gave a special status and made sure the man felt he owed everything to his captain. There was no going back to the ranks for Yefreytor Tomchek.

Instead of relying on him he took lessons from him, and learned the language during the long Russian winter. This was no period of rest for Z Company, Third Lodz Regiment. Otto took his NCOs to one side and explained through Tomchek that if they wanted to retain their rank in his company, they would need to learn some German. He would meet them halfway, but when the bullets started flying, he couldn't be relying on interpreters.

He drilled them hard, and had the engineers build him a house to practise urban fighting. He knew the British and he understood how they fought, but were Canadians the same? His Colonel seemed to think Vancouver itself would be an easy victory, and the army would soon push south into Washington, but rumours circulated of an enormous Indian army with fearless fighters, deadly with both rifle and tulwar.

"Otto, my good man, this war will be one of rivers."

Oberst Schumann was the kind of man who would address his subordinates by their Christian name, whilst reclining in an office chair with his boots on the desk, a desk he did his utmost not to work at. But it was too damn cold for that so instead both men huddled around a potbellied stove, wearing every stitch of clothing they could lay their trembling hands on.

"Rivers, Herr Oberst?" The name thing didn't work both ways.

"Rivers, Otto, first the Fraser River, which we shall fly over to land on its southern bank. After that, we head south into the US, and bypassing Seattle, we head straight for the Columbia River. Here I expect there will be a bloody battle, one of the decisive battles of the war. Remember, Otto, we are the liberators, the locals are on our side, all we need to do is rearm them and cut off the British forces."

"I really hope it is that easy, Herr Oberst."

That was as far as Otto dared to go, but the colonel knew that he didn't believe him.

"We'll find out soon enough, my boy, the Zeppelins will be here tomorrow lunchtime and we will depart as soon as the groundcrews give the okay."

"They look like rail cars," Tomchek said, staring at the seemingly unending rows of troop transporters.

"Let's take a look," Otto suggested, as he heaved the door open.

"Good afternoon, Herr Hauptmann, my name is Bergmann, I'm the loadmaster of this shuttle," Bergmann announced. He appeared to live in the long, thin box and gestured with the coffee pot he was holding at the cramped space behind him. About eight-feet wide, with wide shelves running along each thirty-foot side wall.

"Excellent, is this a storage variant?" Otto asked with a wave of his hand.

"Well, no, each shuttle takes sixty men. You see, you'll lie down head to foot on the benches and each side has six rows."

Otto stared at the cramped compartments he now understood to be bunks.

"And when it comes time to disembark?" he asked.

"Ach, so. The top three rows of each side will climb down and line up to disembark, followed by the lower three," Bergmann said uncomfortably.

"What if there is an emergency?" Tomchek demanded. Bergmann replied tersely in fluent Russian to Tomchek, whose gaze narrowed at the words. Then smiling at Otto, he pointed at several axes mounted along the rows and wrapped his knuckles on the plywood skin.

"Gott im Himmel," Otto sighed.

"Where do we piss and shit?" Tomchek asked.

Bergmann pointed to a trap door at the very end of the shuttle.

"How many per Zeppelin?"

"On the Bodensee? Six, two rows of three." Bergmann said, glad to be back on firmer ground.

"That's overloading the Zeppelin," Otto exclaimed.

"Ja, Herr Hauptmann, you are right that it used to be fifteen tonnes, but we have a dispensation from the Admiralty to increase that to twenty tonnes in wartime."

"You mean when transporting Russian troops!" he countered.

"I couldn't possibly comment. If it's okay with you, Herr Hauptmann, I have some final checks to complete."

"No, Bergmann, it is not okay, and I will be back here in twenty minutes with my company to see if we can actually fit."

Otto watched as each man filled into the cramped shuttle and wedged himself into a bunk. It was a wretched sight and conditions would not be different for him or any of the other officers, nor for Bergmann and his colleagues, for that matter. Schumann, who would arrive later, was not interested in the welfare of Russian peasants and a handful of social-climbing farm boys. Otto had no choice; refusal was desertion and desertion was death.

All he could do was spend an hour rehearsing their exit procedure until his men stood an outside chance of escaping in an emergency. Otto ordered a hot meal and scrounged a double ration of vodka for every man. It was a sixteen-hour flight and he wanted them to sleep for as much of it as possible.

"This is madness!" Kapitanleutnant Gunter 'Glucklicker' Neumann said, with all the emotion that strict naval discipline would allow.

"I don't like it any more than you do, Gunter, but this has come down from the top, and word on the Strassen is that Buchholz is something of a dilettante physicist. Apparently, when he showed his calculations on air displacement to Planck and Einstein, they concurred. Besides, they are only Slavs."

"I don't know what to say to that, Herr Fregattenkapitän. Of course I will follow your orders, but I would like my concerns noted, because this seems like an unnecessary risk to human life."

"To subhuman life, Kapitanleutnant," his superior sneered, with a notable change in attitude. "Your concerns are noted, as are your racial sympathies towards the Slav."

Neumann threw up a parade ground perfect salute and again, within the bounds of naval discipline, he stormed from the office and out onto the vast, frozen plateau filled with hundreds of Zeppelins and thousands of the infernal shuttles. He didn't give a damn for racial purity or for Buchholz and his schoolroom scribblings; this was war and Glucklicker Gunter knew war. Then he recalled the medal that hung at the Reichskanzler's neck and thought again. This man, whatever his shortcomings, had once been an officer too, had led men into battle, so he too must understand the burden of command.

At one hundred twenty metres long and eighteen wide his instrument of war, the Airship Bodensee, loomed menacingly overhead. Though far from the largest in the Imperial Naval Airship Division, she gave him an immense feeling of pride every time he gazed upon her bluff lines. Hung like the testicles of a great beast were the four powerful Maybach engines that propelled her through the sky and protruding ominously from the main gondola were the barrels of the eight MG08s that protected her. He thought of his orders and of his crew, resolving to do his best for them and for the wretched souls swinging beneath.

Bergmann supervised loading, because that's what these men were to him. Cargo.

He had them shuffle down the aisle and crawl into their assigned space, until the soles of their boots were an inch from the helmet of the next man. When all fifty-eight men were confined to their bunks, he smiled at Otto nervously and produced a pair of folding chairs, setting them aside.

"Just a moment Herr Hauptmann," he said, holding a finger aloft and disappearing. Bergmann emerged with a cart filled with hot stones. With thick gloves he placed them throughout the length of the narrow corridor. "We will push them through the latrine hatch when they cool," he said, answering the question on Otto's lips. Unfolding a chair and setting it down, he gestured Otto inside, then swung the front of the shuttle closed before climbing onto the roof.

Otto could hear him rattling shackles and checking fastenings as his footfalls reverberated around the flimsy box. In the darkness, Otto watched through an open hatch in the flat roof as the great silver behemoth blocked out the sun. Men began to shout commands and the shuttle lurched, then swung gently from side to side.

A short while later Bergmann dropped down through the hatch, rubbing his hands against the cold. He unfolded his chair and fell into it with an exaggerated sigh, finding sleep almost instantly. Otto listened to the snoring of over fifty men as they swayed gently, and he studied his map by torchlight. This Zeppelin was carrying his entire company, all crammed in like sardines and hopefully resting. Before long, sleep claimed him too.

Otto jerked awake in his chair to the sound of a telephone, which Bergmann answered holding the handset whilst stifling a yawn.

"Ja, alles in Ordnung. Schön, tschüss."

He replaced the handset and rose from his chair, stretching his arms.

"One hour," he said solemnly before walking to the far end of the shuttle and throwing the rocks through the open hatch.

"Wake up," Otto called in Russian, "wake up there."

He watched as each man struggled against the confines of the inhumane space. They woke up and his patience left him.

"Tomchek, hand me that axe." Otto instructed the men on the upper bunks to climb down and to help him dismantle the shelving and pile the wood up underneath the lowermost bunk.

"Herr Hauptmann, please, I will be sanctioned for this, please!" Bergmann pleaded.

"I'm sorry, Bergmann, but this could be the last hour of these men's lives and I won't have them spending it penned in like cattle."

When they had finished, two benches on each wall remained and the men had room enough to sit comfortably— though still shivering   and prepare themselves for the coming battle. Bergmann sat in the corner, staring at the wreckage of his shuttle, his sole responsibility and the source of all his future woes.

"Come with us, I could use a man who speaks Russian and who knows, you might like it?" Otto suggested, noticing Bergmann's dejection.

"Okay," he said after a long silence, "okay," he repeated, nodding his head.

He began to rummage through the tiny compartment in which he stored his worldly goods and produced a Luger in its holster with some ammunition.

"This is all we get," he apologised.

"That will do just fine, welcome to Z Company," Otto said, awkwardly offering a hand to shake in the cramped corner. "I wish there was a way to see down, without sticking my head through a latrine."

"The roof hatch," Bergmann exclaimed, as though Otto hadn't known it was there in the first place. "You'll want to bundle up against that wind."

As his head emerged from the hatch, Otto's face was assaulted with a blast of icy air, colder than anything he had experienced in Siberia.

"It's the altitude," Bergmann shouted in his ear as he pulled Otto up.

Watching the man move about, thousands of feet in the air, Otto realised that he might have underestimated Bergmann. He climbed with the agility of a teenager and showed no fear as he practically ran up the cables that suspended the shuttle from the Zeppelin, checking the security of his load. Otto looked at it now, an impossibly large flying machine that had traversed the whole of

Asia to pick him up and set him down thousands of miles away in less than a day. Remembering his reason for standing up here in the freezing slipstream, he lay on his belly and let his head hang out over the edge.

Below him were the snow-covered Tantalus mountains to the left, and Vancouver Island to the right, the contrast between these natural wonders against the vast, grey, blue mass of the Pacific Ocean inspired awe in Otto Kessler.

Beauty existed in many forms back in Germany, even in Siberia, but this was unlike anything he had witnessed before, and he felt humbled by its majesty. The coastline wound on southwards in a ragged sweep until the mouth of the Burrard Inlet. This was where they would be set down to face an unknown number of either British regulars or Canadian militia. Otto didn't know whether to expect a cake walk or the fight of his life, but he was determined to find out in time to give his men an outside chance of survival. He tugged at the flaps of his watch cap, adjusted his stolen flying goggles and burying his numb hands deep inside the sheepskin he wore beneath his greatcoat, he prepared for a prolonged period of discomfort.

After checking over his pintle-mounted MG08 and working the action a few times against the cold, Bergmann returned below and lit a fire with the splintered remains of his career.

As the cold slowly seeped into his very bones, Otto surveyed the ground below and took in the beauty of alpine lakes and snow-covered meadows nestled amongst the craggy peaks and raging rivers of the Pacific Mountain range. Occasionally he would see a logging camp or some kind of mining operation,; little more than a cabin and a tool shed. Otto risked a look at his map and recognised the Salish Sea.

Soon smoke began to billow from the roof hatch and Otto turned to warm his hands whilst he peered out into the mist over the harbour, trying to figure out what awaited his company on the other side. Eventually, just as he was able to make out their assigned landing zone, Kitsilano Beach on the north coast of the city, a strange noise caused Otto to search about in the hazy half-light of the predawn sky.

It was so quiet at first, an innocuous buzzing that Otto barely noticed over the thrum of the Zeppelins, but soon the sound rose until it became an all-pervading din, filling the ears of every soldier, sailor and airman in the invasion fleet. A black cloud of Avro 504D anti-Zeppelin fighters emerged from the mist that hung over the Fraser Valley.

Otto heard the familiar rattle of the Nullachtfünfzehn above his head and he craned his neck to see disconcerting jets of flame leap from the water-cooled machine guns of the Zeppelins. Now that his attention was not concentrated purely on the ground or perhaps because the planes had some effect on the clouds, he was able to see the immensity of the invasion fleet. Hundreds of airships carried thousands of troops and spewed millions of bullets at the approaching armada of planes. Otto looked to his left to see the loadmaster of the next shuttle was manning his gun, oiling the working parts, and readying it for imminent action.

The hail of lead produced by the Zeppelin fleet was devastating, ripping through wing and fuselage like paper. Some burst into flames and plummeted onto the jagged rocks below, whilst others produced plumes of thick, black smoke, choking the pilot and his comrades nearby, and yet some pressed on doggedly, determined to defend their home. At first it was just one or two overly keen flyers firing their Very pistols prematurely, but when the majority judged that they were in range, hundreds of flares rose high and sored through the air in flaming arcs that lit up the dawn sky and showed each man the precise location of his target.

Planes dodged and weaved, climbing high to avoid the tirade from the Zeppelins, and though each airship did have at least one roof gun, they couldn't fire. The five tonnes of additional cargo lowered their ceiling considerably, making them unable to reach sufficient altitude to vent their excess hydrogen, so the roof gunners could not risk firing without risking the entire airship. Consequently, the machine guns hung limp and useless in their pintles, whilst the men who manned them looked for other tasks somewhere deep in the bowels of the gas-filled behemoths.

When the pilot of the lead aircraft dropped an incendiary bomb on the airship Sassnitz, Otto looked on in horror as the great whale-like beast began to glow, lighting up what remained of the night. He fired wildly in the general direction of the planes as the fireball spread from bow to stern, spurred on each time it enveloped a new gas cell. The entire airship glowed like the sun for a moment until the fire within finally ate through the outer skin and flames consumed it, burning so hot that the aluminium frame began to melt. Only then did the whale falter, ceasing its elegant passage as the mess of cables and white-hot metal was pulled down by the weight of its cargo.

Otto watched the shuttles drag the flaming remains of the Zeppelin down as men jumped from their would-be coffins into the icy waters of the bay. In every direction the scene was repeated as bombs and flares hit their mark. Airships yet unscathed took evasive action only to collide with a burning comrade, catching the inferno second-hand. Otto looked up at his own, the Bodensee and prayed for the first time since school.

Never throughout his time at the front, crawling through putrid mud on his belly for hours just to drag a British officer from his bed in the night, or cowering in a dugout during a French bombardment, had he ever felt the need to call for help from a deity of any sort. His prayers were answered in the form of rain, which fell by the gallon down the sides of the Bodensee, misting in the slipstream and soaking him to the skin.

Neumann looked on in disbelief at the carnage about him and realised how helpless he was, how little control he had over the situation, until he slowly realised that his next move was the first step down a path to a place from which he could not easily return.

"Drop ballast," he ordered, "all of it, lose excess fuel and any other stores. We shan't need it if we go down."

"Ja, Herr Kapitan," Stindt said with a curt nod, before directing Bauer to the speaking tube to pipe all hands with the same order.

"Freiburg, find us a few possible landing sites," Neumann said as the airship lurched skyward with the loss of ballast.

"Ja, Herr Kapitan. Might I say that if you intend to drop the er, the cargo, we should do it sooner, so they land in the sea and so that they don't have as far to fall," he said nervously, fully aware of his overreach.

"Thank you, Freiburg," Neumann said stiffly, unready to acknowledge, or at least to voice his ghoulish intentions just yet.

For a long time, he stared out of the window into the night at the fate of the Bodensee mirrored as other captains failed to act. "You are of course correct. Do you think they can survive the fall now?"

Freiburg made a show of looking down from the gondola, his young features lit up by the glow from his burning comrades, and Neumann's mind was made up.

"Jettison the shuttles but warn them first."

The briefest of glances from his first leutnant was all the reproach he would ever have from a man such as Stindt. The order was relayed, and the specially designed release pins were allowed to fall into the sea, followed seconds later by the six boxes filled with Russian men and German officers.

The airship climbed at an alarming rate, pushing well above the ceiling of the British planes and the Bodensee's gunners were able to prey on them from above, finally pushing back after the carnage of the morning. Above the clouds, Neumann found other ships, and felt slightly better about his impossible choice. Beneath the flyers pushing their machines to the limit in an effort to reach the Zeppelins, were the thousands of men they had cast into the sea, in a bid to save their own lives.

No one had bothered to teach Otto Kessler how to swim, but swim he did, thrashing him arms wildly against the surging current, fighting against the weight of his heavy winter clothing. Despite this, the salty taste of death filled his mouth, then his lungs, and he could feel his life slipping away until fatigue finally claimed him. Weightless below the surface of the waves, he fought with his last ounce of strength not to give in to the primal urge to inhale.

"The invasion was successful, Herr Reichskanzler. We now have a foothold in Canada and our Russian divisions are moving south into Washington as we speak."

"The butcher's bill, Herr General?" Rudi asked, wearily dragging his hands down his face in an effort to remove the fatigue of three days spent hunched over his sand table.

"Ach, so." General Ludendorff hesitated momentarily to fidget with his cuffs, then looking up, he said, "Half, Herr Reichskanzler… Sixty thousand men."

"Sixty thousand men in one morning? What happened?" he demanded angrily.

"The Royal Flying Corps were waiting for us. The Zeppelins could not climb high enough to avoid the fighters, so many dropped their troop shuttles into the sea, whilst others went down in flames refusing to do just that."

"No, the theory was sound, the–" Rudi paused as it hit him, "the extreme cold weather, he had not accounted for the extreme cold. Gott im Himmel," he cried, pacing his spacious office in the Kanzlei. "How many airships remain?"

"Fifty, Herr Reichskanzler and they continue to shuttle men from Alaska to the American front. There is another matter."

"Out with it, man," Rudi spat at the general twenty years his senior.

"The Japanese have landed at Anadyr and their navy is attacking our troop ships. Admiral Scheer has dispatched U-boats to escort the convoys."

"Give me some good news. What of the Western Front?"

"Well, Herr Reichskanzler," Ludendorff boomed, pride buoying his usually dreary countenance. "The French are on the run. Many have fled to Spain or across the Atlantic to the new colony in the southern United States. Similarly, the British have retreated north across the channel, and France will be ours by the end of the month."

"Why didn't you lead with that?"

"You summoned me to discuss the American invasion, Herr Reichskanzler."

"Of course. Take a seat, General, and join me for a cognac," he beamed, pouring two glasses and handing one to Ludendorff. As the glasses changed hands, their fingers connected for the briefest of moments, and Rudi watched the knowing flash in his general's eyes. What he didn't expect was to gain some knowledge of his own. The documents he'd sent back from Munich in 1962, the Kaiser's army sweeping through Europe and crushing all who stood in its path, and a bomb, the plans for which he remembered. He had, however, never known the outcome of the scheme.

"Clive!" Rudi shouted, finally making the connection between the British spy in Munich and the man with which his life had become inextricably linked.

"What, what is happening to me?" Ludendorff said stiffly. "I think I must excuse myself, Herr Reichskanzler."

"Sit down, General, you are going nowhere," Rudi said, taking a seat in the second of two armchairs positioned by the magnificent fireplace as Ludendorff obeyed, a faraway look in his eyes.

"Who is Rudolf Kessler?" he said finally.

"I am. Tell me about the bomb, General?"

They talked for hours, filling one another in on the events of their various histories and as Ludendorff let the words spill from his mouth, he found a place of comfort in the chaos and he eyed Rudi and his position with a newfound thirst, for the office was his at one time and he would have it again.

"Where is it?"

"I don't know," she croaked.

"Tell me, whore!" The interrogator slapped her loose-jowled face with the back of his hand, cutting her with his ring.

"I never knew of any bomb," she insisted, jutting out her chin in defiance.

"Rüdiger, assemble the probes!" He gave it a dramatic flair every time he said it, knowing for some it was enough, but the hard, green eyes of this one told him he was going to have a fight on his hands. Braithwaite was silent as she watched Rüdiger's ministrations from her position tied to the chair.

Her greatest fear over the last three years of confinement was that the most powerful man in the German empire, the man she had bent to her will and whose every waking move she had controlled, would decide one day to visit upon her the hell she had manufactured for him. So for every day that did not happen, for every day she used the bucket in her cell when she felt like it, for every night she slept unmolested, she was grateful. Braithwaite understood the gravity of her sins, the treatment she truly deserved, and she had come to accept that if it existed, hell was undoubtedly her destination.

The man she genuinely feared, the man who would exact the kind of revenge ¬– the very thought of which had her pacing her cell in the dark hours before dawn – was Clive. If, when the British army marched along Unter den Linden, through the Brandenburg Gate and down into this cold, damp dungeon beneath Prinz-Albrecht-Strasse, if her records showed she hadn't talked, then Clive might just let her go home.

"Fertig, Herr Oberst," Rüdiger said, offering his superior the electrodes.

"Nein, Rüdiger, I want you to do it today, you have earned it," Schöenfeld offered.

"Jawohl, Herr Oberst," he said, rounding on the pathetic creature before him, naked and bound to the chair, "Zip Zap Zop," Rüdiger sneered, tapping the electrodes together with each syllable, causing sparks to fly and land painfully on her bare skin.

Utah, 1915

The train thundered down the tracks and Olga carefully removed a signalling mirror from its pouch at her belt, guarding it jealously from the light of the hot Utah sun. Two cairns, made of smooth, flat rock, had been placed to mark the point at which Sandy must detonate his charges and from Olga's vantage point, they aligned to show her exactly when to signal.

The spot she had chosen was one-hundred yards before the point at which the train had disappeared the last two times. Olga lay with one leg resting on Jemima's to allow silent communication through a series of predetermined messages. It was her task to watch the possible jump point, rifle trained on the track, ready to kill whoever approached.

Chester and Braxton lay in wait amongst the hoodoos to retrieve the teleportation equipment once the operation was neutralised. Olga brooked no discussion once they were out of the door on an operation and tactical hand signals or telekinesis were all that were permitted. She drove them hard, the velvet glove discarded long ago, but she also kept them alive and helped them to disrupt the unending waves of reinforcements arriving from the Mexican border.

This was their home, and whilst each had personal reservations about these united states and the way its citizens had treated them in the past, all could agree that a foreign imperial power would be unlikely to treat them any better. Besides, when this charming German woman entered their lives six months ago, they'd had nothing but the clothes on their backs and the meagre rations doled out by the occupation in Saint George. The Mexicans at least showed an equity of the contempt the held for all; man, woman or child, no matter their creed. This was particularly hard for Braxton to take as a formerly respected veteran and of course, a white man in a world where that was seen as some sort of accomplishment.

Olga spoke in the affected German accent even to Chester, although she left out the smattering of German words she often added when addressing the others. Her cover was far from impenetrable, but among this group, where discovery would likely mean death, despite all that she had done for the wretches, it was enough.

Chester, another white man used to a level of deference no longer afforded to him, even as Olga's man, was struggling more because this was a world in which he had very little to offer. A lawyer living outside of the law, but it was the law of Colonial Mexico and not Washington DC that he anxiously circumvented. He found the manual labour assigned to him demeaning and Olga rode him just as hard as the others, despite the fact that she was riding him and not the others. Gradually, over the last six months, Chester had come to resent Olga and to his shame, those she seemed to favour, although this favour was of course perceived. Olga took her operations seriously and only ever gave tasks to the individual most capable.

Sandy flinched, turning his eyes from the blinding light that fractions of a second later, he knew to be the signal. Automatically, he drove the plunger home and watched as his own signal travelled at one hundredth of the speed of light along the wires he'd buried under the cover of darkness. He must have been getting good at this, because the ground erupted in a chain of explosions beginning under the wheels of the locomotive and working backwards along

328

the underside of the train in a perfectly synchronised dance of mangled steel, smoke, and flames. With the engine, coal tender, and the first three carriages turned on one side and grinding to a halt in the dust, the remaining cars piled in behind. Wood splintered and men screamed as the mile-long train slowed from sixty miles per hour to zero in a terrifyingly short time.

Sandy was already running for the truck when Olga spotted the first operator darting out across the desert, but before she could raise her leg to kick Jemima, she heard the crack of the rifle and watched his head explode, forward momentum causing him to continue on for another few paces before, like the train, he piled into the dust.

Men began to emerge from the wreckage of the train, damaged and confused, some with rifles, even fewer with the presence of mind to use them. Further back, however, Olga could hear orders carried on the wind. Soon, organised men with clear heads and loaded rifles would descend on her position, and by then she needed to be gone.

According to plan, Sandy edged the truck out towards the suspected position of the teleporter and as expected, another operator emerged. He ran towards the truck, waving his arms and shouting something inaudible, then he dropped like a string-cut marionette before Jemima slid back her bolt and chambered another round.

From the far side of the truck, Chester and Braxton appeared, jogging steadily and concentrating on the ground. Though they were little more than stick figures to Olga, she could see Chester stoop for a moment and then as he stood up, he appeared to pull something.

Crawling backwards, Olga left her rock and together she and Jemima moved swiftly in the direction of the truck. The shouts and groans from the mangled bodies in the wreckage, drowned out the pounding of boots on the hard desert dirt and shouts of men as they salvaged guns or rescued their trapped comrades. Soon this momentarily dazed giant would wake and wipe out Olga's team with one meaty fist.

When she reached the truck, Chester was loading the last of the components whilst Sandy helped Braxton onto the flatbed. Jemima climbed onto the roof and began to check over the crudely mounted and hard-won Lewis gun.

"That's the last of it," Chester panted, sweat pouring down his face and coating his bare arms.

"This is going to change everything," Olga said coolly, patting Chester on the back. "Let's go!"

The petrol engine roared as Chester scrambled up the tailgate and Olga settled into the passenger's seat. Overhead, the Lewis gun began its familiar staccato rattle as Jemima did her best to deter the force assembling at their backs. Olga looked over to Sandy, his deeply lined face a mask of concentration as he navigated the treacherous terrain, and she fought the urge to brush away a stray hair that had fallen from his ponytail. Instead, she turned bodily, kneeling up and peering through the tiny rear window at Chester cowering in the load bed. Braxton stood over him, one hand on the frame, the other aiming his huge Colt Peacemaker. As Jemima sprayed bursts into the mass of pursuing soldiers, Braxton took carefully aimed shots with his revolver.

"Here," Jemima called over the roar of the engine and the hammering of her own gun as she passed the old rebel her thirty aught six. Braxton nodded in thanks and immediately took up a fire position, expertly making every round count.

"If this wasn't so verdammt desperate, it would be funny," Olga remarked as she urged the painfully slow truck to reach sixteen miles per hour.

"Ain't nothing funny about this," Sandy said flatly, without taking his eyes from the ground ahead. He tapped a huge, wizened finger on the glass cover of the fuel gauge. "Must've taken a bullet."

"Scheisse." Olga dragged a hand over her face and wracked her brains for a solution. "How did they power that thing out here in the desert?"

"I hope you ain't askin' me?"

"No," she said in her affected German accent. She checked her thirty-eight special and snapped the cylinder back into place before stuffing it into her belt and flinging open the door. She clambered out and edged along the running boards as hot lead bent the air around her and filled her nostrils with cordite. Crouching in the truck bed she cast about for a power source until her gaze fell on what looked suspiciously like a pair of batteries.

"What are you doing back here? You got a death wish?" Chester called over the din.

"Those swine shot out our fuel tank. If I don't get this working, we're about to be very dead or very captured." Olga shouted, as she picked off a particularly fast young rifleman.

"If we use it, we can't take it with us... What if we send them through it?" Chester shouted, jerking a thumb over his shoulder at the pursuing army.

"That could work," Olga mused, staring hard at the apparatus bouncing around in the truck bed and at the deadly cloud of dust that, for now, was falling behind. Exhausted, their pursuers dropped to one knee to deliver a parting volley at their quarry, but at the very limit of effective range, the three-oh-three did little more than bounce off the tailgate to frighten Chester.

"We have until our fuel runs out to figure out how to make that work. Braxton!" she shouted. "Did Sandy leave any of that dynamite? There in the crate at your feet, you old fool."

Testament to the respect he held for Olga, Braxton ignored the insult and began rummaging about in the crates for the sticks of homemade explosives.

"Chester, see if you can get this working. I'm going to build some IEDs to slow these Schweinehunde down and buy us some more time."

"You got it, Colonel," Chester said with a mock salute. Olga's head snapped around and he shrank visibly as her eyes seemed to burrow deep into his soul, silently reproaching his insubordination.

"This here crate is fuller 'an a cathouse on payday, there's twenty some in this'n and I rustled up one or two from Sandy's satchel."

"That's a lot of dynamite... I think I have a plan," Olga said quietly, and then leaning around to the driver's window, she said, "Sandy, pull up here and put the truck at an angle to the track, like it's broken down."

"Sure, I think I see where you are going with this," he said, wrenching the wheel over and braking gently, and then for good measure he blipped the throttle, causing a backfire and plumes of smoke to emanate from the exhaust. Olga peered through the dust and heat haze to see that the beleaguered Indians were about a mile away.

Twenty minutes, she thought.

"Jemima, get that Lewis gun up onto the high ground. Braxton, help her with the ammo, then get yourself installed somewhere useful with that rifle."

Braxton hesitated because he didn't want to fetch and carry for a black woman, but such was his compulsion to please Olga that he swallowed seventy years of ingrained racism to heft a crate and hump it up the hill behind Jemima.

With Chester's help, Olga set off with the teleporter about thirty metres away behind a substantial hoodoo.

"What the fuck is your problem?" Olga hissed. Her forearm had come up from nowhere and now it pressed hard against Chester's throat, his back to the hot desert rock. "Don't fuck with me, or I will end you, and no one will bat an eyelid. This is my outfit, my operation and it's under sufferance that I allow your dead weight to be carried."

"It's not your war though, is it," he gasped as she let up slightly. That earned him a painful dig to the kidney and as Olga stepped back, he slumped to the ground, coughing and spluttering the dust.

Olga had no idea how to work the device, so she just stared at it, breathing heavily as the adrenalin subsided. It consisted chiefly of a large suitcase containing batteries, a series of lights, switches, and three round dials in one corner. Bending forward, she confidently flipped an important looking switch. Lights blinked and capacitors whined as the device seemed to power up. The metre or so of space between two identical fire-hydrant-shaped terminals began to wobble.

When the tear in space time opened, Olga watched mesmerised as a full-scale battle raged before her. Men darted from slit trenches into the teeth of enemy guns, Zeppelins sailed through grey skies as mosquito-like planes harried their bombing efforts. The familiar smells of mud and blood and cordite filled her nostrils and a part of her felt the pull, the desire to be back in the shit with her life on a razor edge. The feeling was visceral, a need to kill and to test her mind and body to the very limits of human exertion. As suddenly as it had opened, the tear closed and she was back in the desert, back in her current reality and back with fucking Chester, the pussy.

"Why did you do that?" Chester whined.

"Why did you do that?" she mocked.

"What is wrong with you?"

"What's wrong with me? Nothing is wrong with me you, little bitch, I'm the fucking glue!"

"The what?"

"The goddamn glue that holds this outfit together. You, on the other hand, are little more than my scratching post. And lately, Chester, lately I feel that particular itch less and less."

"You really have lost your grip on things, Olga."

"Just go and see if Sandy needs a hand," she said dismissively. Chester felt the bruise at his throat and decided to comply.

Olga powered the device down and gathered it up in her arms. It was awkward more than heavy, but she struggled with it to a position just behind the high ground which Jemima had occupied with her Lewis gun. Olga found her arranging the ammunition to make reloading as quick as possible.

"Where's Braxton?" Olga asked. Jemima's nod tracked across to a rocky promontory with a commanding view of the area and the approaching troops.

"That old rebel has a death wish."

"Mmm," was all she got in reply. Jemima was a stoic woman, but the two had had heated words over the outcome of the civil war and the subsequent Emancipation Proclamation. Braxton's family had grown rich on the backs of people like her grandparents, and he'd laid down his life to keep them in chains. The common cause they both fought for now was only enough to keep blood from being spilled.

Olga's eyes darted from the old man to the dust cloud that would soon be within range and was brought back to focus when Jemima chambered a round on her Lewis gun.

"He knows not to fire until you fire?"

"I told him, that don't mean he'll listen, he's a stubborn old fool," Jemima said, without looking up from her ministrations.

"Olga."

She turned to see Sandy at the foot of the hill giving a thumbs up and a nod. A broad grin stretched across his leathery face and transformed it. Olga found him handsome in that moment, and something of what she had once felt for Chester stirred within her. She dismissed it because he was old enough to be her father.

"Give me a hand here, alter Mann," she said, smiling at Sandy as she jogged down the slope. A dusty old map had been folded and stuffed into a gap in the suitcase. She freed it and found that the whole of the western seaboard was broken down into grid squares. The northings and eastings corresponded to the numbers on two of the dials, the third had the word 'Alt' engraved into it and each point showed intervals of two hundred and fifty.

"The way I see it, we have two options. We can stay here and try to drop this entire army into the Pacific Ocean. Or you can nip back to base camp and bring the spare truck to get us all out of Dodge," Olga said, looking at Sandy for his thoughts.

"Live to fight another day," he said laconically.

"Genau, let's get this infernal contraption set up to take you home and hopefully, we can hold them off long enough to made good our escape."

On her belly, Olga crawled up the slope to Jemima's position, just as she began to let loose on the hundreds of soldiers that had filled the valley. Olga suddenly felt like she might not be the ferocious guerrilla fighter her team saw when they looked to her for guidance. Breathing in deeply of the hot, dry air that reeked of war, she steeled herself, summoned up the blood of her warrior father and her fearless great grandmother. Laying a reassuring hand on Jemima's shoulder and feeling her body vibrate with the recoil of the gun, she slipped away back to Sandy, her brow furrowed in consternation.

"I set it like you said, but all I see is darkness. Cold, damp rock."

"Let me check," she said, forcing patience for the relic of another time, wrestling with technology beyond even the greatest contemporary minds. "It's good, but I still don't get what this one's for?"

Her fingers ran over the ridged surface of the dial, and she wracked her brains. Alt, what could it mean?

Bugger it, she thought, turning the dial clockwise one increment. The destination changed before their eyes from dark rock to wet soil. Another and the soil became grass and trees where their camp was visible and more importantly, the spare truck.

"Go on then, old man, get that truck started and I'll move these... these fire hydrant things."

With due trepidation, Sandy stepped through, grunting with approval as he realised he was, in fact, back at base camp. Olga waved curtly and flashed a smile before shutting the device down. The earth shook and the air pressure changed as the blast from

Sandy's IED thundered through the valley. Olga wanted to assess the damage, to find out how many men were close enough to the unlucky one who opened the truck door and detonated the dynamite, but she had a job to do and where was Chester?

Each terminal had a dial on top and when she had placed them far enough apart to allow for the width of a truck, Olga fired up the device and tried turning one. The tear grew in height until it was both wide and tall, allowing Sandy to drive the truck through and out of nowhere, Chester appeared and climbed into the back.

"Fall back," Olga bellowed at the top of her voice.

She crawled up the slope with her rifle and surveyed the carnage below. The dust was gone, supressed by gallons of blood. Entrails, limbs and screaming men littered the valley, but yet more pushed on, weary but determined, vengeance in their hearts. Braxton's deadly, accurate fire continued picking men off and Jemima's steady, rhythmic shooting slowed enemy progress significantly. Olga flashed her signal mirror at Braxton and she watched with acute irritation as he waved her off like a bug.

"Go, take the gun and mount it on the truck, and send Chester up for this ammo."

Jemima didn't need to be told twice; she was gone before Olga built up her fire position. Although it had been the hoard of blood-thirsty invaders in Jemima's crosshairs, Olga had her weapon trained squarely on Braxton Bedford Lee, the obstinate old fool who would be captured, tortured, and would eventually lead them right to her position. She watched him for a moment, allowed him to take the shot he was clearly building up to and as his arm came up to draw back the bolt, she exhaled and squeezed her trigger. His finely-tuned senses heard the shot – the sound of his own rifle from the wrong direction, and his body tensed in the split second before

337

hot lead bore into his shoulder, ricocheting around his torso and tearing up his vital organs. Her second shot burrowed through his brain and extinguished his life.

Olga rolled clear and hurtled down the slope to the truck, turning her ankle in a narrow crevice. She howled with pain at the same time as the Lewis gun started up again, meaning Jemima could see the enemy and that Olga had minutes before she was captured. She knew that, not content with torture, these men would likely rape her, and that thought had her subconsciously wrapping her fingers around the grip of her thirty-eight. All the time wriggling and pulling to free her foot.

Chester lingered at the back of the truck, unwilling to run the gauntlet to help her, his weak mind calculating whilst her strong body heaved with fear. Olga watched in disgust as the man she shared a bed with, the man she had once lusted after, finally showed his true colours. The antipathy she felt towards him, combined with the fear of capture and the adrenaline already coursing through her veins, boiled over into a blind, uncontrolled rage, and gave her the strength she needed to pull herself free.

She was just in time to see Chester finally convince Sandy to drive back through the tear and to safety. Olga limped towards the truck as the sound of the army at her back grew ominously louder and the draw of her pistol and the sweet release it would offer grew stronger. They had never discussed it, but even the echo of the trauma experienced by Carla in another 1945 had marred her life and driven her to drink, perhaps even to national socialism and into the arms of Adolf fucking Hitler.

Olga collapsed to the ground by the device, surprised to feel an intense pain in her side, and when her hand clutched at the area, it came away covered in hot, sticky blood. This was it; she was alone and minutes away from either suicide or a fate worse than death. She looked at the suitcase handle, then at the terminals, half in this plain and half in their mountain hideout. Without thinking too hard, she slammed the lid shut. Grabbing the handle and using the case to stand, she hobbled towards the tear, taking care not to pull on the wires. It was so simple, like turning a sock inside out, she and the device would both step through and both be home free and back at camp.

Rounds struck the earth at her feet as the soldiers bore down on her, taking pot shots as they ran. Olga shuffled on as her heart worked overtime to pump blood out onto the ground at her feet, her boots squelching with every laboured step. She fell through the tear and with her last ounce of strength, yanked the wires from one terminal, causing the rip to close and the danger to abate.

~

Olga woke to the sound of hushed voices and the smell of burnt coffee.

"I ain't saying that I don't believe you, Chester, I'm saying that I want to hear it from her mouth. When she's fit and well."

The voice was Jemima's and it was the last she heard as she drifted back to sleep.

"It was only a flesh wound, but she's damn lucky the fever didn't take."

Through bleary eyes Olga could see Jemima leaning over her, fussing at the sheets and pillows. Groggily looking around, she saw the rest of her team, minus Braxton of course.

"Okay, she's awake, I'll ask her," Chester said impatiently.

"Hold your damn horses, child, she's just woken up after a gut shot!" Jemima reproached him.

"I don't care, she's a goddamn British spy and she's been lying to us the whole time."

"No," she croaked.

"Then explain this."

Chester dangled a British army paybook between his thumb and forefinger as though it were an item of dirty laundry. She knew she had ditched it in back in Gainesville with the rest of her incriminating belongings. Chester must have kept it as some form of insurance.

"I have never seen it before in my life," she said defiantly and with perfect sincerity.

"You can drop the act, Colonel Brathwaite, we know you're British."

Chester was looming over her now, brandishing the evidence like a weapon.

"That says I'm a male Colonel in the Engineers and my name is K. Braithwaite," Olga retorted.

"Yeah, that don't prove much of nothing," Jemima added.

"I found it amongst your belongings," Chester sneered.

"A trophy. I kill British officers all the time, I thought it might come in handy one day." She eyed Sandy, then Jemima. "Tell me neither of you never took something from a kill?"

They murmured affirmation and nodded.

"Okay then, how about this?" Chester produced a letter and began to read it aloud. "Dearest Olga, are you in good health? Splendid work recently, drop by the old place one weekend so I can bring you up to speed on the latest gossip."

"And what exactly does that prove?" Olga said haughtily.

"That a well-to-do Englishman writes to you in a familiar way and invites you to drop by the old place to catch up on the latest gossip." Chester affected a British accent for the last part, before shooting a triumphant glance at Olga.

"Let me ask you something. What is it you think I did before the war? What do you think I did that prepared me for the work we do now?" She waited for an answer, but none came. "I worked for the German government, for the Prussian Geheimspolizei."

"Lies," Chester shouted, "you're a goddamn British agent and you were sent here to sabotage American infrastructure ahead of the invasion."

"Quatsch, I am a German citizen. I have been helping you kill British soldiers for over half a year. Why would I do that?"

"Listen, we all know what you did to Braxton," Jemima said, speaking for the first time in Chester's favour.

"We had an agreement—" Olga intoned, the panic rising in her voice.

"No," Sandy cut in, "you made that rule, none of us much cared for it."

"Just admit it, Colonel Braithwaite—" Chester began to say, before Olga cut him off with a tirade in perfect German.

"Nein, ich arbeite für die Preussische Geheimpolizei, mein Name ist Olga Felsen und ich bin hier, um zu helfen, die verflucht Invasion zurückzuschlagen und eure Freiheit von der imperialistich Tyrannei zu gewährleisten."

No, I work for the Prussian Secret Police, my name is Olga Felsen and I'm here to help repel the damn invasion and ensure your freedom from imperialistic tyranny.

The words were fluent, spoken with vehemence and candour, but both Sandy and Jemima seemed to be unconvinced and were now looking doubtfully at Olga.

"Except those soldiers are not British, they're Indian and you Brits see colonial soldiers as expendable," Jemima intoned, the pain of betrayal heavy in her voice.

"That is true that the British feel this way and I'll admit that the Germans feel that way too. Not me, but the Schutztruppe have done terrible things in the name of Lebensraum."

Olga's voice was weak, her strength was fading, and the pain from her wounds seemed to have enveloped her; she knew she was fighting a losing battle.

"You have been lying to us the whole time!" Chester bawled. "And now you'll say anything to save your Limy neck!"

"Nein, I am Deutsch! Ask me anything about the Fatherland, anything," she said in desperation.

"I'm sorry but that dog ain't gonna hunt, we can't be takin' risks like this, not with our freedom at stake," Jemima lamented. "You gotta get on outta here, soon as you can walk."

"Ha, we can't just let her walk, she's a killer," Sandy spat, "and if we cut her loose like this, she'll die out there in the desert anyway."

"She can't be allowed to leave, to report back to her superiors or worse, to lie in wait for us to..." Chester trailed off, unwilling to say the words aloud.

"True," Jemima said, her narrowed eyes searching Olga's face.

"I'll go to the future," she pleaded, "the time from whence I came!"

Weltenzerstörer, 1920

Carla huddled for warmth in the layers of furs that surrounded her as the open-topped Mercedes Knight tourer bumped along the country lanes toward Broadlands. They were well inside the occupied zone, hundreds of miles from the fighting in the north. People were saying that Clive had overcommitted himself in the States and neglected home defence. Clive had been meeting with Madero in Mexico City when the U-boats had devastated the British Home Fleet as they sat in the harbour.

The invasion force, not depleted by heavy fighting in Russia this time around and meeting far less resistance, stormed through the south of England, bypassing London and only halting at the River Severn in the west. London was now surrounded by a ring of steel, a city under siege which seemed to be holding out for an impossible amount of time.

In the Midlands, the men and women of Birmingham had looted the factories of the famous Gun Quarter and armed themselves against the invading Hun. The plucky Brummies still held out, and the north continued to supply men and raw materials to maintain both use and manufacture of the weapons.

"Drive straight past the house around to the barn at the back," Carla shouted over the noise of wind and engine combined.

"Jawohl, Frau Göring," the driver replied.

Carla had married the dashing young infantry officer with movie star looks during a period of leave, after which he had transferred to the Fliegertruppen where he was an observer with aspirations to fly one day. She had wrestled with the knowledge of what he had done in another reality.

She had convinced herself that he was guilty more of weakness and complicity than any hands-on role. Carla was an intelligent woman who knew that this was no argument for innocence, but for her it was starting to feel like it was enough. After months of soul-searching whilst her betrothed risked his life at the front, she realised that she didn't care, she loved him and with Rudi in charge, none of that would happen, but human beings struggled to be honest with themselves and if she had been able to admit the dark, disturbing truth of her heart, she would have known that the danger, the knowledge of what the man was capable of when tested, had lit a fire in her that burned for him and him alone.

The barn was abandoned, Clive's men had clearly left in a hurry. The matting where Olga had practised martial arts was still there, soiled and peeling at the edges. Dust eddied about the rafters, highlighted by shafts of low winter sun. At the far end, on the workbenches built for her brother, lay the innocuous components that together could make a powerful weapon.

"Go to the house and find a study or file room, bring anything that looks like it could be plans or designs to the car," she said to her driver. The man shuffled away with a brief word of assent, his wooden leg causing him to bob rhythmically to the left with each step. Walter Bolle had been Göring's batman at the front and had been wounded at the same time. Charged with the protection of his fiancée, Bolle had accompanied her from Germany for this mission of the upmost importance.

With no need for secrecy after Rudi's appointment to the Kanzlei, Carla had ordered the microfiche turned into full-sized documents. However, she kept them in the safe of her permanent suite at the Adlon.

She flipped through the file folder now, looking for Rudi's time machine plans and found the cover page with the words Rudi's Zeitgerät written in a childish hand. Using the sketches he had made along with others he'd struggled to draw from his foggy memories of the time he spent under Braithwaite's influence, she'd found a lot of what she needed amongst the scattered parts. This would have been much easier for Rudi to do himself, but of course, he was running an empire at war.

Carla loaded the car herself and drove it around to the front of Broadlands, gazing with mixed emotion at what had once been a place of safety for her and her family. She stared up at the window of Olga's old room, watermarked and beginning to succumb to the ivy that had moved in since its abandonment. Olga had probably done the right thing. She had, unlike Carla, refused to get into bed with the Nazis and Carla should have admired or at least respected that, but her guilt had become distorted into a hatred of the woman and all associated her with.

Britain, Clive, sailing and to some extent, family. She had made it clear to Göring that she would not have children by doing the only thing a woman of the Reich could do about it. She had pretended to be barren. This did not quell his lust for her and they still made love with a mutual vigour and passion that some men lost when they discovered there was no heir to be had. She went to great lengths to prevent pregnancy, taking her temperature and monitoring her fertility cycle as best she could.

"My dear Carla," Rudi beamed, flashing an increasingly rare smile, "do you know what this is?"

"No, should I?"

"No, no one should, it wasn't invented for another thirty years."

Rudi sprang up from behind the huge mahogany desk from which he ran his empire and paced the office, feverishly leafing through the sheets of designs and scanning the notes. "This was Clive's secret weapon, this." He rounded on his sister. "This, Carla, will win us the fucking war!"

"Herr Müller," Rudi said, shaking the man's hand and watching as the memories flooded back, "I have heard only great things about you, my good man. You will be my chief technician on this project."

The sheer vanity and obsequiousness of the man prevented his showing even the slightest emotion, so Müller simply thanked the Reichskanzler and allowed him to move on as he recalled the construction of the Little Boy, the mission to bomb Petrograd and his horrific death. Ludendorff ran the project and with all involved having the edge of temporal echoes to aid them, it was a matter of weeks before a prototype was ready.

"Korvettenkapitän Neumann, this is Major Geiger and General Ludendorff, they have a mission of the highest importance for you and your crew."

Horst Buchholz had taken up riding when his doctor prescribed exercise after a stress-induced coronary episode had caused him to collapse alone at his desk in the Reichskanzlei.

"Now, your heart could heal, but there is a further matter I must discuss with you. We call it diabetic neuropathy, Herr Reichskanzler and I'm afraid we will have to take the fingers on your right hand."

"What causes diabetic neuropathy?" Rudi asked, absentmindedly inspecting his nails.

"Are you not concerned about losing your fingers, Herr Reichskanzler?"

"It happens every time. I already lost my toes, so I suppose I have come to see it as something of an inevitability."

"I'm sorry, Herr Reichskanzler, I don't understand."

"I don't expect you to, you are a mere Doktor of medicine, not Quantenphysik. The intricacies of the subatomic realm are for greater minds than yours, my good man."

"Do you mean to insult me, Mein Herr? Because I can leave if my advice and practice are not of interest to you?"

"Sit down, Doktor, before you find yourself practising on the inmates of Sachsenhausen instead of the great and good of Charlottenburg." Rudi's cold eyes fixed the old man with his small halfmoon spectacles and irritatingly neat goatee. He could ruin this man with a flourish of his gold-plated pen, but it would bring him no joy and Rudi knew it. He had tried to take pleasure from the suffering he inflicted daily on the unfortunates that crossed his desk, but the truth was that he was hollow.

The void in his soul from Olga's sudden departure on that train was a vacuum that no amount of excess would fill. He had tried it all: women, gambling, drinking, torturing Braithwaite, depraved assignations with inmates at one of his many camps and the amassing of large sums of money. None of it had touched the sides.

"How are you sleeping, Herr Reichskanzler?" The doctor asked, snapping Rudi back from his reverie.

"Hah, I drink until I pass out, that's how I sleep."

"Surely you understand that you cannot go on like this, Herr Reichskanzler?"

Rudi didn't reply, he simply leaned back in his chair and pressed a hidden button under his desk. His smile unnerved the doctor, who began to pack away the notes he'd made, shuffling the papers nervously. When the door opened, the old man spun around with such force that he lost his balance.

"What is this?" he demanded.

"Herr Reichskanzler?" Schöenfeld asked, his keen eyes darting from master to prey as a malevolent smile spread across his face.

"Oberst, is Rüdiger with you?" Rudi asked genially.

"Natürlich, Herr Reichskanzler," he said, stepping aside to allow the young man to join him at the door to Rudi's office in the Kanzlei.

The young man stood stock still, his broad shoulders and perfect posture making Schöenfeld look old by comparison. His youthful face, however, was pale and drawn, an echo of some childhood illness perhaps.

"Rüdiger," Rudi said, a note of joy in his voice that had not been there before. "How are you, my boy?"

Rudi struggled to his feet and limped over to greet his hatchet men. Although only ten years Rüdiger's senior, Rudi's hunched shoulders, his limp, his scars, and the chunks of flesh missing from the fingers of his right hand, showed a far older man.

After exchanging pleasantries and offering all three of his guests a drink, Rudi turned to the doctor.

"Doktor Neidhart, I have decided to offer you clemency," Rudi said, as though speaking to an old friend.

"Clemency, Herr Reichskanzler? What have I done to require clemency?"

"Don't come the innocent with me, Doktor, you know very well what you are accused of and if you continue with this charade, I will withdraw my offer and the Oberst will drive you directly to Sachsenhausen."

"Ja, Herr Reichskanzler," Neidhart said, knocking back the rest of his cognac with trembling hands and avoiding eye contact with Rudi.

"Good, now, I offer clemency only if you have the stomach to perform the amputation of my fingers right here, this very minute," Rudi said, silencing the doctor with his grotesque hand. "Rüdiger, your cleaver."

Rüdiger deftly worked the buttons of his greatcoat and opened it to reveal an array of blades hung from hooks in the lining.

"Ever prepared, like a boy scout," Rudi said with glee.

"Vielen dank, Herr Reichskanzler," Rüdiger said, his voice devoid of emotion.

"Now, you have thirty seconds," Rudi announced, as he slammed his hand down onto the desk.

Schöenfeld produced a watch and a Luger, the watch he held in the palm of his left hand and the Luger he held to the back of Neidhart's head. Rüdiger grasped the doctor's wrist and placed the stained handle in his reluctant grasp.

Neidhart's eyes darted from his Kanzler to the boy, to the cleaver in his hand.

"Fifteen seconds, Doktor," Schöenfeld whispered.

Neidhart raised the cleaver with a quivering hand and, pausing for the briefest of moments, he brought it down hard.

Rudi inspected the familiar deformity and nodded curtly to the doctor before limping to the fireplace and kneeling before it. Rüdiger was sweeping up the fingers and Neidhart had slumped into a chair, the colour drained from his face.

"Make him watch," Rudi demanded. Schöenfeld placed an iron hand each side of the doctor's face and with practised fingers, he parted the man's eyelids. Rudi smiled and thrust his bloodied stump into the glowing coals, cauterising the wounds. The smile remained and he showed no sign of pain or discomfort as the stench of burning flesh filled the office.

Clive stood staring out into an empty desert. He wore a black worsted suit, his jacket draped over a chair and his shirt sleeves rolled up. Still, sweat dripped from every pore and seemed to pool in the toes of his black Balmoral boots. The back of his shirt clung to him, and his thinning hair lay in limp strands, matted to his liver-spotted pate.

"Sir Gerald?"

"What?" he snapped, as the vice at his temples seemed to tighten.

"Hold this glass to your eyes." The speaker was Harry Mosely, a brilliant physicist who had turned down a position at Cambridge to join the Royal Engineers. When Clive had caught wind of this, he'd snapped him up and shown him the plans he'd been sitting on for nearly twenty years.

"Thank you, is it ready?"

"Just a moment, Sir Gerald, I have to synchronise both the singularity generator and the firing switch. There we are, and... fire."

The flip of a switch, the simple making of an electrical circuit was all it took.

If Clive had been able to see the bomb go off, he would have expected to see the ground open up and swallow it whole before closing again with equal rapidity. He was, however, too far away, so he didn't hang around, and stepping though his own tear in space time, he collapsed into one of the armchairs in his office at number ten Downing Street roughly forty-five minutes in the past – he wanted a moment to himself before he had to deal with the aftermath of his actions. The city was under siege, but Clive had evacuated all civilians and only maintained a few regiments of reserve artillery to keep the Bosch busy whilst he perfected his gadget.

The phone rang and Clive answered.

"Ah, Winston, how did it go? Excellent, do hurry back, I've got a bottle of '25 Perrier-Jouët on ice."

Moments later the First Sea Lord stepped into the anteroom, shaking an umbrella before placing it in a stand and opening the door as the champagne cork popped.

The broad grin spreading across his jowly face was lit up by the light of a thousand suns. Blinded, both men dived to the carpet and cowered as the glass from the high sash windows flew across the room, followed by all manner of debris from the street outside. The change in pressure deafened Clive and as the building collapsed around him, he knew this was it, thirty years of scheming and lying, planning and killing were for naught. He had murdered his own father in cold blood with a straight razor, only to fail, leaving behind him an empire in ruins and an island under siege.

As Henry Clive lay dying in the rubble of Downing Street, his last thought was one of bitter malice towards the man who had bested him, but then he smiled, remembering through the fug of his fading brain the likely fate of Rudolf Kessler.

"Herr Kapitän, we have lost elevator function!"

Moments later, the nose of the Bodensee dropped, and she headed straight for the River Thames at an alarming rate.

"Drop ballast, throttle back all engines and let go that Verdammt bomb!" Neumann cried over the tumult. The thrum of the motors calmed, and water coated the windows of the gondola as Müller's voice could be heard through the speaking tube.

"We are not over the target, you buffoon!"

"Müller, this is Neumann, drop that bomb this moment, we are about to crash."

As he said this, a flare from a Very pistol hit the gondola, smashing the window and lighting up the inside for every pilot in London to see. Almost instantly the steersman crumpled to the deck as bullets peppered the crew. Stindt's head flew back and he spun to stare Neumann directly in the eyes for several moments before falling. Bauer rushed to take control of the Zeppelin and was rewarded with a chest full of lead and a slow, painful death from a punctured lung. Neumann watched as they drove hard at the mass of glass that was Waterloo Station, but at the last moment the airship climbed, having dropped its mammoth payload.

Müller had pulled the lever and the great three-meter-long bomb tumbled from the Zeppelin. They were too low for optimum detonation, and once the fifteen seconds elapsed, the altimeter closed the firing switch, igniting the charges. This, in turn, launched the hollow uranium projectile down the two-metre gun barrel at a velocity of three-hundred metres per second, whereupon it collided with more uranium and the chain reaction began.

This process took less than twenty seconds and at that very moment, the airship Bodensee and her crew were vapourised, to become very much more than just a footnote in the history of the Great War.

As per doctor's orders, each morning Rudi would limp from the Reichskanzlei to the Tiergarten in order meet his groom, Bernhardt Faulkner. He would lead a palomino Arab, a mare who reminded Rudi of Strudel. He hadn't realised how much he'd missed his old cavalry mount, or the simple pleasure of riding, the connection between horseman and beast.

This had fast become his raison d'être. When he sat in his office, steadily ploughing the furrows of paperwork left by Hitler, a farm he never wanted nor asked for, he dreamed of Rosenknospe. When the idea of her smell filled his nostrils, he longed for the feel of her lithe muscular body beneath him in the cool morning air, steam rising from her hot flanks and her pungent breath. It wasn't only the horse; he spoke with Bernhardt of banal matters and enjoyed the absence of urgency that filled every other waking moment.

He knew he would die in office. He knew he would never love again, just as he knew that this, right now in the Tiergarten with

Bernie and Rosenknospe was as good as it was ever going to get for him. Often, they would pass by the bronze statue of Hitler commissioned by the DAP following his martyrdom. The strength of the bond he had formed with a man capable of such evil, such naked hatred, had plagued Rudi and he looked to Gustl for strength.

But Gustl hadn't known what Hitler would become, what he would do, Rudi had and he'd fooled himself into thinking he could steer him away. Instead, he was sucked in by the unique combination of charisma and impetus that had fooled millions.

Rudi looked about him in confusion as the wind seemed to increase, and the gentle susurration became an all-pervading roar. Rosenknospe whinnied and shuffled her feet nervously whilst Bernt looked at him, genuine fear in his dull brown eyes. Leaves were whipped up into miniature tornadoes before saplings and branches began to fly through the air at an alarming speed.

"We need to get you to safety, Herr Reichskanzler," Bernt called over the howling wind. But the reins were torn from his hand as Rosenknospe reared violently, crying out in terror as she sensed before the men that Hitler's effigy was beginning to topple, to rock on its stone plinth.

Rudi was thrown backwards from Rosenknospe, landing hard, the breath forced from his lungs. He stared up into the face of Adolf Hitler as it grew larger. The statue crushed his torso and Rudi lay motionless and dazed as consciousness slowly returned to him and he began to process what had happened. His heart pounded as it struggled to maintain pressure, filling his chest cavity with blood. The trauma of the impact and the resulting exertion caused Rudi's heart to fail and to stop supplying oxygen to his brain. He watched the sky darken behind a panicking Bernt, before he too faded from view and all was black.

Epilogue

Henry Clive had ripped a hole in the very fabric of time, then dropped an atomic bomb into it. Rather than tumble through the skies over Berlin, the nuclear weapon's firing circuits were immediately triggered when exposed to the singularity, causing it to fire and detonate instantaneously.

The Mexican desert was torn open violently, as a singularity with a gravitational pull over one trillion times stronger than that of earth began to consume matter at an unimaginable rate. Soon the entirety of Central America had been sucked into the gaping maw of the black hole. The mass of the void increased and the speed with which it devoured the earth slowed as the radiation produced countered the black hole's intense gravity, generating a whirlpool between North and South America.

The great mass of water from both the Pacific and Atlantic Oceans was drawn to the event horizon, only to be driven over land, flooding the deserts in the north and the rainforests in the south. The photons orbiting created a glowing ring brighter than the earth's sun. This blinding light stood in stark contrast to the absolute black of the hole itself, as hurricane force winds tore through the northern states and the Amazon with devastating effect. The winds from America ravaged shipping and ran it aground as the oceans receded at the coast of Europe. The draw from the west caused the waters of the Mediterranean to rip through the Strait of Gibraltar, flooding both Tangier and San Roque.

A week later, Olga stood at the precipice, having set the machine herself which she held in one hand whilst she flexed the other for want of a weapon. The truth was that the others were scared of it, they had seen what it could do and were wary of the consequences. In short, they wanted the contraption and the interloper gone from their lives for good.

"I'm sorry you couldn't trust me, but you'd do well to cut out the deadwood, because Chester will get you killed," she said coolly, in a faultless British accent before stepping through the rip to Berlin in the year 1961.

Olga watched from her Mercedes as Henry Clive stepped out onto the Kurfürstendamm and inhaled the warm night air. This was Clive, but not as she knew him, scuffed shoes, loose tie, and unkempt hair, he seemed calm and unburdened. Although his bearing still bore the hallmarks of a seasoned operator; eyes darting about and avoiding the subtlest of potential threats, Olga felt sure that this was Clive's first go round on the carousel of living and dying that she was now all too familiar with. She screwed a silencer onto the barrel of her Walther as he sauntered away towards the ruin of the Gedächtniskirche.

Olga let him reach the corner of RankeStrasse before stepping out of the car, her pistol safely concealed inside a tan rain mac. Her heels struck the cobbles and reverberated around the deserted damm.

"No, thank you Shatze I'm not looking for any company," Clive said casually as he turned to see the source of the noise. "And I'd get yourself indoors, it's about to rain."

"Ha," Olga barked humourlessly, "You'll get what you're given Henry my boy!"

"Who is that? Harriet? How do you know my name?"

"I know a great deal more than that Henry Clive; I know your deepest, darkest secrets."

She was metres away from him now, close enough to smell his cologne and his sweat.

"I warn you, I'm not afraid to strike a woman, I learned that the hard way during the war."

"Just you try it old man," she said, bringing the pistol to bare and keep well beyond his reach.

Clive stood his ground in the shadow of the ruined church, sizing up his assailant with an expert eye.

"I don't suppose you brought that just to make a point, did you?" he said fatalistically. "I know those eyes; I see them every morning in the mirror. Tell me, have you killed so many that you've lost count? So many that it no longer leaves you reeling from the knowledge that another human being has ceased to exist because of something you did?"

"Come on let's get on with it," she said with a nod and slight movement of her pistol.

"Oh," he said with delight, "you've begun to enjoy it, haven't you my dear?"

"I'm certainly going to enjoy this one," she said impatiently.

"Come now, if I'm to die this night, surely I might be afforded some last rites?"

"Try me?"

"I have three things I would ask of you."

"Get ready to hear me say no."

"The first is easy; a cigarette?"

"Fine," she sighed, "keep moving, that's it, through that gap in the fence. Now. Kneel, place one hand on your head and retrieve the cigarettes and lighter with the other."

Clive rummaged and Olga prepared to shoot him even though she didn't want to, not quite yet anyway.

"Slide them under the fence and lie face down with your hands interlocked behind your head."

A lit cigarette fell to the floor next to his face and Olga nodded for him to return to kneeling.

"The second thing?" she demanded.

"Tell me why? Lord knows I've done plenty to deserve it, but what particular act of violence, malevolence, or spite affected you so much that you come here tonight to execute me on the KU-Damm?"

"I'll answer that in good time, what's the third request?"

"Just a ruse my dear. The vain hope that I might stall you long enough for a passer-by to save my bacon. I suppose you should get on with telling me what I've done to deserve your wroth."

"Up," she said nonchalantly, with a jerk of her gun. "Turn around and walk forward."

Olga squeezed through the gap in the fence and came up behind him, pressing the tip of her silencer hard into the small of his back. With her teeth, she removed the glove form her left hand and placed it on the bare skin of Clive's neck. He stiffened and she stepped back, while a carefully placed boot to the knee put Clive back on the ground.

"What the bloody hell was that? Some new Hallucinogen?"

"No, Clive, that was a glimpse of what you are capable of, and the reason why you must die."

Olga put two rounds into the back of his head and one more into his torso where the heart might be.

If he had one, she thought.

Walking briskly back to her car, tears streaming down her face as she stifled the violent sobs that threatened. Sitting behind the wheel she finally broke down and cried for every life she had taken, both on Clive's orders and otherwise. She cried for the time wasted without Rudi in her life, for the repeated failures and for the suffering her meddling had caused so many millions of people.

This time, though, this time would be different. She started the engine and Del Shannon's 'Runaway' was playing on the American station. As she pulled away a summer thunderstorm descended onto the city and rain beat hard on the roof on the car, she wound down the window to smell the air let her hand dangle as she sped along Unter den Linden towards the frontier and the eastern the sector.

~

As the S train rattled and the dim carriage lights flickered, Olga clasped Rudi's hand in hers and rested her head on his shoulder. She had made this journey many times, but she knew this would be the last – Clive was dead and nothing but that snake Torsten stood in their way now. Tonight she would have what she needed and he too would be added to the litany of collateral, of necessary sacrifices for the greater good.

Olga had relived that fabled day at the Müggelsee for a final time, but the knowledge of all that gone before; Rudi's betrayal and his rise to power hung in the air and soured their treasured memory. She tried to tell herself that this was not the man who had done all those terrible things, who had cosied up to the likes of Hitler and Himmler. Allowing his own sister to marry Göring after Olga had ended Carla's affair with Hitler by putting 9.7 grams of supersonic lead between his eyes.

As before, they had taken the rowing boat to a quiet spot on the far shore and made love in the heat of the Berlin summer, but it had felt hollow and neither had truly enjoyed it. The love was there, but the strength of feeling, the passion and the belief that nothing could ever come between them was dulled. Was it an old blade that could be worked and honed back to a semblance of its former glory, or was it a dying star – a glowing shell, a pale imitation of its former brilliance?

The singularity consumed in all directions, pulling at the Earth's crust, mantle and eventually the core itself. As it ate its way through the centre of the planet, the bed of the Indian Ocean opened up, draining it like a bath. From space the Earth was two blindingly bright rings of light separated by violently swirling clouds. From Berlin, it looked like the Götterdämmerung as fires caused by primitive electrics were faced with unimaginable forces of both wind and water. Bridges collapsed, small animals and birds disappeared over the horizon, along with anything not bolted down.

In a damp basement on Hackenberg Strasse, in the Berlin neighbourhood of Aldershof, Carla Göring fired up the contraption she had stolen from Broadlands. The batteries were crudely built glass jars filled with acid and the interface turned her stomach with its apparent simplicity. She set the year and turned the coordinates to zero. Outside the world burned, screaming, drowning, and pulling itself apart. She could not know it, but implosion was moments away. Carla inhaled deeply, picked up the suitcase and touched her finger to the metallic toggle switch. Exhaling, she fought every instinct in her body and flipped it.

The phased singularity tore another hole in spacetime and Carla stepped through into 1961.

"I don't need you to speak for me, Rudi, I'm not tired, I'm very much awake...It's you who needs to fucking wake up! The East is not a socialist utopia, it's a totalitarian nightmare," Olga screamed, pacing the room in frustration.

The rip closed behind Carla and she stared into the face of Torsten Schweighöfer – the rat who had destroyed her life ¬– guilty by association was the watchword of the Stasi in 1961 and Carla Kessler had been picked up the following day along with Lothar and her mother. All three were reduced to quivering wrecks in the basement of Normannenstrasse, before Carla was taken alone to Hoheneck Women's Prison, a forced labour institution with grey walls, grey uniforms, and grey-faced inmates with broken souls.

Meek was her defining characteristic in those days and meek was not compatible with that place, a place so dark and depraved that the inmates did not menstruate. This was not an intervention from the sadistic guards, this was an internal protest from every woman on every wing and in every cell. Carla did not believe it until she experienced it for herself, when her humanity was already gone, taken from her piece by piece, and this gift, the reserve of women, the innate ability to create life was the only part of her they couldn't take.

But now it was gone too.

She thought back to her relationship with Göring and finally accepted that this affliction – the inability to bring forth life – had been with her ever since that version of her endured this ordeal in her first life.

"Carla? What are you wearing? Where did you get those furs?" Rudi demanded as Torsten mentally added another item to his report for the Stasi. Carla and Olga locked eyes as each acknowledged the other as the anachronism they so obviously were. Her fingers wrapped around the Baby Browning in her coat and without taking it from her pocket, she fired two rounds into Torsten's chest. The smell of cordite, burning hair and human shit filled the cramped basement and smoke wound its way lazily upwards from the blackened hole in Carla's coat.

"What have you done?" Rudi roared. Carla stepped towards him and touched his youthful face with her gloved hand.

"He was planning to betray you both to the Stasi, if you don't believe me, go and look at those papers on your workbench," Carla said. Setting the suitcase down and turning to Olga, wrapping her arms around her sister; the woman she had lost all those years before.

The reaction was almost instant and as she removed the needle, Olga slumped against her, clawing at Carla's chest as she fell to the basement floor, a rictus enveloping her.

Rudi turned to see the muzzle flash of his sister's weapon as she shot him in the stomach. He crumpled with the pain and staggered back, his searching hand bloodying the papers behind him and sending them across the room.

"Why?" he cried, "we were going to…to change it all, to fix it, to…save…millions."

Carla watched her little brother as he tugged at the sodden shirt, contemplating his injuries. She looked down at Olga, paralysed but conscious, her green eyes darting from the man she loved to the woman she now despised.

"Can you hear me Olga dear? Look at me if you can hear me."

Olga's eyes bore into Carla with a hatred that belied her predicament and caused Carla to step away for fear that she would suddenly spring up and tear her limb from limb.

"We don't have long," Carla announced as she regained her composure.

"You don't know what you've done!" Rudi croaked, pale faced and despondent.

"You will never truly appreciate the irony of that statement, dear brother," she said, as she stooped to open the suitcase and produce a large bottle of accelerant.

"No, you don't understand—"

"Oh, but I do, Rudi, more than you will ever know," she cut in, dousing the papers and the chalkboard with the pungent liquid. "You see, I was dragged into your crusade against my will at the tender age of fourteen. This bitch kidnapped us and together with that bastard Clive, they brainwashed us into believing that we might save the world from Hitler and Stalin, from atom bombs and mass genocide. But Henry just wanted it all from himself, and she…"

Carla nudged Olga's prostrate form with a pointed boot, curling her lip in disgust and pouring the last of the liquid onto her clothes. Rudi groaned, unable to form words as he realised he would die watching the woman he loved burn before his very eyes.

"I want you to understand something," Carla said, tossing the empty bottle and slumping down onto the sofa next to Torsten's body. "This meddling will never work, history does not want to change, the scales of death, destruction, and suffering must be balanced. I've seen it all, every eventuality, and the world always ends up worse off than it was when you began. The best thing I can do is to kill you now, before you can start down this path of misery and heartache. Olga only exists because of a world you created from that lab in Munich, she lives to play out your God fantasy, it's not fair to keep putting her through that. This has to stop."

"But…you and Muttie…"

"Yes, I know and that fate befell millions of us, we were beaten and raped by the Red Army and it was horrific, the pain and trauma of that day will never leave me. That, however, is what happened, what really happened, it's not a fragile manufactured reality that leads to the world literally imploding."

"Imploding?" Rudi rasped.

"Yes brother, a singularity opened up in the Gulf of Mexico and destroyed the planet."

Carla produced the pistol from her pocket and checked it was loaded, before placing it on the arm of the sofa and patting herself down for a lighter. With a flick of her thumb the top swung open and she stared at the striking wheel, psyching herself up for what came next. With a deep breath she stood and span the wheel, causing a yellow flame to erupt and dance before her eyes.

Breathing out, she flung the lighter at the base of the chalkboard and everything became very real very quickly.

Flames engulfed the room and Carla snatched up the pistol to fire a second round into her brother before turning it on Olga, sending one round point blank to the back of her head.

Smoke filled the room as she brought the pistol up, pressing the barrel to the roof of her mouth.

Sirens wailed outside and Carla screamed before squeezing the trigger one last time.

Thank you to anyone that helped me with this and the other two books, you know who you are.

J. G. Jenkinson is a father, engineer, history nerd and a sailor. He emerged from the burning wreckage of his scholastic career unscathed, but with very little to show for it. This led him to the recruiter's office and over a decade with the British army. As promised, he saw the world, just not the bits of it you might find on a mood board. The army taught him to sail, ski and fence – badly. After a couple of trips to Helmand, the novelty wore off and he sought a living on the Canadian Prairies as an agricultural mechanic. He wrestled steers, drove trucks and fished on frozen rivers. After and interesting year running a farm, he returned to England and found that surveying would fund his writing habit. He recently took up boxing and judging by the state of his nose, he has a long way to go. Now he splits his time between a wind farm in the North Sea and his home in Worcestershire which he shares with his wife and daughters.

jgjenkinson.weebly.com
instagram.com: @author_j.g._jenkinson
facebook.com: @paperbackwindfarmer

Printed in Great Britain
by Amazon